Secrets in the Sky

Secrets in the Sky

Pauline Wiles

This novel is a work of fiction. The names, characters and incidents portrayed are the product of the author's imagination. Any resemblance to real persons, living or dead, is purely coincidental.

Author's Note

This story begins in spring 2010, two years before *Saving Saffron Sweeting*.
In keeping with its English setting, the book uses British spelling and grammar conventions.

Acknowledgements

My courage in attempting a second novel came almost entirely from the response to the first. To everyone who praised *Saving Saffron Sweeting* in person or online, thank you for the impetus to continue writing.

For *Secrets in the Sky*, special recognition is due to Rachel Bennett, Namita Dalal, Susan Latimer and Martina Munzittu for providing plot inspiration, cultural advice and professional tips.

Nancy True was the winner of my contest to name a Cambridge college – thank you, Nancy, for the convincing suggestion of Trewe College. Similar thanks go to Gwen, who won the opportunity to name a character in the book. She and canine winner, Murphy Grace, each feature in a scene.

I am especially grateful to qualified pilots Maxine Burrell and Darius Wiles who painstakingly reviewed all mentions of planes and flying. As such, any deviations from actual aviation procedures were retained by me for the convenience of the plot.

Beta readers Brianna Bocian, Christie Goeller, April Harris, Sharon Nelson, Joanne Phillips, Martha Reynolds, Jane Ritz, Emma S. and Laura Williams were worth their weight in Hobnobs for the excellent feedback which enabled final polishing of the plot. And proofreader Jude White once again amazed me with the quality of her work and incredible eye for consistency. Any remaining errors are mine.

Finally, the only thing worse than living with a wife who's writing a book is living with a wife who's writing a second book. The indefatigable patience of Darius Wiles is behind every sentence on every page. Thank you.

Secrets in the Sky

Chapter 1

I race up the gravel path towards the village church and skid to an inelegant halt. I'll be so glad to get these shoes off.

Kit is waiting in the arched doorway, shifting from foot to foot and looking from her watch to the sky. Thunderous clouds have been creeping closer all morning, and now they're convening right above the steeple.

'Where the hell've you been? They're starting!'

As she speaks, I hear the solemn notes of the organ and recognise the first bars of 'All Things Bright and Beautiful'. Beside us, a clump of yellow daffodils nods in time to the hymn.

Wol loved daffodils.

My sister doesn't wait for me to answer, but wrenches open the ancient door. I'm grateful for the cover of the music as we tiptoe inside. The church is comparatively dark and I stumble down the step, then creep along the side aisle behind Kit to the end of the front row. Heads turn. The villagers' mouths are moving only approximately in time with each other, and Mrs Hughes from the doctor's surgery can be heard an octave higher than everyone else. Violet, the old busybody who runs the post office, bestows a withering glare over her hymn sheet.

Mum would probably like to wring my neck, but with Kit between us, she has to be content with leaning forward and shooting me a look which would freeze a volcano. I shrug back: guilty as charged. But at least I've started facing facts.

The last ten days have passed in wretched numbness. Perhaps this morning wasn't the best time to go and see Mr Baggit, but I was desperate for something to take my mind off the service. Then, realising I'd cut it too fine, I risked life and limb cycling at breakneck speed back from Cambridge. I bought this vintage dress yesterday in a panic, when I realised I have absolutely nothing black in my wardrobe, and the full skirt kept catching in my back wheel. I probably looked like a witch on a mission, and now I'm a witch with sweat trickling down inside my bra.

Beside me, Kit is pretending to sing, but she can't hold a tune and knows it. Her hair's shorter and darker than last year and she's wearing remarkably large sunglasses. Her neat charcoal trouser suit suggests she didn't have to dash to the shops yesterday. Although twelve years younger than me, I'm pretty sure she's already developed a sensible capsule wardrobe.

The congregation is on the fourth verse, but I'm not thinking about tiny wings or ripe fruits. I've finally stopped panting, but still catch my breath as the enormity of saying goodbye to Wol threatens to engulf me. As I inhale, the sweet scent of lilies fills my lungs. There are two huge flower arrangements by the ancient stone pillars, underneath the hymn numbers displayed in wooden slots. And there are flowers on the coffin too: three wreaths in a clashing combination of white, pink and yellow. The first is from mum, the second, Kit and me. I don't know about the third – a friend of Wol's, maybe?

As the hymn dies away, Kit uses the cover of shuffling feet and awkward coughs to hiss, 'Where in God's name were you, Soph?'

I reach surreptitiously into my bag, wondering if God is preparing a lightning strike for her blasphemy or my tardiness, or both. As the vicar climbs the steps to the pulpit and begins his remarks, I find the solicitor's sheet of provisional calculations and pass it to her.

Kit frowns and tucks it into her hymn sheet. Her eyes widen as she scans the short document. Then she turns to me and mouths, 'Holy shit!'

There's an immediate disapproving wallop of thunder from above, making most of the congregation jump.

And now I'm not only late for my great-aunt's funeral, but am also fighting a hideously inappropriate urge to giggle. I bite my lip, dig my fingernails into my palms and look up at the soaring rafters of Saffron Sweeting's fine medieval church. My search for divine guidance is unsuccessful, but I spot some sacred cobwebs and after a few moments a hollow calm settles on me. I force myself to focus on the vicar's words and his urging that we should be grateful for Wol's long and worthy life, even as we mourn her. He doesn't call her that, of course: he uses her real name, Doris.

'Let us pray,' he finishes.

As we position our little embroidered hassocks and sink to our knees, Kit passes the heavy cream paper back to me.

'You'll get some too, apparently,' I whisper.

She leans closer and speaks from the corner of her mouth. 'I had no idea she had money.'

'No,' I reply. 'None of us did.' I pause. 'But I'm not letting this change me.'

'Right,' mutters Kit. 'Good luck with that.'

Chapter 2

'Miss Campbell,' pronounced Mr Baggit, when I finally arrived at his office this morning, before the funeral, 'you are an elusive young lady.'

'Sorry,' I said, picking at the flaking brown leather on my chair. 'I've had a lot going on.'

This was true; there had been an avalanche of logistics for the funeral, including bringing Wol's coffin back from the Lake District. But I was on the defensive because I'd been avoiding this meeting. It took me several days to even open the post, never mind deal with it. When I didn't respond to Mr Baggit's first two letters, the phone messages started coming.

The solicitor puffed up his cheeks, offended by the implication that his business could be unworthy of immediate attention. He began shuffling fat manila folders on his desk. I gazed around, taking in the huge bookcase, the certificates, and the narrow sash window with a view of an equally narrow Cambridge alley. He still hadn't located the right file and I noticed there was no computer in the room. No wonder he couldn't find anything.

'Ah. Here we are,' he announced, nodding so vigorously his glasses slipped down his nose. He cleared his throat. 'Miss Campbell. For the last thirty years I have acted as solicitor to your great-aunt, Miss Doris Campbell.'

I waited, shifting in my chair and resisting the urge to check the time. Mr Baggit was in no hurry and had already kept me waiting. With the funeral at two o'clock, things might be getting tight.

'My condolences for your loss,' he said, and paused again.

I kept my eyes down. Loss suggested I had misplaced my keys or had been trounced again at Scrabble by Wol. I swallowed as I realised she would never again beat me to a double-word score.

The solicitor cleared his throat again. 'Your great-aunt was a methodical woman. I am able to inform you she left clear instructions in her will.'

My God, I thought, we haven't even cremated her yet. Was he that keen to collect his fee?

'However, there's good news and bad news,' Mr Baggit continued.

I hate it when people say that. There's never any truly good news: they're just trying to pretend that the least bad part is something to celebrate.

'Really?' I replied sharply. 'I thought my great-aunt dying after a minor hiking accident was bloody awful news.'

But Mr Baggit didn't react. Perhaps he was used to highly strung relatives. 'Firstly,' he said, 'let me deal with the bad news.'

I ground my teeth again at his words, but kept quiet.

'Miss Campbell, you have been residing with your great-aunt at the property...' he consulted his notes, '...at the cottage known as The Gatehouse, Hall Rise, Saffron Sweeting?'

'Yes,' I said. Wol's cottage was outside the village, and marked one of the original entrances to the much grander Saffron Hall. Was he going to tell me off for not paying the council tax?

'And Miss Campbell, are you aware this property was not owned by your great-aunt?'

Not owned by Wol? 'Er – I dunno.'

When mum and I had first moved to Saffron Sweeting, I was so small I only cared about a warm bed and clean pyjamas. And when I moved back into Wol's house a couple of years ago, the topic of ownership never came up.

Mr Baggit adjusted his glasses. 'In fact, the house was owned by a Miss Edith Ralph, with whom Wol lived when they were both teachers at Saffron Sweeting School.'

'Yes, that rings a bell,' I said.

Edie and Wol, both spinsters, were lifelong friends and

often referred to as a pair in family conversations.

'And when Miss Ralph died, she left your great-aunt a life interest in the property. Do you know what that means?'

I shook my head, wishing he would get to the point.

'It means that Doris Campbell had a right to live in the house for as long as she wished, but upon her vacating it – or upon her death – the property passes to Miss Ralph's heir.'

'Okay,' I said. Did he think I was hoping to inherit Wol's cottage? It hadn't even crossed my mind. 'No problem.'

Mr Baggit steepled his fingers and exhaled. 'You understand, Miss Campbell, you will be required to vacate the property at your earliest convenience?'

'Oh,' I said in a small voice. 'Right. Yes, of course.'

It was nothing to get upset about. Single, with no ties and few possessions, I would find somewhere else easily enough. Still, Wol's death had been a bitter shock and I could do without this on my plate as well.

'Good, so that's out of the way.' Mr Baggit cleared his throat again. Perhaps the dust of these ancient legal tomes was getting to him. I longed to reach into my bag and offer him a fruit pastille.

'Miss Campbell. The deceased named you as a beneficiary in her will.' He leaned forward and pushed a heavy, cream piece of paper across the desk. But I was staring at him, struck by the word *beneficiary*. I might be rotten at Scrabble, but I knew what that meant.

'I will have to liquidate some shares and bonds,' Mr Baggit said, 'And you should in no way rely upon this estimate as more than a good faith approximation.'

What kind of mumbo jumbo was that? No wonder his throat needed constant clearing.

Mr Baggit tweaked his glasses as he peered down at the papers. 'However,' he said carefully, dragging out each syllable, 'I estimate that when the estate is tied up and expenses have been met, you could possibly inherit something in the region of thirty thousand pounds.'

I gave a high laugh. 'There must be a mistake,' I said. 'Wol didn't have any money.'

He sat back in his seat. 'I realise this may come as a surprise,' he said, 'but I assure you there is no mistake. The house, of course, is not part of her estate, but there is a cash bequest for you and also your sister.'

'No,' I repeated. 'Auntie Wol didn't have money. Or stocks or bonds. She had a parrot.'

Mr Baggit raised his eyebrows before consulting his notes. 'Ah, yes,' he said, tapping his fountain pen on the page. 'Stanley the parrot.' He gave me a twinkling look and I realised this decaying old solicitor wasn't as dusty as he seemed. 'I was coming to him.'

~~~

As the long black car stops outside the pub and mum helps Violet clamber out, I ask Kit if she's coming in.

My sister, who hasn't taken her dark glasses off once during the whole funeral, looks at the two women on the pavement. 'Better not,' she says quietly, then adds more loudly, 'I have an assignment due tomorrow.'

'Okay,' I say, feeling tearful again. Briefly, I envy Kit the ability to melt quietly away. But since my own journey is a mere five minutes up the road to Wol's cottage, I'd better settle for my usual tactic of hiding in plain sight.

Having paid their respects in church, most of the mourners skipped the crematorium and headed straight from the service to the Saffron Sweeting pub. So by the time I enter The Plough, Wol's wake bears more resemblance to happy hour. Despite the questionable quality of the catering, the villagers have demolished most of the sausage rolls and are making inroads into the sandwiches. Behind the bar, Fergus is pulling pints cheerfully.

I know my mother is furious I was late for the funeral, but she held her tongue while Violet was around. Now, I waste no time in putting some distance between us. She's too busy anyway, shaking hands like minor royalty opening a hospital wing. In her prim navy suit and hat, she spends precisely thirty seconds with each person, before gliding on to the next.

Pushing my way through the throng, I hear pieces of conversation about Wol.

'I was about nine when she almost took my eye out with a stick of chalk,' comes a stranger's voice.

'Not only was her chalk like a guided missile, Miss Campbell had eyes in the back of her head,' says a second voice as I reach the crowded bar.

The first speaker nods. 'Wasn't her nickname The Owl?'

Auntie Wol, or Miss Campbell as most of her former pupils still call her, taught at the village school for thirty years. She had a sixth sense for mischief and commanded the absolute respect of her class.

'Heart of gold, though,' says the second person.

This was true. Wol took a genuine interest in every child, moulded their individual talents, and made learning a journey rather than a chore. I should know, I was one of them.

'Yes,' agrees the first. 'Give her a box of Jelly Babies and she was putty in your hands.'

'Sophie.' There's a nasal voice at my shoulder.

I turn to find a grey-haired man in thick-rimmed glasses. He looks familiar. The postman, perhaps? Or the milkman?

'Very sad to hear about Doris.' He inclines his head dolefully.

I manage a stiff nod.

'Still,' the nasal man continues, 'she had a good innings.'

Crass git, I think, bile rising. We're not playing cricket and she didn't have a good innings. Wol had years left in her and tripping on a stony footpath in the Lake District was *not* a fair ending. How am I going to get through this?

'Yes,' says the man, nodding again. 'Quite right.'

He has the nerve to pat my arm as I turn away. There

seem to be dozens of strangers in the room and I fend off more cricket-inspired platitudes. Several people profess to have known me since I was knee-high, but not one of them do I recognise. Crowds make me nervous at the best of times.

Despite the throng, I can't dodge my mother forever and I know I'm lucky she doesn't come to the village more often. Mum reaches my side as Fergus is pouring my whisky. I know she thinks it's unladylike for me to drink spirits, but she doesn't say anything and orders a glass of white wine. Rather than hang back and wait for her to pay, I get my purse out. It's the least I can do, after the news I got earlier. She looks surprised, but waits until Fergus moves to serve another customer before speaking.

'Well, Miss Sophie,' she begins, 'you'd better have a cast-iron excuse for being late for auntie's funeral.'

Miss Sophie means I'm in trouble, but I knew that already and I don't want to squabble with her today. I've just watched Wol's coffin glide through ominous black curtains in a building where smoke wafts from the chimney all year round.

'I was at the solicitor's,' I say. 'Maggot or Rabbit or whoever he is. He kept me waiting, then I had to bike back.'

'Mr Baggit,' mum says automatically. 'And I wish you'd use your car, like normal people.'

I ignore the dig. I can't stand being stuck in traffic, and parking in Cambridge is impossible. 'I have to move out of Wol's cottage.' Saying it aloud makes it real.

'What? Didn't she leave it to you? She talked to me one day and I thought that was her plan.'

'Apparently, it wasn't hers to leave.' I fiddle with a piece of hair, the same rusty brown as mum's. We've been mistaken for sisters more than once: the same pale Celtic skin, a few mortifying freckles. Kit doesn't look much like us; she's more like her father.

My mother frowns. 'Oh, Lord, I didn't think of that.'

'She, er, left me some money, though. And Kit.' My tone

is almost confessional: I'm not sure Wol specified anything for mum. On this point, at least, I can come clean.

But she just nods. 'Auntie more or less said she planned to skip a generation; I told her I understood.'

It's true that mum's done well at the bank and owns a little place in Norwich. Still, that was a significant gesture by Wol and I feel a new lump in my throat.

'So,' says mum, 'Edith Ralph owned the cottage?'

'Yeah. Wol had something called a life interest, that's all.'

'Do you remember Miss Ralph? She was still alive when we moved down from Scotland, but in the hospice already.'

I shake my head. 'I was too little, I suppose.'

Mum didn't exactly abandon me while she rushed out to rekindle her career, but I certainly saw more of Wol than my mother in those first years after we found a home with my great-aunt. Although a stranger to me when we arrived in Saffron Sweeting, I soon discovered Wol was kind, wise and funny. Her schoolteacher strictness imparted a sense of security and I suspect she invented extra homework projects to distract me from mum's long work hours.

'Yes, you were little.' Mum sighs, staring at a spot beyond me. 'I don't know what I would have... Wol was very good to us.'

Now I feel guilty. Mum was fond of Wol too; she just hasn't shown it much recently. Which is definitely for the best. The last thing I needed – need – is her showing up in the village for visits.

'Can I have another?' I ask Fergus.

He smiles and produces a second whisky.

'I trust you'll be walking that bike of yours home?' he says with a wink. 'The fuzz hang around after funerals, you know.'

I promise him I'll wheel the bike, or at least ride it on the pavement. I don't mention I may need a third whisky before I go back to Wol's cottage alone tonight.

'Didn't Kit look nice?' Mum says to no one in particular,

while eyeing my vintage outfit.

I shift my weight to my left foot, so I can ease my blistered right heel from its shoe.

'And she's so diligent about her studies,' mum continues, looking at Fergus now. 'She's in her first year, you know, at Nottingham.'

I stiffen. I'm pretty sure Kit's never been in The Plough, but I don't like this conversation.

'How's Anthony?' I interrupt, knowing I'm highlighting her boyfriend's absence. 'Couldn't he make it?'

'He's fine.' Mum's mouth tightens. 'Very busy.'

Hmm, I think. Is the pompous git losing his sheen? Anthony's a stuffed shirt businessman, running for election as a Tory MP in Norwich. His political stance was yet another headache for Kit and me last year. 'Pity,' I say.

Mum turns, but I keep my expression neutral. Still, she seems to sense it might be time to end our conversation.

'Despite what you think, she's proud of you,' Fergus says gruffly, after mum floats off to shake more hands.

'I don't think so.' I swirl the luscious liquid in my glass.

'She is,' he says. 'Whenever she's in here – which admittedly isn't often – she mentions your glamorous jet-setting life. Told me how pleased she is that you've settled in a job at last.'

I catch his eye and he winks again. Unfortunately, Fergus sees and hears everything from behind this bar.

'Right,' I say, my jaw clenched. 'Excellent.'

I bite into a ham sandwich, thinking I should make a token effort to mop up the whisky. Between my appointment with Mr Baggit and the dash back to Saffron Sweeting, I missed lunch. 'Fergus,' I say, 'these taste like the undertaker sponsored them.'

As his face falls, I regret being mean. After all, he just tried to boost my morale.

'Sorry,' he says, 'my chef walked out. Went back to Croatia.'

'So who made the sarnies?' I ask. 'They're not Brian's,

are they?'

Brian runs the village bakery and couldn't produce desiccated crusts like these if he tried. I'm one of his biggest fans.

'I did,' Fergus replies.

'Oops.' Now it's my turn to apologise. 'Sorry. Shitty day.'

'I know,' he says. 'Here, have some Twiglets.'

I take the snack gratefully, thinking that Fergus, with his cheery discretion, would make an ideal boyfriend. A pity he's old enough to be my dad. And I've never gone for men with red hair.

Roughly at the moment when a python of grief has wrapped itself around my neck, but before the whisky anaesthetic has kicked in, I hear a female voice.

'Sophie. I'm so sorry about Miss Campbell.'

'Thanks,' I mutter, barely glancing up from the Twiglets.

There's a pause. 'Remember me?' she asks.

Now I look at the tall figure. 'Bloody hell! Bella!'

Finally, in this tavern full of false friends who've shown up for free sandwiches and superficial conversation is someone who really has known me since I was knee-high to a grasshopper.

'What are you doing here?' I say, which is somewhat daft, considering we're at a funeral.

'I'm moving back to the village,' she replies. 'I heard about Wol.'

At age seven, all the other kids at the Saffron Sweeting School had formed friendships already. I was the outsider, the arrival from Scotland with the sing-song accent. I didn't know a soul and they giggled when I read aloud.

'Leave her alone,' Bella had said from her desk by the window, where the swallows were nesting outside.

The giggling turned on Bella, who grew pink but set her chin firmly. Within the week, I moved desks and had a view of the swallows too.

'It's brilliant to see you,' I say, meaning it.

She smiles, her luminous smile which hasn't changed in twenty years. And that's when my face crumples.

'What did I do?' she says to Fergus as I abandon the Twiglets in favour of my last tissue.

'Nothing,' I snuffle. 'You didn't do anything. I'm glad you came.'

Nonetheless, I start to put my brutal shoe back on. It's time to go. Bella's lovely, but fifty old friends coming out of the woodwork won't compensate me for losing Wol.

In fact, the fewer old friends in my life, the better.

Chapter 3

Considering I pride myself on not having many possessions, I seem to be lugging an awful lot of stuff. It's ten days after Wol's funeral, and I'm exhausted.

Bella and I decided it would be fun to move into her Uncle Mike's house together, and both of us declared we didn't have much to transport at all. We would be finished by lunchtime and spend the afternoon settling in and catching up.

Instead, we're hot, crabby and one of us is emotionally shredded.

On the bright side, her uncle's house is extremely comfortable, possibly the poshest place I've ever lived. It's close to the river in a hidden corner of Saffron Sweeting, and a lilac clematis climbs proudly up the cream plastered exterior. The house appears old, but has been carefully modernised. Inside, it's airy and expensively decorated.

'Wow,' I said, when Bella first persuaded me to take a look. Compared with Wol's quirky nest, with two rooms upstairs and two down, this was a palace. 'How did you swing this?'

'I'm only house sitting,' she said, looking smug nonetheless. 'He hasn't decided whether to sell and move to Spain. Or Slovenia. Or somewhere.'

'Is he gay?' I asked, pointing to the swagged silk curtains in the lounge.

Bella laughed. 'Divorced. Not long ago.'

When she'd initially suggested I share the house, a day or two after Wol's funeral, I was still hungover from grief. Grumpily resistant, I planned to stay out of everyone's way while I licked my wounds. But, with my finances pitiful, and no immediate sign of a cheque from Mr Baggit, my next best alternative was to live with my mother. And there was no way that was going to happen.

'If I move in, there's a condition,' I said eventually, when Bella had weakened my resistance with a lemon drizzle cake, served warm in Uncle Mike's glossy kitchen. The zesty lightness reminded me, she'd come top in cookery class at school. A housemate who could cook might be a nice thing. Wol couldn't make much except omelettes, and my star dish is beans on toast.

'What's that?' Bella said.

'Stanley comes too.'

'Stanley? Who's Stanley? I thought you were single.' She looked confused.

'Stanley,' I tutted, sucking lemon icing off my finger. 'You *have* been introduced. Stanley is my newly adopted parrot.'

This morning, the appointed day for our move, we began at Wol's.

'Just bring your bits and pieces, then come back another day and look at the rest,' Bella said sensibly as we packed my first batch into her Vauxhall Corsa. 'You can't possibly sort through all Miss Campbell's things today.' She was reluctant to give up the name by which she'd known Wol.

I, on the other hand, was reluctant to give up everything else. 'All right,' I said, contemplating changing the locks on Wol's cottage and making Mr Baggit evict me. 'Should I bring the kettle, though?'

'No, Sophie,' Bella sighed. 'We already have two kettles, a teapot and a coffee maker.'

Our second trip was from Saffron Sweeting to Bella's old place, a bedsit in a side street near Cambridge railway station.

'Pooh,' I said as we tramped up three flights of stairs. 'No wonder you're moving out.'

'The fire wasn't so bad,' she replied, her few extra pounds making her more breathless than me. 'But then the fire brigade discovered asbestos, so the landlord has to kick us all out while it's fixed. I don't mind. It's time to move on.'

'You haven't lived here since university, have you?' I asked.

I was embarrassed at losing touch with Bella so easily after school. I suspected she wasn't the disorganised one, who misplaced addresses and never got around to phoning.

'No. I lived with Owen.' She handed me a box, packed far more neatly than mine, with a yellow label on top. 'For six years.'

'Six?' I almost dropped the box. 'Wow.'

I stared at her, but her face was hidden behind her blonde hair as she bent to pick up a bundle of plastic dress carriers.

'Come on,' she said. 'We've still got loads to do.'

Now, we're trudging up Uncle Mike's gravel driveway with an assortment of boxes, bags and a couple of bin liners.

'Sophie,' Bella says. 'this weighs a freaking ton. Did you pack the kitchen sink?'

I too am surprised at the weight of my belongings. 'Sorry,' I say, 'I think you've got the dresses in there.'

I call them 'the dresses' rather than 'my dresses' because I've never actually worn most of them. They're vintage treasures, collected at flea markets and car boot sales: irreplaceable. The fabrics and attention to detail are stunning, but they don't quite fit me. Women must have been a different shape in the fifties and early sixties; the dresses need an hourglass shape to fill them, whereas I'm a scrawny rectangle. Still, one day maybe I'll get a boob job or find some way of making them look good. In the meantime, I'm content with unwrapping and stroking them occasionally.

'Whoops,' I add as a rolled up vintage map escapes from its tube. I'm carrying three under one arm, a faded globe nestled in the other.

'Well, the maps make sense,' Bella says, performing an agile save with her knee. 'Given your job and everything.'

'Yes,' I echo. 'My job.' That part, at least, is true.

The spring day is taunting us with unseasonal warmth;

the back of my shirt is sticky as I dump the maps and globe in the living room and head back to Bella's car. She's done an expert job of wedging a bag of shoes down the back of the driver's seat. I'm leaning in, being tickled by a potted fern on the back seat, when I hear the gravel crunch under the tyres of another car.

'Sophie!'

The trill is familiar; my head clunks the roof of the Corsa as I straighten in surprise.

'Mum?'

Sod, what's she doing here? Did I tell her I'm moving today? Surely I wasn't daft enough to mention my new address?

'I thought you girls might want some lunch.' For once, my mother is dressed casually. She's standing in front of an old Volvo, an unlikely company car. Still, her words are welcome. I run a dusty hand through my hair and discover I'm starving.

'Hello, Ms Campbell.' Bella appears in the driveway and waves at mum. From what I remember of Bella's family, she has a normal, friendly relationship with her parents. Both of them.

'Hello, Bella dear.'

Has my mother reached the age where she calls people 'dear'? How embarrassing.

'I brought you girls some Cornish pasties. Oh, and someone to help with your move.'

I'm still looking at Bella, who blinks, then smiles politely. But did she just pull her stomach in too? I follow her gaze to the Volvo. And standing there, holding on to the driver's door as if braced for a quick getaway, is Joey.

'Hi, Sophie,' he says uncertainly.

He looks good. Really good. He's older, of course: thirty-one now, same as me. He's a little heavier, his dark hair an inch longer. In the intervening years, I had almost forgotten my Latin lover with the Cambridge accent. With an Italian mother and English father, Joey – full name

Giuseppe Williams – was a potent blend of Mediterranean sex appeal and British familiarity.

And the last thing I want to think about right now is his sex appeal. I wipe my hands on my jeans, tuck a hair strand behind each ear, and feign nonchalance.

'Right,' I say, my voice a notch higher than usual. 'Joey. Yes. Hi. How are you?' Then, not waiting for an answer, 'Gosh, mum, you brought Joey.'

'Yes! I bumped into him just the other day.' She beams. 'I told him you're an air hostess now, and terribly busy!'

Oh, she really has excelled herself this time. Ten years ago, they were thick as thieves, but I never dreamed that his relationship with my mother lasted longer than the one with me.

Joey decides it's safe to let go of the car, and shuts the Volvo's door.

'Right,' I say again. 'Excellent. Well, don't just stand there, bring in the grub.'

Mum, swinging a bag, doesn't wait to be asked twice, and strides into my new home as if she, not the absent Uncle Mike, were the owner.

Bella follows and Joey fetches another grocery bag from his car.

With a longing glance in the direction of Wol's cottage, I linger by the front door, kicking my toe against the boot scraper.

Why? I think. Why did you have to die?

And why on earth have all these people from my past started popping up again?

~~~

'I could sleep for a week.' My head flops back on the sofa in our new living room.

Bella rolls her shoulders. 'I'm not going to be able to move tomorrow.'

I look across at her. 'The worst part was lugging your books down all those stairs.'

Even when we were small, Bella adored reading.

'I love my books,' she retorts. 'I curl up with them at night and they rarely disappoint me. Not like men.'

'Fair point,' I say.

'Although Joey was super useful today. Great biceps.' She yawns, which sets me off too.

True. The extra pair of strong arms, plus the huge capacity of his Volvo, was indeed wonderful. Joey smiled and whistled through the tedium of moving unique treasures (mine) and random junk (Bella's) from two locations to a third. He flirted with us equally, and even kissed mum on the cheek when I got rid of her after lunch. Then, in the late afternoon, when he spied the suitcase containing my underwear and offered to unpack, I wasted no time in dispatching him.

'You could thank me by buying dinner,' he said softly as he washed his hands at our kitchen sink, then snaffled the remaining flapjack from lunch.

'Don't be cheeky.' I flicked the tea towel at him. 'Whatever promises my mother made to get you here, you can take up with her.'

He paused in the doorway, dark eyes running over me. I'd forgotten how they always used to gleam. 'Good to see you, Sophie.'

I smiled, not wanting to appear ungrateful. 'Bye, Joey.'

'So what happened between you two?' Bella says now.

'Oh, I dunno.' I wriggle my tongue between my teeth. 'We were together, off and on, through college.'

'Really?' Bella's all ears. 'Was it serious?'

'No,' I say hastily. 'He was just... a boyfriend.'

Joey was funny, energetic, wickedly attractive, with a jaw that could have been chiselled by Michelangelo. All the girls adored him. We egged each other on with practical jokes, laughed ourselves silly on numerous occasions, and shared a bed with increasing regularity as graduation approached. But we weren't *serious*.

Bella looks unconvinced.

'You know...' I continue, 'I had the magazine job in London, Joey was going to work for the bank...'

The sentence trails off. With a serious crush on London life, I couldn't wait to immerse myself in the world of the magazine. Arriving at work at noon, strap-hanging on the Tube, buying Sunday's newspaper on the way home on Saturday night: these all held a special thrill. And whatever Joey was up to, he didn't take long to forget me, either.

Bella nods. 'Even at school, we all admired you, Sophie. You were obviously going places.'

I look at her, then drop my eyes. Bella's so generous and open. Unlike some of my college friends, who turned catty when I snagged a coveted job at a travel magazine, Bella never seemed resentful.

'And now...' she carries on, 'it must be amazing, seeing all those exotic places...'

I jump up. 'Flipping heck, I forgot Stanley. He'll be starving. Where did his seeds end up?'

Bella doesn't notice the change of subject. 'He's not the only one who's starving. Shall I make cheese on toast?'

~~~

After we've eaten some delectably gooey Welsh Rarebit – if that's Bella's idea of a snack, I'm going to adore living with her – she comes downstairs from a visit to the bathroom.

'You don't have many beauty products,' she says sleepily. 'Or haven't you unpacked yet?'

'Er, I think I did,' I say, looking at multiple remote controls for the television and deciding I'm too tired to battle them tonight. I'm glad I'm not alone, but I still miss Wol horribly. At this time of night, we'd be having tea and a bedtime chocolate digestive.

'Oh,' Bella says. 'I thought air hostesses wore a lot of make-up, you know? They always seem so dolled up. I thought you'd have tons of duty-free cosmetics and perfume.'

I chew on a fingernail which is free of nail polish, has

never seen a professional manicure, and is the exact opposite of dolled up. 'It's not like that, these days...'

'Oh. Right.' She flops down on the sofa. 'I guess I won't be stealing your Clarins and Clinique, then.'

I give a thin smile. My entire collection of beauty products would fit in a shoe box; my sole indulgence is some anti-frizz hair stuff from Percy & Reed. Lucky Bella: her hair is smooth and obedient. Mine takes one look at the English weather and declares a fiesta.

'And you'd better show me what Stanley likes to eat.'

'Stanley?' I rub the offending nail.

'Yes. For when you're away.'

Away. *Away.* I've been so stupid. In the fog of pain from losing Wol, I've let someone get close enough to see my routine, my every move. And there is no routine, there is no every move.

'Bell.' I take a deep breath and wait until I have her attention. 'We were – good pals at school, right?'

Bella frowns. 'Er, yeah...?'

'I'll never forget you sharing your crayons with me that first month, when I was the only one in the class with none.'

Her face is blank. 'I don't remember that.'

I carry on. 'And that day when I ate an entire Easter egg, then had to sprint to the toilet with my hands clamped over my mouth, you ran ahead to open doors for me.'

'Did I? Yuk.'

This is going nowhere. 'Look,' I say. 'You were a wonderful friend. And you've been great, since Wol died. Offering me somewhere to live, and everything.'

Bella tenses. 'What's going on? This sounds like the speech guys make when they dump me.' She sits forward. 'Didn't you like the Welsh Rarebit? Too much mustard?'

'No! I mean, yes, the Rarebit was fine,' I say. 'But there's something you need to know.'

I see her fingers drum on the sofa, but she signals me to continue.

'I don't have... a strong relationship with my mother,' I

say slowly. 'She's got the wrong end of the stick about something, and I've chosen not to correct her.' I speak carefully. If I can make Bella understand, she might not kick me out of her uncle's house and then pick up the phone to mum.

'Okay...' Bella's blue eyes are still on me, but she's poised to make a physical escape, should my next words be an axe-murdering confession.

'It's a bit embarrassing, but I'd really appreciate it if you'd – well, if you wouldn't tell her.'

'Tell her what?' Bella is impatient now, in the way we all get when, no matter how bad the news, the anticipation is worse than hearing it.

'I'm not actually an air hostess.'

Bella's staring, waiting for more. I show her my palms to signify that's it.

'That's it?' She gets the gesture perfectly. 'You're not an air hostess?'

I shake my head, face screwed up as if someone's about to throw cold water over me.

'What are you, then? What do you do for a living?'

'I edit travel guides. I work freelance.'

'So you do travel? You write guide books?'

'No.' I wish. 'I don't visit the places or write the books. I just change word choices, organise the information better, make grammar suggestions.'

My job's so glamorous, I spend hours cutting and pasting phone numbers and hotel room rates.

'But – after college – you worked for a big magazine. A travel magazine, right? That's when we lost touch – when your career took off.'

Ironic words. 'It never really took off, as such.' As the office skivvy, my most exciting trips were to the cafe on the corner to fetch coffee.

Bella's lips are pursed. 'And your mum thinks you're an air hostess?'

'I almost was. Got the job, started training, everything.'

Perfectly true. 'When it didn't work out, it was... a really bad time to tell her.' I grimace.

'So she thinks you're flying around serving drinks and pointing out emergency exits?' Bella's brow eases slightly.

'That's right.'

After my other short-lived jobs, including the food-poisoned cruise ship and the hotel which fell into a Cornish tin mine, I was in danger of becoming a family joke. I didn't need more ridicule. Or, worse, maternal questions.

'And Wol knew about this?' Bella asks.

I nod. 'I did a distance learning course, and switched to guide books.'

'What about others in Saffron Sweeting? Haven't they let on?'

'Not as far as I know. I... keep to myself, and mum doesn't come to the village much.' I push away the thought that she's now been twice in two weeks. She probably bought today's pasties at the bakery, where I'm a regular customer.

Bella rubs her nose. 'It's hardly crime of the century.'

I wait for the rest of her verdict, taking my nerves out on the scraggy fingernail.

'Soph... you talked about crayons and throwing up at school?'

'Yeah?'

Where's this going?

'Do you remember the stuff you did for me?'

'Like what?'

Why this tangent?

'Like, when Derek called me Bella the Blimp, and you stamped on his foot and he limped home crying?'

I smile. 'Yeah, okay, I do remember him.'

'And you got detention for a fortnight, but you told him if he said anything like that again, you'd break more than his toes?'

No answer is needed. Derek was a prat.

'And you must remember potholing in the Peak

District,' Bella says.

'The caves? Yes, so?'

'Where I literally got stuck underground, and everyone panicked, and if it wasn't for you, we might all still be there now?'

Slowly, I nod. 'You weren't really stuck... just a bit scared.'

'You practically saved my life.' Bella's face clears. 'So, if you need me to accidentally forget to mention your occupation to your mum – well, I can do that.'

'You can?'

I want to cry. This is the first time since Wol died that I've had an honest conversation with anyone. Then I catch myself. According to Bella, I'm a courageous, cave conquering, chauvinist clobbering champion. That's a lot to live up to.

And I don't want to let her down.

Chapter 4

Poor Stanley. Bella may be happy to pick up her friendship with me, but she is less than thrilled about welcoming a parrot into her life.

With hindsight, it was a mistake to plonk Stanley's cage on the kitchen counter on moving day, but I was exhausted and we hadn't discussed a permanent spot for him. I picked him up in a hurry, though, in response to Bella's curled lip.

'That's so unhygienic,' she said.

'Fine,' I shrugged as I looked around for somewhere better. After a short tour of the ground floor accommodation, I offered him a side table in the lounge and took his silence as acquiescence. There, I hoped he'd feel like part of the family and might enjoy watching television. I'd been worried he was pining for Wol and might start to suffer from some parrot psychiatric disorder. He'd certainly been shrieking less since Wol died, although he still used his favourite command, *Feed me*, at regular intervals.

But while Stanley appeared tolerably content with his new home, Bella wasn't convinced.

'He gives me the creeps,' she complained yesterday. 'I feel like he's listening the whole time.'

I considered Stanley, who was on his perch, enjoying a sojourn outside his cage. It was true, he did spend many hours with his head tilted, one eye half shut. If he wasn't preparing to die of grief, it was possible he was composing his memoirs and we were going to feature one day in *Parrotgate*.

'We can't just turf him out,' I said, thinking not just of the bird but of Wol entrusting him to me.

'I know.' Bella sighed. She's not a mean person – in fact, she's more likely to get trodden on by others. 'I'll try to get used to him,' she said.

Unfortunately, getting used to him does not yet extend

to buying his nosh. I was out for a bike ride, taking advantage of fleeting sunshine after days of rain and hoping that punishing my legs would slow the churn of my mind, when I got a text from Bella:

Need parrot food.

~~~

So now, I'm standing in a pet shop in Newmarket, wondering how to cheer up a bereaved parrot.

It's the week before Easter and the shop is busy. I hustle through the section of cat scratching posts and past the cages which supposedly contain small rodents. All that's visible is beige sawdust, so presumably the inhabitants have gone to ground. At the end of this aisle, a throng of adults and children are gathered around a pen. A sign announces a special deal on Easter Bunnies. I can't see any actual rabbits: they're probably hiding from the onslaught.

'No, Crispin, darling, you mustn't pick them up,' purrs one of the mothers.

'But mummy, I want a WABBIT!' comes the shrill reply.

'Daddy will buy you a rabbit, if you're a good boy,' says the defeated-looking father, and I wince on behalf of the bundle of fluff.

'If you're here for a bunny, you'll have to join the queue,' comes a dry voice beside me.

I turn and see a tall, broad-shouldered man, standing with folded arms. He's wearing jeans and a frayed red shirt. He jerks his head towards the rabble.

'No,' I reply, distracted by a sudden squeal from the pen which I hope was a child, not a rabbit. 'I'm here for a parrot.'

'A parrot?' the man repeats. 'An Easter parrot?' He lifts one eyebrow.

I've always admired people who can wiggle their ears or raise a single eyebrow. I take a closer look. He's older than me, but not by much. He has an outdoorsy face, and floppy, light brown hair. From the line of his forearms, he's in good shape. Underneath the agile eyebrow, he's regarding me with interest.

'Oh,' I say, feeling foolish. 'No, of course not an Easter parrot. And I don't want to buy one. I already have one. I, um, inherited it. Him.' Naturally, I'm babbling.

'You inherited him?' The eyebrow has come down again and he unfolds his arms. He's wearing sturdy gloves and obviously works in the shop.

'Long story.' I try an awkward smile. 'I need parrot food and maybe a toy or something.'

Now he knows I'm not here to abuse baby bunnies, the man's tone softens. 'Bird stuff is that way.' He points to the other corner of the shop.

I nod and turn in that direction, thinking that if he has a problem with people buying rabbits, he shouldn't sell them.

The array of bird pampering products is dizzying, but I locate a book on parrot care, two large bags of seed which seem appropriate, and a millet spray for Stanley's cage. Given that he's heard everything Bella's said, I don't want him feeling unloved.

While I wait in the queue behind rabbit families, I notice red shirt guy again. He's making several trips out the back of the store, each time carrying a big sack on his shoulder. He's manoeuvring through the crowded shop with ease, one hand balancing the load.

A couple of minutes later, I find myself with an astonishingly large credit card receipt, one manageable plastic bag, and two worryingly heavy bags of bird food to transport home on my bike. I kick myself for not coming another day in my car. As I consider my purchases, the shop guy passes.

'Excuse me,' I say, 'I don't suppose you do delivery?'

He stops and turns. This time, the other eyebrow is up. Darn, I want to learn how to do that.

'Pardon?'

'Delivery? I was hoping – um – I just have my bike, you see.' I nod down at the bird food, feeling foolish for not considering logistics before I handed over my Visa card.

He looks at me blankly for a minute. Really, I think, it's not like I'm asking for the moon. Hasn't he heard of good old-fashioned service?

Red shirt guy looks down at Stanley's food by my feet, then, slowly, all the way back up to my face. I turn pink but don't know why. I'm sure my request is reasonable. His expression changes from blank to something else. At first, I think he's amused, but that seems unlikely, so I assume that's his helpful face. I suppose, if he's working in a pet shop, he might not be the brightest of buttons.

'Where are you heading?' he asks.

'Saffron Sweeting. Do you know it? It's not far.'

Now, he smiles. 'That's fine. I'm going that way.' He bends down and picks up Stanley's weighty nosh bags as though they were two feathers. 'What's your address?'

I tell him.

'I have to go to Oak House first,' he calls over his shoulder, already on his way out of the shop. 'You know, the bed and breakfast?'

I do know. It's run by a homely woman who knows Bella from way back. Oak House seems popular with tourists, although I can't think why they'd want to stay in a quiet spot like Saffron Sweeting, instead of Cambridge itself.

'Right. See you later,' says red shirt guy, and he's gone.

~ ~ ~

But I don't see him later. The bike ride home only takes me forty-five minutes, but by that time Stanley's food has arrived, along with a dozen eggs for Bella. I remember that her bed and breakfast friend keeps chickens.

'A hot guy was here,' Bella says. 'With eggs.'

'How original.' I open the fridge in search of a cool drink. 'Did he charge for the delivery?'

'No.' Bella frowns. 'Why?'

'Oh, just that he didn't seem very willing.'

'Well, he was perfectly charming when he was here.'

Bella's smirking. I give her an are-you-serious look and she tosses her head back. 'Come on, you must have noticed he was lovely.'

Now that Bella mentions it, the pet shop guy was good-looking, in a dense kind of way. 'I was more interested in making sure Stanley doesn't starve,' I say.

Bella scrunches her nose at the mention of our green housemate, who continues his habitual gnawing of a branch. Then she changes the topic. 'And Lorraine's invited us to her Easter party. You'll come, won't you?'

'What party?'

'At the bed and breakfast. She does it every year, apparently. It's a brunch buffet. I'm going to bake something.'

'Uh, I dunno.' I'm mixing Robinson's lemon barley with water and ice cubes. Then my phone buzzes with a text from my mother: *Are u still coming to Easter service with us? Wear something nice pls.*

Oh, hell. Pompous Anthony wants to parade into their local church with a perfect-looking family like a US presidential candidate, rather than a wannabe member of parliament. I'll have to put up with remarks about Kit being wonderful, and dodge questions about my fake job.

I drop the phone and beam at Bella. 'Easter brunch? Sounds brilliant. Can I help bake?'

~~~

My nerves are double edged: firstly, because it's so long since I went on a date, and secondly, because the date is with Joey. Something tells me this is a dangerous idea, but when he phoned a few days after the move, I found myself saying yes.

'Of course you should go!' Bella exclaims, when I express my qualms. 'It'll do you good. You haven't been anywhere social since Miss Campbell died.'

'I haven't felt like it.' Wol's been dead barely a month. 'Anyway, I've been to the pub.'

She grunts. 'That hardly counts.'

'But he's my ex,' I say. 'Do you think it's a good idea to go back to someone?'

Bella grins. 'Depends who the someone is.' Then she sees my face. 'It's just one date. And, Soph, he's hot.'

She's right: ten years after I last saw him, I was surprised how great Joey looked on our moving day. The tight black T-shirt revealed muscles he definitely didn't have in college.

'Go and get ready.' Bella flicks her fingers at me. 'Then I can settle down with Trevor.' She picks up the cover for Stanley's cage.

'Who's Trevor?' I wonder what she doesn't want the parrot to witness. Then I see the DVD in her hand: *Brief Encounter*. 'Right,' I add. 'Understood.'

Bella loves those old romantic films, where nothing much happens except a lot of sighing and gazing. If my Saturday night choice is Trevor Howard or Joey, the decision is pretty easy.

~ ~ ~

Joey closes his menu and leans forward. 'I wasn't sure you'd come.' He runs molten brown eyes over me, doing that twinkling thing again. Clearly, he's a mind reader.

'Well, it was kind of you to help us move.' I smile down at my menu. 'I assume I'm paying for dinner.'

'Seriously, Sophie.' His hands are fidgeting and I see him interlace his fingers to keep them still. 'We've got a lot of catching up to do.' He lowers his voice. 'I want to hear it all.'

I pick up my wine glass, then put it down again. The last thing I need this evening is to get drunk and tell it *all*.

'Oh, it's water under the bridge,' I say, which, considering the restaurant is perched alongside the River Cam, overlooking Magdalene College, is an apt metaphor. Cambridge won the Boat Race today, beating Oxford by a narrow margin. The mood amongst diners is celebratory, with light blue clothing much in evidence.

Joey shakes his head. 'That's why we all thought you were so cool. You were going places and not afraid of the unknown. I bet I seemed dull, staying here, not even moving out of my parents' house.'

'Not at all,' I say reflexively.

'I want you to know,' he carries on, 'it took me longer to get my act together, but things are going well.'

I can believe it. He's relaxed, confident and smiling in that sexy way which melted hearts in college. *My* act, though, isn't at all together. My act is like knitting, after a kitten's played with it for an hour.

'Anyway,' Joey says, drinking his wine, 'I kept in touch with your mum. When she mentioned you were in Saffron Sweeting, I thought I'd come and say hello.'

'You did more than keep in touch with her,' I say teasingly. 'She thinks you're terrific.'

He grins and I wonder again how he managed not to blot his copybook with mum.

For the first year or so that we were together, I avoided introducing Joey to my mother. But inevitably, they met. Before long they'd bonded over some fantasy stock market game, although it's hard to say who had less real cash at the time. The summer Joey and I graduated, there was a memorable evening when I refused to see *Gladiator* as it was reportedly too violent, and mum went with him to the cinema instead. That was a little unnerving, actually.

'She's a shrewd lady,' he says, catching a waiter's attention. 'Like her daughter.'

As I headed to London after college, Joey joined the management training scheme at mum's bank. She was in charge of the programme. But within a couple of years, he left to start his photography business.

'Still, she had every right to be annoyed with you,' I say.

Instead, by the time Joey decided to be the next Lord Lichfield, my mother was such a fan, she got him a contract taking shots of all the personal financial advisors. That promising start was the last I heard of Joey's career, until now.

The waiter arrives. I order monkfish and Joey goes for lamb steaks, suggesting we split duck breast with melon to begin.

'Sounds fantastic,' I say. A love of food was something else we'd had in common. 'So, are you still doing portraits?'

'People shots, yes,' he says, 'but not so formal. Kids in their natural environment, paparazzi-style shots of hen nights, weddings...'

'Women want you at their hen nights?' I'm surprised.

'Oh yes,' he says, with a suggestive grin. 'It's quite the thing.' He coughs. 'I behave like a gentleman, of course.'

'Of course,' I laugh, and we both know his definition of a gentleman is pretty modern. 'Well,' I say, 'I'm glad you're doing well.' Then, as my stomach rumbles, I ask, 'Do you have a studio?'

'Not yet,' he says. 'But I'm hoping it won't be long. You noticed all my gear crammed in the car?'

I could hardly miss seeing, as he drove us into Cambridge, that photography equipment was spilling out of the Volvo.

'So,' Joey's eyes light up as a basket of bread arrives, but he nudges it towards me first. 'How about you?'

I take a piece gratefully, hoping this will shut my stomach up.

'What have you been up to?' he persists.

'Oh... well,' I stall, forgetting my usual avoidance tactics for conversations like this. 'It isn't as glamorous as everyone thinks.'

That's perfectly true. My life is nowhere near as exciting as *anyone* thinks. Book editing isn't what I dreamed of, but the flexibility has come in handy.

'You obviously love exploring different countries and cultures,' Joey says.

'I do.' I smile. This is a statement I can agree with wholeheartedly. 'I adore visiting new places.' There's nothing false in that, either; it's just that these destinations are either on British soil or I visit through Google.

'Although, I thought you worked for a travel magazine?' Joey has wolfed down his first piece of bread. I can pack away the carbs myself, when I get going.

'For a bit,' I say. 'But I'd only been there a year before September 11th.' I pause, swallowing hard at the memory of the news that lunchtime. 'Things were obviously terrible in the industry after that. I hung on for a while, till they made me redundant. Mum didn't tell you?'

It's no secret, and, although I was devastated at the time, with hindsight, it was inevitable.

'I think your mum said you left,' he says. 'She didn't exactly broadcast that they gave you the heave-ho.'

'I'm sure,' I say dryly. Mum treats my career failures like dirty laundry, not to be washed in public. And in fairness, there are rather a lot of them. I decide to skip over the puking cruise ship and collapsed hotel.

'So, I worked for a travel agent... and then of course SpeedyJet...' I let my voice trail off.

'That's great,' he says. 'Taking the world by storm. We knew you would.'

I cringe. Is he remembering me or someone else? I run my mind over our college friends, wondering if he's got me mixed up with another girl. Still, back then, I did have big hopes, big plans for changing the world. In the last year or so, and especially in the weeks since Wol left me, I've not been sure I can change a light bulb.

The arrival of our food saves me from further melancholy. I'm probably over hungry. Violet, being nosily helpful, proffered a leaflet about grief which advised against getting hungry, angry, lonely or tired. I'm not sleeping much and my blood boils when I think about the hospital's procedures after Wol's fall. But at least tonight I'm tackling the hunger. As for the lonely part? Perhaps Joey can help with that too.

As we both attack our plates with gusto, I turn the

subject by asking about his family. I recall his parents own a building firm and he has three boisterous sisters, collectively known as 'The Anas'. Joey confirms that yes, he's still living at home, which has been his best option while bootstrapping his business. His parents are still arguing joyfully on a daily basis.

'As for my sisters,' he says, 'Viviana's got three kids, Fabiana is set to be a famous handbag designer and Luciana – the youngest – just qualified as a plumber.'

I'm only half way through my entrée when I see that Joey's eating has slowed. He's looking at me with at least as much appreciation as his lamb.

'You don't look a day older,' he begins, and I wonder if he realises I'm now at the age where that is a precious compliment. Bella was so shocked by my lack of skin care routine, I've been wondering if I should explore the world of Estée Lauder.

'But you look more...' his gaze travels over me. 'Well, you look good,' he finishes.

I take a glug of wine. Hopefully, with some food inside me, I can now afford some Dutch courage.

'Thanks,' I say, which is what Wol told me was the best answer to any compliment.

I must be out of practice at hearing nice things. In the last few years, there's been a dearth of attractive men flirting with me across a restaurant table. There was Vince, who sold advertising at the magazine, but he was more interested in himself than me. And I always seemed to end up paying for dinner. Then, a couple of years ago, there was Liam, an incredibly buff Australian with a love of rugby. He finished with me, just as I was considering buying a ticket to follow him Down Under. A boat ticket, of course. It's a good thing he ended it before I made it to the docks in Southampton: I would have been seriously pissed off to arrive in Perth after weeks at sea, to find he'd changed his mind.

'I mean it, Sophia.' Joey adopted this variant of my name in college. 'Your lifestyle must suit you.'

My lifestyle features a quiet English village, hours in front of my computer, a glut of pastries from the bakery, and countless wakeful nights wondering where, precisely, I went wrong. But I'm not sharing that.

'Although,' he goes on, 'I'm surprised you chose Saffron Sweeting.'

I stiffen. Joey was never top of the class in college, but he's not dim. It doesn't take a genius to deduce that my job as an air hostess doesn't add up. Finding I'm no longer hungry, I place my knife and fork together.

'But then again, SpeedyJet are at Stansted, aren't they? I suppose it's only half an hour down the M11.'

He's answered his own question, with no input needed from me. I exhale and murmur, 'That was delicious.'

'Good,' he says, smiling in the lopsided way I recall from a decade ago. He was never short of female admirers in college, and I'm sure he wasn't heartbroken for long – if at all – when I left for London. I'm flattered he's interested again now. I don't care about his professional success, or what car he's driving, or whether he's living with his parents. But it's a long time since I've found myself sitting opposite eyes that molten and a smile that sexy.

The food, wine and candlelight are dulling my reflexes. Maybe I could revisit my feelings for him. Maybe I want to revisit them.

Joey leans closer and reaches for my hand. 'So tell me,' he half whispers, 'before we tackle dessert, what's your tip for avoiding jetlag?'

Caught off guard, I meet his gaze with apprehension. Joey's such good buddies with my mother, there's no way I can admit to him I'm not an air hostess. It would be like making a chink in a sea wall at low tide: a harmless looking hole, but deadly once the water rises. So, as I mutter something about herbal tea and circadian rhythms, my only thought is there's no hope for us at all.

How can there be, if it's only our first date, and already I'm lying?

Chapter 5

When Bella leaves for church next morning, my head is firmly under my pillow. She doesn't believe in God any more than I do, but she says she plans to throw herself into village life, including midnight mass at Christmas and the Easter morning service. I'm more interested in an extra hour's sleep before I lick out the middle of several Cadbury's crème eggs for breakfast.

Yellow fondant filling notwithstanding, I'm ravenous by the time we arrive at Oak House for brunch. With its old walls and latticed windows, it's one of the most attractive buildings in the village. Lorraine is smiling broadly as we step into the large hall, where the smell of beeswax competes with brunch.

'Happy Easter!' She hugs us both. Then, spotting the simnel cake Bella made yesterday, 'Ooh, lovely.'

I haven't been inside Oak House before, but follow Bella towards the dining room. There's enough food to feed half the village, which is lucky, because they're here: gossiping, quaffing and behaving like they've had no social life since December. Which, actually, might be close to the truth.

Etiquette would suggest we find a drink, then circle the room and garden to exchange pleasantries and ask after people's health. Happily, neither Bella nor I believe in party politeness, at least, not until we've taken care of business. Like two synchronised swimmers, we dive for the buffet. Each of us takes a plate in our left hand, our elbows positioned at matching angles to deter any competition. Lorraine has done an amazing job with plump sausages, wedges of frittata, croissants and fruit. To drink, I spy Bloody Marys and Bucks Fizz as well as huge pots of tea and coffee.

'Next time I invite you to a party, don't look so miffed, okay?' Bella's plate is already heaped as she grins at me across a massive platter of kedgeree.

'Point taken.' This beats grinding my teeth while mum and Pompous Anthony make suggestions about my life. A second text from my mother, in which she promised news to share, sealed the deal of me going nowhere near their own Easter service.

Deciding it's still a little early to get stuck into the breakfast cocktails, Bella and I saunter out to the garden to perch on a bench and eat.

After munching for ten minutes, I stretch and remember my manners. 'I'm going to say hello to some people.'

Bella nods. 'I'll see if Lorraine needs any help.'

Once I've chatted with Brian from the bakery, dodged Violet's pointed remark about missing church, and managed small talk with a serious-looking man who I think runs the library, I meander towards the kitchen. Here, Bella and Lorraine are chinwagging while our hostess mixes something in a huge bowl.

'Just doing some shortbread,' Lorraine says, her arm muscles flexing. 'You never know who might want a piece.' She turns to Bella. 'Have you said hello to the chickens?'

'Not yet. I must thank them for the eggs,' Bella replies.

It's a pity Stanley doesn't lay eggs, I think. She might look more kindly on him.

'Tom's going to build them a new house. He measured up when he brought the feed over.' Lorraine reaches into a cupboard, pulls out chocolate chips, and adds a sprinkle to the bowl.

'Tom?' I ask. Does she mean the pet shop delivery man?

'Yes. My brother-in-law. He's here somewhere, I think.'

Bella looks up from browsing Lorraine's cookbook collection. 'Lorraine's husband died a few years ago.'

Lorraine nods. 'Tom's been very good to me. Helps with some of the man tasks.'

'Nice,' Bella says.

I decide this isn't the time to assert that women are as

capable as men of building chicken houses, if we put our minds to it.

'Actually, we met him,' Bella adds.

Before Lorraine can answer, a brunette floats into the kitchen, her long apple-green dress rustling silkily.

'Am I allowed in here?' she asks, entering anyway.

Something about her makes me look down, and I see she's barefoot.

'Of course!' Lorraine turns from spreading the pale shortbread mix into a baking tin. 'Meet Bella and her friend Sophie.' She looks at us. 'This is Rainbow. She and her husband stayed here last month. Now they're renting a house in the village. They're American.'

You don't say, I think. As I reach across Lorraine's kitchen table to shake the guest's hand, her armful of bracelets jingles.

We discover Rainbow is from Los Gatos, in California. I've never heard of it, but apparently it's near San Francisco. Well, that explains the happy hippie chic. Bella asks if she's on holiday.

'No, more of a sabbatical. Mitchell – my husband – is here for work.'

'He works for, what is it, a medical firm?' Lorraine says.

'Genetics,' Rainbow clarifies. 'He's doing a feasibility study of moving staff to Cambridge.' She sounds bored, as if she has to explain this to everyone she meets.

'It's quite exciting,' Lorraine says. 'Lots more lovely visitors.'

'And you, Rainbow?' Bella asks. 'Will you be sightseeing, while you're here?'

'Jeez, no,' Rainbow laughs. 'At least, not the whole time. I run workshops in healing.'

Based on her lack of shoes, I assume she said *heeling*. 'Cool,' I exclaim. She must be some New Age cobbler. 'You should talk to that man on Cambridge market who makes clogs.'

There's an unusually long pause.

Then Lorraine speaks. 'Rainbow is a professor over there,' she says, bending to put the shortbread in the oven.

'Adjunct professor.' Rainbow looks pleased, nonetheless. 'At the University of Santa Cruz.'

Wow. You can get a degree in shoemaking now? They didn't mention that when I opted for geography. Sensing the conversation is too kooky for me, I retreat to the dining room, where I contemplate the simnel cake but decide on a bowl of apple crumble. From there, the mild outside air beckons.

The morning's April showers have abated and Lorraine's garden, though not large, has a carpet of spring bulbs under a majestic oak tree. At the end, reached by a path of stepping stones, I can see what must be the chicken shed. I pause on the uneven brick patio, surveying the view.

'Did you know you've got custard on your nose?'

I turn sharply. I hadn't realised anyone was standing there, much less looking at my nose.

'Oh,' I say, checking with the back of my hand and finding I have indeed garnished my features with crumble. 'Thanks.' Then I see it's the guy from the pet shop. What did Lorraine say his name was?

'You're welcome.' He gives me a mischievous grin but then makes an effort to straighten his face. He puts out his hand. 'I'm Tom.'

I move the bowl to my left hand so I can shake his. It's a firm grip. 'Hi. I'm Sophie. Thank you for bringing my parrot food yesterday.' Absent-mindedly, I take another spoonful. The apple chunks are firm but tender, the crumble topping not too sweet, the hint of cinnamon just right.

'No problem,' he says. 'Would hate for him to go hungry. And it doesn't look like you'll be taking any crumble home for him.'

I let the spoon drop to the bowl. 'Sorry,' I say. 'Am I being rude?'

He shakes his head. 'No, you're fine. Lorraine does make terrific crumble.'

I nod. 'You should have some. Then nobody can accuse me of eating it all.'

'Right,' he says. 'In that case, I must do my bit.' He looks at me, his head on one side. 'Can I bring you anything, Sophie? Something else to dab on your nose?'

I can't help but laugh, shaking my head. 'Thank you. But I'm fine.'

He heads into the house and for some reason my head wants to turn to follow his progress. Frowning, I make myself focus on the garden instead.

'Sophie! It is Sophie, isn't it?'

I see a chubby woman in her fifties, with a mass of golden hair, advancing across the lawn. She looks familiar, but from where?

'I thought it was you.' She beams. 'So nice you're out and about again.'

She must mean I've been keeping my head down more than usual, since Wol died. I give her a blank smile, still not sure where –

'Marjorie! From the bank? You know – your mum used to work with me.'

'Oh, right, hi.' Yes, of course, the Saffron Sweeting bank. Mum did indeed work there, before she got promoted to branch manager in Colchester.

'I'm terribly sorry about your great-aunt,' Marjorie says. 'She was such a part of the village, Miss Campbell. Of course, I'm a tad too old to have been taught by her –' she giggles '– but she taught my Eddie and did a wonderful job. I often said to her, Miss Campbell, you've done a wonderful job. My Eddie would be illiterate without you.'

'Right,' I say, baffled by this deluge. I prefer to bank online, and now I remember why: going into the Saffron Sweeting branch always takes far longer than it should.

'But it's wonderful news about your mother,' Marjorie continues rapidly. 'I saw her at Miss Campbell's funeral and she dropped a hint. She couldn't say anything then, of course. She wouldn't, I mean, she's too professional.'

'Huh?' I look down at my empty bowl. I could definitely manage seconds. With extra custard.

'We only found out officially last week. I bet you're thrilled, it'll be so nice to see a bit more of her in the village, won't it?'

'I'm sorry?' What is this blonde chatterbox gabbling about? I've never met anyone who can talk this fast, when not standing at an auction podium.

'Your mum, being promoted to area manager. That's such an honour, isn't it? I said to her, Erica, what an honour! She'll be here much more often now, we'll be able to have lunch together, like old times.'

I blink and stare. With the speed of what she said, I may have missed the finer points, but I'm pretty sure I heard that my mother will be spending more time in the village. Oh, crap.

'Oh, and here's Tom,' Marjorie trills, unaffected by my dismay. 'Tom, we met earlier, remember, I'm Marjorie?'

If he's got any sense, he'll scarper back through those patio doors, I think.

He doesn't. He strolls over amiably. 'I remember very well,' he says. 'Hello again.'

'And do you know Sophie?' Marjorie asks. 'I work with her mum. She's an air hostess. Sophie, I mean, not her mother!' She laughs at her own joke. 'Sophie, this is Tom Vine.'

I cringe at Marjorie's gushing introduction. Now, I think, he'll drop his spoon, apologise and retreat hastily.

But he doesn't move.

'Really?' He looks at me. 'No, she didn't mention that.'

'Oh, you two have met? Well, that's lovely,' Marjorie beams.

I nod. 'We met in the pet shop, where Tom works.'

Something flicks across Tom's expression. But he doesn't say anything, just takes a spoonful of crumble and looks at me. He's still looking, when Marjorie chimes in.

'Pet shop? Oh, you mean the garden centre, I expect?'

Then, seeing me frown, 'Tom's family owns the Vine chain of garden centres, don't you, Tom?'

'That's right.' He nods.

Vine, I think. Vines. I know those garden centres: they're all over East Anglia. Wol liked to go sometimes, for bedding plants and the senior citizens' afternoon tea.

A flush circles my neck. 'I thought you worked at the pet shop in Newmarket,' I say.

One of Tom's eyebrows lifts a fraction.

'I thought you were the delivery guy,' I mutter, addressing his shoes.

Marjorie gives a peal of laughter. 'Oh, no, dear, what a mix-up. Tom's the Managing Director of Vines, aren't you?'

Oh, God, and I made him deliver a load of parrot food. When the brick patio doesn't oblige by swallowing me up, I open my mouth to do the only appropriate thing and apologise.

But I can't get a word in as Marjorie ploughs on. With Tom watching me with amusement, I shut my mouth like a goldfish.

'Although, he was telling me earlier, he tries not to spend too much time at the garden centre, because his real passion is flying! Isn't it funny, you two have that in common?'

Flying? *Flying?* Oh, sod. Double sod. Sod with wings on. I turn scarlet and pray he'll think I'm merely mortified about mistaking him for an errand boy. This party has been a total disaster.

'Yes, Sophie works for SpeedyJet,' Marjorie rushes on, and if I had any dessert left in my bowl, I would throw it at her to shut her up. 'Very glamorous. Her mum's so proud of her. Did you know that, Sophie, how much your mum talks about you?'

Marjorie's words barely register. If my mum does talk about me, she's bragging about a career which doesn't exist. She wouldn't be proud of me at all, if she knew. I smile weakly.

Tom looks at Marjorie, then back at me. 'I wouldn't have guessed that,' he says slowly. 'Usually, I can spot cabin crew, but with Sophie, I had no idea.'

'Well, isn't that funny,' Marjorie beams, then spots Tom's apple crumble. 'Ooh, I must try some of that,' she says. 'Excuse me, both of you.'

And before I can react, she sashays off towards the dining room.

'I'm terribly sorry,' I say, to Tom's shirt rather than his face.

'Don't worry about it,' he replies. 'It was an easy mistake to make.'

All I need to do is make another quick apology, then leave him standing there. But my feet don't move.

'I wouldn't have pegged you as cabin crew,' Tom says again. 'Mind you, it's a few years since I flew commercial. I'm an instructor now.'

'Oh,' I say lamely, 'that's nice.'

'What do you fly?' he asks, conversationally. 'Short haul or long?'

I'm having an invisible panic attack. Of all the topics I never, ever like to talk about, it's my fictional flying job. 'Short,' I say, miserably, and so quietly he has to strain to hear.

'And what's the fleet mix?'

The what? What is he talking about? Why did I come here today? I wish with all my heart I'd stayed home with Stanley. Then I decide he's asking about the planes. 'Um, Boeing.' I tug at the collar of my shirt. 'It's awfully warm for April, isn't it?'

It's not actually warm at all; from the look of the sky, it could rain again at any minute. A curious look crosses Tom's face, but then his glance drops to my neckline. I can hardly object: I started it, and I'd rather he was occupied by my minimal cleavage than asking about my even more minimal flying.

When he looks up at me again, his eyes are darker than

before. 'Shall I get you a cold drink?'

'No,' I say, finally gathering my wits. 'That's okay, I should be leaving. It was nice to meet you. Meet you properly, I mean.' I turn to go.

Tom nods. 'You too. Take care.'

And as I walk unsteadily towards the house, head swimming from the humiliation of our conversation, I sincerely hope he doesn't see me stumble and trip over the threshold. But I don't dare look back to make sure.

Chapter 6

'Good news!' Bella says to me, a few evenings later. 'I've got a job!'

'I thought you had a job,' I say. Bella works for one of the Cambridge colleges, planning events and conferences.

'Yes.' She throws her bag on the sofa and hangs her rain mac over the back of a dining chair. On Easter Monday, the weather turned soggy and it's been alternately drizzling and pouring all week. 'But they cut my hours to part time. So I talked to Fergus.'

'Fergus? At The Plough?'

'Yup. I'm going to work behind the bar, and he says I can meddle in the kitchen too. Lord knows he needs some help there.' She leans down to remove her boots, then places them neatly on newspaper by the back door.

'Oh,' I say. 'Congratulations. Shall I dig out some wine?'

After we've toasted her success with a nice burgundy which doubtless belongs to Uncle Mike, Bella peers at me. 'Why the long face?' she asks. 'What with you and the weather, it's like a film noir. And did you even get dressed today?' She gestures at the voluminous green dressing gown I'm wearing.

'Yes,' I snap, although it's true there are plenty of days when I negotiate for editing work in my pyjamas. 'I walked to the village earlier, got caught in a downpour, and treated myself to a hot bath.' The rain somehow made it easier to cry and I'd lain in the bubbles missing Wol. Eventually, I hauled myself out and borrowed this robe from the back of the bathroom door, thinking Bella must have put on considerable weight if her clothes are this size. Poor thing.

Right on cue, she opens the fridge and starts pulling out ingredients.

'Sorry...' I add. 'It's just that since Wol died, things seem to have got complicated.'

'What things?'

I lean my elbows on the kitchen counter. 'Before, when she was alive, it was just the two of us in her little cottage. I worked from home, kept my head down. Nobody took any notice of us.'

Bella picks up a knife and starts dicing an onion. 'And now?'

I sniff, and not just from onion fumes. 'Now, all kinds of people are turning up, asking questions.'

'You mean like me?' She smiles.

'You're okay,' I say. 'I don't mind you.' And you're cooking my supper, I think. 'But there's Joey. He was nowhere to be seen, until Wol died.'

'Are you seeing him again? Here, can you peel these?' Four big potatoes roll in my direction.

'He phoned and suggested a drink.' Doubt creeps into my voice.

'Good! That's encouraging. Don't use that knife, you'll slice yourself. Try this peeler.'

I do as I'm told, taking the potatoes and Y-shaped peeler to the sink.

'I'm not sure I want to be encouraging,' I say.

'Why not? He's dead hunky, and he likes you.'

Oh, he is hunky, I absolutely can't deny that. Even more than he used to be.

'Well, he thinks I'm an air hostess, and I can't tell him I'm not.'

'Why not?' Bella flings the onions into a huge frying pan.

'Because he's so thick with my mum, he's bound to let it slip. Especially since she's got herself a bloody promotion and is descending on the Sweeting branch once a week.'

Marjorie's news at Lorraine's brunch rattled me so much I phoned my mother, which is something I seldom do. Mum assured me joyfully that the rumour was true: she would be in the village far more often and, when my flight schedule allowed, would be sure to pop in to see me.

'It's a nightmare,' I tell Bella now. 'She'll be dropping in, questioning why I'm always here when I'm supposed to be gone half the time.'

'Sophie, I know I promised to keep that a secret,' Bella begins, 'and I will,' she adds, seeing my reaction, 'but is it such a big deal? So, they booted you out of stewardess training. You can tell your mum, she'll get over it. Daughters come home with worse news.'

She's right about that. Still...

'I can't tell her.' I jab stubbornly at a potato with the peeler. 'She mustn't know they kicked me out.'

'Well... could you try again? Or did you find you don't want to be an air hostess?'

'I'd love to,' I sigh. 'It's my dream job.'

'So, unless they found out you're a terrorist or something... try again. Find a different airline. Keep at it.' She turns back to the fridge. 'Do you want carrots in the shepherd's pie or peas?'

The peeler barely misses the tip of my finger. The onions, now sizzling happily in their pan, can't be blamed for the tears welling in my eyes.

'I can't keep at it,' I insist. 'I can't just try again.'

'Why ever not?' asks Bella.

'Because...' I wipe an eye with the back of my wrist. It's actually a relief to tell her. 'Because I'm terrified of flying.'

~ ~ ~

Bella looks incredulous, but before she can respond, there's a brisk knock at the front door.

Bugger, I think, who the hell's that? Surely not someone trying to sell us solar panels in this weather? Bella's busy concocting our dinner, so I gather myself and head for the door.

When I open it, I find a tall woman with wavy auburn hair standing with her back to me. She's wearing a chic navy suit with a peplum jacket, which shows off curves like Jessica Rabbit.

Then she whirls around on one heel and proclaims, 'At last! *You're* the one sleeping in my husband's bed!'

With that, she steps forward, and thrusts out a hand. Instinctively, I take a step back, but then notice her wide, mischievous smile.

'I'm so pleased to meet you,' she says. 'I'm Amelia.'

I shake her hand cautiously. Her grip is enthusiastic and she's wearing a huge cocktail ring which winks at me, despite the gloom outside.

'I'm sorry,' I say, apologising immediately for something I haven't done. 'But I'm not sleeping with your husband.'

But I'm really thinking: Joey – the scumbag – is he married and hasn't told me?

'No, darling, not *with* my husband. Just in his bed, right? And I should have said ex-husband.'

'Umm...' I'm still not getting it.

'You're house sitting, correct? For Michael Hargraves? You're wearing his dressing gown, you know.'

Now I get it. Bella's Uncle Mike. And this is *his* dressing gown? Ugh. I hope it's been washed.

'Well, I'm Amelia Hargraves. I own the estate agency in the village.'

'Oh,' I say. The penny drops. I've seen her occasionally in the post office and the baker's, always dressed beautifully and talking in that deep, posh way. 'Sorry. Yes. Would you like to come in?'

Amelia strides past me happily, not needing, of course, to be shown the way to the living room. I shuffle after her, making sure the belt of Mike's dressing gown is tied securely.

Amelia's standing in the middle of the room, head swivelling as she assesses her former home. Even though I am entirely blameless in the sleeping-with-the-husband department, I still feel awkward.

'Where the bloody hell did that come from?'

She's looking, of course, at Stanley, who opens both

eyes, lifts one clawed foot off his perch and echoes 'Bloody hell!' at the top of his voice, adding 'Feed me!' for good measure.

'He's temporary,' I say. Great. Now she's taught Wol's parrot how to swear. Some guardian I make.

'I like him,' Amelia says. 'He's feisty.' Then she turns to me. 'So, you're Bella's friend?'

'Yes,' I say. 'I'm Sophie. Bella's in the kitchen.' I gesture with my head.

'I'll say hello in a minute.' She waves her ring-adorned hand again. 'But it's actually you I came to see.' She's started digging in a beautiful leather briefcase. 'Erica – your mother – asked me to bring you these.'

'Bring me... oh,' I say as I see that she's holding several sheets of paper, all with the Hargraves & Co heading in bold green ink, matching my dressing gown. Upside down, I make out a photo of a cottage.

'That's right, isn't it?' Amelia asks brightly. 'Erica said you've had a windfall and you're looking to buy a house? You've picked the *absolutely* perfect time of year.'

Great, I think, taking the house details. Mum's meddling. Again. She might claim to be fine with Wol leaving me money, but she still has an opinion on how I spend it. Shouldn't she be busy, out knocking on doors with Pompous Anthony, persuading people to vote for him next month?

Bella rescues me. 'Aunt Amelia!' she exclaims, coming through from the kitchen with oven gloves in her hand.

'Bella, darling!' The two of them hug.

'Will you stay for a glass of wine?' Bella asks. 'And I'm making shepherd's pie, although it won't be ready for a while.'

I grit my teeth. I can hardly object to Bella inviting her aunt for supper, especially as this might technically still be her house. Not to mention her wine.

'I'm not supposed to touch alcohol for a bit,' Amelia says, 'but some shepherd's pie sounds jolly good.'

As I fetch Amelia a Coke, I cross my fingers that Bella understands how vital it is that my fear of flying stays under wraps, just like my job. But the two of them are off, chatting happily, discussing family, the weather and the village. Amelia is vivacious, waving her hands around and calling me 'darling' even though we've only just met.

'My sincere condolences for your great-aunt,' she says in a more subdued tone as Bella mashes the potato for the top of the pie.

I nod my thanks.

'I don't suppose you know who's inherited the cottage?' she asks, without guile.

'The solicitor said he couldn't tell us yet,' I say.

'We've no idea,' Bella chips in. 'But we're all intrigued. It was rough on Sophie, being kicked out. Like something out of Downton Abbey.'

This reminds me, I need to summon the fortitude to start going through Wol's stuff. The new owner won't wait forever to get their hands on her cottage.

'Hmm.' Amelia looks thoughtful. 'Well, darlings, do me a favour and keep your ears open, will you? There's a pretty good chance they'll want to sell.'

~ ~ ~

It's not until I flop down beside Kit that I realise how weary I am.

She's come by coach to pick up Wol's car, left to her in the will and just released by Mr Baggit. It's her Easter break, but she's stayed in Nottingham to do work experience.

'You're sure you don't want the Morris?' she asked me on the phone.

'No,' I said. 'My car's fine.'

My red Fiesta, in fact, is far from fine. The exhaust hangs low to the ground and I haven't trusted it since it broke down on Mill Road Bridge last year. But I much prefer bombing around town on my bike and, in any case, a car will be useful for Kit. I'm only slightly envious of the vintage panache supplied by Wol's powder blue Morris Minor. Maybe, when the dust settles, I'll buy it back from her.

After last year, we've formed an understanding that the less Kit's seen in Saffron Sweeting, the better. So, I pick her up from the bus station and we head out of the city centre towards Newnham. Leaving Wol's car at Sheep's Green, we stroll the short distance to the river.

'I've always found it strange that there are cattle grazing in the middle of town,' Kit says as we step around a cow pat and find ourselves a bench beside the slow flowing Cam.

'It's some ancient bylaw,' I reply. 'And I like this part of the river. The punts seem more intrepid: they've shunned the postcard views of the Backs to head upstream, like pioneers.'

I gesture at the numerous boats on the river, their occupants taking advantage of the first decent day this week.

'Either intrepid or plain daft, if they think they can make it to Grantchester before teatime.'

'Talking of which, let's eat. I'm starving.'

We dig into the white paper bag I picked up that morning from the Saffron Sweeting bakery.

'How's uni?' I ask.

'Brilliant,' she replies through her cheese and pickle sandwich, then tells me about her classes and her promising grades. 'Even maths isn't too bad.'

Maths was Kit's weak spot all through school, and almost derailed her college applications. Mum found a tutor, a gentle young man from India called Ravi, just in time.

'And four of us are getting a house together next year, which will be fantastic,' she continues.

'Sounds good. Anyone special?'

She shakes her head, eyes on the river. 'No. Which is fine. I'm so grateful to have this opportunity... I don't want anything to complicate it.'

'Fair enough,' I say, relieved she's doing well. From a young age, we could all see Kit's potential. This is the perfect path for her: she'll probably invent the robot that cures cancer, or at least cleans your house for you.

'How are you doing?' she asks.

I shrug and bite into sausage and chutney on a wholewheat bap. 'I'm okay,' I reply mechanically, feeling better as I chew.

Kit pauses with her sandwich, and looks at me. When I don't say anything further, she prods, 'You sure about that?'

Dearest Kit. How can she be twelve years younger, but more than twenty years wiser? Despite her mistakes she's so steady and calm now. Yet she's still a teenager.

I bite my lip and have to look away. 'I miss her so much,' I whisper.

Kit puts her arm around my shoulders and gives a quick squeeze. 'I know,' she says. 'I know you do.'

'I never told her, she was more like a mother to me than...' I give a half sob. 'I wish I'd said that.'

I understand why mum was gone so often and I try not to blame her for it: after my dad left, she had to make ends meet and I know that was tough. But Wol never once treated me like an inconvenient house guest. She behaved as if I were a precious equal.

'Wol was a wise old thing,' Kit says. 'I think she knew. She certainly knew what she did for me.'

'I should have talked to her more,' I say. 'There's so much I don't know, about her life. We had time, all those evenings we played Scrabble or did the crossword or watched the stupid Antiques Roadshow.'

'Look, it's only been a few weeks,' replies Kit. 'This was always going to be a horrible time for you.'

There's a pause, punctuated by a collision between two punt-loads of tourists. This sparks much shrieking, arm waving and an exchange of navigational suggestions between the boats.

'Sorry,' I say. 'Have a flapjack.'

'You don't need to be sorry,' Kit says. 'It's not like we're a conventional family. You and Wol – you were all I had for a while there.'

Which is why I'm so relieved she's blazing a trail now. I take a deep breath. Kit's right, losing someone like Wol was never going to be a picnic.

'But it's not just her dying,' I begin, stuttering over the word, which tastes wrong on my tongue. 'It's everything else.'

'What kind of everything else? Work?'

My current editing project involves applying the house style to draft chapters on the south of France, which is ironic as it's one of the few places in Europe I've actually been.

'No, work's okay.'

I tell Kit about mum now having a pretext to visit whenever she wants, that she seems to think I'm going to buy a house with my inheritance, and that Joey has come out of the mist like the Mary Celeste.

'Yeah, mum can be a pain. But I don't agree about Joey. Wasn't he the Italian guy who turned up on Valentine's Day with actual red roses? I thought he was dreamy.'

'My God, Kit, you were – what – eight? I can't believe you remember Joey, let alone anything else about him. That's scary.'

'So it *was* him with the flowers?'

I had forgotten the roses: my first, and the only ones ever hand delivered by a guy on Valentine's Day. 'Yeah.'

'And you're seeing him again?'

'It looks like it,' I say. 'If you can call a quiet drink at The Plough seeing him.'

I think Joey planned something more elaborate for our second date, but I wanted to downplay the occasion, while I worked out whether I liked him, and if so, whether the risk was worth it.

'Okay,' I admit. 'It was a date. We spent a couple of hours at the pub, just talking. He's a pretty successful photographer now, you know.'

'Nice,' Kit says.

'But he's scarily chummy with mum,' I add. 'I can't let my guard down with him.'

Kit nods slowly. 'Right,' she says. 'Yeah, I see.'

Neither of us says what we're both thinking. And it hits me that since Wol died, Kit is the only person on the planet who could possibly guess my line of thought. I realise how precious she is to me, and how scared I am of losing her too.

But Kit's thoughts are less sombre. Smart and practical, she's moving on with her life.

'Well,' she says after a few moments. 'you don't need to let your guard down.' She grins. 'If Joey's half as tasty as he used to be, you can let other things down instead.'

Chapter 7

Waving Kit off in Wol's beautiful blue car doesn't lift my spirits. I need to make my way back to Saffron Sweeting, but it won't be long until Bella finishes work. If I go on Park and Ride with her, maybe she'll cheer me up a bit.

According to this plan, I perch patiently on the wall opposite Trewe College, where Bella works, and watch Cambridge flow past me. It's hard to spot the genuine university undergraduates amongst the visitors, gaggles of English language students, and Cambridge townsfolk. Pedestrians spill off the pavement into the cobbled street, bikes weave around them, and in turn, drivers navigate the throng with surgical precision.

At five past five, I wave as Bella emerges from the elegant arched doorway of the Porter's Lodge.

'Kit came for the car,' I say. 'Thought I'd keep you company going home.' I've forgotten that I'm really the one who wants company.

'I wasn't sure you'd part with it,' Bella replies.

'What? The Morris Minor?' I exhale. 'No, it's okay. Wol left it to her, and it'll be handy for Kit to have wheels this summer.'

'Still, I saw how you looked at that old thing.'

Have I been mooching over the car? Is that why my mood matches its paintwork?

'You're a lovely sister, Sophie,' Bella says as we amble along Trumpington Street. 'I wish I had a sister.'

Bella has two brothers, both mad about rugby, who used to tease her mercilessly about her shape. I hope they've cut that out, these days.

'I wasn't always thrilled about it,' I say. 'I was almost a teenager when Kit was born. She was a hell of a shock.'

That's putting it mildly. Mum remarrying two years before was bad enough – no girl should wear peach frills at her mother's wedding – and I was still dazed when Kit entered the picture.

'It's a big age gap,' Bella agrees, stopping at the polite behest of a Japanese man, to take his photo.

'It wasn't just the gap,' I say. 'They were suddenly this perfect little family. I was left over from a marriage she wanted to forget.'

But it wasn't only the marriage mum wanted to erase. I was nine when I overheard her close to tears one night, telling Wol that eighteen was far too young for motherhood and she wished she'd had the guts to take care of the problem. I didn't know what she meant, but her bitter words festered inside me. Then, a couple of years later, I found a magazine article and finally knew for certain how she felt. That night, I tried to run away from home.

Bella's pace slows outside Fitzbillies, her attention understandably drawn by the famous Chelsea buns in the window. 'Well, you're a great sister to Kit now.'

'The little family wasn't as perfect as it seemed,' I say.

My stepdad owned a petrol station and worked long hours, claiming it was cheaper to stay open all night than to pay the extra insurance. Mum was doing well at the bank and, with friction creeping into their marriage, she threw her energy into her career. 'When they were home together, which wasn't often, we had to duck to avoid the low-flying sarcasm.'

'You escaped to college,' Bella says.

'Yup. But Kit was stuck with it.' We're outside Corpus now, near the bizarre grasshopper clock. 'And then there was the rhubarb accident.'

'The what?'

'Rhubarb. I don't know who grew it or gave it to us in the first place. I was in my last year at college, so Kit must have been about nine. She was home alone, as usual, and tried to microwave it.'

'Oh.' Bella had started to smile at the rhubarb tale, but hesitates now.

'Somehow she dropped it,' I say. 'Scalded all down her legs. She was in terrible pain... finally made it to a neighbour. She doesn't wear skirts, even now.'

'Poor little thing!' Bella stops, a hand over her mouth.

I sigh. 'From then on, although I wasn't physically living at home, I decided I had to do a better job of being there for her.'

I meant it. I still mean it. Kit's had enough to deal with. But now, she's doing so well. She deserves to enjoy plain sailing for a few years. And if I can stop stuff rocking her boat, I will.

~ ~ ~

Despite Kit's advice to throw caution to the wind with Joey, I'm still hesitant. But the next afternoon, when I get back from a bike ride to find him in our living room having an intellectual chat with Stanley, I do wonder if it's a sign. No, I tell myself, just a sign I need to be careful.

'I hope Bella let you in,' I say mildly, thinking I might have to explain to my housemate that I'm not wild about surprise visitors.

'She did.' He flashes me his sexy grin, then turns back to offer the parrot a celery stick. 'Then she went to work. At the pub, she said?'

I nod.

'So it's just us, then,' Joey says. He stretches, T-shirt tight across his torso. The effect isn't lost on me. With the distractions of the last couple of years, it's been a while since I felt a man's arms around me. Wol, of course. Kit, certainly. But a man?

I could really use a hug right now, I think. Still, I fold my arms. 'Don't get any ideas,' I say. 'And your only chance of getting a decent dinner disappeared with Bella.'

He shrugs. I remember his easy-going nature from before.

'That's okay,' he says. 'We could order pizza or something?'

'Fine,' I say, 'if you don't mind it taking an hour to get here and the delivery guy whining when he does.'

Saffron Sweeting is a bit of a trek for the Cambridge pizza restaurants, and they seem to find the village extraordinarily hard to navigate. We're not so far out of the way their sat nav won't function, but they act like they've had to deliver a Hawaiian to Oahu itself.

'I wanted to ask you something,' Joey says, after we've located a pizza leaflet and placed an order big enough to feed six.

People only say that if they think there's a good chance you'll refuse: if a question is innocuous, they come straight out with it. I try not to let him see me tense. What does he have in mind?

Joey crosses to the French doors and stands looking out at the long garden. 'That white shed or summer house thing. It's really pretty.'

I frown. He's admiring the garden? 'Er, it's a gazebo, I think.'

Joey turns to me. 'I have an engagement shoot next week. I was wondering if I could do some of it here.'

'Here?' I let out a big breath: he's simply asking a favour for his business. 'Oh.'

I look out at the garden, where the slanting afternoon sun is casting long shadows. Joey's right, it is attractive. Like the house itself, another clematis scrambles up one side of the wooden structure, splashing white flowers with bold purple centres. Under the trees, daffodils still nod bravely, but I notice with a tug that they're past their best. Wol won't see them bloom next year.

'We should ask Bella,' I say. 'But, yeah, I don't see why not.'

'Would you mind –' he begins, then stops himself.

'What?' I'm more relaxed about this conversation now I know it's about photographs.

'Can I take a few shots, while we wait for the pizza? I want to test the light, plan the best gear for the day.'

'Do you have your stuff now?'

He nods. 'It's in the car. It mostly lives in the car; there isn't room at mum and dad's.'

'Okay,' I say. 'Well, help yourself.'

Joey grins and heads for the door. Then he stops. 'Would you mind coming outside too? It'd be much easier, with a human in the shots.'

So that's how we find ourselves together in an English garden, late on a cool spring afternoon. Dew is about to form, and the scent of grass is so heavy, it almost settles on my skin.

Joey takes a few shots, fiddles with a light meter, then pauses, his eyes on me.

'What?' I feel self-conscious.

He glances away, sheepish. 'Looking at you through the lens...' he says, 'it reminds me of the first time I saw you.'

Until then, I'd been slouching placidly in front of the hedge, enjoying the fresh air and anticipating the pizza toppings. Now, I'm like a young deer, with gangly legs that don't feel right, no matter where I plant them.

'Oh,' is my lame reply.

'You remember, babe?' he says.

I nod. I was outside the library, brandishing a placard, demonstrating with a cluster of other students. What was our gripe? Student loans? The threat of tuition fees? I'm not sure, now. But I remember Joey turning up, on assignment for the student newspaper, wielding his second-hand camera. This energised my little group: we began chanting and posturing with renewed zeal.

And I remember the first time he called me babe too.

'You looked so gorgeous,' Joey says now, looking down at the camera he's turning in his hands. 'With your raggedy skirt and black boots, and those pouty red lips.'

I start to laugh, but then see he's not joking.

There's a pause. I say, 'Where do you want me?' and immediately cringe at my choice of words.

But he doesn't leer, or wink, or do any of the things the

old Joey might have done.

'Here,' he says instead. 'Can you put your hand here, on this pillar?'

I do as I'm told, leaning on the gazebo, and wait for the thudding in my chest to settle.

The camera clicks and whirrs, clicks and whirrs, as he takes shots of me standing with my arm on the gazebo, arm by my side, facing the camera, looking away, looking back over my shoulder.

Just as I'm wondering how he can possibly need so many, he stops.

'Yeah. I thought so,' he says. 'You're still beautiful.'

And that's how, as the sun sinks down over the hedge, we're left in shadows which steal across our faces. Lulled by the sense that nothing in this leafy place is real, all I hear are clicks and whirrs as I let him adjust my hips, my shoulders, then my hair. And then, with no sound in the garden except the first distant hoot of an owl, I surrender to the twilight and let Joey kiss me.

Chapter 8

'This really isn't my cup of tea,' I mutter as we meander through the village towards Amelia's house. 'I don't want to see crowds of people at the moment.'

The shadow of the malt house falls over us, stretching almost across the main street. It's my favourite time of day in the village, when the lime rendered cottage walls glow softly and the street lights seem to bow their iron heads to begin their night's work.

'It'll be good for you,' Bella says. 'You're chained to that computer all day. And it's not a crowd. Just a handful of women getting their nails done.'

I cast a wistful glance towards the pub, looking so enticing in the twilight. If I have to risk conversation with village residents, I'd much rather do it in the dark, beery atmosphere of The Plough.

'Anyway,' says Bella, 'whoever heard of an air hostess who doesn't like her hands pampered?'

I grunt and move the Tupperware box of cheese straws, baked by Bella this afternoon, to my other hand. We've been invited to a manicure party, hosted by the glamorously scary Amelia.

'It's a friend of mine, darling,' Amelia said as she dropped by unexpectedly again, waving fingernails which as far as I could tell were already perfectly polished. 'She's recently qualified and has a new mobile business. She's doing nail parties to spread the word.'

'What fun,' Bella said, ignoring my head shaking. 'We'd love to.'

'Super,' said Amelia. 'God knows, so little happens in this village, we have to make our own entertainment.'

We've reached Amelia's house now: an elegant single-storied building, where the river leaves the other side of the village. 'We should have brought Stanley,' I say. 'He could do with getting his claws trimmed.'

'You're not going to be a grump, are you?' Bella says, lifting the shiny door knocker. 'You can't hide away like Miss Havisham, you know.'

If I knew who Miss Havisham was, I might be able to come up with a pithy retort. Bella's always talking about fictional characters as if they're real, and although it stings me to admit it, I'm rarely sure what traits she's discussing. Wol did a better job of instilling a love of reading in Bella than in me. So, while I'm still struggling to remember whether Miss Havisham spent her time hanging out of a window in *Wuthering Heights* or was perhaps the sinister housekeeper in *Rebecca*, we find ourselves welcomed into Amelia's lair.

Okay, so lair is a bit unkind as we're in no danger and she doesn't seem to have a motive except to send us all home with gleaming nails. But the house is intimidatingly stylish, its impeccable renovation paired with contemporary furnishings in quiet colours and expensive fabrics. There are so few real possessions lying around, it looks like the set for one of Joey's photo shoots, rather than anyone's actual home.

'We're in the kitchen,' Amelia says. 'Getting high on varnish fumes.'

I skulk behind Bella, wishing I'd done a better job of wriggling out of this. It's bad enough dodging Joey's idle questions about my job without other people adding their own curiosity to the mix. This week's been worse than most. A pesky Icelandic volcano has been spewing ash into the air, causing flight chaos, and everyone wants to chat about it. What's more, Bella's pinned a fake trip schedule to the fridge, showing my travel for the next month. Apparently, I'm going to Rome, Budapest and Glasgow – twice.

'Bell,' I said when I saw it, 'we can't do that. It's... downright deceitful.'

'I know,' she replied. 'But you did say how important this charade is. If you're going to lie, Sophie, you have to go all in.'

I left the roster on the fridge, but was also left with an uneasy feeling that this was getting out of hand.

'Everyone, this is Bella,' says Amelia to the women around the large kitchen island. 'Bella's my niece. Sort of. Oh, sod, it's complicated. And this is Sophie.'

There's an impressive spread of wine, nibbles and vibrantly coloured varnish bottles on the dark granite top.

'Who don't you know?' Amelia asks, not waiting for an answer, 'Lorraine, of course, from Oak House... and here's Cassie, she's married to Brian at the bakery. Holly's doing our nails – oh, and Rainbow, she's new in Saffron Sweeting. One of my clients.'

We all say hello. I'm relieved that Lorraine's here; she's friendly but no glamour puss. I won't be the only one who doesn't know one side of an emery board from the other. Cassie is extremely pretty but seems shy; I'm not sure I've even noticed her in the village.

'We've met Rainbow,' Bella says. 'At your brunch, Lorraine.'

'Terrific,' says Amelia. 'Grab yourself a drink. There's juice, if you don't want the champagne punch.'

Oh, I want the punch. Definitely. On closer inspection, Cassie has her hands in a big bowl of water, and Lorraine's are covered in what looks like mud. There's a bowl of olives in front of Rainbow: I'm not sure whether she's going to eat them or skewer one on each fingernail. I look down and see she has one foot in a bucket.

'I'm gonna get my toes done instead,' she drawls.

'Right,' I say politely, remembering her bare foot philosophy. If she's going to dance around the village like a woodland nymph, it makes sense she wants groomed tootsies.

'Oh, you have blue!' Bella cries, planting herself on a barstool and seizing a bottle of nail polish. She sees my wrinkled nose as I take the stool next to her. 'Sophie,' she says loudly, 'would you be allowed blue or is it against the uniform rules? Or how about this one? It's called Ash Morning.'

I glare and grab a cheese straw. 'I'll just watch for a while, I think.'

Bella rolls her eyes but her expression softens, and she turns to chat to Lorraine about mud. Or scrub. Or whatever they're calling it.

Amelia is sipping what looks like half a pint of tomato juice. 'Holly,' she says, 'our hands are in your hands. Work your magic, darling.'

Holly looks nervous as she picks up one of Amelia's elegant paws. 'You'll want to take that off,' she says, gesturing at the enormous rock on Amelia's right hand.

'Good lord, no,' Amelia replies. 'It's only out of a cracker. I made a pact one night with a *very* wicked friend. I'm not allowed to take it off until I get my next shag.'

Lorraine gapes. 'How long's it been on there?'

Amelia smirks. 'Oh, about three years.'

We all laugh. Maybe this won't be so bad, after all. As Holly starts to remove Amelia's current nail colour, I chew a nail and calculate how long it's been since I had sex. The answer shocks me and I reach for a top-up of punch, resolving to ask Bella about Miss Havisham.

An hour later, I've cautiously allowed Holly to shape my nails and apply a silver polish which actually looks quite sleek. Bella is entranced by her newly blue talons and our hippie American friend's feet look good enough to eat. Well, if you like feet, that is.

'Any news on your husband's staffing study, Rainbow?' Amelia sounds deliberately casual.

Rainbow shrugs. 'No clue. To be real honest, his work bores the pants off me.'

'Well,' says Amelia smoothly, 'I'm sure he sees what an ideal location we have here.'

Bella catches my eye. She was remarking the other day on the number of *For Sale* signs in the village, which have been in place for a while. No doubt Amelia would like the property market to pick up a bit.

'How are you getting on with your counselling plans?' Lorraine asks.

Rainbow frowns. 'Work permits are a total bitch.'

We make sympathetic noises. 'What sort of work do you do?' asks Cassie.

'I specialise in fears and phobias,' Rainbow answers.

Based on our previous conversation about shoemaking, I wonder if I heard correctly. Fear of what? Fear of blisters? Fear of turning up to an event in the same shoes as someone else? Is that why she shuns them altogether?

'Goodness,' says Holly, bent over Amelia's nail art. 'How impressive.'

'If you can't work, what will you do?' says Amelia.

Rainbow's face brightens. 'There's nothing to stop me running pro bono sessions. I've been developing some new workshops; I have one I'm ready to trial.'

'What kind of workshops?' asks Lorraine.

'Well, originally I offered claustrophobia,' Rainbow says lightly, 'and agoraphobia. Recently, a huge growth area has been mysophobia. That's the fear of germs,' she adds, glancing at the manicure tools arrayed on the kitchen island.

I'm starting to realise she's not talking about stinky feet and that I might have got the wrong end of the stick about shoemaking. Good thing I didn't mention the clogs again.

'Wow,' says Bella, which suggests she's not keeping up either.

'But I'm totally stoked about my new workshop,' Rainbow says, pausing to pluck a rum truffle from the box brought by Cassie. 'Thanks to Lorraine, I found an awesome co-instructor. It's gonna be ground-breaking.'

'That's nice,' Cassie responds politely. 'What's it for, then?'

Rainbow says something which sounds like *tear-off-my-hand-o-phobia*. I snigger, wondering what stupid fear these paranoid Americans can come up with next.

'Pardon?' Even Amelia is getting the giggles now.

'Pteromerhanophobia,' repeats Rainbow.

'Bless you,' I say, louder than I intended, then try to cover up by coughing into my punch. How many top-ups have I had?

'Sorry, er, what's that then?' Holly manages a straight expression.

Rainbow sighs, as if dealing with English country bumpkins is far beneath her IQ. But her answer wipes the smirk straight off my face.

'Pteromerhanophobia is the fear of flying.'

Chapter 9

On the walk home from Amelia's, Bella and I are both tipsy enough that dodging puddles and coming up with new names for phobias keeps us occupied. But the cool spring night inevitably sobers us up, and as we scurry inside, we're both shivering. I put the kettle on and by the time I've made Ovaltine, Bella has been upstairs, donned tartan pyjamas, and is back.

'You know, Soph,' she says, 'it's perfect.'

'What's perfect?' I pretend not to know what she's about to say.

'Rainbow's flying thing –'

'No,' I interrupt. 'No way.'

'But it's just what you need,' Bella begins again. 'You're scared of flying. She can fix that.'

'I'm not *scared* of flying,' I reply, louder than I intended. 'I'm downright bloody *petrified*.'

'All the more reason –'

'I told you. No freaking way!'

Bella purses her lips and goes to sit on the sofa. I stay standing, keeping my options open.

'So, let me get this straight.' Her voice is hushed but firm. 'You've admitted being an air hostess is your dream job. You even *got* the job, but lost it because of your phobia. Now you spend all day Googling fun places, instead of actually visiting them.' She gestures at my laptop on the dining table. 'You're sneaking around your mother, because you're too ashamed to tell her.'

'I'm not ashamed, exactly...'

'So why not just tell her? Why is it so disastrous if she knows?'

'Please, Bell. If she finds out I'm scared to fly, I'm toast.'

'But why?' Bella demands.

'If she knows that, she... can work other stuff out. I'm

sorry. That's all I can tell you.'

For several long seconds, I can see the hurt in her face. Then she flicks her hair and keeps talking.

'And you're lying to your scrumptious new boyfriend, because he thinks you work at thirty thousand feet, whereas you've never been higher than the top floor of Marks and Sparks.'

'Look,' I try again. 'I know it's not ideal –'

'Not ideal?' Bella snorts. 'It's ridiculous. And now the chance to cure your phobia has dropped into your lap, and you won't do anything about it?'

I set my mug down with enough force to splash Ovaltine over the side. 'I'm not letting a nut job hippie from San Francisco mess with my head.'

'She's not a nut job and she's not *from* San Francisco. She's got all sorts of degrees and she *cures* people, Sophie. I don't get it. This would kill several birds with one stone.'

'And kill me in the process,' I snap. 'Stop meddling, Bell. Sort your own life out, before you poke your beak into mine.'

I feel bad as soon as I say it. There's nothing wrong with Bella's nose but she thinks it's too pointy, and Beaky was one of her nastier school nicknames.

But Bella's skin is thicker than it used to be. Either that or she's still sloshed. She just stretches out her fingers to admire her shiny blue nails.

'It's your loss. But I don't know how long you can keep this up, Soupie Campbell. This would solve your problems in one fell swoop.'

So I'm not the only one stooping to childhood name calling. Knowing I'm in danger of losing this debate, I slink away to bed.

~~~

The next day, and the one after, I find that Bella's college job and her shifts at the pub make avoiding her easy. I simply have to make myself scarce in the late afternoons, when she's home for an hour or so. And that isn't hard: I take myself off to Wol's cottage in the grounds of Saffron Hall, and pretend to sort through her possessions.

In reality, I thumb through old copies of *Radio Times*, rearrange the airing cupboard, eat three tubes of Smarties from the larder, and stare at the wallpaper in my old bedroom. Every time I make an iota of organising progress, I glimpse an object or detect a scent which punches me in the solar plexus.

In every room I find Wol's homemade notepads, made from scrap paper fastened with a bulldog clip. Her favourite Jelly Babies are stored not in their bag, but in an old, clean coffee jar. From here, she dispensed three for each of us, every evening. You'd never know she had money. When I find her long-lost penknife I even call out to her, and the answering silence makes me whimper.

Still, I tell myself, it's a start.

~~~

'Brian,' I say, late on Thursday afternoon, 'I don't know what we'd do without you.'

Weary from stewing in my own thoughts, I'm longing for the comfort of the pub. But since Bella's due there any minute, I choose the next best thing to alcohol: pastries.

He grins at me. 'The feeling's mutual. You're one of my best customers.'

I look at the paper bags on the counter. My haul includes a sausage roll, a cheese scone, two flapjacks, and an individual custard tart. 'What?' I say. 'Is everyone else on a diet?'

Brian passes my change. 'No charge for the custard tart,' he says. Then he adds, 'It's nice to see you smiling, Sophie. I know this last year hasn't been easy.'

My smile stays intact, but I fidget with the bags. I've kept a low profile in the village, but it's a small place and people like to talk. How much have they figured out? Is Bella right, that it's only a matter of time before someone twigs?

Unaware that another customer has come into the shop, I turn and nearly walk straight into a man's chest. Before I can register that it's a firm, appealing chest in a grey sweater, I sidestep.

'So sorry,' I prattle, 'I had no idea you'd come in.'

'That's okay. Hello again.'

It's Tom Vine.

Fortunately, I'm not so flustered I drop all my purchases, but the custard tart does get squashed as I clutch the paper bags more tightly.

'I almost covered you in tart,' I say, then reproach myself as I realise how awful that sounds. 'Custard,' I mutter. 'I meant – custard tart.'

Tom smiles broadly. 'I must say, the conversation around you is never dull.' There's laughter in his eyes.

I risk looking at Brian, who is having trouble keeping a straight face. 'Well, it looks like you two already know each other,' he says.

'Oh no,' I reply, trying to recover an ounce of poise. 'I throw custard tarts at everyone I meet.'

'I bet that's popular with your passengers,' Tom says. 'Or do they only get that in first class?'

Am I imagining it or has his expression changed to something more inquisitive? Is he testing me? Because if so, I'm not stupid. I have done some elementary homework on my supposed employer.

'SpeedyJet doesn't have first class,' I reply, lifting my chin. 'It's strictly a budget operation. See you later, Brian.'

And with that, I turn smartly and exit the shop. Well done, I think. Nicely dodged. And no actual lies were told. SpeedyJet is indeed a low-cost airline. It's just that I don't actually work for them.

My self-congratulation lasts only a minute.

'Hey!' comes the call as I'm passing the red phone box by the post office.

I stop. Even without turning, I'm sure it's Tom. Slowly, I look over my shoulder. He's gaining on me quickly, thanks to the long strides which usually accompany long legs.

'Can I walk a short way with you?' He's not even breathless.

'Er, okay,' I say, but I'm wondering why. I give him a sidelong glance, then resume walking, gripping the pastry bags as if I'm afraid he might mug me.

'I'm early for a dinner engagement,' Tom says, as if I'd asked aloud for further explanation. 'And I wanted to apologise.'

'For what?' I ask, thinking of the little trap he set for me. If indeed it was a trap. Surely he can't suspect me? We haven't had a full conversation about airlines or flying. I'm being paranoid.

'For laughing about the custard tarts,' he replies. 'I just liked the way you phrased it.' He stops walking and says, 'Here. I bought you some more.'

Too polite to keep walking, I halt. We're opposite the malt house, which, despite its decay, is still noble.

'Some more?' My hands are already full of paper bags, but he's offering another.

'More custard tarts. In case you really did squash what you bought.'

Is he teasing? My eyes dart from side to side as I weigh his tone. Then I look up at his face, but nothing indicates he's pulling my leg. There's no smirk, his mouth is pleasantly neutral, his jaw resolutely still.

'Oh.' Why am I noticing his mouth and jaw anyway? I look away.

'I bet you're glad they've opened the airspace again,' Tom adds conversationally. 'Been a tricky week for you?'

He's talking about that volcanic ash cloud which has supposedly grounded me without pay. Little does he know I've been tapping away on my laptop, as usual.

'Yes, it's great that's, um, sorted out,' I mutter. 'Thanks for the tarts.'

'Well, these are good, but they probably don't compare to what you get in Lyon.'

'Lyon?' What's he talking about now?

'You make trips there, don't you? And Vienna? They really know their pastry in Vienna.'

'Right,' I say. 'Yes.' Oh hell, I think, I'm supposed to have first-hand knowledge of the cake shops of Europe. I take the bag, arrange it amongst the others, and turn to walk again, hoping we'll part here.

But Tom falls into step beside me once again. 'Mind you, I think Germany's underrated. Cologne, for example: *Kaffee und Kuchen* by the Rhein on a Sunday afternoon.'

I gulp. I don't know if SpeedyJet flies to Cologne. Or Vienna. If he's trying to trap me, he's going about it the right way. 'Well,' I stammer, 'we don't usually spend long at each turnaround. I don't see as much of these cities as people think.' If I wasn't now juggling five white paper bags with hints of grease seeping through them, I'd be crossing my fingers, both for the fib and in the hope he accepts this explanation.

'Hmm,' Tom says, 'I hadn't thought of that. Sorry. You must hate it when people assume your job's glamorous. I used to get that, when I was with BA. I know it's damned hard work, what you do in the main cabin. A hundred times harder than us, sitting up the front, flicking switches and chatting to air traffic control.'

Now I feel awful. He's praising my fictional job and apparently doesn't suspect I'm a complete fraud.

'No,' I say, half turning to him as we walk. 'That's not true. I couldn't fly a plane, not in a million years.' That part, at least, is straight from the heart. I see him smile, but he says nothing. I quickly take in the rest of his appearance – smart jeans, the sweater, a collared shirt underneath.

'Where are you going for dinner?' I ask, thinking that a good-looking pilot is probably booked every night of the week.

'Ahh.' He looks sheepish. 'Well, Oak House, actually. Lorraine's kindly feeding me.'

'Oak House?' Not a hot date, then. I stop beside one of

Saffron Sweeting's prettiest cottages, looking back the way we've come. 'But that's the other direction.'

Tom shrugs, then puts a couple of fingers to his temple, as if thinking hard. 'Er, yeah, now you mention it, I suppose it is. You won't tell, will you?'

Something in his voice, or possibly the way he's looking at me with a touch of pleading, makes the corners of my mouth twitch. 'Tell what?'

There's a scented honeysuckle twisting up the cottage wall, and in the breeze the loose ends nod as if they're intrigued too.

He jerks his head in the direction of Lorraine's bed and breakfast. 'That my navigation skills are so deplorable, I allowed a magnetic companion to lead me completely off course.'

The twitch becomes a smile, but I tell myself sternly it's nothing to do with being called magnetic. I press my lips together and shake my head solemnly. 'Your secret's safe with me.'

After all, I'm really good with secrets.

Chapter 10

Why don't I feel like going home? I'm bonetired and, thanks to Brian, dinner is taken care of. All I have to do is walk the last quarter of a mile, pop some raw vegetables and nuts into Stanley's feeder, then I can collapse on the sofa and eat until I turn the same colour as the parrot.

But the conversation with Tom has made me restless. He's a nice guy, seems genuine, and was just trying to have a simple chat. And there was I, treating it like a game of chess, trying to stay one step ahead, reading hints and accusations into everything. Not to mention trying to avoid telling blatant lies about my fictional job.

Sighing, I change course towards the river. Well, locals call it a river, but it's a large stream, fuller at this time of year than in late summer, but still tame enough that cars can cross it at the ford. I love watching them do this, fascinated by their faith they'll make it through without mishap, and secretly longing for someone to get stuck.

I find a bench to sit and let the world flow by. The evening is cool, and to the casual observer the river is quiet, but as I begin my slow, satisfying assault on the sausage roll, I hear blackbirds and the occasional call of an unseen moorhen. The water itself babbles and gurgles, determined but unhurried, punctuated by leaves and small twigs. I feel my shoulders relax and my mind settles.

I don't want to do this, I think. I don't want to fib to kind, decent people. I'm exhausted from keeping my guard up and trying to remember which city I supposedly flew to last week. Is Bella right? Is Rainbow's happy-clappy course an ideal opportunity to remove some deceit from my life? Maybe I should consider it.

The sausage roll was delicious. And either Tom nicked the bag with the cheese scone when he offered me the extra custard tarts or, more likely, I've polished that off without noticing. As a Jeep rolls through the river with ease – no entertainment there – I decide I'm too thirsty to sit here any longer. A huge mug of tea is in order, before I move onto dessert.

Calmer and ready to apologise to Bella when she gets home tonight, I hop off the bench, brush the pastry morsels from my jeans and stride purposefully towards home.

But as I round the corner at the end of our road, I see a distinctive, battered Volvo reversing out of our driveway. Hells bells, it's Joey. And he thinks I just flew to Barcelona. I freeze, realising that the moment he turns the car, he'll see me. I'm standing next to a thick beech hedge. There's nowhere else to go. With a squeal, I drop the remaining bags of cakes and dive in.

The hedge is dense and scratchy. There's a sharp branch sticking into my ribs, a leaf is tickling my left eye, and there's a stinging irritation halfway down my other cheek.

I peer out from my leafy disguise. The Volvo is now stationary, just down the road. Dammit, what's he doing here? And why has he parked there, like a private investigator?

Telling myself to calm down, that he's probably making a phone call, I wait.

And wait.

~ ~ ~

Bella comes home shortly after the pub closes.

'What in the name of God happened to you?' she asks.

I'm lolling on the sofa with one foot propped up, my ankle the size of a cricket ball. There is a deep scratch down my right cheek, which has only recently stopped bleeding. One of my eyes is puffy and might be black tomorrow. And I'm pretty sure I've still got beech leaves in my hair.

I answer in a self-pitying slur which has nothing to do with my evening escapade and everything to do with the brandy I've downed since finally arriving home.

'I got back and Joey was –'

'Jesus Christ, Sophie!' Bella's eyes are like saucers.

'Oh – no – not like that.' I sit up and flap a grazed hand. 'No, not Joey.'

'Well, who then?' Bella sits down on the edge of the chair opposite, still gaping. 'You look like crap.'

I already had a pretty good idea that might be the case. 'For some reason, Joey was here when I got home. And since I told him I was going to Barcelona, I decided I couldn't let him see me.'

'So he didn't –'

I shake my head, which hurts, so I stop. 'No, I told you, nothing like that. I hid in a hedge for a bit, but he parked that bloody car of his outside and looked like he was staying there.'

Bella leans back, her face changing from outrage to curiosity. 'Go on.'

'And I was tired and thirsty, but I didn't want to come to the pub as you and I weren't... anyway, I thought Joey might show up there too. So I decided the best thing was to sneak in the back way.'

'The back way? What back way?'

'Yeah, exactly.'

Bella's identified the problem with my cunning Baldrick-style plan to avoid Joey. There isn't a back way to Uncle Mike's house. The end of our garden borders some allotments, where villagers without space of their own grow runner beans and marrows.

'So I thought I'd scoot across the allotments and hop over the wall,' I say, my chin tucked into my chest, just as I used to when I thought Wol was about to throw chalk at me.

Bella's frowning sympathetically but I can see her nose twitch. 'The wall. The, er, ten foot wall? And, how did that go?'

'Do you really need to ask?' I mutter, waggling my ankle and then wincing.

'Well,' she says, getting up, 'I'm going to make you a

nice cup of Rosy Lee, but before I do, have you anything to say to me?'

I shift awkwardly, hoping the tea might arrive with a side helping of paracetamol. 'Bell, I'm sorry.'

She nods. 'Fine. Anything else?'

'Like... what?' I'm stalling, knowing full well what she means.

'Like doing Rainbow's fear of flying course. So you can stop pretending to be an air hostess and actually be one.' Bella folds her arms, puts her head on one side, and waits.

In the time since I moved back to Saffron Sweeting, I've done a good job of keeping out of people's way, avoiding idle conversation and shunning social gatherings. But lying to friends, avoiding my mother and pretending to Joey I'm out of the country is ridiculous. And scaling – then falling off – a gigantic wall to reach my own house is both ridiculous and painful. I can't perpetuate this charade much longer.

'All right,' I say. My head is throbbing and I'm talking fast, before I change my mind. 'All right. You win. I'll do it.'

~ ~ ~

As the results trickled in on the night of the General Election, I was so chuffed that Pompous Anthony failed to win his parliamentary seat, I agreed to see an obscure indie film with Joey.

Never mind, I think as we come out of the Arts Picturehouse the following Saturday. I can take this opportunity to talk to him. I've been playing my cards so close, I've accidentally-on-purpose forgotten to tell him that I've inherited a tidy sum from Wol. Tonight, I decide that although I obviously can't confide in him about the other stuff, I can at least mention the money.

'What did you think?' Joey asks. 'Of the film?'

It was in Danish. I barely knew what to think. 'Um, the photography was good.'

To me, it didn't look real, but the critics had raved about the quality of the cinematography and hence Joey was keen to see it. Who am I to judge the cameraman's skill? And now that the tedium is over, I can afford to be generous.

'Yeah, that was brilliant,' Joey replies, reaching for my hand. It feels strange, but we're a couple now, aren't we? This is what couples do: amble through Cambridge on a May evening, hand in hand.

'Pity about the story, though,' I say, then wonder if I should have phrased that more carefully, in case Joey thought the plot was brilliant too. But almost immediately, I decide I'm not trying to impress him. I don't actually care if Joey thinks I'm clueless, because I didn't see the point of an artsy film. 'Was it sponsored by the Danish architecture commission?'

'You're right,' Joey says. 'Sorry about that.'

'That's okay. I loved the bit when she drowned herself and the credits rolled.'

Joey laughs. 'You've got a twisted sense of humour, Sophie.'

'Not as twisted as that lot,' I say as we turn the corner into Free School Lane and are met by the unlikely spectacle of an old-fashioned metal bedstead travelling up the road on squeaky wheels. A rowdy squadron of students are in close attendance, but their purpose and destination are a mystery.

'You'd think they'd have their minds on exams,' Joey says as we pause to observe these proceedings.

'Like we did, you mean?'

Although Joey and I studied together in Cambridge, we didn't attend the actual university. Our college was a former polytechnic, now under the title of the University of East Anglia, and it's where you go if you're not brainy enough for the real deal. So it's not like we're reliving some idyllic Cambridge youth.

'Good point,' he says, still watching the creaky progress of the bed. 'Do you think they'll winch it onto a roof somewhere?'

I smile. 'I'd forgotten about that.'

One of our more meaningless pranks, carried out on a

night similar to this, was to hoist a motorbike and its sidecar onto the roof of a lecture hall. We were all besotted with Wallace and Gromit and, if we'd had more time, would have completed the vignette with stuffed figures. It wasn't even an original caper – Cambridge students managed to get an entire car onto the roof of the Senate House in the late fifties – but we derived weeks of amusement from the episode.

'I laughed so hard, I almost fell off that roof,' Joey grins. 'You were fearless.'

'I wasn't fearless,' I protest. Why does everyone think I'm so gutsy? I'm just a big coward inside.

'Is your ankle okay to walk to one of the pubs up here? Maybe The Eagle?' Joey asks.

'Fine,' I say. 'It's much better.'

He thinks I skidded and fell off my bike. Yet another lie. At this rate, I won't be seeing Wol again in the next life. Time to start trying to untangle things a bit.

'So, I wanted to mention...' I begin, hoping he hasn't already had a preview of my finances from my mother.

'Mmm?' he says, stepping into the road so I can stay on the pavement as we navigate a tangle of toppled bicycles outside one of the university buildings.

'When Wol died, she left me some money.'

He doesn't answer, just glances my way and nods. Our pace is leisurely, conversational.

'Not a huge amount,' I continue. 'But a nice nest egg.' Oh no, why did I say that? It makes it sound like I'm getting ready to hatch a family.

'I figured she might have done,' Joey says easily.

'Really? But I didn't know she had any money. No one in my family has any money.'

'Someone did,' he replies.

'It just feels so weird. I can't get my head around it.' This is true. With moving house, Joey turning up again, and my mother closing in on the village like a cold war assassin, I've given no thought to what the inheritance means for me.

'How much are we talking?' Joey asks casually.

Hesitantly, I tell him the estimate.

He lets out a short whistle. 'Wow, Sophia, that's great.' He drops a kiss on the top of my head. 'Isn't it?' he prompts, when I fail to answer.

'Of course it is,' I reply. 'I don't mean to sound ungrateful.' How much further to the pub? I badly need a pint.

'Oh, babe, don't worry. I know you miss Wol, but this is terrific news.' Did his grip on my hand just tighten? 'For you, I mean. Terrific news for you. It'll open up possibilities you never knew existed.'

That, I suspect, is precisely what I'm afraid of.

Chapter 11

Rainbow's home is one of the most beautiful in the village: symmetrical and dignified, on the main street near the malt house. It even has a dovecote in the front garden. From what Amelia said, the owner decided it would be more lucrative to rent it out to visiting Americans than to sell.

As I ring the bell, my heart is thumping as if I had run here from Cambridge. And I'm both thirsty and in urgent need of the loo. But there's no going back now. Rainbow was ecstatic when I told her in a stealthy whisper that I would like to join her fear of flying workshop. And although I'm terrified of others finding out, she promised that confidentiality was the most important rule of group therapy. I almost fled when she called it group therapy: my family's had its share of chaos but as far as I know, no one has ever sought professional help. We'd much rather suffer in silence.

'Honey, come on in!' Rainbow, businesslike in a black linen dress, welcomes me into her sitting room. It's a refined space, with pale cream walls and pale cream furniture. In fact, it looks as if everything arrived on the same day from a warehouse, all tastefully coordinated by a designer who knew neither the house nor its inhabitants. But I suppose that's what you get, when your husband's company is paying the rent.

'Hi, Sophie,' says a second voice.

I didn't realise someone was already here.

'Good grief! Fergus? What are you − ?'

Awkwardly, I look at The Plough's landlord, who appears equally embarrassed.

'Same as you, I expect. Learning to fly.' He answers the obvious question.

'Well, this is going to change your life,' says Rainbow, 'but we're not actually going to teach you to *fly*.'

'Bella made me come,' Fergus says. 'She's in charge of the pub tonight. Chased me out with a broom.'

What happened to the meek, malleable Bella I knew as a child?

'You know, then?' I say, through the corner of my mouth.

'What – that you have a flying phobia?' Fergus nods.

'Shit,' I say, before I can help myself. 'So you know...'

'That you're not an air hostess? Yeah, I figured. I hear things, you know, in my job.'

I did suspect that Fergus knows a thing or two about village life that he doesn't let on.

I sit gingerly where Rainbow indicates. 'Do – others know?'

He shrugs. 'I wouldn't worry about it. Kenneth's theory is you work for MI5, and Violet claims you're undercover for the Inland Revenue. But Bernard Pennington-Jones says you might just be a tree-hugger.'

'A what?' I'm too startled to be mortified that half the village has rumbled me.

'You know, a conservationist type.' Seeing me sag, Fergus adds, 'Cheer up, at least he didn't say high-class prostitute.'

'In Saffron Sweeting? Not likely.' I glance at Rainbow, who's busy with a flipchart on a wobbly easel. 'What about you? Are you afraid of flying, or is Bella forcing you to make up the numbers?'

'Effing petrified,' Fergus replies. 'Almost made a flight to Majorca divert last summer.'

Next to arrive is a middle-aged woman, who is bulky enough to unbalance most aircraft. She sinks heavily into the chair closest to Rainbow. To my amusement, she then takes out her knitting. I'm dying to know if she's in the right place or whether she took a wrong turn on her way to *Advanced Fair Isle* in the village hall.

Fergus and I exchange glances, then eye Rainbow, like a pair of naughty schoolchildren in the headmistress's study.

What punishment does she have in store?

'Who are we waiting for?' Fergus clears his throat.

'The technical guy,' I say. 'Some old fossil is going to teach us flying stuff, while Rainbow picks our subconscious to bits.'

Rainbow is especially proud of what she calls the bi-sentient nature of her 'program'. According to her research, if we learn the physics of flying, including how planes stay in the air, while at the same time confronting our neurolinguistic fears, the series of classes stands every chance of curing us. By week five, apparently, we'll be happy to board a Cessna for a short flight over Cambridge.

Oh – my – God. Just thinking about this is causing my ribs to tighten and my ears to ring. I don't care how magnificent King's College Chapel is, I have no wish to see it from the air. Fergus looks a bit green around the gills too.

But before The Plough's landlord and I can agree a Thelma and Louise style escape, Rainbow jumps up.

'Here he is right now!' she exclaims, heading for the front door.

I crane my neck and look out of the window in time to see an athletic-looking man stride up the path. He's wearing dark trousers with a tailored white shirt and has giveaway stripy epaulettes on each shoulder. I can't see his face: the evening sun is behind him and he's wearing aviator style sunglasses. But there's something about his walk which looks confidently capable. Maybe they teach that commanding chin up gait in flying school.

Fergus and I sit up as he enters the sitting room. Even knitting woman pauses, her needles frozen mid stitch.

Rainbow beams at her pilot friend, tossing her head so her hair falls attractively over one shoulder. Technically, he's late, but she doesn't seem to care, turning delightedly to us instead. 'And I'm thrilled to welcome my *very* talented co-instructor for this course, Captain Thomas Vine.'

My constricted ribs release with a whoosh which pulls my jaw towards the floor. The ringing in my ears ceases and

I'm left with a pin drop silence. There's a split second in which it might – just might – have been possible to fling myself behind the sofa and then crawl out of the room unnoticed. Like most split seconds in my life, it passes unseized.

Tom Vine takes off his sunglasses and turns to smile at us. As I lock eyes with our pilot instructor, one eyebrow lifts unmistakably.

'Sophie?' he says, and in his face I see both surprise and confusion. 'What the hell are you doing here?'

~ ~ ~

Whatever words of inspiration Rainbow uses to begin her course are lost on me as I squirm and wait for my cheeks to cool. Then I pull a notebook from my bag and doodle diligently for a few minutes. Okay, so this is highly unfortunate, given that I've now had two conversations with Tom in which he thinks I'm an air hostess. But they were short conversations and I didn't *actually* lie to him.

Satisfied it could be a whole lot worse, I risk lifting my eyes to the group. Tom sits next to Rainbow, listening politely, not looking my way. His legs are stretched in front of him, his hands resting loosely on a clipboard in his lap. Since I know Bella will want a full report, I steal a quick look at his brown arms under the short-sleeved shirt and confirm my suspicion that the stripes only serve to accentuate his broad shoulders.

I swallow and focus on Rainbow, which is fortuitous as at this moment she declares, 'Let's all introduce ourselves. Just say your name and why you're here.' She beams at knitting woman, who lays down her work.

'I'm Ingrid. I've never enjoyed flying but I manage it sometimes, if the doctor gives me something.' She gives Rainbow a slanting look, as if afraid she'll disapprove of medication. Personally, I doubt Rainbow has a problem with mood altering substances. 'But now my daughter's moved to Canada and I want to visit. I can't be drugged for that long, so here I am.'

Rainbow nods with the whole top half of her body. 'Thank you so much, Ingrid, for sharing that.'

Oh, crumbs, I think. This really is touchy-feely.

Fergus shifts in his seat. There's a fifty-fifty chance his turn is next. When Rainbow nods to him, I offer a smile of encouragement.

'I'm, umm, Fergus,' he says, and coughs. 'I run the pub in the village. But I'd like to, you know, go on holiday, like normal people.'

'Hi there, Fergus.' Rainbow waits, smiling like an expectant crocodile.

'I, um, had a bit of a scare on a charter flight last year.' He's fidgeting badly. 'There was terrible turbulence, like someone smacking the plane hard from the side. Then a pause, then another smack. We made these tiny, repeated drops. And each time, I kept thinking, this is the one where we'll keep falling and falling.' He coughs. 'You know. Bit embarrassing.'

I join in with the general nodding and give Fergus a quick pat on the arm.

'Thank you for sharing that, Fergus,' Rainbow says. 'We'll talk about turbulence, won't we, Captain Vine?'

'Absolutely.' Tom nods.

I wonder how old he is and decide probably late thirties.

Rainbow speaks again. 'And Sophie? Tell us about your fear of flying.'

It's on the tip of my tongue to clarify I don't have a fear of flying, I have a fear of crashing, but I think better of it. I glance at Tom and look away quickly. 'I'm Sophie. I've always wanted to travel but...' Damn, this is harder than it seemed when the others were speaking.

Rainbow waits, then says, 'Remember, everyone, this is completely confidential.'

'It has to be,' I say, looking at the others to make sure they understand too. When they nod, I continue. 'I did take one short flight, to Nice, the summer I finished college. It was awful – I didn't sleep for two days after. I came home by train and ferry.'

'Go on,' says Rainbow.

'The next year was 2001. As in, September 11th, 2001.'

I'm looking at the carpet now but I sense the room go still. Fergus and Ingrid need no explanation of the effect that day had on nervous fliers. For months, I couldn't even look at a plane passing overhead.

Seconds tick by. 'It took me five years to try again. I'd managed to get a job at a travel agency and they were kind enough to send me to a convention in Berlin.'

'And?' Rainbow nudges.

'I missed the flight. Deliberately. I was at Heathrow with time to spare, but I couldn't do it.'

I look across at Tom's shoes, but they're still. When I flick my eyes up to his face, he's looking at me in amazement. He opens his mouth as if to say something, then jerks his gaze away.

I swallow the guilt that rises. It doesn't matter what he thinks, I tell myself. It doesn't matter if he thinks I'm a liar, a freak, a nut job, or all of the above. *It doesn't matter*. He and Rainbow just need to fix me.

'The silly thing is,' I say, 'my grandad worked with planes. In Scotland, where I was born. He was crazy about them.'

And although I was only four when he died, he was crazy about me too. After my father left us, grandad stepped in. My memories of him are blurred at best, but losing him was far more of a blow than losing dad.

'Well,' says Rainbow, 'we're gonna make your grandaddy proud.' She launches into a description of what's ahead and how this revolutionary approach is going to give our brain cells a whole new outlook. I'm relieved to hear we don't have to go anywhere near an actual plane at first. Before that, we'll do some guided visualisations, and possibly hypnosis if needed. In addition, Captain Vine is going to explain the different parts of a plane, what happens during take-off, and how collaborative minor miracles keep it in the air. He doesn't actually use the word miracles, he calls it *lift*. And he predicts, once we've been on a short flight with him and are starting to feel comfortable, we can even take the controls for a few moments.

The group rustles at that suggestion. Sounds similar to those made by a baby hyena may have escaped my throat. I'm gripping the cushion of Rainbow's rented sofa with white knuckles. Looking at me, you might think we'd taken off already.

'I know that all sounds a bit daunting,' Tom says, looking around the group. 'But you'll get there. Once you know the physics of what's happening, and what to expect, the fear will disappear. I plan to show you that the most dangerous part of flying is the car ride to the airport.'

Rainbow is looking at Tom with professional respect and a smidgen of something else. She keeps her gaze on him as she says to us, 'You really are in the most excellent hands.'

Despite my white knuckles, I have enough functioning brain cells to wonder if Rainbow would like to be in his hands too.

After almost an hour of squirming discomfort, Rainbow declares our first meeting over. 'You all did so great!' she declares, bracelets jangling. At one point, I was trying so hard to block out the gut-wrenching description of what was ahead of us, I started counting them. 'Great job!' she repeats, as if expecting us all to jump up and start high-fiving each other or start a Mexican wave. In more British style, we look at our knees, then each other's knees, then get to our feet in an awkward Anglican ripple.

It's dark outside, and much cooler now. I tug my insubstantial denim jacket around me, say goodnight to Fergus, and hunch my shoulders as I set off at a brisk pace.

'Sophie! Wait a minute,' comes a voice.

I don't need to turn to know who it is. I keep going, but

a fraction slower, resisting the urge to bolt. Before I've walked twenty yards, Tom is beside me. He's not wearing a coat, and the moonlight picks out the white of his shirt.

'This is a joke, right?' he asks, and catches me lightly by the arm. 'You're keeping Fergus company or... something?'

I shake my head. 'No. It's for me.'

Tom frowns. 'But... we talked about your job.' He lets go of my arm.

'I'm sorry,' I say. I want to turn and scuttle, but don't.

'You're honestly afraid of flying?'

'Shh!' I hiss, peering up and down the road. 'We can't talk about that here.' This time I do start walking. It's cold, the air is damp, I want to be in bed with the covers over my head.

'I don't understand.' Tom strides along with me, taking one step for every two of mine. 'Why would you –'

'I'm sorry,' I say again.

'I thought we were getting to know each other. Why did you –'

'Look,' I interrupt. 'It's complicated. I got in – in over my head in something and now I need you to stick to Rainbow's rules and not tell anyone. Not *anyone*.'

'Are you in trouble?' he asks.

A tall hedge looms beside the road and I slow my pace. 'No,' I sigh. 'Not anything you'd call trouble. But please, Tom, you mustn't tell a soul.'

With this, I stop and turn towards him. I need to make sure he understands. Our eyes meet. In the shadow from the hedge, I can't tell if his are green, or brown, or somewhere in between.

'Okay,' he says slowly, then, more quietly, 'Okay, Sophie.'

'Thank you.' I release the breath I've been holding.

Tom's eyes are still on me. Just as I've been looking at him for confirmation, he seems to be searching for answers in my face. I shiver through my jacket. If he's cold in his shirt, he doesn't show it. A wafer of moon catches one side of us, highlighting his cheek and jaw. For some reason I want to reach up, touch him, apologise again.

'It's a shame, though,' he says in a half whisper.

There's a change so infinitesimal, I'm not sure who moved. Did I lean in and lift my face to his? Or did he step forward and duck his head? Either way, his mouth is inches from mine and I'm spellbound.

Next moment, Tom steps away, gives one shiver, and shoves his hands in his pockets as he turns back towards the main street.

When he speaks, his voice is as blunt as his words. 'We weren't getting to know each other, were we? I really don't know you at all.'

Chapter 12

Joey is acting strangely. Normally laid back, he navigates life with his easy charm, which works equally well on his parents and traffic wardens, and on one occasion a tax inspector. It's one of the reasons I was never sure how keen he was on me in college. If he was smitten, he never showed it, if jealous, he never griped, and if heartbroken when I left for London, he gave no sign.

But in the last few days, he's been restless and distracted. And when he shows up on my doorstep before ten in the morning, I know something's up. Hastily, I shut the lid of my laptop to hide the work I'm doing.

'Sophissima! Good. You're awake. Come on, I've got a surprise for you.'

Sophissima? That's a new one. Even allowing for his buzzing energy, I feel that's taking his Italian heritage a little far.

'Where are we going?' I dig my heels in. Like many people with something to hide, I dread surprises.

'Not far. Bring a jacket, it's chilly out.'

Oh. A local surprise. Not the Eurostar to Paris, then.

As he marches me towards the village centre, the puzzle grows. It's too early for a surprise date, and in any case, there aren't many venues in Saffron Sweeting which are date-worthy.

'Close your eyes,' he commands as we pause outside the library.

I comply. I don't know what he's up to, but his enthusiasm has me intrigued. Joey propels me by one elbow, checking at intervals that I'm not peeping. I'm not, which almost costs me grazed knees as I trip on the curb and lurch forward before he catches me.

'Sorry, babe. Almost there.'

'Joey,' I tut, 'what the hell are you doing?'

'Here,' he says. 'Don't look yet.'

We stop and I hear the clinking of keys. Then he leads me through a narrow gap and I sense the space around me grow darker. A door closes. I sniff and am reminded of Brussels sprouts and pea soup.

'Giuseppe.' I get stern. 'You're freaking me out.'

'Ta-da!' he proclaims. 'You can look now.'

I open my eyes. We're in a dim space, the lights not working. Behind us, next to the door we used, slits of light suggest a boarded-up window. As my vision adjusts, I see shelving on the walls and, in the corner, some disintegrating cardboard boxes. On one, there's a picture of carrots, on another, a cauliflower. That explains the odour.

'Okay.' I turn to Joey, trying not to look deeply disappointed with my surprise.

His lips are clamped, like a child who's scared he'll give away a phenomenal secret. But his eyes are shining and he's jiggling from one foot to the other. He looks adorably boyish.

'Well?' he says, unable to resist any longer.

'Well,' I repeat, looking around me and wondering what practical joke is underway. 'We're in the vegetable shop.'

'The *former* vegetable shop,' he corrects. 'Isn't it great? Do you like it?'

'Like it for what?' The words are barely out before I start to cotton on.

'My new studio,' Joey declares, throwing out his arms like an explorer discovering Fiji. 'Don't you see it, Sophie? The location is perfect, the size is ideal and back here –' he drags me towards the rear of the shop '–will make a fantastic dark room.'

'Oh.' I can't think what to say.

His chin dips – he was expecting more enthusiasm.

'Gosh. Well. Yes, it's, um, it's great.'

But I don't get it. How can an old vegetable shop in a village like Saffron Sweeting be an ideal location? It's not as if hundreds of people walk past every day.

'Obviously it needs a few repairs,' he says, 'but my dad'll help with those.'

Indeed, a father who's a builder could come in handy.

'Amelia said if we like it, we should move fast,' Joey says.

The nasty smell is lingering. I can't imagine anywhere less inspiring. Then I chide myself for not being more supportive.

'Sorry,' I say. 'Just takes some getting used to.'

'I know,' he says. 'I've barely slept since I found out about it.' He takes both my hands in his, twirling me around like a kid on a skating rink. 'I can tell you're over the moon.'

I gulp back a squawk, thankful for the low light.

'I knew you'd love it,' Joey says. He drops his head and gives me a bold, urgent kiss. Surprised, I stiffen, then just as I'm starting to relax and enjoy it, he pulls away.

'That's what's so great about you,' he grins. 'You've always been willing to take a risk.'

'Take a risk?' Why is my tongue so knotted that I keep repeating things?

'Yes.' He pauses, puts both hands on my upper arms and looks at me so intently, I'm scared of what he'll say next. 'Sophie,' he begins, 'we've known each other a long time.'

No, we haven't, I think. Not if you skip the years in the middle, when we didn't know if the other was alive or dead.

'And nothing would make me happier...' Joey continues.

No way, I think. We've only been going out a few weeks. This time.

'... than having you as my business partner.'

Business partner! At least I manage not to repeat that aloud. I fear the relief is plainly visible on my face as I relax in his grip.

'We'll have a proper partnership agreement. All official.' Joey's still talking, smiling as if I've already said yes. He releases my arms in acknowledgement of the done deal.

Have I missed something? Did I get drunk one night

recently and agree to this? I step towards the front window, looking up at the tatty ceiling in case it's about to collapse.

'But why do you want a business partner? I don't know anything about photography.'

He laughs. 'Of course you don't, silly. You'll be my financial backer. You won't have to get your hands dirty.'

His financial backer. I swivel on my heel, skidding on an old piece of plastic underfoot. Joey needs cash to get his studio off the ground. My cash.

'You'll do it, won't you? You and me, in business together?'

My jaw goes slack. Never mind drunk, I would have been absolutely legless before forgetting this.

'I knew it!' Joey's elated. Maybe it's the murky light, or maybe he's mistaking my expression deliberately. 'I knew you'd say yes. It's going to be brilliant.'

~~~

'I need some time to think about this, Joe,' I say after he's locked up the vegetable shop and we're walking the short distance towards the estate agency. 'In any case, I haven't got the money yet.' My mind is racing, trying to find a way to let him down gently.

But Joey's barely listening. He now has one arm around my shoulders and we're making awkward progress, as my pace is a heavy trudge while his is practically a skip.

'Isn't it perfect?' he says, gesturing at the deserted Saffron Sweeting street. 'The ideal location, but with really reasonable rent.'

I cough to cover a groan. The sum he's mentioned doesn't sound even faintly reasonable. For a backwater like this, in fact, it sounds like daylight robbery. As he continued to gesture around the crumbling vegetable shop, pointing out where he would store equipment and woo customers, I asked through gritted teeth what investment he had in mind. His glib answer – acknowledging the high cost of quality equipment – made me wince. How on earth could a few camera lenses and a couple of lights on sticks cost that much?

When we reach Hargraves & Co, I try to detach myself, but he hustles me down the step and into the office. Amelia looks up from her desk.

'Joey, darling,' she says, putting a coffee mug down and blotting her lips with an index finger. 'How did it go?'

'We love it,' he says, going over to her desk to surrender the keys. Then he parks himself in one of the visitor chairs, looking businesslike.

'How marvellous.' Amelia smiles encouragingly. 'I am pleased.'

'Actually,' I say, 'I'm going to take a couple of days to think about it. And I don't have the money yet, you see.'

Joey has pulled out some paperwork – for the shop, probably – and is studying it carefully. I've no idea if he's heard me as he doesn't acknowledge my guarded tone. Amelia, however, has sharp eyes, despite her easy manner. She says nothing but nods to me, her impressive auburn hair bobbing.

'Right,' I say. 'I must get back.'

'All right, see you soon.' Amelia flicks a paper clip at my boyfriend. 'Joey, do pay attention, Sophie's leaving.'

Joey looks up, as if he'd forgotten I was there. 'Cool. Okay,' he says. 'I'm going to stay and talk contracts for a bit. All right, Soph?'

'Right,' I say again. 'Yes, of course. Bye, then.'

Considering the zeal with which he hauled me out of the house this morning, I find it a bit strange he doesn't get up to kiss me goodbye.

~~~

Fergus has offered to host our next fear of flying workshop in the upstairs room at the pub. I'm not sure Rainbow is thrilled about her anxious pupils having such ready access to alcohol, but she accepts graciously, admitting that her husband wants to watch something called an NBA Playoff at their house.

So, to avoid drawing attention to our meeting, we sneak up The Plough's old oak staircase.

Tom shows up, this time wearing a plain sweater and jeans. He nods hello to everyone, but I have trouble meeting his eye. I'm not sure whether he's disgusted with me or indifferent.

'You're not in uniform tonight, Captain Vine,' Ingrid says coyly.

'Shh,' he replies, 'I'm hoping Rainbow won't notice. And call me Tom.'

'Does she like you to wear those stripes, then, Tom?' Ingrid giggles.

'She wants you lot to have confidence in me.' He pauses. 'I'd been doing some commercial work last week and was dressed accordingly.'

'Oh, well,' says Ingrid. 'We don't mind what you wear, do we?' With this, she beams at Fergus for confirmation.

Tom chooses that moment to look at me and I drop my eyes in a hurry. I'm saved from awkwardness by Rainbow marching in, accompanied by her portable easel.

'I'm so thrilled you're all here,' she declares as she grapples with the flip chart at the front of the room. 'This evening,' she continues, once our nervous rustling has subsided, 'we're going to start our introduction to the physics of flight.'

She stresses the words as if they're the eighth wonder of the modern world. Which I suppose they are. Still, I'm not in the mood for a science lesson and can't see how a few fancy diagrams are going to stop the stampede in my stomach.

'Then,' Rainbow continues, 'we'll be sharing more about our fears, how they began, and how they make us feel.'

On second thoughts, the physics bit sounds just grand.

'Captain Vine, over to you,' she says as sweetly as Scarlett O'Hara at a Twelve Oaks barbecue.

I suppress a tut. She and Ingrid are so obvious. Are we here to get over our fear of flying or to ogle the hunky pilot?

Who'll be next to flick their hair at him? Fergus? I fold my arms, set my chin and resolve to pay attention to the principles of flight.

~ ~ ~

Okay, my mind does wander a few times from the complex diagrams which Tom is showing us. As he explains concepts like air pressure and lift, his easy, calm voice makes me forget he's using words like take-off, airborne and flight. When he says them, even runway and wing don't sound so terrifying. And who knew that each commercial plane gets struck by lightning about once a year, emerging unscathed? Is it possible that with him at the controls I might feel safe enough to give it another try?

When he introduces our first hands-on exercise, which is to make paper aeroplanes with varying dimensions, I look around incredulously. This must be a joke, surely? How does Rainbow expect us to get over our fear of flying by constructing aircraft from coloured sheets? It's like asking Titanic survivors to applaud a paper boat.

But no, Ingrid lays her knitting to one side. Fergus – the swot – has even made his first few folds. I bow my head and start creasing my pale blue paper as instructed, but am secretly planning how I'll relate this to Bella.

When our mini missiles are ready, there is brief chaos as planes of different pastel hues whizz around the room with varying degrees of success. Fergus is mortified when his plane nosedives immediately and Ingrid teases him about keeping it up. I pray Rainbow hasn't heard, in case she decides our fears correlate with sexual repression or some other Freudian codswallop.

Next moment, I too am hanging my head as my plane stays up for barely two seconds, before ditching straight into Tom's lap.

'Nice shot, Sophie,' he laughs.

Oh my God, I hope he doesn't think I did that on purpose. I didn't point it at him – how can it have made that beeline for his crotch?

As the other planes either dive or swoop to the floor again, Tom stands up, holding my creation.

'Okay,' he says. 'Why didn't this one stay in the air?'

Great, now he's picking on me, planning humiliation in front of the little class. I slouch down in my seat, shoulders tensed for the onslaught.

'Ash cloud,' Fergus pipes up, and I look at him gratefully. I know I'm not the only one who's freaked out that commercial planes are now allowed to fly through dense clouds of stuff which could clog their engines and send them plunging to the ground.

Tom shakes his head. 'Well,' he begins, 'for one thing, it wasn't travelling at sixty miles per hour before take-off.' His tone is unexpectedly kind and I risk stealing a glance as the others laugh. He gives me a ghost of a smile and carries on. 'And another thing, we were deliberately mean to you with those instructions.' He gestures to the flip chart. 'We made you put the folds in the wrong place.'

Fergus looks relieved that his engineering skills weren't at fault, and I soften a little too. Maybe Tom isn't picking on me. In fact, he selects a fresh sheet of paper and brings it, with my battered blue plane, to the table beside me. Then he bends to demonstrate.

'Make this fold here instead –' he's next to my elbow, tucked in the gap between Fergus and me, and I watch his hands make surprisingly deft creases in the paper. '– and you'll get a much bigger wing in relation to the body of the plane.' He holds up the result. Frankly, it looks the same to me.

'The wing is bigger, so there's more lift, and it's more able to support the weight.'

Never mind the weight, I've just caught Tom's aftershave, or whatever it is that makes him smell fresh but earthy. Of course, he would smell earthy, he owns several garden centres. Joey, by contrast, smells of spices from his mum's cooking and a designer scent from his bathroom shelf.

Tom straightens up, and launches the plane towards the other end of the room. Comparatively speaking, it does glide more easily, before hitting the window and tumbling to the floor.

The others clap, but I look up at him, giving him a small nod of understanding. He holds my gaze for a second before returning to the front of the room and addressing the group.

'Plane manufacturers know this stuff,' he says. 'Believe it or not, they do actually make sure the wings are big enough to support the rest of the aircraft.'

His audience looks sheepish, and as I check the other faces, I know that all three of us privately doubted that Airbus knows anything about mathematics at all.

'If you don't believe me,' he says, 'I'll take you hang-gliding on Sunday and you'll get a better idea of how wings work.'

Strangely, none of us call his bluff on this point, but the atmosphere in the group is a few notches lighter now.

'Thank you, Tom.' Rainbow can't resist a smug smile. Perhaps she's spotted the chink in our collective scepticism. 'Now,' she continues, 'let's switch things up and start to confront the fear we're holding inside.' She places both hands on her chest, between her breasts. Fergus shifts uncomfortably beside me and I hope Rainbow doesn't expect us all to grope ourselves in the same place. No way am I doing that in mixed company.

But Rainbow looks entirely earnest. 'Just as the paper plane can't fly if it's too heavy, y'all can't fly if you're carrying the weight of fear inside you. Research shows that addressing our fears openly is the best way to let go.'

Our shuffling is almost deafening. It's okay for her, she's American, but does she expect this trio of Brits to discuss our deepest feelings?

'I know this can be hard,' Rainbow says, and I can't help but snort.

Trying to cover up, I suggest, 'Maybe we can have a

drink first?'

Rainbow's lip curls and she shakes her head in disappointment. 'Sophie, honey, alcohol and narcotics are not the answer.'

'Right,' I say. 'Sorry.' So much for trying to lighten things.

'I want you all to close your eyes,' Rainbow says confidently.

We look at each other, then obey, although I bet I'm not alone in peeking through a slit in one eye.

'Picture yourself in an airplane, getting ready to fly somewhere on vacation,' Rainbow instructs. I gulp. I do not want to picture that at all. I would rather picture a parking ticket, an ingrowing toenail or a Benny Hill repeat on television.

'Say this out loud, or whisper if you like,' Rainbow continues. 'Tell us any words that describe how you feel.'

'Scared shitless,' says a male voice.

The group giggles and all three of us open our eyes, thrilled at this diversion from the task.

Rainbow summons a positive expression, like a mother presented with a toddler's artwork. Tom scratches his ear and stifles a grin.

'Excellent, Fergus,' Rainbow says bravely. 'Now, everyone, try again.'

We settle again, and after a moment I hear 'Breathless', which must be Ingrid, followed by a gravelly 'Dying!' which sounds like Fergus.

Then, between them, they keep going, like a tap has been turned on. 'Choking,' comes a voice, then 'Panic', 'Hijack' and 'Crash'.

'Sophie?' prompts Rainbow gently. I open my eyes, confused. I said my words, right? I said *trapped, terrified, sick* and *hollow*, surely? I felt all those things as I pretended to be crammed into the window seat of a charter flight at Gatwick. Then I realise I didn't actually say any of them aloud. I look round the room, see Rainbow's expectant look, and encounter compassion in Tom's face. I squeeze my eyes shut again, and twist my arms around me.

Finally, I breathe out. 'Alone,' I whisper.

Chapter 13

Rainbow might not approve of dulling our fears with alcohol, but there's no stopping us once the class ends. Like children rushing out of school at the afternoon bell, we tumble from the meeting room downstairs to the pub itself. We're greeted by a warm, yeasty aroma of beer, with undercurrents of fish and chips.

Bella's working tonight and fixes our drinks. Rainbow causes confusion by asking for something called Kombucha, and has to settle for a shandy. I nod hello to Amelia, the estate agent, who's eating nearby with an incredibly good-looking man. They're sitting with knees almost touching, and she just fed him a chip.

While I wait at the bar for my whisky, Tom moves into the gap beside me.

'I promised I'd give Rainbow a lift home,' he says.

'Right,' I say. 'Of course.' I don't mention the proximity of Rainbow's house: I've heard that Americans don't like to walk.

'So, you ride your bike everywhere?' Tom says, while Bella's pulling his pint. She's taking special care to fill the glass to the top without creating too much foam.

'Pretty much,' I say. 'I prefer it to driving.'

'It keeps you fit, I expect,' he adds.

I glance sideways. Surely he's just making polite conversation? He didn't just skim his eyes over my body with that remark? Nonetheless, I can't think of a witty response. I wave my five pound note at Bella in the hope she'll stop caressing his beer and hurry up.

'And your job must keep you lovely and fit.' My housemate has heard our dialogue and joins in cheerfully. I'm grateful for the intervention. 'Sophie said you own some garden centres,' she adds.

'Well, my family does,' Tom smiles.

'And you're a pilot too, you must be awfully busy,' Bella says. I wait for the next part, but she stops short of asking if he's too busy to have a cup of coffee some time. I suspect she wants to, but Bella's got old-fashioned notions about men making the moves. Maybe once I know Tom better, I'll drop a hint. He's nice enough and Lorraine spoke warmly about him. Bella could do far worse.

The wannabe fliers settle down to decompress and munch on salt and vinegar crisps. Rainbow picks up a bag of pork scratchings but drops them when she understands what they are. As a vegan at The Plough, she'll have to go hungry. I, on the other hand, am perfectly content. The murmuring Monday night chatter, punctuated by the thwack of darts, is soothing. Ingrid gets out her knitting and adds a rhythmic click-clacking to the mix.

'Well, Tom,' says Fergus, 'you must think we're a right bunch of twits.'

'How do you mean?' Tom looks at Fergus over his beer.

'Our silly fears, I think he means,' Ingrid supplies. 'We know it's illogical, we just can't help it.'

I hush them, nervous of our conversation being overheard, but no one pays much attention.

'Confronting it is the only way to overcome it,' says Rainbow. 'That's why we're here.'

'Even so,' Fergus persists, 'if Tom spends all his time zooming around like Biggles, he must think we're bonkers.' His mood is glum. Perhaps he thinks real men shouldn't have phobias.

'Not at all,' Tom says. 'Most of us are scared of something illogical.'

Ingrid pauses her needles. 'I bet you're not scared of anything, Tom.'

Rainbow smirks too and they both wait expectantly.

'You'd be surprised,' Tom says.

'Oh, go on!' Ingrid nudges him on the arm.

'Why can't I be scared of something?' Tom asks.

His tone is light, but did his fingers just clench? There's

a pause, then I ask, 'Are you?'

He looks at me, and in our cosy corner of the pub, his hazel eyes are dark.

'Are you scared of something?' I repeat, full of curiosity now.

'Yup.' Tom takes a swallow of beer and sets the glass down. 'I'm terrified of mice.'

Ingrid and Fergus laugh: they think he's pulling their legs. But as I look at his face, I'm inclined to believe him.

I change the subject. 'So, Rainbow, how are you liking England?'

'Oh, I'm having a ball,' she replies. 'There's so much history, it's awesome.'

Ingrid nods. 'That's true, we are spoiled with our heritage.'

Rainbow frowns. 'I'll never understand your funny little ways, of course, but I love Cambridge. And this village is just the best.'

'Really?' I ask. 'What do you like about it?'

'Y'all know each other. People look out for each other. And Saffron Sweeting is so peaceful.'

Personally, I wish people didn't look out for each other quite so much. It's not easy, avoiding attention in a village like this. And it's only become harder since Wol died. Without thinking, I sigh.

'You don't like it here, Sophie?' Tom asks, apparently finished thinking about mice.

I shrug. 'It's okay. But I've lived here off and on since I was little. I'd like to try something new.' I drop my voice. 'I've always wanted to travel.'

'What kind of off and on?' Ingrid asks.

'Mum and I moved here from Scotland when I was seven. So I went to school in the village. Then we lived in Norwich for a bit, but I came back to Cambridge to study.'

Rainbow looks flabbergasted.

'Not Cambridge University,' I add quickly. I don't want her thinking I'm an elite scholar. 'The former polytechnic.'

'And then?'

Why is Tom interested? Do they teach small talk in pilot school too?

'Oh, you know...' No sense publicising my ghastly curriculum vitae. 'I spent the next few years trying to build a career in travel and time ticked by.'

Ingrid looks at Tom. 'How did you come to be a flying instructor?'

He smiles. 'I've always had a thing about planes. Couldn't get enough of them, as a kid. Every birthday, I begged to go to Duxford to see the World War II bombers. But after I left British Airways, I got drawn into the family business.'

'The garden centres?' Ingrid asks. 'They're terrific. I love Vines.'

'Yes. But they're a lot to manage.' Tom nods. 'My parents are getting older, they hoped my brother and I would step in. I didn't mind grubbing around in the compost or the accounts.' He drinks some beer. 'It just wasn't my true passion.'

'So...?' Rainbow prompts.

Tom looks away. 'My brother, Alistair, died suddenly. Heart attack.'

He's talking about Lorraine's husband. We murmur our sympathies.

'And I realised,' Tom says, 'life really is too short. I could be dead tomorrow. I knew I had to admit that my priority was flying.'

'What about your parents?' asks Ingrid.

'They weren't thrilled initially, but I think they understand. They were devastated to lose Alistair too. I'm still involved with Vines, just less than before.'

'Lucky for us,' Rainbow declares, smiling at Tom skittishly.

'Strange, though,' Fergus muses, 'that our fear can be Tom's passion.'

'Great point, Fergus!' Rainbow seizes on this. 'Anything

worth going after in life is likely gonna be scary at the same time.'

We let that sink in, then Ingrid picks up her glass. 'In that case,' she says, 'I suppose we should drink to fears and passions.'

~ ~ ~

What's got into Bella this morning? She's going to be outrageously late for work.

After awarding myself a lie-in, I'm sitting at the kitchen table having breakfast, but Bella's still upstairs in the shower. What's more, it sounds like she's whistling Beethoven. Has she lost her marbles? She was fine last night, when I left the pub. Bella's supposed to be the steady, sensible one. If anyone is allowed to be harebrained, it's usually me.

I've guzzled a bowl of Frosties and am still hungry. With my head deep in the fridge, I'm looking for bread when I hear a cough behind me.

'Bell,' I call, 'is there any of your marmalade in here?'

'Just coffee for me, thanks,' comes a male voice.

I bang my head on the fridge shelf before spinning around. 'Who the bloody hell are you?'

'Bloody hell!' repeats Stanley, making me jump again. I send up another apology to Wol for his new vocabulary.

Then I turn my attention to the tanned, fair-haired man leaning in the kitchen doorway. His arms are folded complacently and he looks entirely comfortable in our house. Oh, wait, it's not our house.

'Sorry,' I say. 'You must be Uncle Mike. Hi. I'm Sophie.' I pull my dressing gown a bit tighter, for the sake of decency.

He's younger than I expected, closer to our age than to Bella's parents. There must be an age gap in her family, like Kit and me.

'Nice to meet you, Sophie.' He crosses the kitchen and shakes my hand. His hair is wet from the shower and he's wearing grey business trousers with a white shirt. The clothes look sharp, matching his confident manner. 'But I'm not Mike.'

I drop his hand and back away, eyes flicking around the kitchen for a defensive weapon. The knives are too far away, but I could squirt him with washing up liquid. That might buy some time.

'I'm Scott,' he continues. 'I'm, er, a friend of Bella's.'

'Bella?' I repeat.

He nods, looking sheepish now. 'Scott Jones,' he says, and produces a business card, which he hands to me.

'How do I know you're a friend of Bella's?' I say, one hand reaching for the Fairy Liquid, just in case. 'You heard me say her name – you could be making that up.'

He sits down at the table. At least that makes it less likely he's going to lunge at me. 'We met last night, in the pub.'

'Wait,' I say. 'Don't move.' I reach for my phone to call Bella. 'There's a guy here. Is he yours?' I demand as soon as she answers.

'Hi, Soph.' She clears her throat. 'Um, yeah, that's Scott.'

'Really?' I put my soapy weapon down. 'Why didn't you say something?'

She coughs again. 'It happened a bit, um, fast.'

I turn to assess Scott. He is extraordinarily good-looking, definitely out of Bella's usual league. If it wasn't for his slightly wonky nose, he could easily be on an advertising billboard. He looks back at me, head on one side, presumably curious about the conversation.

'Gosh,' I say. 'Right. Okay. I'll give him some coffee, shall I?'

'Yes, fine,' she says. 'Oh, and Sophie?'

'Mmm?' I'm still regarding this handsome apparition with disbelief.

Bella lowers her voice. 'Could you possibly try to get his phone number?'

~ ~ ~

I find sharing breakfast with a strange man deeply unsettling, but Scott doesn't seem to feel awkward. When I refuse to make fresh-ground coffee, he settles for a big mug of tea, and asks politely for a paracetamol.

'Did you have a heavy night?' I ask sarcastically, then wish I hadn't. I don't want to hear about his time with Bella, especially if he misunderstands and thinks I'm talking about her weight. I stick my head in a cupboard to avoid looking at him, and am rewarded with the elusive marmalade.

'Drank a bit too much,' he says smoothly. 'If you're making toast, can you pop a slice in for me?'

So now I'm supposed to wait on him too? I turn to glare, but he's wearing such a charming expression, I bite back my grumble and put two pieces of bread in the toaster. Darn, I wish I looked that good with a hangover.

'You live in the village?' I ask, after a pause. I can't think of any other reason he'd be in our pub.

'No, London.' He adds sugar to his tea. 'I had some business nearby and stopped off to see an old friend.'

'Oh. Right.'

'Feed me!' commands Stanley from the corner as the toast pops up. Great, now the parrot's bossing me around. I make a point of helping myself to marmalade first. Wait a minute, I think, is this the man who was drinking with Amelia last night?

'Did I see you at The Plough with the woman from the estate agency?'

He's spreading Bella's sweet, orangey concoction on his toast and doesn't meet my eye. 'Yes.'

That's all – a single, clipped word. I say nothing, but I'm suspicious on my friend's behalf. If he was being fed chips by Amelia earlier in the evening, how did he end up in Bella's bed? I chew my toast and look across at Stanley. But he's busy preening himself and apparently has nothing to say on the matter. It's a pity that parrot doesn't talk when asked.

Chapter 14

So much for my Saturday lie-in. According to the text messages now filling my phone, my mother is sorting through things at Wol's cottage and I'm late on parade. Again.

'And I don't mean wistful gazing at old tea towels,' were the words mum used when I agreed to join her. 'We need to get that place spick and span before the new owner turns up.'

My week was busy: fact checking a guide to Canada, with a tight deadline. Still, it was a relief to keep out of everyone's way and not draw further attention to myself. Joey thought I was flying, which got him out from under my feet and his nose out of my business. After a few peaceful days, I'm not looking forward to a morning in close proximity to maternal questions. Last night's homemade cocktails with Bella aren't helping either. At least it's not just me with a hangover: Bella clumped out of the bathroom looking horrible too.

Wearily, I text back: *Sorry. Be there soon.*

~ ~ ~

After a shower, I feel clean but not human. I can't stomach breakfast, but I decide to stop at the bakery and buy something for later. Brian's wide smile lifts my spirits, and as I leave the shop with a currant bun in a paper bag, I decide I could manage just a little of it.

Five minutes later, I leave the bakery again, having inexplicably found myself bun-less and in need of another. Then, with a notion of redeeming myself with mum, I venture into the estate agent's.

'Hello! I was just thinking about you.' Amelia looks up from behind a tower of papers.

'Oh.' With her shiny hair, pristine make-up and taupe dress, she is the glossy opposite of my hungover shambles. 'That always makes me nervous.'

'Are you here to sign the lease? Hang on, I'll find it.' She starts to look through the stack of folders.

'Um, no, actually,' I say hastily, and watch her elegant hand, complete with coloured cocktail ring, pause in its search.

Amelia looks up, quizzical.

'Sorry.' I shift to the other foot. 'I need a bit more time on that.'

I expect her to look irritated, but she smiles instead. 'No problem,' she says. 'It's a big decision.'

I exhale. 'It is,' I say. 'I don't want to... rush into it,' I add feebly.

'Of course not, darling. Going into business with someone is huge.' Amelia smiles. 'It's easier to get divorced, these days, than end a partnership arrangement.'

Oh God, I think, is it? My face must have given me away, because she adds, 'Although Joey's great, of course.'

'Yes,' I say. 'Great.'

Amelia winks. 'Don't let him push you around. Between you and me, nobody else has shown much interest in the shop. The economy, and all that.'

There's a pause. I wonder if she should be telling me this. Shouldn't she pretend that eager entrepreneurs are fighting over it?

Amelia's phone rings and she glances at it, then back at me. 'So, how can I help?'

'I was wondering if I could borrow some of the cardboard boxes from the grocer's.'

'Boxes?' She looks puzzled.

'I'm helping mum clear out my great-aunt's cottage. We haven't got enough boxes.'

'Oh, I see.' Amelia gets up from her desk. 'Yes, no problem. I'll get you the key.'

She's pretty trusting, I think. Although there's not a lot

of mischief I can do in a worn-out shop filled with cardboard boxes. 'Do you want to come and supervise?'

'Supervise? Good lord, no. But I'll walk with you – I need some stamps.'

Amelia disappears into a back office, and returns with keys and her purse. She gestures to the front door and, once she's locked it, we set off down the street together.

'Have you heard from the new owner, then? Of Miss Campbell's house?' she asks.

'Mum asked the solicitor,' I reply. 'A cousin from America's inherited it.'

'Hmm, really? How interesting.'

I sense she's filed that piece of information away.

We reach the post office, and Amelia tuts at the 'Back in 5 minutes' sign on the door. Which is funny, as she's just left a similar notice at Hargraves & Co.

'Darn,' she says. 'Where the devil has Violet got to? Maybe I'll come with you after all.'

'There she is,' I point. Violet is a few yards away, peering through the letterbox of the green grocer's. Next to her, a man has his back to us.

'Violet, darling, you're playing hooky,' Amelia calls out.

Violet stands up; both she and the man turn. It's Tom. He looks as surprised as me. Embarrassed, I twizzle a still-damp piece of hair.

'Amelia!' exclaims Violet. 'Just the person.'

'What's going on?' Amelia asks. 'Why aren't you at the post office?'

'Hi,' Tom says quietly to me, and I give him an awkward nod before folding my arms, then unfolding them and tucking my thumbs in my pockets.

'I was hearing noises,' Violet replies.

'Oh yes?' Amelia pulls a comical face.

I smile, despite the embarrassment of bumping into Tom. What's he doing in the village again?

'What kind of noises?' I ask.

'Strange yowling,' Violet replies. 'I was just telling this

nice young man, I think they're coming from in here.'

'And I said, the Sweeting Werewolf is back.' Tom's smiling at Violet.

'Gosh, what a bore,' Amelia grins, glancing at Tom. Then she looks more closely. 'Hello there, I'm Amelia Hargraves.'

As she shakes her beautiful mane, I feel a prickle of something I can't identify.

'Nice to meet you.' Tom's voice is neutral. He looks back at me. 'Not flying today?'

'Who? Me?' I say, like an idiot. Clearly, he meant me. 'No,' I add, and look down at the shiny toes of Amelia's shoes, but not before I've seen his wry smile.

'Shush!' I'm grateful for Violet's interruption. 'Did you hear that?'

'Hear what?' Amelia's smirking, but all four of us lean closer to the building.

I hold my breath. A faint squealing noise does indeed seem to come from inside.

'You're right.' Tom frowns. 'There is something.'

'Of course I'm right,' says Violet, with the certainty of one who is fast approaching three score years and ten. She has, after all, outlived JFK, John Lennon and Princess Diana.

'Snakes alive,' says Amelia. 'I hear it too.' She straightens and looks at me. 'Well, that's good timing. Here you are, Sophie.' With this, she holds out the key, dangling it between thumb and forefinger.

I take a step back.

'You wanted boxes, remember?' Amelia prompts, with a mischievous gleam in her eye.

'Right. Yeah.' I take the key and swallow. My head is still pounding and now I have to investigate strange noises?

'There isn't really a village werewolf, Sophie,' Violet supplies helpfully.

'But if there is,' Amelia gives a small chuckle, 'be sure to catch him. I could do with a new handbag.'

'Right,' I repeat. 'Will do.'

As I turn the key in the lock, a louder wail reaches us. I bite my lip, then feel a shadow as Tom steps forward. 'I'll come with you,' he says.

'There might be mice in there,' I say.

He stiffens and I glance at him. If his fear of mice is anything like my fear of planes, he should stay here with the others.

Tom blinks, but squares his shoulders. 'That's okay.'

I nod up at him, trying to signal my admiration. Together, we push the door open. I'm relieved to sense him half a pace behind as we step into the shop. We leave the front door ajar and I look around. Everything appears as it did before – scruffy, abandoned, but not harbouring any monsters. There are the boxes I wanted, and I curse them silently for luring me here.

'Are you okay?' Tom asks quietly. 'You look a tad pale.'

I nod without looking at him. 'Bit hungover.'

'Ah,' he says. 'Understood.' Then, casually, he adds, 'Big date last night?'

Distracted, I shake my head. 'Just home with my housemate.'

The mysterious noises have stopped.

'Shall we – er – go through to the back?' I say.

'Sure.' He steps forward to lead the way, and I let him.

'I know you think I'm nuts,' I say as we make cautious progress towards the gloomy rear of the shop.

'No.' Tom stops and turns suddenly, and in the dim light I almost bump into him. 'But I am curious why you're pretending to be cabin crew. It's bizarre, given how you feel about flying.'

'I nearly was,' I protest. 'I got the job, did some of the training before I freaked out.'

'But why even apply, if you're so terrified?'

'I thought...' My face is level with his chest, so close I can see the buttons on the navy cotton of his shirt. 'I was trying to confront it, head on. Stupid, I know...'

Tom's chest rises and falls as he breathes, and, despite the musty air, I smell the tangy, grassy scent I'm starting to associate with him.

'Oh,' he says, and I wait for him to move away. But he doesn't. Instead, he says quietly, 'Not stupid. Brave.'

I freeze, and for a long moment neither of us moves. After what seems like ages, I raise my eyes slowly to the top button of his shirt, then the base of his neck, then throat, chin and nose. Finally I meet his gaze, and the intensity knocks me sideways. His eyes are swirled with green and brown. I release the breath I've been holding and at the same time allow my stare to drop back to his mouth. He takes half a step forward, and lifts a hand to my cheek.

Just as I close my eyes, a single bark breaks the silence. It's incredibly close.

'What the − !' I leap off my toes and my eyes fly open, heart hammering. 'Did you hear that?' I ask, unnecessarily.

Tom looks equally shocked, but recovers. 'I can safely say I heard that, yes.'

He turns and gestures to the stock room. 'Shall we?'

In the windowless gloom, I spot more shelves, plenty more boxes, and a lot more cobwebs. But it's not the eight-legged creatures we need to be concerned about.

'Oh,' says Tom, stretching the syllable.

'What?' I say.

'There.' He points to the corner as a series of squeaks starts up.

'Oh my gosh.' I crouch down to get a better look.

There, on an old pile of sacks, in a cosy corner between two stacks of boxes, lies a black and white spaniel. Her soft eyes are like treacle as she looks at us warily.

Tom drops to one knee also. 'Well, that's quite a werewolf,' he says in an undertone, and I sense from his voice he's smiling.

'Yeah,' I say. 'Terrifying.'

'Terrifyingly cute, you mean.'

'Uh huh.' I nod, unable to take my eyes off them. All six

of them.

Tom retreats to the front of the shop, where I hear him inviting Violet and Amelia to join us.

'What is it?' I hear Violet say. 'What did you find?'

'Come and see,' Tom replies. 'But be warned: if anyone mentions handbags, I'll personally chase them out of town.'

Chapter 15

'Joey,' I say casually on Sunday night, 'what are you afraid of?'

Joey's glued to the television. He, Bella and I are lined up on the sofa. I'm in the middle and he's lolling at one end as we wait for the nineties action film to deliver some excitement.

'Afraid of?' Joey repeats. 'Like what?'

'Like anything. You know. Like needles, or hospitals, or mice.'

Or flying, is my silent fourth option.

He uncrosses his ankles which, despite Bella's wrinkled nose, are on the coffee table.

'Dunno. Nothing, really.'

'There must be something,' I say. 'Snakes? Rejection? Your grandmother?'

Bella chuckles.

'Nope,' he says, and reaches for his beer. 'Can't think of anything.'

Since last week's flying class, I've been thinking about phobias and Tom's admission. Even if the others thought he was joking, I'm pretty sure he is scared of mice. It made me think, is there something inside all of us that we strive to avoid?

'Joey's not scared of rejection,' Bella says. 'He's convinced he's going to be a world-famous photographer.'

Joey doesn't bother to feign modesty. 'Quite right,' he says. 'Just a matter of time.' Then he looks at me. 'Once I get my new studio, that is.'

Blast, I don't want to get back onto that subject. 'But you must be afraid of *something*,' I insist, disappointed by this lack of depth.

Bella chimes in. 'I'm afraid of fireworks.'

'Really?' asks Joey.

'Oh yeah.' I grin. I'd totally forgotten.

'Why?' he persists.

Bella puffs out her cheeks. 'I was on Midsummer Common one bonfire night, for the display. It was mild, for November – my jacket was open.'

'And?' Joey is intrigued.

'A spark went down my top,' Bella admits.

His eyes light up. 'Seriously?'

She nods. 'It hurt like hell. Obviously.'

Joey leans around me, looking at Bella's cleavage. 'Are you scarred?'

'That's enough, Giuseppe,' I say. 'Watch the film.'

He shrugs and turns obediently to the overdue gunfire on the screen, but with his arm around me, begins gently kneading the muscles in the back of my neck. I sit quietly for a minute. Joey likes to keep things simple. Maybe I need more simplicity in my life.

Then I look at Bella, who smiles.

'I'm proud of you,' she murmurs. 'Wol would be proud of you too.'

'What for?' I say in an undertone.

'For tackling your fear,' she whispers, then stops as I put a finger to my lips.

'How about you?' I mutter. 'Will you be addressing your firework phobia?'

She smiles. 'It's not exactly a problem in daily life. My other fear is far more worrying.'

'What other fear?' I'm not aware of anything else Bella hates. Except perhaps Stanley.

There's a pause before she answers softly, 'I'm scared I'll end up alone.' She grabs a cushion and hugs it.

Hearing the catch in her voice, I squeeze her forearm. 'Bell, you won't end up alone. There's somebody wonderful out there for you, I know there is.'

She doesn't answer.

'Has he called?' I ask eventually. 'Scott, I mean?' By my calculation, it's been almost a week.

'No,' she sighs. 'He hasn't.'

~~~

Two days after their discovery, the puppies are the talk of the village. Violet, as self-appointed canine spokeswoman, is holding court at The Plough to update eager fans.

'We've found the owner!' she announces on Monday night.

I'm early for our flying meeting, taking place once again at the pub. Bella's working tonight and the menu has improved considerably since she got her hands on the kitchen and made Fergus change suppliers.

'The mother's from a farm at Wilbraham,' Violet continues. 'Apparently, she likes to wander, and when it was time for the pups to arrive, she took a fancy to our veg shop.'

'What will happen to them?' Bella asks from behind the bar. She's showing a lot more empathy with the wriggling, eyes-closed squeakers than she ever has for Stanley.

'We're looking for homes, obviously,' Violet says. 'I'll probably take one. A friend at Six Mile Bottom wants one too.'

'Didn't the farmer wonder where she was?' I ask.

'Of course he did,' Violet says crisply. 'He just didn't know where to look. Luckily, others were on the ball.' She means herself, of course, not Tom and me who braved werewolves and mice to venture into the vegetable shop.

'What breed are they?' Ingrid is also early for the meeting and is alternating sips of Diet Coke with knitting.

'Spaniels, dear. Not pedigree, of course, but mostly spaniel. The farmer has several running around. How about you, Sophie?'

'How about me what?' I'm devouring a wonderful plateful of Bella's bubble and squeak, with accompanying baked beans.

'You'd like a puppy, wouldn't you?' Violet says, as if she's merely offering me the HP sauce.

'Blimey,' I say. 'I don't think so.'

Bella looks curious. 'I thought you liked animals? You've bonded with that parrot fellow.'

'Stanley's a temporary lodger,' I say. 'A puppy's a different thing altogether.'

'And I expect it's difficult, with your, um, job and all.' Fergus sits down next to Ingrid and shoots me a meaningful glance.

Violet's eyes narrow. 'Of course,' she says. 'Your job.'

Luckily, Rainbow arrives. 'Awesome,' she says, 'you're all here. Sophie, honey, I hope that's apple juice.'

I take a hasty swallow of my Riesling, in case she confiscates it.

Fergus gets up to lead the group upstairs. 'Actually, Tom's not here yet,' he says.

Rainbow gives a Cheshire Cat smile. 'Tom's meeting us there,' she says.

'Where?' Ingrid and I ask simultaneously, looking at each other.

'We're going on a field trip,' Rainbow says.

'What kind of field trip?' I ask again. I'd rather stay at the pub. It feels... grounded.

Rainbow's still grinning. 'We're gonna desensitise you.'

'Do what?' Ingrid clutches my hand now.

I clutch back, hard. I don't like the sound of this one little bit.

~~~

Fergus backs away, so sharply he stands on Ingrid's foot. 'Sweet Lord,' he gasps. 'You don't mean we actually have to get in it?'

Our field trip is a visit to Cambridge airport. We've formed a dispirited huddle on the grass, next to an alarmingly small plane which looks like it's been made from a child's kit. Some of the joins are wonky and appear to be held together by Play-Doh.

Ingrid claims she's coming down with something and says she'd better go home. I look at her pale, sweating face and can hardly blame her, even if the only thing she's coming down with is gravity. Then I remember that Tom and Rainbow arranged this so that they're the only ones with cars here.

Rainbow speaks fluidly. 'You're all doing great. It's scientifically proven that exposure to the thing you're scared of lessens the fear. Let's begin with a visualisation.'

She makes us close our eyes, and this time we have to pretend we're airborne and perfectly serene. As a group, we take slow breaths in, then supposedly picture ourselves floating as we exhale steadily. Personally, I picture myself falling, but I clench my fists and keep quiet. Standing with your peepers squeezed shut is a recipe for dizziness in any case. I half open one, just to get my balance, and am surprised to see Tom with obediently closed eyes too. Is he picturing himself flying or perhaps calmly stroking a little white mouse? It's impossible to tell.

After Rainbow's New Age attempts to calm us, the class turns more practical. Tom moves to the plane and points out the parts he described last week. He tells us how much it weighs and how many square feet make up the wings.

'These are the flaps,' he says, showing us some bits which look like they might fall off at any moment. 'They increase the area of the wing, letting us fly at lower speeds when we need to. And here are the ailerons. To over-simplify things, they help us turn.'

That's all very well, but when he gets out a list and starts doing what look like pre-flight checks, the group grows mutinous. Our nervous coughs almost drown out a cargo plane which chooses that moment to taxi to the end of the runway. We watch it, heads drawn into our necks like turtles, until it's in the air and fading from sight.

Fortunately, there isn't much else going on at the airport and nothing else has taken off since we arrived. Tom's told us that Cambridge is heavily used as a maintenance facility, and by private planes like the ones he flies, but not much in the way of commercial traffic.

'There's no way I'm going in that thing,' Ingrid says. 'It's a deathtrap.'

Tom appears to hide a smile. 'It's not a deathtrap, Ingrid. I was up in it yesterday.' Ingrid looks unconvinced. 'However,' Tom continues, 'you'll be glad to know you're not flying in it. At least, not yet.'

Rainbow nods. 'Today's assignment is that you'll each go for a short ride in the plane with Tom, but you won't leave the ground. Just taxi around the airfield.'

'Think of it like a ride in a Mini,' Tom offers. 'It's bumpy and rattles a lot, but that's all.'

Okay, I think, that doesn't sound so bad. Tom catches my eye and I twitch my head, to show I might consider the idea.

'Good,' he says. 'Now, Fergus, help me check the fuel.'

Fergus demurs but it turns out all he has to do is inspect a little tube which Tom is sticking in various points of the plane.

'We're looking at the colour,' Tom explains. 'Making sure it's the right type in there. And we don't want to see water or sediment.'

Next, he walks all around the plane, pulling on some bits and pushing others, consulting his list as he goes. He's businesslike, yet relaxed.

Then Tom gets inside and occupies himself with the inner controls, which we can't see. But some of the outside parts wiggle as he does so.

'Okay!' He jumps out again. 'Sophie, I have an important job for you.'

I shake my head and inch closer to Ingrid, but Tom is undeterred.

'Come here,' he says, 'and help me clean the windscreen.'

I notice he's holding an aerosol can and a cloth in one hand. He's grinning broadly.

'No way,' I say, but I can't help smiling. 'That's sexist. Fergus checked the fuel.'

'Go on, Sophie,' Ingrid chips in. 'I certainly can't get up there.'

I look where Tom is gesturing for me to climb to reach the plane's windscreen. Even if Ingrid could hoist her considerable bulk up, it doesn't seem a good plan. She might break something – on the plane. She gives me a nudge and I join Tom beside the wing, which suddenly looks far bigger.

'Can you get a foot on there?' He gestures to a small foothold, on a level with my thigh. 'That's it,' he says. 'Now hop.'

I push off with my grounded foot and Tom grabs my calf to boost me further. Before I am fully aware of his grip on my lower leg, I find myself clinging to the side of the plane.

'Okay,' he says, 'rest your other foot here.'

It's certainly not comfortable, and I'm worried it's bad for the wing support, but I'm stable enough, at least for a minute. The aerosol can isn't fancy plane stuff but basic furniture cleaner, and I apply myself to wiping flies off the glass.

'That's great, Sophie,' Tom says from below. 'Use vertical motions, don't go round and round. It's plastic and we don't want to scratch it.'

Plastic? That doesn't sound especially sturdy. What if we hit a bird – a big one, like a goose? I've heard stories of pilots being partially sucked out through broken windscreens and their colleagues hanging onto their legs. But I don't have time to dwell on it as my own legs are cramping and I have work to do. Tom helps me jump down, his hands around my waist as I land, and this time I do consider how that feels. It's actually really nice. But that's probably the relief of being back on terra firma.

'Good stuff,' he says. 'Now the other side.'

We repeat the performance on the far side of the plane, the nose shielding us from the group. When he helps me down, his hands stay around my waist a second longer than necessary.

'I apologise,' he says. 'It *was* a bit sexist to make you do that.' His voice is low and serious and he leans close to my ear. 'But I enjoyed it.'

I gape, then look up to see if he's teasing me. But he just smiles, then marshals me and the rest of the group a safe distance away from the plane.

As Tom and Rainbow decide on the order for our ride, I'm not listening. My legs feel wobbly – no doubt from their unfamiliar gymnastics – and my stomach is full of butterflies at the thought of getting inside the aircraft.

'Right,' calls Tom. 'Fergus and Ingrid, you first.'

I don't know whether to be pleased or dismayed that I'm last.

Fergus looks anything but happy about this prospect, but I sense he doesn't want to be a cissy in front of Ingrid. He's gentlemanly in helping her into the back of the plane, which, given her size, is a game of Twister. Tom helps them both, betraying nothing in his expression.

'We'll make this quick,' Tom says. 'Don't want Rainbow and Sophie getting cold.' He jumps into the pilot's seat and shuts the little door.

Cold? I'm already freezing. At least, I'm shivering and prancing from one foot to another, arms around my torso for warmth or maybe comfort. Is he really going to make us do this?

Rainbow and I wait as more preparations are made inside the plane. Ingrid and Fergus are both kitted out with headphones, and Tom seems to be talking non-stop, pointing to things. Then he opens the window, shouts something that sounds like 'Clear prop!' and with a terrible stutter, the engine and propeller come to life.

Holy smoke, I think, I've seen lawnmowers start more easily. After what seems like ages, but might only be a few minutes, the plane begins to move, and Ingrid – darn her – gives us a wave as they pass. I can't read Tom's face as he's now disguised by both headphones and sunglasses. The little Cessna trundles past us and off down the taxiway.

'This is so great,' Rainbow tells me, when the noise of the plane lessens. 'You're all doing great.'

'Right... great,' I repeat lamely.

'Isn't Tom the *best*?' she says, looking in the direction of the Cessna's tail. 'He inspires such confidence.'

'You think?'

'Hell, yeah.' Rainbow replies. 'I'd fly to the moon with him. Today.'

I smile. 'He does seem very capable.' But I suspect her praise isn't solely for his flying credentials.

Within minutes, they're back. As far as I could see, they simply went down to one end of the runway, turned and completed the loop. Tom returns the plane to the same parking spot.

I grit my teeth. Surely this can't be too bad? I only need to get in, not have a heart attack for five minutes, then go home for a ginormous whisky.

But Tom switches off the engine and opens his window. In the back, Ingrid is glum, and then I spot Fergus, looking like death warmed up.

'Bit of a glitch,' Tom calls to Rainbow. 'Fergus was sick.'

Poor Fergus. I hope this hasn't ruined his chances with Ingrid.

'Sorry, Sophie,' Tom calls to me. 'We're going to have to postpone.'

'Postpone?' says Rainbow.

Dammit, just when I'd got myself psyched up.

Tom nods. 'The plane needs to be cleaned. I'll book another for tomorrow.' He takes off his headset and looks across at me. 'All right with you, Sophie?'

No, I think, it's not all right. You made me clean dead flies with a flannel, I've been standing here shivering for twenty minutes, and I want to get this over so I can go home and drown myself in an enormous hot toddy. And then never go near anything with wings, ever again.

'Sophie?' Tom repeats, and even from this distance, I see encouragement in his face.

I swallow a sob and find my voice. 'Yes,' I say shakily. 'Tomorrow. Fine.'

I'm still having that sodding whisky. I've totally earned it.

Chapter 16

I'm chaining my bike to the railings near Parker's Piece when I see him. Dressed in a charcoal suit and blue shirt, he's coming out of one of the posh estate agents on Regent Street with another man.

I couldn't face Tom or his plane today. I sent a text claiming an overlooked appointment and fled into Cambridge for a couple of hours. And after browsing vintage clothes on the market and picking up a coconut for Stanley, I feel better. I know I'm dodging the inevitable, but I can't bring myself to get in an aircraft.

This, on the other hand, is an opportunity to seize.

'Oy!' I shout.

Either he's ignoring me or the passing open-top bus drowns me out. Damn. I can't just leave my bike unsecured, it won't stand a chance. Hastily I spin the combination lock and detach the front light.

Where did he go? I trot towards the street, in time to see them going into the University Arms. 'Hey!' I call again, but Scott doesn't turn.

Well, I'm not giving up. Bella's been putting on a brave face, but she's trudging around like a deflated balloon.

'I can't believe I actually thought he'd call me,' she said yesterday, pummelling a batch of scone dough. 'How could I be so stupid?'

'It's not your fault,' I said. 'He was utterly charming, even at breakfast. I practically spread the marmalade on his toast for him.'

'I spread more than marmalade for him,' Bella replied miserably. 'I'm never going to find a nice man, Soph.'

'Yes you are,' I said. 'Hang in there.'

But that batch of scones, usually so light and flaky, was like rock. And this morning, before she crawled out of the house to go to work, I heard something which made my heart plummet.

I push open the hotel's big door and look around the lobby, dark compared with the May sunshine outside. There they are: in the bar, documents on their table.

'Excuse me!' I tap Scott on the shoulder and he turns.

'Hi,' I say, then 'Sorry' to the older man.

'Can I help you?' Scott is wary, showing no sign of recognition.

'We met last week,' I say. 'At breakfast. In Saffron Sweeting?'

The older man coughs awkwardly and Scott shifts in his chair, but his face is still a blank.

'At *breakfast*,' I repeat. 'My friend Bella had already gone to work.'

'Oh.' Finally, he nods. 'Sorry, Clive.' He turns to his colleague and shrugs, then glances back at me. 'And?'

A waiter brings their drinks. Scott takes a lazy mouthful of beer.

'And?' Oh sod, I haven't planned what to say. 'And Bella, she's, um, waiting for you to phone.'

Scott stands now, palms turned up. 'Okay,' he says. 'Bella and I had a... pleasant evening... but it's not going to go any further.'

'But –' Oh, this is bad, he's turning away, back to his meeting. 'But it's important. You need to talk to her.'

'Look. This isn't the school disco.' He's annoyed.

'You really have to call.' I plant my feet squarely.

'No, I don't,' he says.

'You do.'

Scott sighs and runs a hand through his hair. 'And why might that be?'

'She's been sick,' I blurt. 'Twice.'

His deep blue eyes flicker.

'I'm sorry,' I say, taking a breath. 'But I've heard her twice now, in the mornings. And I really think you should call.'

~~~

I wake under a weight of shame and foreboding. I had another flying dream. Nothing unusual there: I've had them off and on for months, with variations of planes spinning out of control and crashing. This time, I was back in stewardess training, but standing in front of Wol's blackboard to give the safety demonstration. And when I looked down the rows of the plane, every seat was occupied by a baby.

As consciousness settles on me, I realise I overstepped the mark by telling Scott that Bella might be in the pudding club. I'm still terrified that she might be. But I, of all people, should know the value of discretion.

Then my phone buzzes and as I see the text from Tom, I remember my bigger problem. It's raining and he's offering to pick me up. I text back to protest that surely planes can't operate in wet weather, but his reply is firm. They can, and they will.

~~~

'Did you think I wouldn't show?' I ask as I lift heavy bones into his grey Range Rover.

'The thought did occur to me,' he says, and reverses the car out of the driveway. 'Plus, I didn't want you riding your bike and arriving all wet – you might make the plane rust.'

'Rust?!' That sounds horrific. What if something essential drops off?

'I'm kidding, Sophie.' Tom grins sideways.

I sigh. 'I wish you wouldn't.' Then I add, 'I don't really see the funny side of plane jokes.'

'Fair enough,' he says. 'Sorry.'

'Rainbow's house is the other way,' I say as he turns right at the High Street, towards the shops.

'Rainbow's not coming,' Tom says. 'She said she's seen it all before.'

'Oh.' I process this. 'Right.' I can tell he glances at me again, but I focus resolutely ahead. It's fine. Tom is my fear of flying instructor. This is purely professional.

'So, what's new in the life of a grounded stewardess?' Tom asks.

Now, I look at him. He has a nice profile, with a relaxed driving style: one hand on the wheel and the other resting loosely on the gear stick. The windscreen wipers make a comforting swooshing as we drive out of Saffron Sweeting. The car smells of leather seats, with a hint of garden shed, presumably from Tom's job. I feel so insulated in here; I wish we could keep driving and never reach the airport.

'Look,' I say, 'I didn't mislead you deliberately, when we met.'

'No? Seemed like you did, from where I was standing.'

'My mum thinks I'm an air hostess and so does half the village.'

'So, if you're not, tell them.'

'I can't.'

'Yes, you can. You say: mum, I'm not an air hostess.'

I pause. 'She mustn't know I can't fly.'

Tom checks his blind spot before pulling out to overtake. 'Why on earth not?'

I look down at my lap. 'I can't tell you.'

There's silence. From the corner of my eye, I see the sceptical look he shoots me.

'But if you could fly, things would be better?'

'They would.' I nod. 'I can hardly bear the idea of getting in that plane, but yes, it would make things much better.'

'Right,' Tom says. 'Let's see what we can do about that.'

~ ~ ~

After picking up the keys from the flying club, Tom parks his Range Rover close to all the little planes.

'You know,' I say, 'we don't have to do this today. It's very kind of you, but I watched the others and I'm fine. I can just move on to next week's class.'

He shakes his head. 'Nice try.' His voice is muffled as he

pulls a waterproof over his head. 'You wait there, I'll get the plane ready.'

The rain is lighter now and, despite the droplets trickling down the windscreen, I can see Tom carrying out the same checks as before. I wish he wouldn't do all this stuff: surely it's not necessary, if our wheels are staying firmly on the ground.

He hops up to wipe the glass, and I find myself with the same view of his backside as he had of mine. Well, if he checked me out, I'm sure as heck going to peek at his behind. As I thought: long, strong legs and his jeans fit him well. In fact, he might be in better shape than Joey. Nonetheless, he's about to make me get in a plane. One of those thoughts is enough to make my mouth dry and my fingers tingle.

When Tom comes back and opens the passenger door, I find there's a woodpecker inside my chest. Not only that, but someone has stolen my knees.

'Don't make me do this,' I say.

'Sophie, it's okay,' he replies. He's standing by the car, one hand on the open door. 'I promise, you'll be fine.'

'Please.' I'm as croaky as Stanley. 'I lost a relative recently, I'm not ready for...' I trail off. And whose white knuckles are those? Oh. They're mine.

When he doesn't answer, I'm forced to look up. Although the rain has slackened to a drizzle, his hair is wet and there are streams trickling down his jacket. In his face, I see equal parts amusement, compassion and something else.

'Trust me,' Tom says softly, and reaches out a hand.

I gulp, and take it.

Compared to the warmth of the car, it's chilly in the plane. And squashed. Tom wasn't joking when he said it was like being in a Mini. He helps me clamber into the right hand seat, and prevents me from bumping my head on the wing as I find I have more legs to coordinate than an octopus.

'You'll get the hang of it,' he says, and removes the

wooden blocks from beside the tyres before climbing in the other side.

'I'm going to be sick,' I say immediately.

'No, you're not,' he replies cheerfully. 'Although after the other day with Fergus, I brought these. This is a different Cessna, by the way.' He hands me a couple of paper bags, with Virgin Atlantic printed on them, then busies himself taking off his waterproof and stowing gear behind us.

'Let's do your seat,' he says, and reaches across to help me slide further forward. The interior of the plane is cramped and he can reach both the seat – and me – easily.

'Seatbelt next,' he instructs, and I fumble as I locate the ends but fail to slot them together.

'You really haven't done this before, have you?' Tom says, and takes care of the fastening. 'Pull that snug,' he says. 'Good. Now the shoulder belt.'

This time, he's reaching across and up, above my right ear. He's disarmingly close and I catch his scent, made stronger by the moisture in the air. Once again, I swallow butterflies as he clips the other seatbelt into the first one. Then he adjusts his own seat and gestures to my door.

'In an emergency,' he says, 'you can open it with that handle.'

I nod, thinking that this is a dire emergency and I should begin escape preparations immediately.

'And I do mean an *emergency*,' he says dryly.

Oh, bum, I think, he's onto me.

'And I'm not trying to scare you, but if the propeller's still turning, head for the back of the plane, not the front. I don't want your lovely face sliced up.'

Yuk, that's gruesome. But I'm distracted: did he just call me lovely? Before I can analyse that, Tom hands me a pair of headphones.

'I don't need these,' I say sharply, 'if we're not going anywhere.'

'No,' he replies. 'But I thought you'd like to hear air traffic control, and they'll protect your ears from the noise.

Truly, it's going to get loud.'

I sit quiet as a mouse, half scared and half interested in what's going on. This tiny plane has a massive number of moving parts. What happens if even one of them fails? I don't want to think about it. I can't, in fact, think about it, as Tom says 'Ready?' then yells 'Clear' from his window before I have time to beg to be let out of this tin thimble with wings.

The engine starts more easily than the day before yesterday, but still stutters reproachfully.

Reluctantly, I pull the headphones over my ears as Tom plugs in the cables in front of me. Then he fits his own headset.

'Can you hear me?' comes his voice in my ears as he twiddles some buttons.

I nod, reminding myself what Bella said about Wol being proud.

'Good. Say something.'

I look at him. I've never had a thing for men in uniform, but in those headphones, with all those controls before him, and my life in his hands, he's making me shy. 'Er, hi.'

'Hmm.' He fiddles with a dial. 'Say something else.'

'Please don't kill me.' If he can't hear me, I can be blunt.

He frowns and reaches for the mouthpiece on my headset, bringing it closer to my lips. His hand brushes my cheek and my stomach leaps. This flying thing has really unhinged me. After all, it's not as if I'm attracted to him, or anything.

'Repeat this,' Tom says, businesslike despite my jumbled reactions. 'Juliet Lima Whisky.'

'Juliet what?'

'Good,' he says, 'I can hear you now. That's part of our tail number. You'll hear it on the radio. When they talk to me, I have to respond, so I won't be able to talk to you.'

'Oh! Can they hear me too?'

He laughs. 'Only if you press this when you speak.' He gestures to the controls in front of me and I resolve not to touch them. In fact, I'm not going to touch anything, especially not those massive pedals which are worryingly close to my feet. Lord only knows what they do.

Tom now has a mini clipboard strapped to one thigh, which strikes me as quite kinky, and he's doing yet more preparation. I watch, fascinated, as the fateful moment approaches. Finally he looks across. 'This will be a piece of cake,' he says. 'We're just going for a saunter along the tarmac.'

I give a frigid nod, my teeth digging into my bottom lip. The headphones must be too tight because my head is pounding. And the seatbelt is surely cutting into my lungs, restricting my oxygen supply.

'Breathe in through your nose and hold for three,' Tom says, then waits until I comply. 'Good. Now out through your mouth ...Great. Again.' He reaches across and squeezes my arm. 'You're doing so well.'

After I've done about four breaths like this, he turns back to his clipboard and starts jabbering into his radio. I hear something like '...request taxi...'

Chatter comes back through my headphones, but I don't catch any of it.

Tom says something else, and this time I make out Juliet Lima as the noise increases and the plane moves forward. Compared to being in a car, we're high, and through the wet splotches on the window, I have a view of the other little planes parked nearby, and the grass and hangars of the airport. To our left, I spot what I think is the runway, with all kinds of lights, and, in the distance, a much bigger plane cloaked in scaffolding for maintenance.

We're not quite gliding along, but it isn't as bumpy as I expected. I can't tell how fast we're going, but we're making good progress down the taxiway.

'All right?' Tom says, still checking stuff.

'Uh huh.' I'm not exactly relaxed, but this isn't so bad.

'Good.' He shoots me a smile.

We're closer to the hangars now, which dwarf us. More gibberish comes into my ears and I hear Tom respond. He sounds so calm and confident, talking this language I don't understand, working his hands, feet, eyes and ears all at the same time. I catch morsels of the words but they mean nothing to me. Then the plane stops and I see him engage a brake.

'Okay,' he says, 'mind your knees.'

He's doing further checks, and I'm bemused that things are moving, apparently of their own free will, including the joystick near my thighs. Is this thing haunted? Tom flicks switches, consults dials, and references his clipboard. Then he looks across at me.

'Sophie,' he says, 'you've done brilliantly. It's not so bad, is it?'

I inhale before answering. 'It's bad... but not as bad as I thought.'

Tom's back on the radio. This time, I catch 'Juliet Lima,' 'request' and something that sounds like 'traffic pattern.' Perhaps I can figure out this strange abbreviated chatter after all.

He smiles. 'For the record, you're much better than the others were.'

'Am I?' In that case, they must have been a right mess.

'So I thought you might like to take off,' he says, so casually he could be suggesting a quick cup of tea.

Caught off guard, I snort unbecomingly. 'Do what?' My eyes widen. 'Take off? You're joking.'

'I'm not joking.' Tom shakes his head. 'You've come this far and you're fine. We can do this right now. I radioed for clearance.'

'You're crackers.' I try to laugh at his teasing, but my throat is so tight, I sound like Mickey Mouse.

'Do you trust me?' he asks.

Oh help, where did he put those paper bags? 'I did trust you,' I say, trying to breathe through my nostrils but taking gulps through my mouth instead. 'But now I think you're insane.'

'No,' he answers. '*This* would be insane.'

And in this tiny plane, with the propeller still whizzing round in front of us, he leans across the cabin, moves the microphone away from my mouth, and then curls one hand around the back of my neck. My breathing gets even shallower, and my heart goes from a race to a flat-out sprint, as he bends to press his lips against mine.

Chapter 17

Tom's mouth is firm but caressing. I give a tiny gasp of surprise, and for a moment I don't move. Then, just as my subconscious decides it would really like to kiss him back, he pulls away.

I stare dead ahead. What the heck happened? Am I hallucinating or did a warm, delicious pair of lips just brush mine? The kiss was amazing, yet it can't have lasted more than three seconds.

'Sophie?' His voice comes through my headphones.

The aircraft engine is still running and we're still stationary, in the middle of a taxiway at one end of the airport.

'Tell me you're okay if we take off?'

I forget I'm in a plane, I forget I'm terrified of flying. All I can think about is how it would feel to wrap my arms around Tom and kiss him back.

'Okay,' I hear someone say. I still don't look at him as I touch my tingling lips experimentally.

Before I can utter another sound, the plane trundles forward and turns onto the runway.

There is a moment's pause, then we pick up speed. The plane reaches forty, fifty miles an hour and just as I come to my senses and open my mouth to scream, I realise the ground is falling away from us. Oh, God in heaven, I'm flying.

'We're up,' Tom says. 'You did it.'

We're still gaining height and I look down and behind to where the safety of the airport used to be. It's already shrinking. The city of Cambridge is to our right, and beyond is the flat expanse of East Anglia. Dimly, I notice how green everything looks.

I utter a few choice words which, if Wol could hear me, would result in Jelly Baby privileges being withdrawn for a month.

Tom laughs. 'We're just going around the traffic pattern, then back down,' he says. 'Don't want to push you too far on your first time.'

The horizon tilts and I swear again. 'Is that normal?' I squeak. 'Is everything okay?'

'It's perfectly normal,' he replies, looking as relaxed as someone on a sofa watching EastEnders. 'We're turning. The plane's fine. You're doing really well.'

'I'm not,' I reply through clenched teeth. 'I'm going to pass out.'

'Just breathe, Sophie,' he says, apparently unmoved by the prospect of his passenger losing consciousness. 'Look, there's King's College Chapel.'

'Big bloody deal,' I say, but am momentarily distracted when I spot Trewe College and the building where Bella works.

'Can you see Saffron Sweeting?' Tom asks, pointing in the other direction. 'There's still some low cloud.'

'I'm not sure,' I say, forgetting to pass out as I try to locate familiar buildings which look oddly different from above. 'That's Anglesey Abbey, though.'

He nods and then says something into the radio. Once again, nothing but jumbled words and numbers come back, some of which he repeats.

'Okay, that's enough for one day. I'm getting ready to take us down.'

He might have tricked me into agreeing to get airborne with that kiss, then conned me into neglecting my phobia with Cambridge landmarks, but I'm on red alert now.

'Down? *Down*?' I've read that more plane accidents happen during landing than any other part of the flight. I'm looking all around, trying to get my bearings from the ground far below. Where did the airport go? How on earth will we find it again? Oh, shit, *where is it*?

The plane tilts again as Tom begins to turn. I hate that part, when the world lurches. He's talking into the radio again.

'A couple more minutes,' he says to me. 'Everything's as it should be.'

And there, ahead of us as the plane levels, I see a tiny black and white strip on the ground, like a miniature liquorice allsort. Can that possibly be the runway?

Tom's adjusting dials and knobs, and the noise in the cabin drops. I look at him anxiously, but his face is perfectly neutral as he refers to another sheet on his thigh clipboard.

Wait till you get me down, I think, then swivel my head as something moves on the wing next to me. Is the wretched thing about to fall off?

'Relax,' Tom says. 'It's just the flaps. They're for landing, remember?'

'I'm never forgiving you for this,' I mutter.

'Fine,' he replies. 'You're still flying.'

I am. Good grief, I'm flying.

Just as the ground fell away at disarming speed when we took off, it's now rushing up to greet us, objects getting larger each second as they approach life-size. Tom's busy making tweaks and adjustments and checking readings, but smoothly, in no apparent hurry.

'We're going to die!' I yelp as the runway fills the windscreen. I clap my hands over my eyes and try for brace position, but am prevented by my multiple seatbelt straps.

'Not today,' Tom says.

And after the softest of bumps, we decelerate.

'Welcome to Cambridge,' says my pilot.

I peek through my fingers as we turn off the runway. Tom brings the plane to a stop and grins at me.

Damn you, I think, you totally tricked me.

But I flew. I actually *flew*.

He doesn't say anything else to me, talking into the radio instead as we begin taxiing again. I'd like to give him a piece of my mind but daren't, in case air traffic control is saying something important. Instead, I dig my nails into my palms and try to concentrate on my ragged breathing, until

Tom parks the plane in its designated spot. Finally, he turns the engine off and gestures for me to remove my headphones.

'You bloody bastard!' I wrench them off my ears. 'I can't believe you did that.' My voice is shrill as the anxieties of the last hour tumble out. 'You tricked me! You act all smooth and caring but you're a freaking con-man. How dare you take off? How *dare* you?' I swallow the next batch of insults and concentrate on not crying.

Beside me, Tom takes his headphones off. 'Sorry, didn't catch that.' He starts winding the cables around them neatly. 'Were you saying thank you?' He's smiling broadly, a twinkle in his eye.

That does it. I put my head in my hands and weep.

'Hey – hey. It's okay. You're fine.'

I feel a hand on my arm but I don't look up.

'Look,' he says, 'just give me a minute.'

By the time he's messed around with the plane and recorded numbers in some kind of log, I'm snivelling into a tissue. Tom gets out, puts the wooden blocks near the wheels and attaches chains to each wing. Then he comes around to my door and opens it.

'Let me help you,' he says, and I grudgingly allow him to untangle my headphones and my seatbelt arrangement. 'Come on.' He leads me, shivering, to the Range Rover, where he rummages in the boot before climbing into the driver's seat.

He throws a blanket across my knees and passes me a silver hip flask. I unscrew the lid and sniff cautiously before taking a swig. It's whisky. Hurrah. I take another glug, and exhale properly for the first time that day. Then I wipe the rim and hand it back to him.

Tom doesn't drink from the flask, just puts the top back on and throws it on the back seat. He seems to be waiting for me to say something, but I scowl down at the blanket and fiddle with its fringe.

'You were fantastic,' he says finally. 'I'm proud of you.'

Why should I care what he thinks? 'You tricked me,' I repeat, but my voice is steadier now.

'No,' he says softly, 'I just distracted you a bit.'

'You shouldn't have kissed me,' I whisper, and when he doesn't answer, I give in and look across.

Tom's watching me carefully, no trace of laughter in his eyes. 'Why not?' he says, looking down at my lips. 'It worked, didn't it?'

I blush, thinking about the kiss. A small but insistent part of me wishes he would do it again. And this time, I'd be ready.

Then I remember reality. 'I have... a boyfriend.'

Instantly, Tom's face changes. He looks away, and there's a long silence, during which I carefully plait the blanket's tasselled edge. A few splotches fall on the windscreen as the clouds, which dispersed briefly for our flight, return.

Then, without looking at me again, Tom puts the car key in the ignition. 'Come on,' he says. 'Let's get you home.'

~ ~ ~

I spend the next day in a daze. Not only am I terrified and perplexed by the unexpected flight, I'm strangely unsettled by the minutes immediately before take-off too.

Having spent months avoiding people, I'm suddenly dying to talk to someone. Bella is temporarily off-limits: I haven't confessed what I blurted to Scott and she's likely to get her knickers in a total twist. I don't know if Tom will have told Rainbow about the flight, and even in her professional capacity, I don't feel like confiding. If I discovered that him kissing me was part of some standard shock treatment for phobias, I'd probably make a speedy and permanent departure from Saffron Sweeting.

Wandering up the High Street with no particular destination in mind, I consider going to the pub and whispering to Fergus in the safety of his bar. But since he lost his lunch while still on the ground, it's insensitive to burden him with my gravity-defying exploits. I pause outside the malt house. Long, low and abandoned, its gloomy decay matches my mood.

Eventually, I reach the school. The person I really want to talk to isn't here; at least, not so I can hear her talking back. We scattered her ashes under the weeping willow trees at the end of the playing field, where it slopes down to the river. Wol gave so much of her life to the Saffron Sweeting School and the generations of children who passed through it, I like to think she'll stick around in some way to keep watch on their kids too. But if she is here, she makes no sign.

Still, if I can't talk to Wol, I can talk to the one other person who knows the tangles of my mind. I get out my phone and call Kit.

'I'm so confused,' I say, when she answers. 'I thought if I could fly, things would be better.'

'What's happened?' she asks.

I tell her about Rainbow's class, and Tom taking me on a ground tour of Cambridge airport which led to the surprise flight. But I don't mention the other surprise.

'That's brilliant,' she says. 'So you're cured?'

'No!' I say miserably, my feet leading me slowly towards Wol's spot by the water. 'I don't feel cured. I feel half numb, half panic-stricken.'

'Why?' asks Kit.

'Before, I thought I was just scared of flying.' I trap a long twig under one foot, and use the other to prise up the end. 'Now, I'm scared of everything.'

There's silence for a moment.

'Soph, I know you didn't get yourself into this originally. And... I'll always be grateful. But it's time to start living the life you want, not continue a work of fiction.'

'I didn't mean to let it go on this long.'

'I know,' she says, 'and you did it for the best reasons. But if flying isn't going to happen for you, maybe you should just tell mum and get it over with. Start a new chapter.'

'Easy for you to say. She already thinks I'm hopeless.'

I hear Kit control a chuckle. 'She doesn't. She says nice stuff about you, when you're not around.'

'Anyway,' I say, 'you know what kind of questions that might unleash.'

Kit sighs. 'You're right.'

Seconds pass.

'Do you regret it?' I ask.

I think I hear her swallow. 'Yes. No.' She stops, tries again. 'I wish... things hadn't happened the way they did. But once they did – happen... I think this was the best outcome.' Kit's barely audible. 'For all of us.'

'Do you think about her much?'

There's no answer. When Kit finally speaks, her voice is brittle. 'Every single day.'

The twig under my foot snaps.

'I'm sorry,' I say. 'I didn't phone to bring you down.'

'It's okay. You've... been carrying too much. Maybe this is a door closing for you, so another can open.'

'I don't want another open door,' I say. 'I was quite happy sitting behind the one I had.'

Now there's a smile in Kit's voice. 'Maybe you're not getting a choice.'

No, I think, not when I'm secured by a three-point seatbelt while a psychotic pilot accelerates to take-off speed.

I puff out. 'I think that's what's so unnerving.'

'Yeah,' my little sister says. 'I know.'

A breeze has picked up; the English spring has a bite to it.

'How did you get so wise?' I say with an edge of grumpiness.

'Do you really need to ask?'

'Sorry.' She's right, that was crass.

Then Kit laughs. 'Anyway, I'm at university. These colossal tuition fees would make anyone wise.'

At least, thanks to Wol, she doesn't need to worry about those fees any more. That had been a concern of ours last summer, that mum might cut her off and not pay.

'Look,' she says. 'I don't know much about it, but haven't you done the hardest bit? With the flying, I mean? The workshop thing isn't over?'

'No.' A grey squirrel lollops across the grass. It sees me, but doesn't change course. 'But I'm still shaking from yesterday.'

I had another night of disturbing dreams – flying, falling, crashing, burning. Even worse, there was one featuring Wol, Kit and me on a magic carpet made entirely of Jelly Babies.

'Well, if it's what you really want, don't give up now. You've always been so brave.'

'I don't feel brave.'

In fact, if Wol were here, I would sit down on the floor at her feet, wrap my arms around her legs, and tell her that everyone's wrong about me being brave. I'm scared, and I'm scared that I'm a coward.

So, by definition, that makes me a coward, right?

~~~

After talking with Kit, I trudge up to Wol's cottage and make lame attempts to finish clearing out the kitchen, sorting larder items into things worth saving and things no human should touch without a bio-hazard suit. It crosses my mind that if the fall in the Lake District hadn't finished Wol off, the tinned pilchards might.

But my thoughts keep wandering and I repeatedly mix up my piles: is the Branston Pickle to be kept or tossed? Is that Fray Bentos chicken pie meant for the bin or my rucksack? At six o'clock I plod home, bringing some chocolate covered ginger as a peace offering.

Unfortunately, but not unexpectedly, I soon find myself standing in the kitchen, hanging my head at Bella's verbal torrent. She barely glances at the ginger before dropping it onto the work surface, from where it rolls with a clatter into the sink. Then she turns to me, eyes flashing.

'You bloody idiot, Sophie. I've never been so

humiliated.'

'Look, Bell,' I begin.

'Scott came to see me,' she snaps. 'I was thrilled to bits. Then I realised I didn't have a clue what he was talking about. He'd only come out of some bloomin' sense of duty.' She inhales and rushes on. 'Dammit, I wanted the floor to swallow me!'

'But I heard you –'

'You heard a hangover, you plonker! And the second time –' she stops abruptly, folding her arms.

I wait, curious.

'The second time,' Bella mutters, 'was a curry recipe which went wrong.'

I have the sense not to laugh, but not enough sense to shut up. 'I was only –'

'You were only bloody meddling! It was mortifying. Mortifying!' Her pitch is rising with each sentence. 'He had no interest in seeing me again. The minute I told him it was a mistake, he took off in that flashy car like the devil was behind him.'

'I'm sorry,' I say ineffectually. 'I really thought you were pregnant.'

'It was too early, you imbecile! Morning sickness doesn't start that soon!'

'I didn't know that,' I reply. 'How would I know that?' But behind my back, I cross my fingers.

'Anyway. I told Scott you'd got the wrong end of the stick.'

'Sorry. I was... trying to help.'

'Well, don't fricking help, okay?' She retrieves the tin of chocolate ginger and starts weighing it in her hands, as if about to take aim. 'Try sorting out your own life before you get delusional about other people.'

Delusional? A bit strong. As for not taking charge of my life, that's a piercing blow. But I know I deserve the dressing down.

'I just... didn't want you to be hurt and alone,' I say.

But Bella just harrumphs. 'Yeah, well, I'm fine, okay? I'm totally fine, being on the shelf all by myself.'

I look at her properly, and see tears forming. 'Bell... Don't.'

She sniffs and I wonder whether to risk approaching for a hug. But I'm still in the dog house.

'I'm fine,' she says again, lifting her chin. 'I'm going to make chocolate mousse. With brandy.'

'Okay,' I say carefully. 'Good. Sounds... good.'

Bella starts to open and shut cupboards with force, seizing bowls and brandishing her electric mixer.

'Yes,' she says briskly. 'Good. And *you're* buying the brandy.'

~ ~ ~

Bella peers into the oven at the individual steak and kidney pies, which are slowly turning golden brown. 'We're doing a trial run. You can come if you want, I suppose.'

This is the most she's said to me in the twenty-four hours since she lambasted me about Scott.

My punishment, which was fair enough, was not being allowed to eat any of the mousse. Most of it she spooned into eight dinky cups and put in the fridge to set. I didn't even make a move to lick out the bowl, knowing that was a treat Bella adored and fully deserved. And now, an equal number of miniature pies are cooling on the counter.

'It's a dinner party, then?' I say. 'More or less?'

'No.' Bella tuts, and I recoil. I'm still treading carefully around her. 'We're starting an underground supper club,' she says. 'They're all the rage in London. But it needs to be hush-hush, word of mouth only.'

'Why?' I say. 'You and Lorraine are fab cooks, why keep it secret?'

'Because she's passed the health inspections, but I haven't,' Bella says, and begins peeling the first of a huge mound of carrots. 'And this kitchen certainly hasn't.' She looks around. 'There's Stanley, for starters...' she trails off ominously and I shoot a nervous glance at my feathered friend. 'So we shouldn't be asking people to pay.'

'Makes sense,' I say. 'How much is it?'

'Nothing, tomorrow night. It's our practice run. Wear something nice.'

Shame on me, but now I understand there's free food, lovingly cooked by Bella and Lorraine, featuring steak and kidney pie and chocolate mousse and who knows what other treats, I'm looking forward to an evening amongst friends. It has to be more fun than my anticipated entertainment tonight, which is watching the United Kingdom lose the Eurovision Song Contest.

'You don't need practice,' I say. 'But, yeah, I can probably find time to come along.'

She gives me a beady look. Bella's no fool.

'Shall I bring some wine?' I say brightly, wondering if Joey has any nice friends we could match her with.

The narrow blue eyes glimmer. I'm not off the hook. 'Actually,' she says, beheading a carrot, 'I was thinking you could do the washing up.'

Chapter 18

This was a huge mistake. I let my guilt towards Bella, plus the hope of escaping my own swirling thoughts, tempt me into risky company. If I had to seek music and conversation, I should have found some anonymous pub in Cambridge, rather than attend a dinner at Oak House. Who was I thinking the other guests would be? Paul McCartney and the Duchess of York? Instead, the first person I lay eyes on is my mother.

'Sorry,' Bella whispers, offering a smoked trout canapé. 'I didn't invite her.'

'Then who did?'

Bella shrugs. 'Lorraine and I asked one each. Then we invited a second guest and told them to bring a friend. That makes eight.'

I'm too distracted to check her maths. 'So I'm your guest?'

She nods.

'Who else did you invite?'

'Joey,' replies Bella, as if it's obvious.

Right on cue, a hand lands on my bottom. I choke on the trout.

'Good evening, gorgeous.' Joey plants a smacker on my cheek. 'Nice dress.'

I obeyed Bella's command and threw my faded jeans in the wash. I'm wearing the only vintage dress which fits me: cherry red with a swishy skirt.

'Joey...' I act pleased, but my heart sinks. 'Er, did you happen to invite my mum?'

'Yup,' he says, oblivious to my discomfort. 'Hi, Erica.'

So, my boyfriend invited my mother to a party as his date. That's too weird to process. I wonder what Pompous Anthony makes of it. Or perhaps he's no longer in the picture.

'Isn't it fantastic about Erica's new job?' Joey grins at mum. 'You two can see much more of each other.'

Joey's close to his own family; he can't fathom that I never knew my dad and prefer to keep mum at arm's length. While I drink my mineral water and try to pretend I'm breathing into a brown paper bag, my boyfriend and mother exchange happy banking banter and compare notes on Russell Crowe playing Robin Hood.

'I'm so glad you're here, Sophie.' Lorraine arrives beside me and I turn, grateful. 'Bella won't tell you this, but your support means a lot to her.'

'Well, you know, anything for a free dinner,' I say lamely. After my last attempt at support, I'm amazed Bella wants to be anywhere near me.

'You know Violet, don't you?' Lorraine beckons our stalwart postmistress.

'I do,' I say, smiling stiffly at one of Saffron Sweeting's most diligent gossips. I remind myself that if I smile a lot and keep a clear head by avoiding alcohol, the evening can be survived. One thing I've learned in the past year is that when people ask a question, they rarely listen carefully to the answer. Mostly, they're thinking about the next thing they want to say. A bland smile, as if the question were merely rhetorical, has extracted me from several tight corners. That, and breathing into my imaginary paper bag, will get me through.

'Yes, I know Sophie.' Violet manages to inject disapproval into my name. 'Sophie, this is my son, Peter.'

Happily, Peter has a more pleasant countenance than his mother. He's older than me, but his cheerful face knocks five years off.

'More wine?' Bella appears with a bottle, and as she smiles at Peter, I notice Lorraine watching. Maybe I'm not the only one who's angling to set my housemate up with an available man.

But my matchmaking intentions are forgotten as Lorraine looks to the door. 'Oh, here's our final guest,' she says. 'How splendid!'

I turn and, with a jolt, see that an imaginary paper bag will be insufficient. I'm going to need a full size sack. Shaking hands with my mother, and about to introduce himself to Joey, is Tom.

He doesn't seem surprised to see me. In fact, Tom meets my dazed stare with a neutral nod. Maybe he did better research on the guest list. The conversation in the room doesn't stop, but for me, sound ceases. For several seconds, I'm frozen. All I hear is the relentless ticking of a time bomb.

Bella, I can trust. We go back a long way. If she hasn't outed me after the episode with Scott, if her idea of punishment is making me wash up, I don't think she'll betray me tonight.

But Tom? In the short time I've known him, I've lied to him, cried on him, and all but sighed into his mouth as he kissed me. I shut my eyes, open them again, and find the room is still here. Five of these eight people think I'm an air hostess, and in less time than it takes to say 'steak and kidney pie', he can expose me. And from where I'm standing, he has absolutely nothing to gain from keeping quiet.

How could I be so stupid as to think I could keep that kind of secret in a tiny place like Saffron Sweeting?

Finally, I take a lungful of air. There's no one between me and the living room door. I need to leave. Now. This house, this village, maybe this county.

In the hall, I trip over a tortoiseshell cat, which bolts, hissing, half way up the wooden staircase. As I regain my balance and reach for the front door knob, Bella steps out of the kitchen.

'What are you doing?' she asks.

'I have to get out of here.' My hiss mimics my new feline enemy. 'It's a bloody time bomb.'

Bella looks stricken. 'You can't. I need you.'

'Why?' I say. 'It's only dinner. You've done it before.' I

open the front door.

'Not like this,' she says. 'This has to go perfectly. Please, Soupie, you owe me.'

I waver. In that moment, Joey appears. 'Oh good,' he says, glancing at the grandfather clock, 'is it time to go through to the dining room?'

Bella gives a stiff nod, still studying me.

'Why's the door open?' Joey asks. 'Are we expecting someone else?'

My appetite's fading fast. But Bella wants me here, and even mild-mannered Joey might get suspicious if I dash off now.

'No,' I say. 'Just letting the cat back in.'

After all, the worst that can happen here tonight is public shame and humiliation. I close the door.

~~~

Bella's watching anxiously for signs that her steak and kidney pies are well received. That curry mishap must really have shaken her confidence. On my left, Joey has finished his pie already. To my right, mum is eating happily, and across the table, Violet is devouring hers too. Peter is making slower progress as he's chatting with Bella, and Tom is chewing thoughtfully. But from their vantage points at each end of the long table, I think Lorraine and Bella can conclude the food is meeting with approval.

Only my plate is barely touched. The little pie smells delicious, but I'm having trouble swallowing.

The assembled guests have discussed the perilous state of the Royal Mail, the mice infestation at Peter's antiques shop, and mum's promotion to regional manager.

'But isn't internet banking hurting you?' Violet wants to know. 'Even crumblies like me are online now.'

'Well, things are a little challenging,' my mother answers, spearing a carrot. 'We're concentrating more on things like mortgages, financial planning and small business loans.'

Joey looks up from the morsels on his plate. 'Erica's advising me on bootstrapping my photography studio,' he says. 'But she's driving a hard bargain – making me put up capital myself, before the bank will lend more.'

Mum gives a wry smile. 'Joey, I've dealt with enough charming young men trying to borrow money to make me cautious. Sophie's dad, for starters. All gab and no graft.'

Even allowing for some one-sided telling, it's true, my dad was a loser. If mum hadn't had her eye on the family finances, we'd have been out on the street long before he actually left us. When Kit was little, she formed the impression my dad had died, until I explained he just didn't want to live with us any more. The last we heard, he was in Glasgow, spending more than he earned at the bookmaker's.

'Can't blame the banks for being careful,' Peter says. 'Not in this economy.'

'Yeah,' Tom says, thoughtful eyes on Joey. 'Seems fair.'

'Absolutely,' Joey agrees, and turns my way. 'That's why Sophie's going to partner with me. Aren't you, sugar?'

I can't really be surprised at him mentioning the business again.

'Um, probably,' I say, stalling. 'But I've been awfully busy. There's still loads to sort out at Wol's cottage.'

'I thought we'd do some more tomorrow, since it's a Bank Holiday,' mum says. 'You're not flying, are you?'

'No,' I say, addressing my napkin. I'm about to go on the offensive and ask after Pompous Anthony, when Lorraine chips in.

'Such a coincidence,' she says. 'Tom flies too.'

I glance in her direction, then the other way to Bella. Has she confided in Lorraine? She promised she wouldn't tell anyone.

'Yes,' Tom says. 'It is a coincidence.' He's holding his wine glass as he looks directly at me. 'Sophie and I have had quite a bit to talk about.'

Here it comes, I think. He's going to tell them. Miserably, I close my eyes, then open them in a last plea for mercy. Tom's still looking at me, but his expression is more curious than malicious. I watch, perplexed, as he raises his glass an inch, then drinks. He puts the wine down, and carries on eating.

'Oh, are you cabin crew too?' asks Peter. 'I have a friend with Virgin.'

'God, no,' Lorraine laughs. 'Perish the thought. Tom's a pilot.'

Violet says, 'Why perish the thought?'

Tom smiles. 'I think Lorraine means I couldn't be nice to people all day. I have huge respect for cabin crew – their job's so gruelling.'

I'm irrationally pleased that he's complimenting my non-existent occupation.

Joey reaches a fork to my plate. 'Babe, don't you want this?' he says, absconding with a chunk of pie.

I mutter that I'm not hungry, and catch Bella's gape of disappointment. I might as well have called her first-born ugly. Great, I'm back in the dog house again.

'But seriously,' Joey continues, 'all you have to do is smile and serve drinks, right? Personally I think it's best you stick to that, Sophia, and leave the technical stuff alone.'

He grins at Tom and Peter, as if sure of agreement from that side of the table. Peter opens his mouth, but Tom speaks first.

'Actually,' he says, 'I know some fine women pilots. I'm proud to share the cockpit with them.' His eyes glint. 'But you might have a point, Joey, that women are more suited to working in the main cabin. They seem to have more patience when dealing with wankers.'

There's a pause. Then Lorraine jumps in. 'You're right, Tom. You'd lose it and tip their drink in their lap.'

Bella is just moments behind. 'Drinks, yes, who needs a top-up of wine?'

'You see?' Joey says, and if he caught Tom's barb, he's not letting on. 'Bella knows how to keep a man happy.' He grins up at her and holds out his glass.

Bella pours more wine for Joey, but catches my eye. I shrug. Joey's hardly my biggest problem right now. I risk a look in Tom's direction, trying to read his thoughts, but he's asking Violet about the puppies. He must have found her soft spot; her normally grumpy face has softened. Tom's eaten most of his food now, and his knife and fork are neatly together. One hand lies casually on the tablecloth, silver cuff links visible at the cuff of his striped shirt. I wonder who gave him those? He moves his fingers, and I think about the ease with which he coaxed the Cessna into the air. Then I think about the ease with which he coaxed my face towards his, and a heat creeps into my cheeks.

'I can think of worse places to seek refuge than the vegetable shop,' Tom says to Violet, his eyes moving casually around the room.

I look away and twist a piece of hair, glad he didn't catch me staring.

'True.' Violet nods. Her gaze lands on me. 'Talking of refuge, Sophie, how's that young friend of yours who was here last summer?'

I don't believe it. No sooner am I off the hook for the flying thing than I have to deflect something else. 'Er, fine, I think. Although really, she was more Wol's friend than mine.'

Violet nods. 'Yes, it wasn't the first time Wol gave sanctuary to a former pupil. She was very good like that.'

'What kind of sanctuary?' Peter asks.

Oh, cripes, can't they talk about the weather?

'Sophie's great-aunt – Miss Campbell, you remember? She stayed in touch with lots of her pupils. Occasionally, if one of them fell on hard times, they'd visit for a while.'

'Wol was one of a kind, that's for sure.' Mum joins in. 'Do you remember, Sophie, a young woman called Sheila who stayed for a bit? It wasn't long after we moved down from Scotland. You'd have been, what, seven or eight?'

I shrug. 'Um, I think so.'

Mum nods to Violet. 'I think her husband was beating

her. Wol didn't ask questions, just took her in.'

'She had nowhere else to go?' Lorraine asks.

'Apparently not,' mum says. 'Some women can't even confide in their families. Wol had such a big heart.'

Despite my anxiety at the conversation, I find myself nodding. And for the first time, the wrenching pain that I've come to associate with talking about Wol is dulled. She did have a huge heart. I'm glad people know that.

But I don't want this topic going further. To my relief, I see Bella place her napkin on the table. The moment she pushes back her chair, I leap up too.

'I'll help with the plates.'

~ ~ ~

Escape to the kitchen is such a reprieve: the air is cooler out here. As I stack plates near the sink, I tell myself the meal is almost over. If things haven't yet fallen apart, I might still get away with it.

'Any room for these?' It's Tom's voice which breaks my thoughts.

I step away from the sink to let him squeeze wine glasses onto the counter. Suddenly, I'm not sure whether it's riskier here in the kitchen or back in the dining room.

'Thanks for helping, you two.' Bella comes in and plonks the bread basket and a gravy boat down on Lorraine's big kitchen table. 'Was it okay? Not too heavy?'

'It was great,' I say, trying to sound sincere, especially in light of my unfinished plate.

'It was delicious, Bella. Thank you,' Tom says, but he's looking at me.

Bella doesn't notice; she's still anxious about dessert. That makes two of us. She picks up a stack of little bowls and leaves the kitchen.

'Thank you,' I blurt. He needs to know how grateful I am. 'I don't ...' I falter. What am I trying to say? 'Thank you.'

He turns from the sink and leans both hands on the kitchen table. 'Sophie –' he says, but stops. He stares down at the table, then lets out a breath as he looks back up at me. I don't move, staring back with a mixture of misery and indebtedness. His frown clears. 'You look stunning in that dress.'

I blush to match the frock; that was the last thing I was expecting. Yet I can't look away.

'There you are!' Lorraine bustles towards the fridge. 'Crumbs, we should have taken this mousse out sooner. What are you two gassing about? Flying?'

Tom blinks. 'Yes. Sorry. Flying talk.'

He turns away.

'Well, since you're here,' Lorraine says, 'carry the cream, would you?'

Tom takes the little jug, throws me one last glance, and leaves the room.

~~~

Bella's chocolate mousse receives praise from all quarters.

'This is absolutely splendid,' Peter says, a sentiment we all echo.

Lorraine and Bella are starting to relax, and, at our prompting, share details of their plans for pop up dinner parties. Even Violet's impressed.

'It reminds me of the sixties,' she says. 'Cambridge was so bohemian, then.'

'We just want to offer good food and a great time,' Bella says.

'We had a great time tonight.' Joey winks at her, licking his lips after his second helping of mousse.

Peter is finishing an extra helping too. 'Terrific job, both of you. Jolly well done.'

This is it, I think. Run for cover while they're all mellow. Tomorrow, I'll make plans to run further. 'Thank you so much,' I say, through a fake yawn. 'If you'll excuse me, I'm going to make a start on my washing up.'

Lorraine laughs. 'Don't be silly, Sophie.'

'I don't mind,' I say.

Lorraine tuts. 'Bella was pulling your leg. Stop being daft. It'll go in the dishwasher.'

'It won't –' I protest, but I'm drawing attention to myself now. Others are stirring, chairs are scraping back.

What now? Can I slip away? Tentatively, I inch towards the door.

'Hang on a minute, Sophie.' My mother's on her feet already. 'If you're leaving, I've got some stuff in my car for you.'

There doesn't seem any point arguing, but I thank Lorraine and Bella, then steal away from the dining room while the others are debating whether they want coffee. They might think I'm rude to leave without saying goodbye, but at least I'm getting out with my secret intact.

In the street, mum's Mondeo is parked a short distance away. The usual night-time hush has descended on Saffron Sweeting; no vehicles are passing and the only sound is a solitary owl hoot.

'What time shall we meet tomorrow?' Mum returns from her car, holding what looks like a shoe box. 'At Wol's, I mean?'

'I dunno,' I say, not caring. 'Two-ish?'

'Fine,' mum replies. 'I was over there today, going through some documents. I thought this stuff was mine, but it turns out it's yours.' She holds the box out, but as I move to take it, she doesn't let go.

'Funnily enough,' my mother continues, 'your passport's in here. I rather thought you would have it with you.'

My passport? She's found my *passport*, of all things? Bloody freaking hell.

'And it's the strangest thing, Sophie.' Mum's tone is crisp and deliberate. 'It seems to have expired two years ago.'

I freeze, looking at my mother, trying to work out how busted I am. She had wine at dinner, which usually makes her mellow rather than argumentative. Can I laugh this one off? Say there's been some mistake? There's a pounding silence as my brain attempts to pick the most promising tactic. But as I gulp for air and inspiration, all I catch is the sweet scent of the lavender outside Oak House.

'Goodnight, both. Erica, it was a pleasure meeting you.'

I jump at the voice behind us. It's Tom.

Mum is momentarily distracted. Whatever grilling she's about to give me, her manners won't allow her to ignore him.

'Lovely to meet you too,' she says.

'Did you both drive?' he asks. 'Do you need a lift?' He's added a dark jacket over his shirt; his hands are in the pockets.

Mum shakes her head. 'My car's there, thanks. I imagine Sophie plans to walk.' She looks down at the box and it seems to remind her of the inquisition. 'I was just saying to Sophie, I found her passport at my aunt's house, and how strange it is that it's expired.'

'Expired?' Tom takes a step closer. His eyes flick from my mother to me. 'Well... I expect that's your spare one, isn't it, Sophie?'

I gawk at him, not catching on.

Tom nods. 'Your spare one,' he says again, stressing the words slightly. He looks at my mother. 'It's quite common for air crew to have two passports. Helps avoid problems, if they have to send one off to get a visa.'

'Oh, really?' mum says. Her eyebrows twitch: she's weighing the idea. Then her gaze returns to me.

'Spare one,' I say, knowing my only option this time is a brazen lie. 'Yup.'

Tom smiles. 'Sounds like Sophie hasn't gone anywhere requiring visas recently. Just Europe, maybe?'

I can't believe he's lowered a ladder and is helping me out of my mire, rung by rung.

'Europe.' I give a pathetic shrug. 'Pretty much.'

'Who knew?' says mum. 'Do you have two passports then, Tom?'

'I used to,' he says. 'But my trips are all shorter now. The planes I fly wouldn't make it anywhere more exotic.'

'Right,' mum says. 'Well, here you are, Sophie.' At last, she hands over the shoe box and I hold it like a defused bomb.

'Thanks,' I say, the galloping in my chest easing.

'And I'll see you at two tomorrow?' my mother says over her shoulder.

She walks away and I finally exhale, watching until she reaches the car. Then I turn to thank Tom.

But he's already gone.

~ ~ ~

'I'll admit, I'm curious to meet him,' mum says the next day. 'Although he may turn out to be some awful, loud American.'

She tells me that the heir to the cottage, Charles Jefferson, is planning to fly across to take a look at his new property. They've exchanged several emails, it seems.

'He can't be much louder than Stanley.' I'm coughing through yet more dust. 'When's he coming?'

Mum straightens and rubs her back. 'He's not sure. Maybe the end of June.'

'Do you think he'll sell it?' I ask wistfully.

'Who knows?' mum says. 'But we've only got a couple more weeks to get this place ship-shape. I'm not having him pitching up and seeing chaos.'

'Why not? What does it matter if there's a mess?'

'Oh, Sophie, don't be so stroppy.' Mum tuts, looking around with renewed determination.

I chew my lip and she sighs. 'I'm sorry, sweetie. I know this is hard for you.'

There's no flying meeting today, because of the 'holiday,' as Rainbow calls it. It doesn't feel like much of a holiday to me. Sorting out Wol's bedroom goes fairly fast, but then I find myself arguing over kitchen gadgets. High on my keeping list is Wol's old whistling kettle.

'You're joking,' mum says, dangling the dented, rusted metal by its handle. 'It sounds like closing time at the coalmine when it boils.'

'She used to make me hot Ribena after school,' I say. 'It reminds me of her. She –'

'She what?' asks my mother, throwing warped Tupperware into a rubbish bag. When I don't reply, she stops and looks over her shoulder.

'She took care of me,' I say, half apologetically.

'Sophie –' mum begins, but pauses as I hold up a hand which happens to contain an egg whisk.

'I didn't mean... anything,' I say. 'I know you were busy working.' There had been one modest income and two mouths, one of which was permanently hungry. 'I don't blame you, or... anything...' I trail off.

Mum looks at the floor for a few moments, then raises softer eyes. 'You were often waiting by Wol's front door, you know. When I came home in the evening.'

'I don't remember that.'

'You were dying to show me your homework, or art, or whatever that day's task was.'

I feel a lump in my throat. I didn't realise I was so in need of her approval when I was little. Even now, Bella's suggested my fear of rocking the boat with mum is because I've lost the other parental figures in my life.

Unwilling to explore those thoughts, I decide it's safer to get on with the task in hand, while turning our conversation back to the new owner of the cottage.

'Do his emails sound like a loud American?' I ask as I lug blankets from Wol's airing cupboard down the stairs. 'I bet an animal shelter would take these.'

'Good idea,' mum calls from the sitting room. 'No, he sounds perfectly normal. But of course you can't tell until you meet someone.'

'Maybe he'll be another hippie, like Rainbow,' I say.

'Do they have hippies in Montana?' she asks. 'I was thinking more cowboy.'

Kit confirmed by text last night that Pompous Anthony appears to be history. And now mum's talking cowboys? Interesting. I dump the blankets near the front door. 'In that case, he might want the blankets for his horses.' I poke my head around the sitting room door.

Mum's perched on Wol's brown tapestry settee, going through her stamp collection. 'Do you think these are valuable?'

'No idea,' I say. 'Nobody collects stamps any more, do they?'

'Maybe I'll ask Peter,' mum ponders. 'You remember, we met him last night? Runs the antiques shop. He seemed nice.'

'Righty-ho,' I reply. He did seem nice, but my interest in Peter – specifically, the possibility of setting him up with Bella – waned last night after his mother confided he was dotty about his girlfriend and planning to pop the question any day.

I pull out a box which is full of Christmas cards Wol received. For a few minutes, we sit in silence.

'Here are some from Charles Jefferson,' I say. 'She sorted them by sender.'

Mum looks up, intrigued. 'Much as I'd love to read those, we'd better put them aside for him.'

'Yeah.' I make a separate pile on the teak coffee table.

'Any from the Campbells?'

I frown, thumbing through. 'A few from grandma. But they fizzle out in the late eighties.'

Mum's face is tight. 'She took it so badly when your grandad was killed.'

I read the last one. 'It just says, *Glad to hear wee Sophie is doing well. Give my love to Erica*. Weren't you in touch, then?'

Mum shakes her head. 'We were never close. She thought –' she reaches for the flimsy card, a scene featuring a large robin, '– she thought your dad wouldn't have left, if I'd tried harder.'

I open my mouth, but close it again. After all, I don't remember why dad walked out, leaving just a letter on the kitchen table. I always thought he just had an overwhelming case of wanderlust. Mum can be annoying, downright fanatical at times, but I doubt that she was solely to blame. He waited until I was seventeen to get in touch and ask how we were doing. Mum sat me down one winter's evening to show me his letter, and we both agreed we wouldn't respond.

But mum is still thinking about grandma as she turns the card in her hands. 'We argued so much after grandad's... accident. Ma wasn't able to show her grief. She just doubled her cigarettes.'

I wait.

'I was so worried about you living in that house. Some nights, I could barely see the television for smoke.' She pauses, biting her thumbnail. 'When Uncle Robbie died and Wol came up for the funeral, we agreed you and I would move south.'

I never realised that mum's relationship with her own mother had been so strained.

'And that's when you got the job at the bank?'

'Not straightaway,' she says. 'I was at a building society in Cambridge, but it closed. Wol put in a good word for me at the bank.'

I'm not overly interested in mum's career. Instead, I flick through the box for my dad's name, but of course there's nothing. He'd hardly be likely to send Christmas cards to his ex-wife's aunt.

'Here.' I pass the cards to mum. 'See if there are any

other names you know.'

Then I reach for the first of several photo albums. There are pictures of Wol's retirement party, and a few of her in front of various American landmarks.

'She travelled around the US after she retired,' mum says vaguely, still with her nose in the Christmas cards. 'Canada too, I recall.'

We were living in Norwich by then, with mum's second husband. I move on to the next album; here are endless school photos of Wol with different groups of children. They're all arranged in the same way, in the playground of Sweeting School. How did she ever keep all the names straight? I turn to the late eighties and find my class. There I am, in a pleated grey skirt and white shirt, all serious. Next to me is Bella, her cheeks plump. Our hands are clasped in front of us, as instructed.

The next album contains black and white photos, many with people's feet chopped off or subjects uncentred in the frame. 'Is this you?' I point.

Mum leans across to look. 'Yup.'

Wow, she was pretty. Her hair is unruly, and she's too thin, but beautiful nonetheless. How come I haven't seen these before?

There's one of me in mum's arms, a bundle of scowling blankets. That's dad beside us, looking proud but awkward. Within two years, he fled.

I turn the pages. Me, sitting on the lap of a Father Christmas impersonator, clutching a doll. Me on a tricycle, in front of grandad's house. Me, helping grandad with a trellis in the garden. I look so serious in these, as if it's vitally important to get the task right. And this one's funny: grandad and I are on the swirly patterned carpet and he's pretending to fly a small wooden plane close to my face. I'm concentrating so hard, I've gone cross-eyed.

Here's grandad on his own. Is he at work? He's wearing overalls, standing proudly in front of a set of massive industrial doors. Who took that one? And here he is, beside an aeroplane. He loved his job so much. Nobody knew more about planes than he did. I slip this one from the album and into my back pocket.

Sighing, I wonder where to put the album. Then, in a triumph of decisiveness, I opt for the shelf it came from. Getting rid of Wol's photos is too personal, too final. As I swing the heavy leather album to the shelf, some paper slithers out. I bend to retrieve it before flopping back on the sofa.

'Fancy a cuppa?' mum asks, already on her way to the kitchen. I'm glad the whistling kettle escaped execution, even if it is on death row.

Then I unfold the yellowing newspaper I'm holding.

Tragedy at Strathblae School. The typeface is old, the photo grainy. The smaller headline reads: *Rogue pilot blamed for crash.*

Three minutes later, I barely register that mum is back with two steaming mugs of tea. Hands shaking, I'm fixated on the brittle news clipping, but the print is now swimming before my eyes.

Mum gets as far as the fireplace before she spots what I'm holding. The mugs clink as she abandons them and comes to kneel beside me.

'Sophie –' she says, then holds her breath.

'I thought –' My voice is jerky. 'I mean – You *told* me it was a car crash.'

'Please, love.' Mum reaches for my hand but I twist away. 'We wanted to spare you the pain.'

I lay the newspaper on the coffee table, smoothing it with trembling fingers. I try again, 'So – this is true? It wasn't a car crash?'

Mum sits back on her heels. 'No, sweetie, it wasn't.'

I raise my head, and when I encounter her sad, steady gaze, my pathetic hope that the media got its wires crossed or made up a sensational story ebbs away. Mum glances down at the paper and I see her shoulders sag. As her own eyes well up, she takes me in her arms and I weep.

Chapter 20

I stumble home, barely seeing where I'm going. The tears come in waves, sometimes subsiding, then starting again. My breathing has become soggy gulps and I narrowly avoid a couple on a tandem as I totter across the road by the school.

Even as mum begged me to stay, to talk, I think she knew I wanted nothing to do with her at this moment. Her protests were hollow as I lumbered to my feet and out of Wol's cottage.

My family lied to me. Mum kept on lying for twenty-seven years. My beloved grandad was killed in a plane crash, not a car accident. And it was his fault. My childhood hero was, in fact, wilful and negligent. Little better than a murderer. At four years old, did I really have no idea? Was I that easy to con? Or did I sense something? Did I suspect the car accident was a cover up? Is this why I'm petrified to fly?

As I pass Rainbow's house, Amelia is leaving. I almost bump into her, but mutter an apology and continue with my head down. She can probably see my tear-soaked face but I don't care. I just want to get home. I hope Bella's there: maybe she can help make sense of this hailstorm of emotion. Maybe she'll make me a hot drink and listen in that quiet way of hers, before offering gentle wisdom. I feel relief as I turn the last corner before Uncle Mike's house.

But the car on the gravel driveway isn't Bella's. It's a rusty Volvo with tape holding one corner of its front bumper. Joey. He's sitting in the car, listening to music on his phone, but jumps out when he sees me.

'Sophie-kins!' He bounds towards me, then falters. 'Jeez, what's wrong with you?'

I stand where I am, knees wobbling, and shake my head as the next contingent of tears starts up. Is this how everyone feels grief? You think you're okay, over the worst, and then the next wall of pain thunders in, even worse than the one before?

Joey puts his arms around me. The relief of having someone else hold me upright is immense. 'Okay,' he says. 'I'm here, sugar.'

With three sisters, Joey should be used to women having hysterics from time to time. If he thinks it's strange that we're standing in the middle of the driveway while I sob my guts out, he doesn't say so. But as this batch of tears subsides, I do hear his stomach rumble.

'What are you doing here?' I snuffle.

'Thought you pootled off a bit sharpish last night,' he says. 'Was wondering if you'd like to go to the pub.' He pulls back to look down at me. 'I nipped into the estate agent's to upload some photos, and Amelia said she'd just seen you.'

Trust Amelia to be working on a Bank Holiday. I wonder if she mentioned I was in dire need of a handkerchief and nearly squashed her expensive shoes.

'Shall we go inside?' Joey asks.

Good idea. We can hardly stand out here all night.

As I thought, Bella isn't home, although Stanley greets Joey with both a *Feed me* and a *Bloody Hell*. Normally, they're buddies, but for once, the parrot gets short shrift and returns sulkily to gnawing this week's branch.

'Come and sit down,' Joey says. 'I'll put the kettle on.'

It seems he has indeed had practice with his sisters, although I wonder if his Italian roots mean I'll get the cup of tea I'm craving or a strong espresso instead.

His offering turns out to be a mug of instant coffee – nowhere near the standard of Bella's hot cocoa, but still welcome.

Joey sits down beside me on the sofa. 'Do you want to talk about it?'

I don't, but I tell him anyway, staring at the carpet and trying to explain why, after so many years, it even matters.

'Oh,' he says. 'That's tough, I'm sorry.'

I'm not sure Joey fully understands how this revelation has shaken me, and of course I can't mention the flying phobia. But he's making appropriately kind noises, putting his arm around me so I can lean my head on his chest. It feels nice: I decide I'll just hang out here for a bit, with him stroking my shoulder.

After an appropriately respectful interval, Joey asks, 'Have you eaten anything today?'

'Not really,' I mutter.

'Well then.' Joey untangles his arm and nudges me gently upright, so I don't topple as he springs off the sofa with considerable enthusiasm. 'No wonder you feel a bit blue.'

He strides through to the kitchen with fresh purpose, and despite myself, I have to smile. One of the reasons I like Joey is his shared belief in the healing power of food. I hear him opening cupboards and the fridge, then doors bang shut again, drawers clang, and saucepans begin rattling. Call me shallow, but I find the thought of a man cooking extremely beguiling. Maybe there is a future for Joey and me.

After fifteen minutes of banging and crashing, and at least one 'Whoops' and one 'Bugger' from the kitchen, he returns to the living room and places a tray on the coffee table.

'Heinz tomato soup, with toast,' he announces. 'With my special addition: chunks of cheddar.'

I sit up. Okay, so he's not Jamie Oliver, and I'm not sure that opening a tin and heating it on the stove qualifies as culinary prowess, but it smells good. Joey has cut the bread thickly, and has been generous with the butter, now forming tempting pools on the toast. My stomach decides to postpone my nervous breakdown and growls with interest. 'Thank you.'

After we've polished off the soup and toast, Joey returns to rummage in the kitchen. He comes back bearing leftover brandy chocolate mousse, still in its large mixing bowl. He dips a finger in, licks it, and frowns.

'What's wrong?' Fear that the mousse might have gone off already distracts me from my despondency.

'Not enough brandy.' He heads for the cupboard where he knows we keep the booze, and liberates the bottle of Rémy Martin. He pours me a large glass, then settles the mixing bowl on his lap. We eat together, sharing a spoon. By the time we finish, it's astonishing how much better I feel.

'Poor you,' he says, filling my brandy glass again.

'Poor me,' I smile. I'm warmed by soup and brandy, there's a delightful fuzziness to my problems, and Joey's presence is snugly reassuring. I nestle into his shoulder in hazy contentment, then decide that nuzzling his neck would be even better.

Not surprisingly, this doesn't last long before Joey twists around to kiss me, and that doesn't last long before I'm kissing him back. Predictably, he doesn't waste much time before starting to run his hands under my top. Not to be outdone, it seems imperative that I help him take off his shirt. By the time he leans me back on the sofa and begins undressing me, we're both careless enough that when we try to change positions, we land ourselves on the floor in a giggling heap of limbs and half discarded clothing.

And, sure enough, *that* doesn't last long before we both agree that we'd be a whole lot more comfortable upstairs, in bed.

~~~

'So I came home last night and found a bra in the chocolate mousse,' Bella says. 'And I don't think it's mine.'

I raise my head from my hands. She's actually dangling a chocolate-dipped lacy bra from one finger.

'You're right,' I say, speaking at a pace to match the thumping in my brain. 'It's not yours.'

Bella sits down at the kitchen table. 'Did you and Joey – ?'

I nod, but only once, because the movement triggers a dizzy nausea.

'Wow, you look awful,' Bella says. 'Like someone died. Again.'

Bella's not known for her wit but she's hit that nail on the head. I accept her offer of a breakfast smoothie. Then I tell her about mum finding my passport, me finding Wol's photo album, and mum finding the decency, after all these years, to tell me the truth. Then I concede that this led to Joey finding his way into my knickers.

'Okay, so the thing with your grandad, that's terrible,' Bella says, when I'm finished. 'But it doesn't mean he was a bad person, just because he... died in bad circumstances.'

I suck the last of the smoothie through the straw, hopeful that yoghurt, strawberries and wheat germ can turn my life around, or at least my day.

'He was the closest thing I had to a father,' I say, swallowing a fresh jolt of pain along with the drink. 'Dad was such a loser, but grandad read me stories and made me a dolls house and always had time for hugs. I can't believe he'd do something that terrible.'

'And you don't remember anything fishy at the time?'

'No. Maybe. I'm not sure. I've been thinking so hard about it, I'm not sure what I remember and what I might just be imagining.'

Bella nods, tilting her own glass to reach the bottom. 'False memories. I've read about them.' She looks at me quizzically. 'Did he ever take you flying with him?'

I shrug. 'I dunno. But it would make sense, right?'

'Wow, yes.' She exhales. 'It most certainly would.'

There's silence as we both think about the effect on a four-year-old of learning, or even sensing, that flying could kill someone she loves.

'What about Joey?' she asks. 'Was it him I heard leaving around six this morning?'

'Probably. I had my head under the pillow.'

Bella looks at my slumped posture and doleful expression. 'You're having second thoughts?'

'Yeah.' I put a hand over my eyes. 'I pretty much

decided I couldn't let things go any further between us, until I shed a few of the lies I seem to be living.'

'But you did? Let things go further?'

I can hardly ask for privacy now Bella's found my underwear in the dessert she made. It was damn good mousse too. I hope we ate it all, beforehand.

'Further? You could say that. In fact, you could say, all the bloody way.'

Bella's lips twitch but she's too loyal to laugh. 'Well, don't worry,' she says, 'I won't go chasing after him to announce you're pregnant.'

'Thanks,' I say dryly. 'You're a true pal.'

I consider telling her about the kiss with Tom, which so far I've avoided mentioning. But I decide it wasn't important.

'You need to hydrate,' she says. 'Have some orange juice too.'

'You don't have to wait on me,' I say. 'Dinner was great, by the way.'

'You left pretty suddenly,' she says, pouring a huge glass of juice. 'Hey, where's all the bread gone?' Then, seeing my face, 'Oh, never mind, forget I asked.'

'I couldn't take the heat,' I admit. 'I thought someone was bound to rumble me.'

Bella puts the two remaining crusts of bread in the toaster, then turns. 'So, what now?'

Despite the juice, my throat is dry. 'I think it might be best if I... go away.'

'What do you mean?' she frowns.

'You know. Move. Go back to London, maybe. Make a fresh start.'

Her mouth drops open. 'You're not serious.'

'I told you, I can't take the heat any more. I need to get away from here.'

'You're taking the mickey.' Bella folds her arms.

'No.' I test the words. 'There's nothing keeping me here now.'

The little Cessna glides forward, turns onto the runway and, with a glance from the pilot at his rigid front-seat passenger, picks up speed. This time, I'm not stupefied from being kissed, and nerves grip my chest as the ground starts to race by. The nerves uncoil into a serpent, but as it rises up and threatens to choke me, Tom eases back on the yoke and the plane glides effortlessly into the air.

'Oh, shit!' Fergus gasps.

I swallow the serpent and keep quiet. Tom is trying to talk to air traffic control and he doesn't need two of us displaying our four-letter vocabulary. I saw the view last time, and though it's spectacular, my eyes are on our pilot instead. The plane is turning away from the airport, but still climbing under Tom's careful hands.

'You're doing really well, Fergus,' Tom says now.

We level off and the sun glints alongside us.

'Wow,' Fergus responds. 'Thanks, man.'

'How about you, Sophie?' Tom's voice comes through my headset but he doesn't look round. That's perfectly all right: I'd much rather he pays attention to what he's doing.

'I'm okay,' I reply. 'I was watching what you did.'

'Good,' says Tom, then adds, 'next time, you can have a go.'

Ha, ha. What a ludicrous thing to say.

~~~

'I'm so proud of y'all!'

Rainbow might be a hippie fruitcake, but her enthusiasm is catching. A balloon bursts – I'm not sure whether by accident or on purpose – and she shrieks, then regains her composure. 'You faced your deepest fears and overcame them! There's nothing holding you back now!'

And with that, our graduation party is officially underway. The small group giggles self-consciously and Ingrid applauds. But no matter how we try to play it down, we're swelling with pride. Today, we actually did it. We're on a giddy high from looking into the jaws of death and

'You'd leave Saffron Sweeting? Truly?'

I nod. This isn't so hard to grasp, is it?

'But, Soph –' Bella really does sound shocked. 'You've come so far already. If you can conquer your fear of flying, you can actually get a job as a stewardess.' She holds up her hands. 'After that, what's the problem?'

'I can't,' I say. 'I can't conquer anything. Look at me.' I gesture to my pyjamas, as if they are a reliable indicator of my overall psychological state.

'No,' Bella says, an edge to her voice I haven't heard before. 'I won't let you. You've come so far already.' Behind her, the toast pops up, but she doesn't move. 'You have professionals helping you. That Tom guy's lovely and Rainbow isn't completely doolally, now that we know her. And then there's you.' She stops.

'What about me?' I say, sulky but curious.

'When I first met you,' Bella says, 'you were the most courageous person I knew. Nothing seemed to scare you. You wouldn't let something like this get in the way of your happiness.'

Well, I'm scared now. I'm a spineless coward and I'm throwing in the towel.

'It's not as simple as that!' I get to my feet. 'My grandad killed himself in one of those things.' As I finish, my voice cracks.

'I'm not saying it's going to be easy.' She softens. 'It might be incredibly hard. But think how much you have to gain.'

I sniff, but I stay where I am, holding onto the back of the chair. To be honest, I'm not really in a position to storm out. I might throw up on the way.

'Wouldn't you like to go to dinner parties and not be afraid of idle questions?'

I look up at the ceiling.

Bella waits, then continues. 'Wouldn't you like to tell your boyfriend how your day went at work? And even if your father's long gone, wouldn't you like an honest relationship with your mother?'

There she goes again, reminding me that for all my bravado, I don't want to admit to mum I've changed jobs yet again, and especially not the reason why.

'Soph?' she says. 'If we don't count your dad, you've only got two blood relatives left.'

Three, I think, but that line of thought is hardly helpful.

Silently, I'm ticking off the boxes. *Yes* to being able to chat openly with Brian, Amelia and even the overpowering Marjorie. *Yes* to having a boyfriend who knows what I do for a living. *Yes* to not having to lie to my mother, even if she's told some huge porkies herself.

Bella tuts. 'Stay right there,' she commands, then beetles off upstairs. I hear footsteps above, in my bedroom. When she clatters back down, she's carrying one of my vintage maps.

'Wouldn't you like to own a passport that hasn't expired, and be able to use it? Wouldn't you like to visit these places, not just write about them?' She's unrolled the map and is jabbing at random continents.

I don't answer, but I reach out to stroke the beautiful map. It's so full of mystery and promise. I lick my lips as I run a finger from Brazil to Bolivia.

Bella's wasted in her steady university job. She should be an MI6 interrogator, or prosecuting barrister, or at least an investigative journalist. She has the unswerving knack of knowing when someone's about to crack. *Yes*, I would like to wake up in Saffron Sweeting and go to bed in Santiago, Stockholm or Singapore. *Yes, yes, yes.*

'You can do this,' she says. 'I know you can. Running away won't solve anything.'

I take a deep breath, grip the chair tighter, and force myself to speak. 'Okay,' I say finally.

'You'll stay in Saffron Sweeting?' she demands.

'Yes,' I croak. 'I'll stay, if you'll have me.'

'And the flying classes? Promise me you'll try to fly?'

I grit my teeth, knowing these tremors will have to

subside at some point. 'Yes. I promise. I'll go back to the classes.' I raise my chin, blinking hard. 'And I'll fly.'

Chapter 21

'This is beyond awesome! Can't y'all feel your dreams coming *alive*?'

I think Rainbow's been inhaling the Pritt stick. She's behaving as if our haphazard attempts at collage are Fantasia in technicolour.

The group is gathered in our usual room upstairs at the pub, putting final touches to what Rainbow calls vision boards. Our homework was to collect photos and brochures of places we would visit, if only we weren't too scared to purchase the plane ticket. We've spent the last forty minutes sticking these onto pieces of poster board, which we're supposed to take home and display prominently. Not only that, but we had to bring one thing we will need for our trip and – this is the best part – something which *smells* like our destination.

My board is a mish-mash of world destinations, since I want to go pretty much everywhere. I brought along a Russian phrase book and a jar of Bella's curry powder. Fergus wants to go to Morocco, and brought sun tan lotion. Since Ingrid's daughter is in Canada, she brought a furry hat and maple syrup.

I admit, cutting and sticking has been therapeutic. I must have had my head down, trying to trim around the outline of Sydney Harbour Bridge, because I didn't notice Tom walk in. But I look up, and there he is, sitting quietly, watching Fergus and Ingrid stick photos of beaches and a beaver to their respective boards.

Just as I register Tom's presence, his head turns and our eyes meet. I yank my gaze to another part of the room, but not before he gives me a silent nod. It must be raining again: his hair is damp and there are beads of water on his navy sweater. From the corner of my eye I see him reach for the hem, hands crossed, and pull it over his head. In the split second that the wool is covering his face, I steal a look as his T-shirt stretches across a toned torso. The movement reveals a sliver of stomach, and I swallow hard.

I look around the room, convinced that the two other women must be holding their breath too. But Ingrid is working quietly, while Rainbow gives Fergus hearty encouragement.

Then she turns her attention to me. 'You're doing great, Sophie, I love it.' She leans in. 'Did you mean to cut that bridge in half?'

I stab at my board with the glue. 'It's symbolic,' I mutter.

Rainbow returns to the front of the room and raises her voice. 'Okay, finish up. Now, I want y'all to take your board home and put it somewhere you'll see it every day.'

I nudge the two pieces of Sydney Harbour Bridge together and pat them apologetically. Someday, I'll see you for myself, I think.

'Before we end tonight,' Rainbow continues, 'I want us all to share our feelings from last week.'

Great. More touchy-feely stuff. We all fidget like crazy. Can't she see we don't want to talk about it?

But she's good at her job. Gradually, she coaxes a few words out of us.

'I felt safe enough on the ground, but I don't think I could take off,' says Ingrid. 'There were so many buttons and dials, what happens if one single thing goes wrong?'

Tom speaks up. 'Ingrid, it may look complicated, but it's not. There's quite a bit of redundancy built in.'

Ingrid listens politely but her eyebrows are knitted together.

'Besides,' Tom leans forward, 'I've had loads of training for when something does play up. It happens. It has happened. It's fine.'

'I'm sorry I threw up,' Fergus says. 'I'll try to be better next time.'

'Don't worry about it, mate,' Tom shakes his head.

Fergus mumbles his thanks. Since I'm next to him, and haven't spoken yet, heads turn my way. I pretend to pick glue off my fingernails.

'Sophie?' Rainbow is gentle but firm. 'What do you want to share, from last week?'

Absolutely nothing, I think. I'm not telling them that Tom kissed me, then took me a thousand feet above Cambridge. I give a fleeting shake of my head, hoping maybe Fergus will get the message and divert Rainbow's attention. But no, he just jiggles his feet unhelpfully. In the pause, I risk looking at Tom for guidance, but he's studying the floor.

'In your own time,' Rainbow says, looking at her watch.

'There is something about flying,' I say slowly. 'Although not from last week.'

Rainbow tilts her head. Ingrid is nodding, and I see Tom glance up. But I can't look at him; I can't look at any of them.

'When I was small, we lived with my grandparents,' I begin. 'My grandfather was... he was really special to me.' I pause for air. 'He died – he was killed – when I was four. I always thought it was a car crash.'

I stop as my voice wobbles. I don't think I want to continue.

'And was it a car crash?' Rainbow prompts.

I shake my head. Moments pass.

'It was a plane crash,' I say, just above a whisper. 'He... worked with small planes. In Scotland. He was at work and slipped out for a quick flight in a plane he wasn't authorised to use.'

No one in the group is fidgeting now. If they're counting down the seconds until they can rush downstairs for a gin and tonic, they're not showing it.

'They think grandpa knew he was in trouble and was aiming for a rough landing in a field behind a school.' I'm addressing everything I say to Sydney Harbour Bridge, picking at the corners of my collage.

'Go on, Sophie.'

'Except he probably didn't realise it was a school. And he didn't know, because it was rainy, the children had been kept inside at lunchtime.' I take a gulp and Fergus pats my arm. 'The plane came down badly and clipped a classroom, which – which collapsed.'

A shocked rustle runs around the group.

'Oh, God,' says Ingrid.

I steal a look at Rainbow; even she's stunned.

Tom clears his throat. 'How bad?' he asks.

'Two of the children were seriously injured.' I swallow the bitterness in my mouth. 'Although my mum says they recovered...' I have to believe she's telling the truth about that.

The group still waits.

'But in getting them to safety,' I finish hoarsely, 'their teacher was killed. Her body was recovered the next day.'

~~~

My defences must be down. There's no other explanation for letting him catch me out so easily.

I spend the following morning ignoring a looming work deadline. Instead, I'm engrossed in the website of the Air Accidents Investigation Branch, where I've discovered I can access details of every plane crash in the UK for decades. With a thrill which shocks and disgusts me, I click on report after report of human error and mechanical failure. Although presented in starkly objective terms, it makes disturbing reading. Yet I gorge on the material until I can barely think straight.

Realising that sometimes the internet can do more harm than good, at lunchtime I meander into the village for fresh air and a pick-me-up from the bakery. I've chosen wisely from Brian's cabinet – a sandwich, piece of ginger cake and bag of mini meringues – and am standing outside, deciding if the weather is okay for picnicking by the duck pond, when I see Joey. He's going into the estate agent's, his old Volvo parked right outside. We haven't planned to meet, but he's obviously seen me, so I wave.

He doesn't wave back. A frown crosses his face, and he stands for a couple of seconds. Then he shakes his head as if to get rid of a buzzing fly, and disappears into Hargraves & Company.

Well, I think, he's working. Or maybe he's embarrassed to see me, because he hasn't called since we ended up in bed the other night. I haven't called him, either: I'm still ambivalent about letting things go that far. Frankly, if we could slow down until I manage to land a real job with an airline, I would breathe far more easily. Alternatively, if Joey's simply in a strange mood, that's fine too.

So, I don't think any more of it, and I settle myself happily on the bench by the pond, in a patch of dappled shade. And that's where I am, brushing crumbs off my jeans, when Joey sits down beside me about twenty minutes later.

'Sorry,' I say, 'I didn't save you any cake.'

'I don't want cake,' he says, stretching his legs and not looking at me.

He's definitely behaving strangely. Surely sleeping together hasn't freaked him out? I've yet to meet a man who is seriously troubled by a quick roll in the hay. Or can he sense I'm regretting it?

'Last week...' Joey begins.

Wow, he is freaked out. That's more startling than England beating Italy at football.

'... when I made that soup for us, I noticed your schedule on the fridge.'

'Right,' I say, thinking, what schedule?

'So today's Tuesday, yeah?' He tucks his thumbs in his belt loops.

I nod, a sick feeling sliding into my belly, which can't be blamed on Brian's baking.

'According to your fridge, you should be in Istanbul. Due back tomorrow.'

Istanbul... Oh, boy. I purse my lips and look to the ducks for inspiration. Now would be a good time for them to start tap-dancing or playing cricket. But the waterfowl, perhaps in a strop because I didn't share my sarnie, fail to oblige. With Joey looking directly at me, I concoct the inevitable lie.

'Uh, things are still a bit messed up,' I say. 'From the ash.' Except they're not. Flights are back to normal.

Joey scratches his nose. A decade ago, I used to find that a cute indication that he was thinking. Now, I find it an altogether unwelcome sign that he's evaluating my words.

'Are you seeing someone else?' he asks eventually.

'No!' I'm so surprised, the words come out as a half giggle. 'I should be so lucky,' I say, and instantly regret that part.

A male duck chooses this moment to jump on another male and hold his head underwater. Charming. Much flapping, quacking and re-assertion of the pecking order follows.

Joey can hardly miss the scene before us, but he doesn't react. 'I was just in the post office,' he says, apparently changing the subject. 'Violet's a terrific pal of mine, since that dinner party.'

'Really?' I say, thinking that Joey's acting as though he's a couple of pence short of a first class stamp today.

'Uh huh. And she says, she hasn't once seen you in your SpeedyJet uniform. Not once, in all these months.'

Violet. That pointy-nosed old biddy. Has she really been keeping tabs on me?

'She must have done.' I decide I can bluff through this. Still, I never actually got a SpeedyJet uniform. I left the training programme, in disgrace, before it was issued.

'Not once,' Joey says.

'Well, I often change at Stansted,' I say. 'My uniform's not comfortable to drive in.'

'Yeah. That makes sense.' Joey nods, seeming to accept the explanation. 'Still, can I see it?'

'See what?' I pull my knees up and hug them.

'Your uniform. I bet you look sexy in it. Purple, isn't it?'

His eyes are on me again, and they contain a glint which could be a boyfriend's affection or could be for an entirely different reason.

'Um.' I wrap my arms more tightly around my shins. 'It's at the cleaner's. In Cambridge.'

Joey gives a small chuckle. 'At the cleaner's?'

'That's right.' I don't like the way this is going. The cake is sitting heavily in my stomach.

Joey stands. 'Show me your suitcase.'

'My what?'

'I want to see your suitcase,' he says, pausing between each word. 'When Viviana was travelling constantly for work, we couldn't move without tripping over it. In the hall, on the stairs, spilling over the landing.'

'So?' I'm still hoping to come through this.

'So, the other night, it wasn't in the hall, or the living room, or the kitchen. Nor was it in the bathroom. And it definitely wasn't in your bedroom.'

'You went round our house looking for it? What kind of weird –'

'Shut up,' Joey says, and his voice is so jagged, I do. 'And go ahead, tell me some claptrap like it's in your car. That's fine. But we're going to your place right now. And you're going to show me a suitcase plastered with *Air Crew* stickers.'

I don't answer, but I twist so I'm sideways on the bench, holding the back with both arms, in case he tries to prise me off.

'Except you can't do that, can you?'

I stare fixedly at the patch of worn grass by the bench. Then I shake my head.

Joey puts one hand on the back of the bench and leans closer. 'You're not really an air hostess, are you?' Now, his tone has softened, like he's just glad to have found the answer.

Finally, I know I have to look at him. I'm a loathsome coward, but I can at least meet his eye. 'No,' I say. 'I'm not.'

Chapter 22

At nineteen, Kit has more poise and quiet self-assurance than I ever will. How has she managed that? Despite my huge head start, I'm floundering more than ever.

'Happy birthday, darling,' mum says, raising her glass of bubbly.

We're sitting outside a Thai restaurant near Covent Garden; naturally, the sun is shining for Kit's special day. After lunch, she's going shopping, and then her friends from Nottingham are coming down. They plan to watch the England match, go clubbing and miss the last train back. At least in that respect she's still younger than me. I get awfully sleepy after eleven these days.

There's a festive atmosphere in London, with the pubs anticipating brisk trade from World Cup fans. In Saffron Sweeting, Fergus has rented a huge screen for The Plough, and we've been teasing Rainbow for calling it soccer instead of football.

'Happy birthday, Kit,' I echo. It's not that I'm envious of her. I just want to know the secret of knowing where you're going in life, and not feeling bad about where you've been.

Kit grins. 'Thank God exams are almost over. One more, then I'm free!'

She's at the end of her first year; nervous but hopeful about her results. Mum and I aren't nervous at all – if Kit doesn't come top of her class, I'll eat Stanley's food for a week.

'I'm so proud of you, darling,' mum says, beaming.

Kit gives a tiny flick of her head in my direction.

'Of both of you,' mum adds quickly, tilting her airborne glass towards me too. 'I'm so lucky to have two wonderful and successful daughters.'

I study my chicken and papaya salad. If only she knew. But at least Kit's future is bright, and it's looking as though we did the right thing.

'Wouldn't you have liked a son?' I can't resist asking. It's crossed my mind that mum's so close to Joey, she might secretly prefer to trade in her elder daughter for a male of the species. 'Like Joey, say?'

I watch her carefully: if he's told mum about my non-existent air hostess job, she'll mention it now. I've avoided Joey since the duck pond debacle, hoping the start of the World Cup would distract him.

But she just looks nonplussed, as if I suggested adopting an abandoned donkey. 'A son? What a strange question, Sophie. I haven't thought about it.' She bites the end off a spring roll. 'But I do like Joey. I'm glad the two of you are... back together.'

Okay, he hasn't said anything to her. Yet. Her words should be a relief, but for some reason there's nothing like your mother's approval to give you doubts about a guy.

'Mmm, yummy.' Mum chews appreciatively, not noticing my silence. 'I'm sure it's nowhere near as good as you two had in Thailand last year, but still tasty, yes?'

She's talking about the round-the-world trip which Kit and I supposedly took. Not a safe topic.

Kit sees me squirm, and changes the subject. 'How's work, mum? Do you like your new job?'

I don't like her new job one little bit. I've seen her in the village three times in as many weeks and I dread an unannounced visit when I'm supposed to be flying. If Joey hasn't spilled the beans, I don't want her working it out on her own. Still, I'm surprised to see mum hesitate.

'It's... fine,' she says slowly.

Kit and I raise four eyebrows between us.

'Well, you know.' Mum looks past the other diners. 'Times are tough for high street banks.' Then she grimaces. 'Whatever you do, don't say anything. You know what Marjorie's like, if she sniffs a rumour.'

We don't need to ask what kind of rumour. I file this away, not knowing whether to be pleased that mum might have less opportunity to visit in future or sorry for the village if another business is under threat.

Our talk turns to shopping options. I can see why Kit likes Covent Garden, with its small stores, vibrant street scene and historic architecture. And I do enjoy a stroll around the so-called market – with my purse clutched tightly in case of pickpockets, of course. But for me, the plaza is too contrived for tourists, the so-called crafts desperately over-priced. If I can slip away from mum later, I might take myself off to East Dulwich or Crouch End, to seek out genuine bargains.

'I forgot to tell you, Kit, I bumped into Ravi the other day,' says mum, out of the blue. 'You remember, your tutor?'

I swallow a piece of papaya, my eyes flicking to my little sister. Of course she remembers.

Kit, glass in hand, manages not to react, murmuring a non-committal, 'Oh?'

Mum nods. She's rightly proud of her role in setting up a pilot scheme at the bank, for their staff to coach kids in maths. It was probably no coincidence her own daughter was in dire need of calculus help at the time.

'He's engaged now,' Mum says. 'To a lovely Indian girl. Their families are over the moon.'

'Is he really?' I say, feigning surprise.

Kit smiles and murmurs, 'Great... nice.'

I'm so proud of her.

Nonetheless, a change of topic is overdue and I might have just the thing.

'You'll never guess who I met the other night,' I say brightly. 'Chuck Jefferson.'

On Thursday, Bella persuaded me to abandon my grumpy screen-staring and accompany her and Lorraine to Pilates in the village hall. She's been so down since the episode with Scott, I complied. My stomach did not take kindly to being crunched, tightened and abused for an hour, but it growled in appreciation at Lorraine's subsequent invitation to sample peaches and homemade frozen yoghurt at Oak House.

I was giving my biceps a work-out with the ice cream scoop when a tanned man in his fifties with salt and pepper hair put his head around Lorraine's kitchen door.

'I'm real sorry,' he said in an American drawl, 'but we're out of hot water.'

He had bare feet and several shirt buttons undone. From the tilt of Bella's head, she'd noticed. As Lorraine disappeared into her utility room to give the Oak House boiler a bashing, I considered offering him some dessert, but decided that, despite his arresting looks, he was too old for Bella. When Lorraine enlightened me to his identity, I was glad I hadn't been too gracious to the new owner of Wol's cottage.

'What was he like?' Kit asks now. 'Do you think he'll sell the place?'

'I don't know,' I admit. 'I didn't talk to him. Now I think about it, I'm not sure I want to know.'

'Well, I do,' says Kit. 'I'd like to know Wol's place is in good hands.'

'He was really good-looking,' I say, 'if that helps. But old enough to be your father. No, grandfather.'

Kit dips her fingers in her glass and flicks water at me.

'When did he arrive?' Mum's face is calculating.

I shrug. 'Dunno. Recently, I think.'

I'm pretty sure Lorraine told us more about Chuck, but our talk then moved on to the supper club she and Bella hope to launch. Through a mouthful of peaches, I asked how they planned to promote it, if it's supposed to be hush-hush.

'Actually,' Lorraine said, 'Tom's wife's doing a brilliant job of spreading the word.'

For some reason, my hand froze above the shortbread plate, and the gossip-worthy details of Chuck Jefferson's arrival floated out of my head.

'Well, ex-wife, I should say,' Lorraine added.

My shoulders dropped. Although, of course, I really don't care about Tom's marital circumstances.

'I didn't know he was divorced,' said Bella.

'Yep, four or five years ago. But she phones me occasionally.'

I didn't like to ask more.

Now, mum nods. 'Hmm. Maybe I'll pop round and see if Chuck needs any help.'

Kit catches my eye.

'But we got Wol's stuff out of there,' I say. 'It's none of our business now.' There's a catch in my voice as I admit the end of the most important era of my life.

Mum shakes her hair back. It seems she can't resist something else to organise and someone else to manage. 'Doesn't matter. I should bring him the keys. He might need some hints on how things are done in England.'

'Well, be careful you don't cross swords with Amelia from the estate agent's,' I warn. 'If she's got wind of the new owner arriving, she's probably beating a path to his door too.'

Mum says nothing but looks off to the distance. At least, I think, if she's sticking her nose into Chuck Jefferson's cottage, she might not have time to wonder about my movements. Then I sigh. Who am I kidding? Sooner or later, Joey will drop me in it. I push some noodles around on my plate and rack my brains for the hundredth time on how to keep him quiet. So far, my best idea is to tell him I'm ready to invest in his studio, and hope he's excited enough to forget about my job. But I'm not optimistic.

The moment mum goes to the loo, Kit leans across the table. 'What's going on? You look like you haven't slept in days.'

She's right about that. The dreams are worse than ever. Last night, I was balanced on one wing of a Cessna, clouds smacking my face with a damp chill so I couldn't see where we were going. Wol was clinging to the other wing, and I could tell she was shouting to me, but I couldn't hear. At first, when I looked at the pilot, it was Tom, but then when I looked again, it was grandad, and I knew with absolute certainty we were going to crash.

I tell Kit that Joey's onto me and it's only a matter of time until he spills it all to mum. 'It's a complete disaster,' I say.

'Damn,' she replies. 'I'm sorry.'

I drink some more champagne.

'What will you do?' she says seriously. Kit's not daft, the cogs of her brain are turning.

I chew my lip. 'If he tells her I've been lying about work, I think I can brazen it out. She'll be furious, and I'm pretty sure he's going to dump me. But if neither of them speaks to me again, I can live with that.'

'Soph –' Kit begins.

'As long as he doesn't find out I'm scared of flying, I think I'm... we're... okay,' I mutter. 'But if he twigs that part, all hell's gonna break loose.'

'Right,' says Kit, her cheeks draining of colour. She takes a breath. 'Look, I feel awful. I'm the reason you –'

'It's okay,' I say, interrupting. 'I'll sort this out.'

She frowns, rolling her chopsticks between her fingers. 'If you need me to – say something –'

I shake my head vigorously. 'No. It's fine. I'll deal with it.'

Kit looks like she wants to continue the discussion, but I see mum emerge from the restaurant, blissfully unaware of the secrets we're sheltering.

'Right,' I say, forcing a jolly tone as I reach for Kit's gift. 'Does the birthday girl want the bumps before or after her presents?'

~~~

I have to reach deep inside myself to find the nerve to seek Joey out, when every ounce of me wants to run in the other direction. But the meal with Kit and mum has made me realise I'll be walking on nails until I know what he plans to do with my secret. My first secret, I mean.

When I track him down on Garret Hostel Bridge, he's in

full photographic mode, with a long lens pointed towards Trinity Hall.

'What are you doing up here like a paparazzi?' I ask.

'Paparazzo,' he corrects me, barely looking my way. 'It's Suicide Sunday.'

That's a bit strong, I think. I've been feeling pretty down about my life unravelling, but I'm not ready to throw myself off this bridge yet. In any case, it's not high enough.

Joey jerks his head towards the college. 'Garden party. Exams are over, lots of celebrations going on today.'

'Oh.'

He's been trying for a while to get more work with the university, capturing quintessential Cambridge days like this. This party must be a daytime version of the May Balls, which, despite the name, are always held in June. It's the time of year when one encounters jubilant groups of students in black ties or ball gowns, wobbling down the city's cobbled streets. And that's at the start of the evening, never mind on the way home.

'Why Suicide Sunday, then?' From what I can see of the party, nobody looks especially depressed. Voices and laughter drift over from the brightly dressed flock. Lucky sods.

'Not sure. Something about stress, and exam results not being out yet.' Joey reaches into his bag, then looks up. 'What are you doing here?'

I may have found the courage to start this, but it's threatening to desert me. 'We, um, need to talk.'

Well, that was sparkling and original. Even without my clumsy lies, coming out with a line like that is enough to make a man sprint in the opposite direction. Lucky for me he's working.

'What, now?'

It's good that he's distracted. 'I'm sorry I didn't tell you the truth about my job.' I jump straight in. 'But I need to know, are you going to spill the beans to my mum?'

Joey's mouth is sulky, but at least he's considering the

question. Unfortunately he chooses not to answer it.

'Why didn't you tell me?'

I pause, then opt for the truth. 'I was worried you'd let it slip.'

'To your mum?' He glances at me, then back across the water to the party, making sure he isn't missing a career-defining shot.

I nod, studying the lazy river with its scattering of punts.

His forehead creases. 'I don't see why that matters.'

I decide to gamble with a part truth. 'I'm not... proud of it, Joe. I was kicked out of air hostess training and it was... really bad timing to tell mum. To disappoint her. Before I knew it, she'd told some people what I do – what she thinks I do – and the chance to say something... passed.'

The timing was indeed horrible. With a figurative footprint fresh on my behind, feeling more in need of a maternal hug than ever, I drove straight from Stansted Airport to Norwich. But on arrival, I found a bank-sponsored reception in honour of mum's fabulous work on the maths mentoring scheme. It had really taken off, and she'd made a bit of a name for herself, giving interviews on the importance of educational opportunities for girls in reducing teenage pregnancy rates. She thought I'd come to congratulate her, not announce my latest screw-up. As the indisputable evidence of her own teenage pregnancy, I lurked in the corner with a tense smile. I simply couldn't ruin her triumph.

'What *do* you do?' Joey asks now. 'I mean, do you even have a job?'

I tell him about the travel guides. Nothing to hide, there.

'No way,' he says.

'No way what?' I squint.

'I thought...' Joey runs a hand through his hair. 'I thought you must be doing something dodgy.'

How strange that people leap to the conclusion of shady

activity.

'I thought you knew me better than that,' I say, before I can help myself.

'I want to know you better than that.' He takes a step towards me. 'Much better.'

Although his tone has softened, and I'm thinking there's hope for my deception yet, I'm still having trouble looking at him.

'Why did you get kicked out of air hostess training?'

Rats. I shouldn't have hesitated. I should have stepped into his arms with pouting lips and big eyes. Shame that puckering isn't my style.

I pause. 'It was... complicated. But I think getting plastered at lunchtime was the last straw.'

My SpeedyJet training went okay for the first couple of days, as we dealt with admin and learned about company structure. But then we began Safety and Evacuation Procedures. We were taken to a mock aircraft and had to act as passengers, even buckling our seatbelts. The trainers pretended to be cabin crew and went through the safety demonstration. I kept telling myself it was only pretend, but by now my pulse was racing as I battled to stay calm. During the simulated take-off, the mock plane made noises and vibrations, and it felt so real, I thought I was going to pass out. Then, out of the blue, the lights went out and the cabin filled with smoke. I screamed so hard, one of the other trainees had to slap me. After that, I screamed some more, threw up, and fled to the nearest pub.

As Joey raises his eyebrows, I scrunch my face. 'Like I say, I'm not proud of it.'

He frowns. 'You're totally nuts, you know.' But his mouth twitches. 'You always were barking mad. It was why I fancied you rotten from the start.'

I smile up at him, uneasy but flattered. 'I fancied you rotten too.' That was true. All the girls at college noticed Joey. He still turns heads in the street.

He's smiling back now, in that casual, melting way. 'I

meant to tell you,' he says, 'I bought a bike.'

I'm wrong-footed by the sudden change of subject. 'What? Why?'

'Seeing as you enjoy it so much.' He reaches out and smooths a strand of my hair. 'I thought we'd do some rides together.'

'Oh,' I say. It's been a while since I've had any pleasant surprises. He was never keen on the great outdoors before. 'That sounds fun.'

Joey's focus is drawn back towards the Trinity Hall party. 'Look, I've more to do here, then I have to get over to Emma.'

'Emma? Who on earth is Emma?' I take a step back.

'Emmanuel.' He rolls his eyes. 'Their ball or thingummy is this evening.'

'Oh.' He's talking about a college which has been around since Tudor times. I'm clearly going nuts. With an effort, I return to the subject which brought me here. 'So, umm, you won't tell mum?'

Joey fiddles with the camera again, then looks at the sky with its wispy but thickening clouds.

'Well, I think it's weird, but no, not if it's important to you.'

A whoosh of breath escapes me. 'Thank you.'

'Anyway, it might be a good thing,' he says, raising the camera and pointing it at me. 'If you're home every day, you'll have more time to work on the studio.'

'The studio,' I echo as the camera captures my dismay for eternity. 'Of course.'

Chapter 23

'Will you help me?' I ask Tom, pulling him to one side before our final flying meeting.

'Sure.' He doesn't hesitate, his face pleasantly curious.

That changes as I hand him dog-eared pages of the official report into grandad's crash.

The accident was non-survivable.

'Where did you get this?' Tom asks, leafing through the analysis.

'Internet.' I've pored over it every night since discovering it.

The whole of the front fuselage was completely destroyed.

He looks up and exhales. 'Look, Sophie, this is hardly the time –' He gestures to Fergus and Ingrid, who are due to take an actual flight today.

'I need to know what happened,' I say. 'This doesn't tell me anything.'

There was no requirement for a flight recorder and none was fitted.

The report is written in plain English, and I've been able to decipher most of the technical terms. But as far as I can see, there's no definitive explanation for what went wrong.

Death was attributed to multiple injuries consistent with severe vertical deceleration.

'Please,' I say.

Tom shakes his head. 'Not now. Sorry. And you shouldn't be thinking about this stuff right now, either.'

I start to protest, but Rainbow, who's noticed Tom and me in a huddle and probably doesn't like it, calls the group to order.

'All right, y'all!' she bellows. 'Show time! You've worked so hard for this!'

Tom shoves the accident report in his pocket and turns dutifully to Rainbow, his pilot's face firmly in place. At this point, we're arranged loosely on the grass next to the plane, but our insides are wound up like a collective rubber band as we eye the Cessna.

Tom steps forward. 'Okay,' he says, his voice reassuring. 'This will be a piece of cake. We're only doing five minute flights. You know the theory. You know that I know what I'm doing.' He pauses, kind but confident, waiting for anyone to suggest he doesn't. Naturally, we keep quiet. 'Right,' he says. 'Fergus and Sophie, you first.'

My stomach twists as I hear my name. Instinctively, I look at Tom, and he gives me an almost imperceptible nod. I try not to think about all those accident reports I've read.

Beside me, Fergus gulps and I turn to him. 'You'll be okay, Ferg,' I say. 'Think about Morocco.'

'Yeah. I'm okay,' he mutters, as if telling himself.

The two of us walk towards Tom and the plane.

'Why don't you sit up front, Fergus,' Tom says lightly. 'Where I can keep an eye on you?'

Fergus falters. 'Uh – um, I'm fine in the back.'

This is weird. I'm rooting so hard for Fergus, wanting him to make it through this, my own nerves are receding. I prod him encouragingly. 'Go on. You've earned the front seat.'

Tom shoots me a tiny wink and the approval warms the ends of my fingers.

'Great,' Tom says. 'In you hop then, Sophie.' He opens the plane's miniature door and I try not to think about the view he's getting of my rear as I scramble into the small back seat. Tom hands me headphones and I busy myself with them, then with my seatbelt. In the front, Tom is helping Fergus do the same.

As Tom makes his checks, I allow myself to study him from my vantage point behind Fergus. I should be tied in knots at the prospect of flying again, but the distraction of looking at Tom's profile and capable hands is surprisingly effective. He's not as good-looking as Joey, but something about that makes him more trustworthy.

Finally, he leans out of his window, shouts 'Clear,' then clangs the window shut and starts the engine. I can't see Fergus's face from where I'm sitting, but his body looks pretty rigid.

'How are you guys doing?' Tom asks, once he's switched on the communications system.

'Fine,' I say, and almost mean it.

He turns round, as if for visual confirmation, and the long look he gives me makes me think of what happened last time I was in this plane. I can't say anything – everything going through my headset can be heard by Fergus too – so I will myself not to look at his mouth. After a moment, Tom nods and turns back.

'Okay, Fergus?' Tom asks.

Fergus replies with a strangled yowl.

'Good,' Tom grins. 'Just keep your feet off those pedals, all right? That's your job today, mate.'

'Whoa.' Fergus is shocked into responding. 'Right. Got it.'

In the back seat, I smile to myself.

We taxi the short distance to the end of the runway, where Tom swings the plane off to the side. 'This is where I make last minute checks,' he explains, presumably for Fergus's benefit. I suspect Tom hasn't told anyone else that he's already taken me for an airborne spin.

I watch him flick levers, twist dials and rev the engine, all the while consulting the clipboard strapped to his thigh. The butterflies inside me are dancing now at the prospect of the flight, but there's something else there too: curiosity. Is this what grandad did? Did he have a checklist? Did he miss something? What the heck did go wrong? My thoughts take my mind off what's happening now, and before I know it, we're moving again, to the brink of the runway.

Tom gabbles into the radio, and answering gibberish comes back.

surviving.

On the wall of the flying club's office, Rainbow has persuaded someone to string a banner reading 'Congratulations graduates'. The mortar boards it depicts aren't right, but we don't care. And that bottle of cheap bubbly she's struggling to uncork looks extremely tempting. Eventually, Tom takes it from her and the cork flies out as if propelled by jet fuel. Rainbow beams up at him and I feel a twinge I don't care to analyse.

'Here, y'all! Group photo!' Rainbow cries.

We shuffle into position under the banner, Rainbow and Tom flanking us. A man in a Shell uniform, whose usual job is to refuel the little planes, takes the tiny camera from Rainbow. With a few rapid clicks, we are released from our pose, but now run the risk of being immortalised on her website. I must ask her not to post us on Facebook or anywhere mum might stumble over it.

'Great job, you guys!' Our effervescent instructor begins hugging each of us. Fergus, clearly alarmed, springs back and nearly squashes me.

'Thank you so much,' Ingrid is saying to Tom. 'You made it look so... complex and yet so effortless. Once we got up there, I – well, I *almost* enjoyed it.'

Tom smiles at her. 'You did really well.' He looks to his left. 'And you, Fergus. I'm glad you stuck with it.'

Fergus looks bashful. 'Sorry about that first time, mate.' He's talking, of course, about the throwing up episode.

'Don't be,' Tom says. 'It happens all the time.'

'And now you have your sick bag ready, it's not the end of the world,' I tell Fergus, and we laugh. Ingrid and I conspired over the purchase of some sturdy paper bags from Lakeland Plastics. I think they're meant to hold homemade fudge, but they'll do the job if necessary.

Fergus risks approaching Rainbow to claim his glass of fizz. Without looking, I sense Tom step into the gap beside me.

'You were a big help today,' he says quietly.

'What? Me?' I check to see if he's being sarcastic. But he seems perfectly serious and I look back down at my drink.

'With Fergus. He was about ready to bolt, you know.'

'Oh,' I reply. 'I didn't – um – do much.' There's a pause, then I gather my wits. 'Can we talk about the accident report now?'

'Look,' Tom grimaces, 'can't you just enjoy tonight?'

'Please,' I say as I see Rainbow bearing down on us, bottle in hand. 'I have to know.'

He holds my gaze for a moment, then looks away. 'All right,' he says. 'Call me.'

~~~

Powered by adrenaline, it doesn't take long for the party to move to The Plough, where I add a vodka and cranberry juice to my earlier glass of fizz.

'Bella!' I clamber onto a velvet-covered stool. 'You're not going to believe this.'

'Believe what?' Bella hands a customer their change and a bag of crisps.

I draw myself up, pausing for effect. 'Today, my friend, I flew.'

Bella's eyes widen and she forgets to stop pouring from the Adnams tap. Beer flows over the edge of the glass and onto her hands. 'You never did!'

'I did too.' I beam around the bar, nodding to reinforce my news. Discretion is no longer top of my mind. 'I mean, Tom did. But I was there. So was Fergus.'

'That's brilliant,' Bella says. 'Bloody good show, Soph!'

I preen, the vodka already history. 'How much is champagne?'

Fergus looks blank. 'I don't think we've got any.'

'Oh.' On reflection, there isn't much call for Dom Pérignon in Saffron Sweeting. The village certainly isn't full of big spenders. 'Never mind.' I raise my voice. 'A round on me, everyone!'

This gets the attention of a few villagers who have

settled in the pub to watch Italy and Paraguay kick a ball around for ninety minutes. But I'm oblivious to the *Gli Azzurri* and I don't stop to wonder where my half-Italian boyfriend is tonight.

'I'm still not sure I can do it again.' Fergus frowns. 'What about you, Ingrid?'

Ingrid inhales. 'Well, I might talk to my doctor about a little something to take the edge off –' she glances at Rainbow, who's at one of the tables nearby, '– but I think I can do it.' She nods vigorously, as if to convince herself.

'Hurrah,' I say. 'Rainbow! Let us buy you a drink!' I rootle for my purse, hoping there's a twenty pound note here somewhere.

'So.' Bella props her elbows on the bar. 'What was it like?'

'Fantastic!' I declare.

'Petrifying.' Fergus proclaims simultaneously. Then he looks at me critically.

'Oh, all right.' I nod. 'My heart was hammering so hard, I thought I might pass out.'

And that was just the time before, when Tom kissed me, comes the uninvited thought. I push that to one side. 'I was scared witless.'

Where is Tom, anyway? Didn't he follow us to the pub? That's a pity, I wanted to buy him a drink too.

'So, are you cured?' Bella asks, glancing around to check the villagers aren't listening.

I pour more vodka down my throat. 'Oh, I expect so! Piece of cake next time!' But I can't meet Fergus's eye.

'Were you up for long?' Bella asks.

'No. Tom said he didn't want to push it too far.' He'd already pushed it far enough with me, after all.

'I must go and help in the kitchen.' Bella squeezes my arm. 'You should eat something,' she adds.

'Not hungry!' I topple off my stool to visit the juke box, wondering why the choices are blurred tonight. Ignoring the grumbles of the football viewers, I select 'Wind Beneath My

Wings' and 'Fly Me to the Moon'. I'm stuck for a third choice and end up with 'Mull of Kintyre'. Well, at least the band is on theme.

When Violet and her lemon-sucking cronies arrive in the pub, I greet her like a dear friend. Reckless from adrenaline and vodka, I regale her with our airborne exploits. Only this time, I'm bolder, the flight was longer, and we climbed higher. Next time I tell the story, I'll be piloting Concorde.

'Very good, Sophie,' she says, clearly perplexed. 'Cheers.' She raises her gin and tonic politely. A few minutes later, she's showing photos of the puppies from the vegetable shop to Ingrid, who coos and sighs appropriately.

At about ten o'clock, Bella comes out of the kitchen, untying her apron. She deposits a plate of chunky chips next to me, complete with tartare sauce for dipping.

'Eat,' she says, waggling a fry at me.

I take a few chips but am more interested in chatting to anyone who'll listen. I'm now mates with Kenneth, who runs the library, and we're debating the Apollo missions. With slurred speech, I confide that since this afternoon, I'm thinking of becoming an astronaut.

'So, tell me more,' Bella says. 'How did you pluck up the courage?'

I tap the side of my nose and try to wink. 'Shh!' I say, loudly. As I lean in, my stool wobbles and tips me into her lap. 'Oopsy – sorry.' I climb back up. 'Fergus, your stool's lousy'. The lousy sounds like 'loushy'.

'What happened, Sophie?' Bella asks again.

I smirk. 'Today, you see – it wasn't my first time.'

Bella's nose twitches, in the way it does when she's trying not to laugh.

'I flew – over a fortnight ago!' I announce in a booming stage whisper.

'Two weeks ago? How come?'

I lower my voice a little. 'He – he kished me.'

'Who? Fergus?' She looks aghast at The Plough's

landlord, now lounging beside Ingrid.

'No, not Fergus.' I snort. 'Tom. Tom kissed me, then suggested we take off.'

'Wow!' Bella gapes. 'What was it like?'

I lick my lips. This vodka is making me parched; I'll switch to whisky. 'Really hot.'

Now Bella frowns. 'No, Sophie, I meant the *flight*.'

~ ~ ~

Bella forbids Fergus from serving me whisky and makes me have a large Coke. But it's too late: the vodka and bubbles mix is prancing around my bloodstream.

I don't remember the rest of the evening. But apparently, I decided to demonstrate the principles of flight to the assembled Monday night drinkers. Apparently, I introduced the importance of lift by scaling a barstool and spreading my arms. Then I commandeered four bags of crisps to act as flaps.

And apparently, that's pretty much where I was when Joey walked in.

Chapter 24

'I don't see what the big blooming deal is,' I say.

It's a glorious English summer day and we're having lunch outside, at a cafe near Magdalene Bridge.

'I just think you might have mentioned it.' Joey stabs his jacket potato. 'I felt like the only one not in on a huge secret party.'

'It wasn't a secret party, it was a spontaneous celebration.' The words are out and can't be taken back.

'Celebrating what, for God's sake?' He's smelled a rat.

I decide if there's no way out, the only way is through. 'Rainbow's been running a course to help people get over their fear of flying. I've been, um, helping.' Tom did say I was helpful on Monday, so the lie is in the implication, not the actual statement.

'Fear of *what*?'

I repeat it.

'That's ridiculous.' He takes a large bite of spud. 'What kind of pillock is scared of flying these days?' A gooey string of cheese trails to his plate.

'Plenty of people,' I snap. 'About six per cent, actually.' This is Rainbow's statistic.

'And you've been *helping*? You, who don't even work as an air hostess and never have?'

A forkful of coronation chicken pauses part way to my mouth. This isn't good. I attempt a withering glare.

'No wonder you're never home. You know I've seen more of Bella than you in the last few weeks?' Joey takes off his designer sunglasses and behind them I detect genuine hurt.

They get on okay and Joey's happy enough to eat Bella's food. And I reckon he cheers her up, so what's the problem?

'I've had a lot going on,' I say. 'My car died yesterday. It stalled outside the malt house and wouldn't start again.' I hope that isn't a more general omen.

'I assume they've been paying you, at least?' He looks over my shoulder at the river, where three punts have collided and separate factions of French and American tourists are attempting to communicate in English. Clearly, it's a foreign language for all of them.

I blush. 'Not exactly.' What business is it of Joey's?

'Huh. You've been helping at some lame workshop for free?'

'It wasn't a lame workshop,' I reply. 'Rainbow has some interesting, um, techniques, and Tom is a terrific pilot.'

'Who the hell are Rainbow and Tom?'

A piece of chicken threatens to stick in my throat. 'The instructors. Rainbow lives in the village. She's a psychologist from America. And Tom's the flying expert. You met him, remember?' I feel my cheeks redden.

'They sound like something off children's television,' Joey sneers. 'Who else is there? Bungle? Rupert the Bear?'

'Don't be like that,' I say. 'They were good. The group trusted them.'

Joey scrunches up his mouth like an obstinate kid. 'So Tom took you flying?'

I pray I don't blush any deeper. 'He took the whole group. In pairs,' I say. That was true, after all.

'And he's a pilot?' The sunglasses are back on.

'Yes. Part time. He runs his own business too.'

Talking about Tom gives me the urge to check my phone again, but I resist. I've called him twice since Monday and left messages about grandad's accident report. But I've heard nothing back. He's obviously not going to help me.

'So he's a right tycoon,' Joey says sarcastically. He's made light work of his lunch and is now eyeing the ice cream choices.

The prudent thing to do would be to shut up right now. Such a pity I'm not prudent. 'I wouldn't say tycoon. His family owns some garden centres.'

'*Garden* centres?' Joey drops the dessert menu and

laughs. 'You're hanging out with a hippie and a flying gardener? No wonder you're not yourself!'

Darn him. I take the bait, like he probably intended. 'What do you mean, I'm not myself?'

'You've been acting really weird, Sophie. You were such a laugh in college, so easy-going. But since... well, since we got together again, you've changed.'

'I have not,' I protest. Have I? Well, if I have, losing Wol was a horrible wrench. Joey can understand that, surely?

He leans across the table and takes my hand. Then he tips his sunglasses down his nose so he can peer at me with his dark brown eyes. 'You have,' he says, stretching out the second word beguilingly. 'It's like all you ever think about... is that money you inherited.'

'I do not!' This stings, although I'm pretty sure I've been obsessing far more over my flying secrets than Wol's will.

Joey strokes the flesh between my thumb and index finger. 'I'm ready to launch a business with you,' he says. 'To move forward together, not just rehash what we had in college.'

What did we have in college? Some drunken fun, exuberant sex and an enthusiasm for the future. Our separate futures.

'You're the cleverest, most go-getting person I know,' he says. 'It'll be great.'

He has a small circle of friends, if I'm the cleverest. The last time he met Kit, she was nine, and even then her brains outshone mine. But the compliment nudges at me.

'Joey...' I say, desperate not to antagonise him further. 'I just don't want to move too quickly on the studio.'

He gives me his best hurt look.

'Sophia,' he says, 'I thought, if you loved me, you'd want this too.'

I look down at my half-eaten lunch. 'Can't we wait a while?'

'What for?' he says beseechingly. 'We've found the perfect place. And we've got the money.'

I bite my tongue and draw my hand away. Then I look towards the railings and the River Cam, wondering if I could hop over the side and make a stealthy escape in a passing punt.

No, I think, *you've* found the perfect place. And *I've* got the money.

~~~

'Sophie? Is that you?'

Tom's Range Rover stops a hundred yards up the road, then reverses back.

'What the hell are you doing?' He lowers his window.

I straighten, taking my bike light from my mouth so I can talk. 'Hi. Nothing.'

'It's half past ten and you decide to undertake bike maintenance miles from anywhere?' He gestures to my bike, upside down, resting on its saddle and handlebars.

Frustration makes me snappy. 'So it would appear. Now if you'll excuse me, I've had a shitty day and I'm busy.'

It's the summer solstice, the longest day of the year, and it only got dark an hour ago. There was no sunset to speak of: it was hidden by stubborn clouds. But it's been a long, long day in other ways too.

I return the light to my teeth, so I have a chance of seeing the inner tube. It's currently hanging out of the wheel, like roadkill. On the back of my neck, the drizzle is getting heavier.

Just go away, I think.

But Tom doesn't go away. He gets out of his car, glancing at the sky as the damp chill settles on him. 'You pick your moments. I almost ran you over.' There's a smile in his voice.

I take the light again and shine it in his face. He winces. Good.

'Well, thank you for not squashing me. That would have been the perfect end to my day. Actually, it would have been the high point. Now if you don't mind, I'm *busy*.'

Today started with an email from my favourite publisher, informing me they'd sent the wrong file for a book on Ireland. Would I mind awfully starting again, and without further compensation? A painful trip to the dentist followed, after which I was supposed to meet with an aeronautical engineering student, unearthed by Bella at Trewe. Unfortunately, rather than give his opinion of grandad's accident over lunch, he stood me up. Then, this evening, I was forced by Joey's mother to attend a handbag show, featuring the work of Fabiana and her class. Too late, I found that purchasing was compulsory in the eyes of Mamma Joey. I was effectively a prisoner until I forked out three hundred pounds for a mock pony skin satchel.

I was still four miles from Saffron Sweeting when I realised each turn of the pedals was getting harder. And my bones were being pounded by every inch of road. I stopped and looked down: the rear tyre was flat. Dammit. For three hundred quid, I could have bought the actual pony, dispensed with my bike and been home by now.

Tom takes a step towards the bike. 'Puncture?'

'Yeah. Bloody thing.' I roll my aching shoulders.

Tom squints at the dangling inner tube. 'I'll give you a lift,' he says.

'I'm fine.' I shake my head. 'I just need to find the hole and patch it and wait –'

'No,' Tom says sharply. He pauses and starts again, more slowly. 'I absolutely admire your independence, Sophie, but this is ridiculous. You're not safe out here.'

'I said I'm fine.' My voice rises. 'I've just had a crappy day and –'

'Shut up,' Tom says kindly. The hatchback of the Range Rover is open; he's lifting the pestilent bike like a toy.

'Hey! I was fixing that.'

'I know,' he says. 'And you can carry on tomorrow. Out here, you'll get hit by a tractor. Or kidnapped by a badger. Or worse.'

'Don't be daft,' I say. 'Saffron Sweeting hasn't had a

murder in twenty years.'

'Good,' he replies. 'And we're not going to start tonight. Hop in, it's raining.'

I can't help but sigh as I sink into the relative warmth of his car and feel a soft leather seat rather than a hard leather saddle under me.

'Thank you,' I mutter. To my horror, I feel tears welling.

If he notices, he doesn't say anything, but cranks the heat higher and turns the car towards Saffron Sweeting. I hunt in my pocket, find a paper napkin from Costa Coffee, and snuffle discreetly as we drive in silence.

'There,' Tom says, switching on the interior car light as we pull into my driveway. 'That wasn't so terrible, was it?'

'Thanks.' I don't look at him.

'Want to tell me about it?'

'You didn't call me,' I say, and immediately hate how that sounds. 'About grandad's accident, I mean.'

'I got your messages,' Tom says. He leans towards me and I stiffen, then feel foolish as he stretches for his jacket on the back seat. He pulls some folded papers from the coat and smooths them. With a sulky sidelong glance, I'm surprised to recognise the accident report.

'So are you going to help me?' I'm talking to the glove compartment.

'Yes,' he says.

'Oh.' I sniff. 'When?'

There's the smallest of pauses. 'How about now?'

~~~

I make tea for my guest, then we sit on opposite ends of the sofa, three feet between us. Stanley is asleep so we keep our conversation low. I tell Tom all I know about grandad's job and the last flight he took. I try to explain my gnawing need to know more, to understand and reframe this part of my history. I don't mention I've spent the whole week staring at my phone.

'Well,' Tom says, moving our mugs to spread the report

on the coffee table. 'There isn't much to go on.'

'I was hoping you'd spot something,' I say. 'I couldn't see anything definitive.'

I scan the report again, but I know it pretty much by heart.

Prior to the flight the aircraft had been refuelled with Avgas 100 to a total of 136 imperial gallons... A deep depression crossed the area with associated frontal occlusion... A witness reported that he had seen an aircraft flying very low... The aircraft hit the ground in a left hand spin... The autopsy did not suggest a medical cause for the accident...

He shakes his head. 'I'm sorry. They say a bird strike is unlikely, but not impossible.'

I nod. 'And the weather was bad, but you said planes don't crash from lightning strikes.'

'I didn't say never crash. And there's this bit, that your grandad wasn't qualified under Instrument Flight Rules.'

'What does that mean?' I ask.

'It means, if there was heavy cloud and he couldn't see where he was going... he could have made a mistake. But we don't know that,' Tom adds, when he sees my face.

'Okay.' I blow on my tea.

'Then there's this part,' Tom says, 'That he was under treatment for mild hypertension.'

'But it also says the drug being used to lower his blood pressure was approved by the Civil Aviation Authority. So that's unlikely.'

'I agree. And I checked with a doctor friend; he didn't think that was it, either.'

I bump my tea down on the table. 'You checked with a friend?'

He nods. 'I asked around. There are people far more knowledgeable about this than me.'

I digest this.

'I wasn't ignoring your calls,' Tom says quietly. Then he clears his throat. 'And I had to go to the Netherlands too.'

'Holland?' I repeat.

'Bulb supplier. Buying trip, for next spring.'

Now I feel bad. He wasn't screening my messages, he was working, and doing research on my behalf. And in any case, what right do I have to be annoyed that he didn't call back?

In an unspoken apology, I fetch the biscuit tin from the kitchen. Bella, bless her, baked yesterday, but is shunning carbs until after an upcoming blind date.

I point to another part of the report. 'I don't understand this oil leak.'

Tom leans forward too. Our heads are close together as we study the wording. 'Yeah,' he says. 'All things considered, that could have been it.'

'And?' I'm hanging on his words now.

Tom meets my eyes, his brow knitted. 'Well, the next bit's here.'

We look down at the page together.

The aircraft entered a spin from which there was insufficient height to recover.

~~~

Neither of us says anything. Tom's still sitting forward, his forearms resting on his thighs. He looks at me, then at the floor.

'Well,' I say finally, summoning a thin smile. 'Maybe getting a puncture wasn't so bad.'

Unsure of what to do next, I make more tea. As the kettle boils, I realise the obvious has been staring at me.

'So what now?' Tom asks as I return.

'You'll think I'm crazy. Shortbread?'

Tom nods and reaches into the tin. 'What are you going to do, and why is it crazy?'

I dip my chin. 'Okay, it's not that crazy. But I think I need to go to Scotland.'

'Scotland?' His tone is surprised.

'The accident was in the local newspaper. I'll go up

there and see what I can find out.'

Tom takes a long drink. 'You make a brilliant cup of tea,' he says.

I smile. Living with Bella, I don't get – or expect – any praise in the epicurean department.

'Look, Sophie, I know this is important to you but... do you think that's a good idea?'

'Yes.' I snap my shortbread, shooting crumbs everywhere. 'Don't try to talk me out of it.'

Tom rubs his eyes. 'Whereabouts?' he asks.

'A little town called Strathblae,' I answer. 'It's south of Aberdeen. I can get National Express. Tomorrow, or the day after.'

'Long trip,' he says thoughtfully.

I nod. 'I don't care. I have to do this.'

Tom sets his mug down. 'I have a supplier near Montrose. I need to meet with him soon. I can take you.'

'Huh?' I've had a long day and my brain is blanketed, like Stanley's cage. 'You mean, in the car?'

Tom smiles. 'No, my intrepid flying friend. In a plane. We'd be there in a jiffy.'

'Oh.' I say. 'A plane.'

Twelve hours each way, on a bumpy, nausea-inducing bus is hardly an appealing prospect. I weigh it against a few hours in a bumpy, nausea-inducing plane, with a kind, capable and – yes – attractive man.

Tom is looking at me expectantly. He stretches his legs in front of him, crossing them at the ankles. I notice his socks are navy. Joey would never wear navy socks with brown shoes. Joey wouldn't take me to Scotland, either.

I shake my head. 'I couldn't possibly.'

'I thought you'd say that.' Tom gets to his feet. 'Well, thanks for the tea.'

Disappointment wriggles through me. I'm shocked to find how much I wanted him to talk me into flying. I tuck both hands under my knees and examine the carpet. For several seconds, neither of us moves.

'Sophie?'

I look up. From my seated position, he towers over me and his hair flops over his face as he looks down. Suddenly, the lounge seems tiny.

Tom shoves his hands in his jeans pockets. 'The offer's still open,' he says in an undertone. 'You don't have to do this on your own.'

I shut my eyes, finally admitting to myself how good that sounds.

Chapter 25

'I won't be able to talk much on the way,' Tom says as he preps the plane at Cambridge.

'Of course,' I reply, pretending to be perfectly calm. 'That's fine.'

His businesslike manner pleases me: it lessens the chances of another pre-take-off kiss. And, as we climb from Cambridge airport and turn north, anyone can see Tom has his hands full. He's in constant dialogue with air traffic control, leading to changes of altitude, direction and radio frequency. At every moment, he's either flying the plane or fiddling with the communications system.

My new-found flying confidence was premature. Not only is this flight far longer than the others, but I find the amount of activity in Britain's airspace thoroughly daunting. The only times I can't spot planes on all sides of us is when we're flying in cloud. And there's a heck of a lot of cloud. This petrifies me – surely, with so much traffic in the sky, the probability of a collision is enormous? I picture us tangling with a commercial plane, either slicing our wing off so we spiral to the ground or a full-on hit, exploding in a fury of fire.

At one point, I realise Tom's having trouble being heard by air traffic control, as he keeps repeating our call sign and waiting for acknowledgement. Oh my God, I think, they can't hear us and they don't know where we are. We're stuck up here, trying to dodge Boeings the size of castles.

'Are you okay?' Tom asks, during a blissful couple of minutes when the cloud is absent and the swarm of other planes has dissipated.

'Umph,' I say. 'Fine.' But my nails are shredded. How I wish I'd taken the overnight bus instead.

And the landing, when we seem to hover over the Firth of Tay until the final moment, is the last straw. By the time

Tom taxis the plane off the runway at Dundee, I would pay good money for one of Fergus's sick bags.

But it isn't just the journey which has rattled me. I'm deeply apprehensive of what I might find in Strathblae. What if there's no information here? Or what if there is, and grandad was entirely to blame? Maybe mum and gran were right to hide it from me.

Tom brings the Cessna to a halt. The airport is even smaller than Cambridge and its relatively clear skies have been replaced by a blanket of grey.

'You don't look too good,' he says, removing his headset. 'Sort of green around the gills.'

'Just a bit... nervous.' I try a weak smile.

'Did you eat breakfast?'

I shake my head. I didn't fall asleep till about one, then slept through my alarm.

'Right,' Tom says. 'First stop, food.'

~~~

As we drive towards Strathblae in his hire car, Tom asks, 'Are you sure you won't need your own wheels?'

'The town's really small,' I reply. 'I can visit the newspaper office easily.'

I look around, struck by the dramatic colour of the fields. Here, the soil is a bright, rusty red, in contrast to the darker tone of the Fens. The houses – mostly cottages – are all made from the same stone. Granite, maybe? The heavy grey of the sky blends into the buildings. There are some mountains in the distance, but here, the landscape is bleak.

'It's pretty on a sunny day,' Tom says, reading my mind. 'The granite contains micas, which sparkle in the light.'

'Hmm,' I reply. 'It isn't sparkling today.'

It's late June, but there's smoke coming from some of the cottage chimneys. Does my family really come from such a gloomy place? I force my thoughts to more practical matters. 'So, what kind of supplier are you seeing?'

'Heathers and other tough stuff. As you can see, this

isn't Tuscany. Plants need to be hardy to grow here. Bill's about twenty miles north of town. So I'll drop you off and come back later, okay?'

'Right. Thanks.'

'But first, we'll get some food.'

'That's okay,' I say. 'Drop me off, I'll be fine.'

Tom looks at me as we turn at a crossroads. The sprinkling of cottages is growing more dense: we're reaching the town. 'No,' he says, 'the minute I let you out of my sight, you'll be off like a bloodhound. By the time I come back, you'll be a pile of bleached bones.'

I laugh. 'You don't have to be so kind to me.'

'I'm not being kind to you.'

His voice is low and something in his tone makes me look at him, just as he glances across at me. I want to search his face for his meaning, but he turns back to the road, squeezing the car to the left to make room for an oncoming tractor. I chew a fingernail and ponder his words.

By the time we've driven down a hill and along the main street, the windscreen wipers are turned on full.

~~~

After breakfast, Tom seems reluctant to get back in the car.

'You don't want me to... stick around?' he says.

'Of course not.' Just as I'm wishing I'd twisted Bella's arm into coming. 'I'll be fine.' I shift from one foot to another, but fortunately he doesn't notice.

'Right,' he says finally. 'See you at four. Call me if you need me.'

I turn purposefully up the hill, in the direction of the *Strathblae Enquirer*. But as I approach the tall granite building, flanked on one side by a solicitor's and the other by a launderette, I sense that something isn't right. It's now late morning, but the heavy wooden front doors are closed.

I grasp the handle of the imposing door and twist. Nothing. I twist the other way, adding a rattle for good luck. No. Locked.

In a cabinet beside the door is a bulletin board, displaying the yellowing front page of the Strathblae newspaper. Frowning, I notice the date is three weeks ago. Then, my heart sinks as I spot a small notice: 'With immediate effect, all business shall be directed to the Press & Journal, Aberdeen.'

Yet I know the paper is still published – I checked online yesterday.

With no backup plan in place, I push open the door of the launderette, glad of the industrious warmth. Here, the only occupant is a young woman wearing a green puffed jacket. Her hair is streaked black and white, reminding me of a badger.

'Sorry,' she says, rolling the Rs delightfully, 'I hannae got any change.'

'I don't need change,' I say. 'I was hoping you might know about the newspaper office.'

'Oh,' she replies. 'Aye, them.'

I wait.

'The paper's moved to Aberdeen,' she says. 'It's all done from there now. They sacked half a dozen folk.'

That's what I feared. 'So, if I wanted to look at the archives, I'd have to go to Aberdeen?'

She shrugs. 'I dinnae ken.' Then, seeing my baffled face, 'I don't know. I expect so.'

Darn it. Aberdeen is another forty miles north. I stupidly expected all the answers to be here, where the accident happened. I didn't reckon on the slow demise of traditional newspapers.

The town library is no better. Here, I find a woman who bears a striking resemblance to Mrs Doubtfire, stationed behind a desk so solid it could serve as a bomb shelter. She calls me 'dear' half a dozen times and takes fifteen minutes to acknowledge her dusty, chilly mausoleum doesn't contain anything of use.

'Oh, no, dear.' She shakes her head, looking as if I've failed her, rather than the other way around. 'We don't have anything like that.'

My shoulders sag.

'You'll be wanting the museum, dear.'

'Museum?' My head snaps up. Why didn't she say so sooner?

Naturally, the museum is located back up the hill, drizzle and all. Cycling isn't keeping me as fit as I thought: my calf muscles complain loudly. I allow myself a brief fantasy that the museum might have a cafe. The breakfast with Tom is still fuelling me, but, now that I'm cold, wet and demoralised, a mug of steaming hot chocolate would be truly welcome.

But cocoa, whipped cream and marshmallows are not in my horoscope this morning. The museum is padlocked, with a brass sign declaring opening hours of Friday, ten until noon, and all day Tuesday. For Pete's sake, this *is* Friday. I consult my phone and groan. Nine minutes past twelve. I've missed the bloody place by nine minutes. If only I hadn't embarked on a wild goose chase around Strathblae first.

I sink down on the museum steps, only to clamber up again as chilly, moist granite greets my backside. What a disaster. I shouldn't have come all this way without more research. Too proud to phone Tom, I now have four hours to kill in this dismal town.

As a drop of rain plops down the back of my neck, I retreat under the lintel of the museum's door. From there, I stare out at the street, wondering where to go next. I wish I'd brought my laptop: at least then I could get some work done. I contemplate the nearest puddle, where each raindrop forms a perfect ripple.

But I count no more than ten new drops before the puddle sloshes and disappears under a car tyre. The tyre is attached to an old blue Vauxhall, with a low-hanging exhaust and terrible rust around the wheel arches. From the car emerges a middle-aged woman wearing a floral nylon overall, plus headscarf and wellington boots. After lugging cleaning supplies up the museum steps, she produces a bunch of keys tied with green twine. By the time she selects one and grasps the padlock, I'm catching on.

'Hello,' I say, offering my brightest smile. 'I'm Sophie. I wonder if you can help me?'

'We open again on Tuesday,' she says, lips firm.

My smile doesn't waver. I will not be defeated by this last hurdle. 'That's such a shame. I've come all this way,' I say. 'I'm not sure I can stay that long.'

Morag, as I later learn is her name, puts her head on one side. 'You're English.'

I have the sense to shrug apologetically. 'I was hoping to research some local history,' I say. 'It's such a lovely town.' Lovely is stretching the point, but I'm hoping she was born and raised here.

No answer is forthcoming, but her dense eyebrows lift infinitesimally. Although the door is unlocked now, she pointedly keeps her mop between me and the entrance. I don't want to start a jousting match.

'It's a bit delicate.' I lower my voice, despite the fact the street is empty. 'I wanted to find out...'

It's on the tip of my tongue to make something up, to tell her I'm the long-lost daughter of the local laird or a geologist who's found gold in the hills behind Strathblae. But with a jolt, I realise there's too much deception in my life. I'm here to learn the truth, not weave more stories.

'It's about the plane crash at the school,' I say finally. 'In the early eighties.'

Morag's hand flies to her throat. She remembers it, then.

'I... lost someone,' I confess.

She stares at me for a moment, then lets her mop fall as she flings the museum door wide. 'You poor lassie. Come away in.'

~ ~ ~

I'm back at our meeting point fifteen minutes early,

umbrella tilted against the slanting rain. I thank my lucky stars when the first car to stop is Tom's.

'How was your –' he cuts his pleasantry short as I flop into the passenger seat, umbrella flapping.

I let my eyes close as my head lolls back gratefully.

'Want to go?' he says. At my nod, he puts the car in gear and turns it.

We're at the edge of town when Tom speaks again. 'You look shattered.'

He's right. I'm damp and deflated.

'Did it not go well?' he asks. 'Fiddle with the heat, if you like.'

I do as he suggests. At least it's still daylight, or the Scottish version of daylight, where the clouds balance on the nearest roof.

'It went... okay,' I say. 'But I didn't find anything I don't already know.'

'Go on,' Tom says.

I tell him about the initial dead ends, then getting lucky at the museum with Morag.

'And the plane crash?' Tom's eyes are on the road but he does seem to be listening.

'It was basically what the newspaper said. I'd got my hopes up that there would be more to it.' I sigh. 'Some... reason, you know?'

'Oh.' Tom glances at me and gives my thigh a spontaneous squeeze. Tonight, in bed with the lights out, I'll analyse that squeeze, but for now I'm occupied with 1983.

'There's no doubt he borrowed the plane without permission. And although he loved to fly, he wasn't especially experienced. He'd logged less than fifty flying hours.' I pause, waiting for Tom to agree how little that was. But he just nods. 'Tom,' I prod, 'you have more hours than that, don't you?'

'What? Yes. Loads. Over a thousand. Don't worry about me, Sophie.' His tone is as steady as always.

I let out the breath I didn't know I'd been holding.

'I wasn't worried about you,' I smile, and the mood in the car lightens. 'I was worried about me.'

'What else?' Tom turns the car onto a dual carriageway. I recognise this; we're not far from the airport.

'Well, there was something in the coroner's report about the plane's records. But... grandad was at fault. There's no getting away from it.'

'I'm sorry,' Tom says. 'That's hard for you.'

'I think it's part of growing up,' I say, watching the intermittent swoosh of the windscreen wipers. 'When you're little, you think your parents and grandparents are perfect, whiter than white. Then you start to detect little flaws. Eventually, you realise they're no more perfect than you are.'

Tom shoots me a sympathetic look but doesn't say more until we reach the small airport. 'Right,' he asks, 'ready to go home?'

~~~

But going home is not on the agenda.

'I think I'll phone for the weather first,' Tom says as we scuttle from the car rental office to the plane. Wind streams across the tarmac, and the drizzle is diagonal.

I know by now that before each trip, pilots phone to find out about the weather and any special instructions. 'They tell you useful stuff,' Tom told us in class one day. 'Like, if there are any skydivers planning to hurtle past your windscreen.' The class giggled nervously but we knew that tangling with a parachutist wouldn't end well for either party. 'I generally like to stay out of the drop zone,' Tom said wryly.

'Sorry.' Tom finishes his call.

'What?' I ask. I've installed myself in my seat, figured out both parts of my seatbelt, and am preparing to plug in my headset.

'The weather,' he says, nodding at the charcoal sky. 'It's crap.'

I lean forward to peer out. It does look pretty evil.

'Crap?' I repeat. 'Is that... an aviation term?'

Tom consults the notes he's made on his clipboard. 'Cloud at a thousand feet, storms likely over Newcastle... Flight not recommended.'

'Not recommended?'

He shakes his head.

'So you can't fly in this?' The possibility of not being able to get home never occurred to me.

He frowns down at the clipboard again. 'I can... but I'd rather not.'

'Right.' I say. It occurs to me that this might be the equivalent of a teenage boy running out of petrol when there's a girl in the car. But then something that could be lightning catches the corner of my eye.

'So what do we do?' I ask, gesturing at the tiny plane as if it might turn into an overnight bus to Cambridge.

Tom puffs air out. 'We can wait an hour and phone again,' he says. 'Or we can give up and find a hotel.'

'A hotel?'

'You want to sleep in here?'

I make a face to show I'm not in favour of Cessna camping. 'Will it be better in an hour, do you think?'

He looks at me for a second before answering. 'Actually, it'll probably be worse. But I don't want you to think I'm making this up to get you to spend the night with me.'

I blush. 'Don't be silly,' I say. 'Of course I wouldn't think that.' What is he, a mind reader?

Tom says nothing, watching me steadily. He's not wearing the smirk of someone who's teasing.

'Right,' I say, when my cheeks have cooled. 'Let's look for a hotel, then.'

Chapter 26

Viewed from the end of its gently curving driveway, the Monboddo Arms offers a proud welcome in the subdued afternoon light. A large country house, it boasts a couple of small turrets and I spot the Scottish flag waving in the stiff breeze.

Inside, the foyer smells of pine trees, clean linen and a hint of whisky. A terrier trots up to sniff our legs, then returns to sprawl in front of an enormous fireplace. Beside the hearth are a pair of huge sofas, occupied by two earnest women in twin-sets and tweed skirts. Each is accessorised with a brooch and a broadsheet newspaper. The place exudes tradition, respectability and Celtic pride.

'I phoned ahead,' Tom says to the young woman who greets us from behind a polished counter. 'Two single rooms for Vine, please.'

Having phoned his supplier friend for a recommendation, his next call was to this hotel. I expected a sour-faced landlady and boiled haggis for supper. Instead, we've walked into thistle-tinged luxury.

Tom is explaining to the receptionist why we're arriving without luggage.

'Oh really?' she says, with at least four Es in the word. But her accent is charming. 'And you were going to fly the plane yourself, you say?' Her smile is far wider than necessary.

I glance sideways at Captain Vine. Joey would be flirting back, without a doubt. But Tom's not reacting. Perhaps he gets this a lot.

'Can we eat here tonight?' he asks as he signs the paperwork.

I nudge my credit card towards him but he ignores it.

'You can, sir. The dining room is open until nine.' Still smiling, the receptionist hands over room keys and gestures to the wide staircase. 'Twelve and fourteen, you can't miss them.'

~ ~ ~

By the time we meet for dinner an hour later, I'm feeling distinctly uncomfortable. I keep my head down as we're escorted to a white-clothed table near the window.

'How are you doing?' Tom asks as a waiter brings a basket of crusty bread.

'I'm horribly under-dressed,' I whisper, feeling the glower of the stags' heads on the wall.

Expecting a day of leg-work and research, I wore chocolate coloured jeans, my favourite burgundy boots and a cream jumper. Despite a quick bath in an ample claw-footed tub, using dollops of lavender-scented shower gel to make bubbles, I don't feel much fresher.

'You look fine,' Tom says. 'Some food will perk you up.'

Right on cue, my stomach growls.

The menu offers high-end dishes, with prices to match. It's a good thing I'm due an inheritance, as it seems we've checked into one of the region's best hotels. My room, far from being a poky single, is spacious and beautifully furnished. It has a sweeping view across the front drive to a pine forest half a mile away. The bed is huge, made up with no-nonsense white sheets and piles of pillows, a soft tartan blanket draped across it. The whole deal is a long way from the running-out-of-petrol routine I initially feared.

'Well,' I say, eyeing the alarming choice of dishes which includes rabbit stew and venison casserole. Not a great selection for fans of Bambi. 'This beats flying home in a thunderstorm.'

Tom nods. 'I'm glad you think so. I'm not... this isn't some ruse, you know.'

I swallow the bread in a hurry. 'Gosh, no.'

'Unless you want it to be.' The corners of his mouth turn up.

I sip my water and feel a smile twitch my lips too. I

ignore the sudden thumping in my chest: I must be really, really hungry. 'Any idea what Cullen Skink is?'

At my response, Tom looks away. Did I imagine it, or did he shake his head briefly? He's obviously not used to philistines who can't read a Scottish menu.

Dinner is simple but hearty: tender meat, vegetables bursting with flavour, and more than a dash of booze in the sauces. The unfortunately named Cullen Skink reveals itself as a delicious soup, made from smoked haddock and potato. We follow this with venison sausages for Tom and roast quail for me, so moist it falls off the bone. The portions are huge – more than enough to satisfy anyone who's been stomping the heather all day. By the time we've shared a creamy, whisky-infused raspberry cranachan for dessert, I'm beginning to unwind.

'I barely asked about your meeting,' I say, noticing Tom push the last of the cranachan towards me. 'Did you get what you needed?' There's no way Joey would do that. When it comes to dessert, he believes in every man for himself. I have a grudging admiration for that philosophy.

'It was fine,' Tom says. 'Not as exciting as your day.'

'If I made my day sound exciting, I was misleading you. I'm afraid it was a waste of time.'

Tom gives me a thoughtful look, then glances out of the window. 'The weather's cleared up a bit,' he says. 'Fancy a walk before it gets dark?'

Some air would be lovely, but I'm sure he's just being polite. 'Don't you want to watch the football? Joey's obsessed at the moment.'

He shakes his head. 'Not tonight.'

The hotel's side exit leads us into some formal gardens.

'Why do you feel it was a waste?' Tom asks as we stroll along a gravel path lined by neat knee-high hedges.

I inhale deeply. The air smells different up here: the rain has released a damp, sweet smell of peat. 'I honestly don't know what I thought I'd find. Maybe I had some pathetic notion that grandad was innocent and I could clear his name.'

'Look,' Tom says, 'accidents happen. Cars, boats, planes... Things go wrong. It doesn't mean he was a bad person.'

I sigh. 'I know.'

'Over a thousand people are killed on the roads every year,' Tom continues, 'but plane crashes get more publicity. We find them more shocking.'

Our feet crunch softly on the gravel. I sense him looking at me, so I nod to show I'm listening. But I'm too gloomy to answer.

'So shocking, people develop phobias,' he says. 'I bet Rainbow's never run a class for people scared to get in a car.'

I smile, lifting my head. 'Good point.'

We turn a corner and are now at the back of the hotel. 'Oh,' I say, startled. 'Wow.'

Before us, the formal gardens end in steps down to a lawn, which in turn slopes to a lake. In contrast to the weather report, the sun lazes as a gigantic orange ball above the water.

'That must be west,' I murmur.

Some straggly clouds remain, but, as if in deference, they keep their distance from the sun.

'Bill said this place was worth it,' Tom says quietly.

I let out a breath. 'Is it the Northern Lights? I've never seen them.'

'No. Just everyday grandeur.'

'Look.' I point to the far end of the lake, where a lone swan flies along the water towards us, its wings beating lazily. It's mere inches above the surface and golden light bathes the creature's white feathers.

We watch for a few seconds.

'How does it do that?' I ask.

'Do what?' Tom's voice is husky. He seems mesmerised by the scene too.

'Fly so close to the water. It's magical.'

He smiles. 'Sorry to break it to you, but it's not magic,

just physics.'

'Yeah? I might have guessed.'

'But it's still impressive. It's called ground effect.'

'What?' I'm only half listening as the swan passes in front of us. Then, as it draws level with a little island in the lake, it sticks its feet out to act as brakes. The landing is ungainly, the magic over. I glance at Tom: he's still watching the swan.

'It works for planes too. When something flies that close to the ground, it gets additional lift. Birds know it's the most efficient way to fly.'

'Huh.' I pause. 'Close to the ground, you say?'

'Yeah.' Tom's not looking at the swan any more. In the evening twilight, his face is turned to me. 'Stay true to what you trust, Sophie, and flying is no effort at all.'

Chapter 27

I'm relieved when the sun drops abruptly below the mountains, rather than lowering itself all the way to the lake. My senses are tingling too much to stand here and watch a picture-book sunset with Tom. Even so, as we look out across the water, a gossamer thread of silence hangs between us. You'd miss it entirely, if you didn't know it was there.

'We should go in.' There, I've said it. Whatever unspoken strand was between us, it's gone.

As we pass the dining room, the waiter is bringing coffee to the staid ladies I saw earlier.

'Sir, madam, coffee for you?' he asks. The lilting Scottish accent still sounds foreign to me.

A hot bedtime drink. Only Bella's cocoa could be nicer.

Tom hesitates.

'I'd like one,' I say. 'But you go up, if you're tired.'

'I'm fine.' He nods to the waiter. 'Two coffees, please.'

'And maybe a wee dram too?' The waiter winks.

I shrug. Scotland hasn't been worth the trip so far, why not see what it offers for a nightcap?

'Thank you for flying me up here,' I say, once we're settled in over-stuffed armchairs, a pot of coffee and two crystal tumblers of whisky before us. 'I don't mean to seem ungrateful, I'm just a bit disappointed.'

Tom swirls the liquid in his glass, studying it, not drinking yet.

I lean forward to take a cautious sniff of mine, then dip my little finger.

'Careful,' Tom says. 'That's the real deal, not some pale imitation from Waitrose.'

'Mmm,' I nod, once I take a mouthful and feel it slide from my throat to my toes. 'Bold.' Then I add, 'No, it's more than bold. Brave, maybe.'

Tom picks up his glass and gestures as if toasting me. 'Exactly,' he says. 'To Sophie. Bold and brave.'

'Nope.' I shake my head. 'That's another thing.'

'Another thing what?'

'I'm not sure I have the nerve to try again as an air hostess. I'm thinking maybe I got this bee in my bonnet about grandad as a form of distraction. Or procrastination or something.'

Tom frowns, but his attention is on his whisky. He swallows and licks his lips.

'You're still having doubts about flying?'

I exhale. 'Part of me still longs for the job. I want to travel, obviously...'

'There are other ways,' he says.

'What do you mean?'

'Just that you shouldn't assume that being cabin crew is the only way to travel. You could consider some other options.'

'What, like becoming a pilot, you mean?' I laugh at my own joke.

Tom just smiles, his face unreadable.

'Anyway, it's, um, a neat solution to my current predicament.' I duck my head as I reference my lie.

'Do you... want to tell me about that?' He looks directly at me now, waiting.

I do want to explain things. He's been kind, he's so easy to talk to, there's nothing to be ashamed of. There's just one problem. 'It's...not my secret to tell.'

'You're protecting someone?'

My silence is confirmation. Although I'm staring at my drink, I hear him sigh and sense him look away.

'But about the flying,' I say, wanting to share what I can, 'thanks to you I'm not as petrified as I was.'

'But?'

'But, well, it's complicated. There's Joey for a start –'

Tom's eyes narrow slightly, but I keep going.

'Joey wants me to invest in a photography studio,' I say.

'Well, finance the whole thing, actually.'

'With your inheritance? That's a lot to ask.'

'I know. Obviously I should be happy to help his dream...'

'But he's not happy about yours?'

'No. Now that he knows I never was an air hostess, he thinks I can just forget it and jump into business with him.' Probably as his chief tea-maker, I add to myself.

We've both finished our whisky and without asking me, Tom nods to the waiter to repeat the order. 'What did Joey say about you coming up here?'

I put two fingers to my temple and make little circles.

As the seconds stretch and I don't answer, Tom grins, then tries to conceal the expression. 'You didn't tell him, did you?'

I did consider mentioning the Scottish trip to Joey. But I haven't seen him this week and, when Italy got knocked out of the World Cup yesterday, I knew he'd be in a strop. Anyway, it was only supposed to be a day – a few short hours. Bella and I have taken longer shopping trips. But under Tom's gaze, I have to admit there's more to it. Joey and I are talking a different language these days. I didn't think he'd understand my need to learn about grandad's accident. And I didn't want to spend the energy explaining it to him, while he looked perplexed or accused me of being selfish.

Earlier, after checking in at the Monboddo Arms, I phoned Bella.

'I won't be back tonight,' I said.

'Crumbs,' she replied. 'Are you still in Scotland?'

'Yeah.' I told her about the weather and the hotel.

'How deliciously convenient. You're holed up in a Scottish castle, sheltering from the storm with Tom?'

'It's not like that,' I said.

'I don't care what it's like. You've just sparked the sweetest fantasy for me.'

'Bell –'

'No, don't interrupt. I'm trying to picture Tom in a borrowed kilt. You lucky sod.'

'What about your blind date?' I asked.

'Disaster. Turns out he's from Poland, here to learn English.'

'So? Poles are okay, aren't they?'

'He had terrible teeth, and his English was horrendous. When he mimed that he's a gluten-intolerant vegan, it was game over.'

Poor Bella. Her ideal man can't be a cake-hater. 'Are you okay?'

'Yes,' she said. 'I think I realised, after the thing with Scott, the right guy will come along when he's ready. I can wait.'

'Good for you.' Whoever it was would be a lucky man.

I checked my phone. 'Look, my battery's low. But if Joey turns up there, will you cover for me?'

'Cover for you?'

I winced, realising how that sounded. 'I don't want... drama. Okay?'

'Soph, I hope you know what you're doing.'

'I'm not doing anything. It's all totally proper.'

Bella sniffed. 'In that case, why haven't you said a single word about your grandfather and what you found out?'

'I have to go,' I said, and hung up.

But I can't hang up on Tom, he's sitting right here, looking at me.

'It's probably none of my business...' he begins.

'Right,' I agree, trying to keep my voice light. 'None whatsoever.'

'Seriously, Sophie.' Tom leans forward in his chair and takes my hand. I'm too surprised to move, and just stare down at his fingers covering mine. His touch is firm, yet gentle, and all I can think about is how it would feel if he moved his hand to my wrist, my arm, and higher. But after a moment he looks down too, and lets go abruptly. I keep my eyes averted, scared of what he might see there.

Tom clears his throat. 'What I'm trying to say is, if you can't talk to Joey... what kind of relationship have you got?'

He's right. Of course. But I can't think about that now.

When I risk meeting his gaze, it's full of kindness and friendship. And more. Definitely something more. If he sees the corresponding curiosity in my face, he makes no move, just blinks and gives me a slow, sexy smile. As I sink back into the inferior embrace of the armchair, all I know is that I feel warmer and safer than I have in a long time. It must be the whisky. Oh good, here's the barman with another.

Neither of us says anything for several minutes. I'm watching the fire and I think Tom is too. The flames dance in graceful patterns, a flicker here, a flare there. How can something so seductive, that brings such comfort, be so dangerous at the same time?

As yet more of the amber liquid heats my insides and loosens my tongue, I turn to Tom with an exaggerated frown. 'What makes you such a relationship expert?'

He makes a face. 'Call it the deep expertise that comes from mucking it up.'

'What did you muck up?'

Tom studies his glass. 'I made a mess of my marriage, for starters.'

'What kind of mess?'

He hesitates, shakes his head.

Lorraine mentioned divorce. That would count, I suppose.

'Come on,' I say. 'You know all about my stupid fears and dreams and stubborn boyfriend. Share.'

'You sound like Rainbow.'

'Yeah,' I smile. 'We're doing collage before bedtime.' I rearrange myself in my chair, my head rocking more than it should as I move. Am I drunk? A bit. But I don't care. 'What sort of mess?' I repeat.

He looks at me, then at the fire. 'I made the crucial mistake of thinking we wanted the same things. We didn't. By the time I realised that, we'd spent so long having different conversations, there wasn't any common ground left.'

'What things? Didn't you want?' Ah, there goes my grammar. Wol would be aiming the chalk by now.

Tom doesn't seem to notice. 'I wanted a family. Victoria kept putting me off.'

Victoria. I roll the name around my whisky-marinated brain and decide she must be fantastically glamorous. I picture the cat-shaped eyes and beauty of Mrs Beckham, then add a Master's degree. I pick a ruthless job, like a venture capitalist or fund manager. Or maybe she's a barrister, striding around the courtroom in a black gown and wig, sharpening her sarcasm for arguments with Tom.

'She didn't want kids?' I say.

'The last two years, I thought we were trying, and she hadn't even come off the pill. She was hiding them in a packet of Weetabix, for God's sake.' The regret in Tom's voice is edged with bitterness. 'It wasn't just that her career came first... her career was everything.'

Mentally, I promote Victoria from barrister to high court judge.

'But – you'd support her having a career, surely?'

'Of course I would. I did. I sweated buckets, helping her get the salon ready to open.'

'Salon?' I say in surprise.

Tom gives me a strange look, but continues. 'She's a hairdresser. A good one. She said she'd worked too hard, winning loyal clients, to disappear to have a baby.'

A giggle escapes. 'Sorry,' I say. 'I was picturing her as a judge.'

'A what?' He looks incredulous. 'Where did that come from?'

'Sorry,' I repeat, trying to look serious. 'I'm really sorry.' I clamp my hand over my mouth so nothing else slips out.

From nowhere, Tom laughs. 'You're nuts,' he says. 'Nuts. But I like you.'

I wriggle, certain now I've had too much to drink, not

daring to say or do anything.

'All I'm saying is,' Tom continues, 'once you lose honest communication, it's like a piece of furniture with woodworm. It looks fine, it seems solid, but it's full of holes. One good kick, and it crumbles.'

There's a pause. I forget to keep my hand glued over my cakehole. Before I know it, a fresh thought is trying to get out. 'But –'

Tom looks at me and waits. He hasn't finished his second whisky, he's had the sense to take it slowly.

'But I've seen the way women are around you,' I say. 'If you want to settle down and start a family, they're queuing up.'

One eyebrow goes up. 'No...'

'They are,' I say. 'Rainbow was constantly making eyes at you. The young lass on the reception desk would take you on a tour of the heather right now. And Bella –' I stutter to a halt.

The other eyebrow joins the first. 'I'm pretending I didn't hear any of that,' he says.

''S no secret. They all fancy you,' I say stubbornly. 'Bella said you'd look really sexy in a kilt.'

Tom's eyes widen but he inclines his head graciously. 'Well, that's, er, very kind of Bella.'

I'm annoyed that he's no longer perfectly in focus. 'Bella would make a brilliant wife. She wants lots of kids. Oodles.'

Tom lifts a hand. 'Whoa,' he says. 'I never said lots. Just one or two.'

'She'd be brilliant,' I say again. 'Let's call her.' I pat my pockets, looking for my phone, which I can't find because it's in my room, charging.

Tom finishes his whisky and puts the glass down on the table. 'Let's not call her. Let's think about getting you to bed.'

But I don't take the hint. 'No,' I say, 'You have to call Bella.'

'I don't,' Tom says. With one smooth movement, he's on

his feet and has pulled me up too. The blood makes a gravity-driven exit from my head and now I'm seeing double. With legs like a rag doll, I sway sideways.

'Whoops,' I say, then 'Thank you much,' as he prevents me making an undignified nose dive back to the armchair. His hands are holding my upper arms firmly as I persuade my head to stop lolling. 'Why won't you call Bella?'

'Because,' Tom says, moving one hand to my back and stepping closer as he starts to steer me across the lobby, 'if you must know, I think I've fallen for someone else.'

Chapter 28

We're at a small crossroads. To our left, on higher ground, is a chapel. The graveyard sits to one side, and from the angle of the stones, I sense it's been there for several centuries. Ahead, the road peters out into rough ground. There's a playing field, with football goal posts. And to the right, nestled behind a stone wall, is the school.

'Are you sure about this, Sophie?'

'Yes.' My voice is clipped. 'Absolutely. I am.'

'Right.' Tom pulls across the junction towards the rough parking of the playing field.

Before he's even switched off the engine, I'm out of the car, tugging my coat tighter as the breeze nips. On the school's roof, its weather vane points north.

~~~

This morning, I woke with a brain as misty as the Monboddo Arms. At least I didn't drink so much last night I can't remember undressing myself. It was definitely me, and I was definitely on my own.

At breakfast, Tom made conversational efforts, but got little response at first.

'I don't suppose you want the kippers?' he said.

My throat tightened and I shook my head. But I did manage some orange juice, followed by coffee and several pieces of plain toast. Tom, meanwhile, made light work of a full Scottish breakfast.

Today, we've both climbed back into yesterday's crumpled clothes. Tom hasn't shaved, and the stubble adds an interesting dimension to his face. He's normally so clean-cut, it gives him a rebellious air.

'So,' he began, when I started to answer his questions, rather than grunting, 'there's good news and bad news.'

I looked at him, cradling my coffee cup. Strangely, the sentence didn't annoy me, like it usually does. 'Go on.'

'The good news is, the weather looks like we can get home today.'

'Great. And...?'

'But I'd like to leave it a few hours. Maybe set off after lunch?'

'No problem.' I was glad of a few hours before getting airborne. I didn't want to thank Tom for this trip by imitating Fergus and throwing up in the plane. 'Have you more business with your supplier?'

Tom shook his head. 'I wondered if you'd like to go to the newspaper office? In Aberdeen?'

I reached for the coffee pot again. 'That's so kind. You don't have to do that.'

'Not really. We've got some time to kill.'

I didn't know if the newspaper would be open to visitors on a Saturday, in its new Aberdeen office. But I did have another idea. I trapped my tongue between my teeth, then decided I might as well ask. 'In that case... would you mind if we went somewhere else?'

~~~

With no school today, the building is deserted. From the road, there's nothing to see, just a wide single storey, with a gable at each end. There are two breaks in the wall, two rough paths leading to the building, and two identical front doors. Etched above one, in the stone, I see *BOYS*. I walk a few paces and make out the matching *GIRLS*. The building looks too old to have been damaged by a plane. If it had been rebuilt, it wouldn't wear this dignity, would it?

Beyond, there's a larger gate, providing access to a shed in the school grounds. As if following an invisible yellow brick road, I lift the metal handle and the gate swings open.

I cross the tarmac, where a few weeds poke through, and round the corner of the building. This is more like it. Back here, there's a playground, with faded paint marking the lines for netball. On one side stretches a new wing of the school, forming an L-shape. It's a dreary box, with no attempt made to blend with the original architecture. On the adjacent side of the netball court is a bicycle shed, painted dark green, empty except for a couple of abandoned bikes. One's missing its saddle and the other, a front wheel.

All this, I absorb in mere seconds, before I notice the corner where the bike shed doesn't join the school. Like the gap in a toddler's smile, the hole is arresting. I cross the playground in a few strides, pulling up short as if I'd arrived at a cliff face instead of a wooden bench under a slender tree.

I lean in to read the brass plaque:

Phoebe Buchanan. 12 November 1983.

Is this it?

'Sophie?' Tom's low voice comes from several yards behind me.

I don't turn. 'Is this... all there is?'

Tom clears his throat. I'm still staring at the bench. It looks new, or at least newish: the varnish is fresh, and unlike the rest of the school's surroundings is unscuffed, free of chewing gum stains and whitewashed graffiti.

'It's a seat,' I mutter. 'It's a bloody seat.' There's a metallic taste in my mouth.

My legs shake, but the last place I'm going to sit is the bench marking the spot where my grandfather's plane smashed into the ground. I sink to my knees and bow my head. But I'm not praying. I'm weeping.

'Hey.' An arm goes around my shoulders. Through my tears, I see Tom's feet and knees. Then he's down on the damp tarmac beside me. 'Hey, Sophie.'

'They put up a seat.' I don't know if he hears through my sobs, but it doesn't matter. What had I expected? A marble obelisk? A rose garden? Edinburgh castle? 'It was a horrible accident,' I say. 'Two people died. And all they did was put up a seat.'

'Look... come here.' Tom puts the slightest pressure on

my shoulder and I allow myself to cave towards him. I bury my face in the stiff waxed cotton of his coat. 'They didn't even list his name.'

'Shh. It's okay.' Tom has both arms around me and I'm holding onto the front of his jacket as if it's a parachute in my own plane disaster. 'It's okay,' he says again.

I don't know how long we sit there, but eventually I'm aware of wet Scottish tarmac soaking through my jeans. As my sobs become gulps which in turn become sniffles, the circles Tom's rubbing on my back get smaller and then stop.

'Here,' he says, handing me a tissue.

'Thanks,' I sniff. 'Sorry.'

'Don't be,' he says quietly. 'I expect coming here made it more real.'

'Yeah,' I whisper. 'I guess.' Was that it? Had I not believed it, until I saw that pathetic wooden bench?

Tom shifts on the ground beside me. Much as I'd like to, I can't hide in his jacket indefinitely. We'll both catch rheumatism or whatever it is you get from sitting on damp ground. I start to pull away, but there's a tug of resistance which makes me look up. His brow is furrowed and his eyes are darker than peat as he leans towards me.

My grip tightens on his coat. The comfort of another human's touch is irresistible.

Then he pulls away, shaking his head as if to get water out of his ears. 'Sorry,' he says, clambering to his feet. 'I'm sorry.'

He pulls me up with him. I'm filled with a rush of loss, which I attribute to a twenty-seven-year-old plane crash. Biting my lip, I turn away. Without a word, I cross the playground, back towards the road, wanting to put some distance between me and the place my grandfather died.

Half running, I reach the car. But I don't want to wait for Tom, get in the vehicle and make conversation. Was he about to kiss me? He might simply have meant he was sorry about the crash. And I practically flung myself at him. On top of that, I've just found the indisputable evidence of my grandad's fatal recklessness.

I circle the car and continue my ungainly lollop to the football field, where I head down one long side of the pitch, past the groundsman's shed. From here, there's a view to distant mountains, tinged purple grey with heather. Half a mile away, some shaggy-coated cattle stand motionless. There's a light wind and the sun is toying with coming out from behind the clouds. I take a few lungfuls of air and feel my pulse slow. There's no sign of Tom; he's correctly deduced that I want to be alone.

Except I'm not alone.

I sense the old man before I turn and see him, leaning on a walking stick. He's beside the shed, hidden from the direction I came. He looks at me steadily from under a flat cloth cap, his features brown and wrinkled. A black dog – a Labrador, maybe – sits impassively beside him.

'Fine day,' says the man, and resumes tugging on his pipe.

I feel a prickle of irritation. Where does a girl have to go to be alone these days? And in my opinion, the weather is far from fine. If this is summer, the Scots can keep their hills, their haggis and their heather. Still, I nod back.

'I saw you over at the school, lassie.' The man speaks again. 'Nobody there today.'

I have to concentrate to catch his words; his accent is thick and he's several paces away, downwind. I shrug and nod again. If he saw me, he saw me. I wasn't doing anything wrong.

'You're an old pupil, are you?'

'No.' I glance past him now, towards the car. Tom is leaning against the bonnet, looking off into the distance. He can probably see me out of the corner of his eye. He made the right call to give me a few minutes alone. Pity this old chap couldn't do the same.

The Labrador yawns and flops at the man's feet. The dog's master sucks on the pipe again, the breeze whipping the smoke away. With the wizened face scrutinising me, I decide I should go. I'm not in the mood for pleasantries.

As I pass the pair en route to the car, I duck my head. I'm pretty sure my eyes are red.

'So you're not here to remember someone, then?'

I jolt to a halt and look sideways.

'Aye,' he says. 'I saw you, looking at the bench.'

Now, I do face him, and something in his stance reminds me so sharply of Wol, I catch my breath. The sweet tobacco smell, less offensive than cigarette smoke, finds my nostrils now.

'I told you. I wasn't a pupil,' I say. 'I've never been here before.' I hear a shake in my voice.

'Aye,' says the man again. 'I believe you, lassie.' Still those beady eyes are on me. 'Well, well,' he says, gnawing on his pipe with apparent satisfaction.

Well, well, what? I think, glancing towards Tom again. He's looking this way now, watching my encounter with this ancient character. But he doesn't move from beside the car.

'Okay, well, it's time I was off,' I say to the old man. This is more courteous than our conversation requires: I could stalk away without another word.

'Right you are, Miss Campbell.'

My feet stop first. Then the wind goes out of my lungs, and finally my head yanks towards him.

The beady eyes are positively twinkling now. 'You are, aren't you?' he says. 'One of the Campbells?'

Wordlessly, I nod.

'I thought so.' He takes his cap off and holds it to his chest in an old-fashioned gesture which hits me in the ribs. 'Aye,' he says again. 'I thought so.'

My skin tingles.

He replaces his cap and begins to walk in my direction. Matter of factly, he says, 'You'll be wanting a cup of tea, I expect.' He whistles to the dog, which struggles up and plods along too. As the old man reaches me, he offers me his arm. I take it, not sure who's the stronger of the two of us. We walk towards the car.

Chapter 29

His name is Dougal. I spend most of the visit calling him Mr Dougal, but I think in fact it may be his Christian name. For a while, I wonder if he's perhaps a family relative, but it turns out he's simply lived in Strathblae all his life.

Tom stiffens perceptibly as the old man, his dog and I approach the car. And although he doesn't comment on the strangeness of the invitation to tea, I do catch the lift of one eyebrow. There's also no question, I find, of me going alone with Dougal.

His house is tiny – not even a cottage, more of a bothy. We fall off the main street directly into a small sitting room which contains a brown three piece suite, a fireplace and a television smaller than most microwaves. Tom follows wordlessly behind the Labrador, Murphy Grace, and suddenly our host's room is uncomfortably full.

The walls are thick with commemorative plates, including Queen Elizabeth's coronation and silver jubilee. There are royal wedding plates too, including Margaret, Anne, and – no surprise – Charles and Diana. But nothing since. No clean patches which might belong to the disgraced Fergie, nothing for Edward and certainly no sign of William. Whoever adorned this home with Britain's monarchy stopped shortly after 1981.

Murphy Grace watches as we settle ourselves, then lies down by the fire, chin resting on his front paws.

'I will nae tease you, lassie,' the old man says, as he places three mugs of tea on a wobbly coffee table. 'I'll get straight to it.'

With that, he proceeds to tease me tortuously, explaining that my questions in town yesterday caused speculation, my interest in the crash heralding our arrival at the school. 'Morag thought you were a Buchanan,' he says, eyes dancing again. 'But I guessed Campbell. Would you like a biscuit with that?'

I shake my head and adjust my perch on the brown and lumpy settee. The tea is the same dark colour, but fortunately I haven't come across any lumps yet. 'You remember it?' I ask. 'You were here?'

He nods. 'It was a terrible day for our town.'

I don't dare speak. Guilt wells inside me and I look at Murphy Grace.

Tom clears his throat. 'Can you tell us what happened?'

Dougal turns to him. 'You're the husband, laddie?'

Despite my preoccupation, I squirm.

'No,' says Tom, without embarrassment. 'A friend.'

'Well,' Dougal says. 'You know the facts, I expect. Hamish Campbell was the pilot. He lost control and crashed into our school.'

I force myself to look up.

'You've seen the seat,' the old man continues, looking at me. 'You know we lost a brave young woman.'

'I'm...' I want to say I'm sorry, but can't utter the useless, insulting words. Instead, I ask, 'Did the children recover?' They were just eight years old. 'Eventually, I mean?'

To my relief, Dougal gives a slow nod. 'They did. Eventually.'

Tom speaks again. 'Do you know what caused the crash, sir?'

'Aye,' Dougal replies. 'A bit of weather, a bit of something else.'

'Something else?' Tom asks, after a pause.

Dougal exhales and takes a long slurp of tea. I follow the gesture, but it's still too hot and burns my tongue.

'Lassie... Sophie,' he says, addressing me now. 'Our town suffered a devastating blow that day.'

I close my eyes. This is horrible. What did I expect, showing up here, as his granddaughter?

'But I think you would nae be here if you weren't suffering too.'

As these words register, I open my eyes again. He's looking at me with wise compassion. I risk a nod, pressing my lips together to stop them wobbling.

'Aye,' he says.

'They told me it was a car crash,' I blurt. 'I didn't know. I was even younger than... than them.'

Dougal reaches down to scratch the dog's ears.

'Mr Dougal,' Tom says quietly, 'you said there was another factor in the crash.'

The old man smiles to himself. 'I've been on God's earth more years than I care to admit,' he says. 'And I've learned, some things are so ironic, they'd drive you mad if you let them. Some folks, they do go mad from it.'

I glance at Tom, who shakes his head. What is Dougal talking about? Please, I think, don't let him be soft in the head. I couldn't stand it if he doesn't actually know anything.

But he does.

'The plane...' Dougal says slowly. 'There was some maintenance... The book... what do you call it...?'

'The log book?' Tom supplies.

'Aye. The log book. The book was wrong.'

'Wrong?' I leap on this. 'What kind of wrong?'

'Och, I dinnae ken,' Dougal says. 'Does it matter?'

I look at Tom. Does it matter?

'No,' Tom says to Dougal. 'Go on.'

Dougal turns to me. 'Your grandad should nae have taken the plane.' I hold my breath as he continues. 'But there's no way he could have known it wasn't fit to fly.'

There's absolute silence in the room as I think about this. 'Why... wasn't that reported?' I say faintly.

Dougal sighs. 'Ah, what harm can it do now?'

The seconds crawl by while we wait for him to continue.

'The mechanic who signed the book was Jock Buchanan. The previous winter, he lost his wife in childbirth. Left him with four wee bairns. The man was out of his mind with grief.'

Tom processes this first. 'This... mechanic... you're saying he wasn't fit to be at work? He made a mistake?'

'Aye, sonny. That's what I'm saying. A howling great mistake. It was pretty clear to us, this lassie's grandfather would nae have taken that plane up, if the book had been right.'

'But – why was he at work, if he wasn't fit?' I fail to keep the edge out of my voice.

Dougal looks impatient for the first time. 'I told you. He had four little ones. How else was he supposed to put food in their mouths?'

So, my grandfather was foolish and irresponsible in borrowing the plane without permission. But he couldn't have known it was a deathtrap. I feel tears welling. Tears for grandad, for the teacher who died.

But Tom's brain is working better. 'Buchanan,' he says slowly. 'Mr Dougal, the name on the bench was Phoebe Buchanan.'

Dougal smiles grimly. 'Clever lad,' he nods. 'I was thinking the brave young lassie here would spot that, but in fairness, she's got a lot on her mind.'

I stop snivelling for a moment to focus on their conversation. Dougal reaches into his pocket and passes me a handkerchief – a real one, and clean too. I take it gratefully, mop my face, then look at him.

'The same name?' I say stupidly. Were they related?

'Aye,' Dougal looks from me, to Tom, and back to me. 'And there's your answer, for why it wasn't reported.'

Once again, I have to remember to breathe. As I wait, Murphy Grace gets up from the hearth and comes to sit beside me, pressing against my leg and nudging his chin onto my knee.

'The Buchanans lived in this town.' Dougal speaks slowly but clearly. 'Jock worked at the base, but he lived here in Strathblae. He'd already lost his wife, and his grief lost him his sister too.' The old man meets my gaze defiantly. 'The townspeople decided it would do those four children no good to have their father thrown into prison. We closed ranks, Sophie Campbell. For the good of those Buchanan bairns, we kept quiet. We sat back, and we said nothing. We let your grandfather take all the blame.'

Chapter 30

'Wow,' says Tom as we drive back towards Dundee.

The clouds have finally cleared; the atmospheric pressure has lightened, along with the crushing in my head. I don't answer for a moment as I blow out through barely parted lips. Then I say, 'Yeah. Wow.'

'Are you... okay to fly?'

It's a reasonable question, given my recent obsession with plane crashes. I wait for the fear to tighten, for the terror to hit between my eyes. Nothing. Slowly, I nod, looking from side to side as if the demons might ride in from our flanks instead. Still nothing. Then I look at Tom. 'Yes,' I say. 'Yes, I am.'

~~~

Tom drops me off in Saffron Sweeting High Street. In contrast to Scotland, it's puddle-free and several degrees warmer. I walk a few yards past the post office, where there's a large sign in the window offering spaniel puppies to good homes, then I call Kit.

'It was incredible,' I tell her. 'Grandad was definitely at fault. But there was so much more to it than that.'

She listens, doing a good impression of sounding truly interested. It's different for her: she wasn't born when it happened.

'That's wonderful,' she says. 'So you're glad you went?'

'So glad.' I sigh. 'Things make much more sense now. I think, even as a tiny tot, I had an inkling.'

I would love to confront mum. I see now that I suspected something terrible had occurred, and I translated that into a paralysing fear of flying. Except, of course, mum can't know I was afraid to fly. If I tackle her about grandad, there's every danger I'll reveal that.

'Even Stanley,' I say. 'It turns out he's another of Wol's waifs and strays.'

Just when I thought nothing else Dougal said would surprise me, he'd revealed that Phoebe Buchanan owned a young parrot, trained to say her name. After the accident, the bird pined for his owner and kept repeating it – *Phoebe, Phoebe, PHOEBE.*

'The family could nae deal with it,' Dougal said. 'Another week, and Phoebe's father would have wrung that bird's neck.'

Stanley hadn't been ordering us to hurry up and feed him. He'd been calling for Phoebe, even after all these years.

'So Wol adopted the parrot?' Kit asks now.

'Yup.' I wonder if we'll ever know all the good things Wol did. If I try until I'm ninety, I'll never be as noble as her. 'They thought Stanley might enjoy living with another teacher.' I'm outside the library now and notice an apple tree. Stanley would love a branch from that: I'll see if I can scrounge one from Kenneth.

'And the trip back?' asks Kit. 'Was it... better?'

'Loads,' I say. 'I was still jumpy, but it was okay. Tom made me help.'

'Help?' Kit sounds a tad alarmed.

I laugh. 'Not hands on. He made me look for other planes and call out their positions.'

Actually, it was fun, using the hours on a clock face to describe to Tom the relative position of other air traffic. I've a feeling he knew perfectly well where everything was before I said it, especially since I kept mixing up ten o'clock and two. But it kept me from freaking out about every little change in engine noise, and before I knew it, we were making the descent over East Anglia.

'At one point, he had me dial in a radio frequency, ready for the next changeover with air traffic control. It was cool.'

Kit gives a whistle. 'So, is there anything standing in the way of your career as an air hostess now?'

I cross the road. 'I guess not. No. I can't think of

anything. I'm going to start applying tomorrow.'

'Cool,' says Kit. 'Well done you.'

~~~

I wish Bella wasn't out with work friends tonight. I would love to relive my trip to Scotland – from Morag to Dougal, the swanky hotel to the sad little school, from my flying terror to the cautious comfort I'd felt beside Tom on our way home. But an evening alone with my thoughts will have to do.

So, as I crunch up the gravel driveway, I'm surprised to see lights on. Then I notice Joey's Volvo. Bella must have let him in. Well, okay. Joey will keep me company, maybe phone for pizza while I have a bath, then I can give him edited highlights of the trip. I recall Tom's views on honest communication, but push the thought aside. Joey will be glad for me, even if I don't tell him everything. He doesn't hold grudges.

I don't call out as I open the front door. If Stanley's asleep, it's best that he stays that way. The house is quiet; Joey's probably playing the latest game on his phone rather than watching television.

'Hey, Joe,' I call softly as I put my head around the sitting room door. 'I'm back.'

Nothing. That's strange. I walk into the room and find it empty, but then catch a movement in the kitchen. Of course. He's peckish and is snuffling through the fridge.

Except it isn't Joey scavenging for a snack. And I'm pretty sure that this stranger *hasn't* just hopped out of Bella's bed. I deduce that because the person with their back to me, standing on tiptoes to reach the cupboard where we keep the breakfast cereal, has slender ankles and toned, hair-free calves the colour of butterscotch. Above the naked calves are equally naked thighs, devoid of cellulite. These, in turn, disappear under the hem of a cream babydoll nightie, short enough for me to see its owner isn't wearing any knickers.

'What the f–,' I yelp. Yes, far from eloquent, but I have, after all, just found a blonde bombshell stealing my Alpen.

'Oof!' She twirls around, a hand flying to her collarbone. 'You scared me!'

The front view is even more stunning than the rear. I take in a pretty, heart-shaped face above an ample chest which is stretching the front of the lace-trimmed negligee. Her rosebud lips pout. 'Who are you? Are you September?' She looks me up and down.

What kind of name is September? 'I live here. Who the hell are you?'

But before she can answer, another voice calls from behind me. 'No carbs, hon! You know they go straight to your hips.'

I spin around. Cripes, another one. A redhead. And oh my God, she's topless.

I'm no prude. I've done my share of youth hostel showers, girl guide tents and, yes, strip poker at student parties. But there's something about a pair of wobbling nipples advancing across the living room – right past Stanley's cage, for heaven's sake – that I find deeply unsettling.

'What the bloody hell's going on?' I shriek. 'Is Joey here?'

Duh. Of course he's here. But why is he using my house for this orgy?

The redhead grins. 'He didn't tell us more girls were coming. Hi. I'm July.' She puts out a hand – a surprisingly formal gesture, for someone with no top on.

Instinctively I shake it, then immediately want to kick myself. Or her. Julie, or whatever her name is. I force myself to look at her lightly freckled face rather than her breasts. She has ridiculously green eyes. They won't look so good when I've scratched them out.

'I don't believe it,' I stutter. 'I don't bloody well believe it.'

The first girl frowns. 'Are you all right?'

Let's hope the wind changes and she gets stuck like that. 'No! I am not sodding all right! How many more of you are upstairs?'

Is the bastard using my bed? That really would be the pits. I'll have to burn my bedding. And maybe the bed too.

'We're not upstairs,' supplies the redhead helpfully. 'We're in the garden.'

Tears and outrage fight for the upper hand. 'The garden? Brilliant. Bloody brilliant.' Great. A Midsummer Night's Nightmare. And I'm the ass.

The first one, the blonde, has her hand inside a packet of Frosties now, but has yet to eat any. 'Is this your first job?' she asks nervously, hoisting herself up to sit on the worktop. The negligee is centimetres away from revealing everything.

'What?' I snap, and swipe the first tears away.

'Your first paid job,' says Julie. 'You seem a bit tense.' As she shrugs her shoulders, her breasts jiggle.

'He's *paying* you?' For Pete's sake, my boyfriend can't just cheat on me? He has to bring in two call girls? 'Jo-ey!' I throw back my head and scream his name. 'Get in here!'

He's there in seconds. 'Sophia!'

Something about his expression is wrong. Yes, there's surprise, but mild, not the all-out shock I expect to see. And no guilt. No horror, no appreciation that he's in the biggest trouble of his life. And he's dressed. Not dressed in the hurried way you might expect, with shirt buttoned wrong and missing socks, but properly dressed, down to his trainers. He looks at the three of us, then takes a hint from the blonde, who jerks her head at me and pulls a face.

'Oh!' he exclaims, coming towards me. 'You're upset.'

'Upset?' I screech, lifting my hand to wallop him. But the nimble little sod jumps back, colliding with the redhead who squawks loudly. I'm treated to a view of the two of them in a tangle of flesh as they steady each other.

'Of course I'm bloody upset!' I'm practically yowling. 'Get your hussies out of my house!'

'Hey!' says the blonde, cramming a handful of Frosties

into her mouth as she jumps down from the kitchen counter.

'And get yourself out too!' I snarl at Joey, ignoring her. I turn on my heel, pausing only to grab my keys. 'You've got ten minutes. If you're here – any of you – when I come back, I'll skin you alive.'

I'm not being literal, of course. I wouldn't know how to go about skinning anyone, dead or alive. But it was a threat Wol used about once a term for the most egregious pupils, and I always liked the gory sound of it. But I am clear that if any of these toerags are hanging around when I come back, I'll kick them from here into Suffolk.

'Soph–' comes Joey's voice as I stampede towards the front door.

I don't turn. I can hardly breathe, hardly see, hardly keep my balance. I have to get out of here.

~~~

I've barely slid to a halt on the river bank opposite Uncle Mike's house when Joey catches up with me.

I'm bent over, clutching my knees, both for oxygen and to combat the dizziness. And because I think I might throw up.

From my upside down position, I don't see much more than his feet and shins.

'Sophie! You've got it all wrong!'

The nerve of it. Has he got some death wish in following me, rather than spending the next nine minutes hustling his hussies out of my home? The moment I stop seeing stars and can stand upright, I'm chucking him in the river.

'Go away,' I hiss through gritted teeth.

'It wasn't what you thought!' He's undeterred, the fool. 'We weren't – you know.' Joey pauses and I hear him take a breath as he collects himself. 'I'm shooting a calendar. The girls are my models.'

A calendar. My lungs are still heaving, but the comets swirling through my vision start to clear. A bloody *calendar*?

'My gear's set up in the garden. It's completely above

board. Come back to the house, you'll see.'

Slowly, I straighten. Joey's a short distance away, out of punching range. Smart lad. He's wearing a look of apologetic innocence. Seeing my glare, he holds both palms up. 'I'm sorry,' he says. 'Sorry you walked in and got a shock. I tried to call earlier – your phone was off.'

This is true. Phones and Cessnas don't mix; Tom made me double check my mobile.

'A calendar?' I make an effort to keep my voice steady. If I do choose to push him in the river, I want it to be a surprise.

He nods, squinting. 'Yeah. We were doing July and August. I wanted a nice garden.'

July and August. Not Julie, then: July. And that explains why the other one – the blonde in the silly nightie – asked if I was September.

'That's so sleazy, Joey.' I curl my lip. 'A topless frickin' calendar? Eww.'

A wood pigeon coos from the trees, as if agreeing with me.

Joey looks down. 'I know. Yeah.' Then he looks up at me. 'But it's a job, babe. It pays well. I don't have the luxury of turning stuff down, you know?'

I'm still trying to digest this. Rather than feeling furious for myself, I'm now outraged on behalf of Blondie and Ginger. 'All the same...' I wrinkle my nose. 'It's demeaning. For all of you. Not to mention outdated. Do those things even still sell?'

'Yeah. They do. Big time. Sorry.'

I say nothing. This is seedy and sordid. It's degrading and distasteful.

'Please. Try to understand,' he says.

It's actually kind of pathetic. 'All right.' I fold my arms. 'I get it. I don't like it, but I get it.'

Joey's face clears and he gives me one of his show-stopping smiles. 'Thank you,' he says. Then, deciding it's safe to approach, he takes both my hands in his. 'I'm so glad you understand. I'd never do that to you. I'd never hurt you like that.'

I don't reply. Joey's a good guy. He acts impulsively sometimes, and photography is clearly the true love of his life. But he's got a good heart.

Joey's looking down at our hands now, his fingers twining around mine. 'You get me, Sophia. And I get you. We both know that things are complicated, not always black and white.'

I frown. What's he talking about?

'Sometimes the end justifies the means, right? We're alike in that way.'

Is he comparing making a profit from soft-porn photos to me hiding my grounded state from the world? It's not the same thing. Is it? I've got damn good reasons for people not knowing about that. But I'm distracted by the thought. Have I been too intent on keeping the secret I was trusted with not to realise the unsavoury path it led me down?

Joey smiles gently now. 'You see? We're a great team. I love that I don't have to explain this stuff to you.'

My mind races as I grapple with whether my lies are as bad as Joey's grubby efforts to advance his career. The moral indignation of a few minutes ago has been replaced by a deeper unease. Does my end justify my means?

'I'm not kidding,' Joey says urgently. 'You and me. We're so good together.'

'Joey...' I begin, then trail off.

Under other circumstances, I would have been more alert. I would have stepped back at the right time, cracked a joke, dropped his hands and suggested pepperoni pizza for dinner. But I'm not alert. I'm rattled, distracted by all that's just happened and the new stabbing of my conscience. So I don't pull away, or laugh, or do anything that prevents Joey dropping suddenly to one knee.

'So good together...' he says, still holding both my hands in his, '...that I was hoping you'd marry me.'

Chapter 31

Bella's face is a picture. If I wasn't so churned up myself, I'd enjoy her look, which is best described as equal parts shock, wonder and joy.

'Oh – my – God!' she gasps, pausing for breath between each word. 'Ohmygod!'

She grabs the nearest thing – a tea towel – and clutches it to her chest as she breaks into a smile. 'You're getting married!'

'Hang on,' I say. 'I haven't said yes yet.'

If finding Joey's half-dressed calendar models in the kitchen knocked the stuffing out of me, this is more like bungee jumping and not knowing if the rope is shorter than the distance to the ground. I feel like I'm in total free fall, not sure whether I'll be yanked back to safety and sanity by my ankles or whether in fact my brains are about to decorate the rocks below.

'You haven't?' Bella switches the tea towel to her mouth. She might be about to gnaw on it. 'Oh.' Behind her, my supper – sausages with onion gravy – is abandoned. She dips her head and looks at me with a piercing *tell me more* gaze.

I explain how I walked in on Joey apparently conducting an orgy in our home, and how explanation turned to apology, which then morphed to a proposal as quickly as a camera flash.

'It was so sudden,' I say. 'I had no idea.'

'No idea?' Bella looks disappointed. 'I always thought, if a man was about to pop the question, I'd sort of... know.'

She has a good point. Not that I've spent much time pondering hypothetical proposals. But shouldn't one have an inkling that a relationship is getting to that stage? Shouldn't a proposal be the cherry on the cake, rather than being hit round the head with a black pudding?

'It never crossed my mind he might be thinking about it,' I say.

Bella frowns. 'It is fast, Soph.'

'Yeah.' Almost as fast as those goals Germany just shot past England, to send them home from the World Cup. 'He said we knew each other so well in college, now we're back together, it doesn't feel too quick.' I taste this explanation, still trying to decide if I like it. Is it sweet, or a little salty... or bitter?

'Oh, of course. You were together ages, back then. Well, that makes sense.' She brightens. 'It's actually quite romantic.'

'What is?'

'You know – you were young lovers, it didn't work out, now there's a second chance... almost as soon as he saw you again, he knew you were the one.' She's fanning herself with the tea towel as if Joey's ardour is heating the kitchen.

I look around for a distraction. This seems a good moment to empty and wash Stanley's seed container. Put like that, maybe the proposal wasn't such a bolt from the blue.

Bella's smiling now, but she senses my unease. 'So, what will you say?' she asks, clearly trying to keep her excitement under control. 'Oh my gosh – did he have a ring?'

'No ring.' I shake my head. No surprise there. Despite what Joey claims, deep down I know he wasn't planning this before I walked in on his grubby little photo shoot.

And Bella's still waiting for me to answer the first part of her question. Which is a tad tricky. Even if I knew what I'm going to say, which I don't, it feels right that Joey should hear it first.

~ ~ ~

No. It has to be no.

Joey's a good guy, he makes me laugh, and yes, we were a great couple back in our twenties. But even with that shared history, it's too soon. To accept a marriage proposal, I'm pretty sure I should feel elated, not panicked.

Nonetheless, this is new ground for me. Now, more than ever, I wish I'd read more of the classic novels which Wol loved and Bella was so happy to devour. Surely, then, I'd have some idea of how to turn down a marriage proposal gently and elegantly.

What would Wol suggest? She'd probably laugh. She might even hoot. Then she'd tell me there are times when we need to solve things for ourselves.

Joey must suspect that I'm not about to fall into his arms in a flurry of rose petals. Even if he hasn't proposed to anyone before, having your prospective bride tell you she needs to think about it, then ignoring your calls and texts for two days, is hardly a sign of imminent wedded bliss. But I owe him an answer in person. So when he suggests tea at The Orchard in Grantchester, I agree.

~~~

I have to admit, as locations go for getting engaged, this one takes some beating. Bella would swoon from the setting alone. We're draped in elegant green deckchairs under the fruit trees, within earshot of Rupert Brooke's famous church clock which might possibly still be stuck at ten to three. Smartly dressed waiting staff have brought us tea, scones and little sandwiches, and Joey is actually paying more attention to me than the food. There are a few other customers, probably tourists considering the scary prices on the menu, but the orchard is so large, our shady spot feels private.

I pour the tea, my hands shaking. If I get this over with quickly, I might then be able to manage a sandwich. Assuming Joey doesn't throw the whole lot in my lap, that is.

'Well,' I begin. 'This is a first for me.'

Joey leans forward, which is no mean feat in a deckchair. 'I know I sprang it on you a bit,' he says. He's clearly been dying to speak. 'But I meant it. We're a brilliant team. You and me.'

I take a breath. 'Joey, this is a humongous compliment.' Oops. Not elegant. 'I'm incredibly flattered,' I continue.

Joey flinches. I was right, he knows this isn't a done deal.

'But we really haven't been together long. I had no idea you were thinking in these terms.'

He shakes his head. 'It's been long enough for me. Not this time around, I'll give you that, but before. We were great together. We *are* great together.'

I take a sip of tea. Ouch: too hot. I waggle my tongue, sucking in air to cool my mouth.

'The thing is, Joe, you don't know me very well. You don't know what you'd be getting.'

If he thinks he'd be marrying the same young woman I was in my twenties, he'd be disappointed. I've given up on a few dreams since then, and made some decisions I'm not proud of.

'I know you plenty well enough,' he smiles.

'You don't,' I protest, and as I say it I start to mentally list the people who know me better. There's Kit, of course. Wol – can I still count her? Bella, certainly: she's in on a few of my shady secrets, yet hasn't breathed a word. Rainbow, if only in a professional capacity, knows more about my fears and what keeps me awake at night than Joey. Then there's Tom. I've opened up more to Tom, shown him more of my true emotions than I have my own boyfriend. I frown, remembering the trip to Scotland. Was it really just a few days ago?

'Wanna bet?' Joey's lips twitch. 'You're not as enigmatic as you think, Sophie.'

Enigmatic? I never claimed to be enigmatic, did I?

He takes my silence as a sign to continue. 'So, you don't work as an air hostess. No problem. I haven't told anyone.'

'I'm going to fix that –' I begin, thinking of the applications saved on my computer.

'Really?' Joey remembers the food and pauses to

demolish a dainty sandwich. 'I didn't think you'd want to,' he says. 'Seeing as you're scared of flying. I thought you'd rather work in the studio, with me.'

Oh, shit. What did he just say? I'm suddenly still.

'I'm not as dense as you think, Sophie. I know you weren't hanging around with that pilot chap and the crazy American to help other people. You're terrified of flying *yourself*, aren't you?'

Despite the tea, my mouth goes dry. I try to protest, but no denial comes to me. 'Was terrified,' I mutter. But my voice is feeble.

Joey waves his hand. 'Forget it. I can tell by your face I'm right. And it's no big deal. Makes it easier, though. You can work for me. With me, I mean.'

It's a good job I didn't bite into a sandwich – I would surely be choking by now. And I barely notice his slip about business arrangements. I'm too fixed on what he'll say next.

'And yeah, your mum thinks you went on a big round-the-world jaunt last year. Which you obviously didn't. Whatever.'

There it is. He's rumbled me. He's led me to the gallows, strung me up, and is contemplating the wobbly three-legged stool on which I'm balanced. Any moment now, I'll be twisting miserably in the wind.

But Joey takes another sandwich, his demeanour as pleasant as can be. 'I know more than you think, and it's fine. As long as you didn't spend last year hanging out with al-Qaeda, I don't care.' He chews and shrugs. 'I want to marry you.'

My hands are gripping the sides of my deckchair. Much as I'd like to struggle out of this impractical seating arrangement, surely invented by someone who never went anywhere in a hurry, I'm frozen. I had no idea Joey knew all this. I had no idea he was smart enough to work it out. I completely underestimated him.

'So...' I force my voice to work. I'm no longer thinking about choosing suitable words, I'm having trouble finding any words at all. 'So, are you going to tell her?'

He doesn't ask who I mean. He doesn't need to. He pauses and pours more tea, an agonising process involving milk, teapot and then sugar. I watch each grain fall into his cup in slow motion, as if my secrets are dissolving in the hot water.

'Please,' I say in a half whisper. 'Don't tell her.'

Joey looks straight at me. Something changes in the back of his eyes. 'Why should I tell her? If you're going to be my wife, my first loyalty is to you.'

Is he so smart he's been playing me all along? Or did my reaction give him the final leverage he needed? I'm not sure I'll ever know.

The summer afternoon would normally be full of gentle noises – the trill of birds in the trees, a car on a nearby road, maybe the chime of the capricious Grantchester church clock. But for several seconds, as I count the individual blades of grass at my feet, there's absolute silence.

Then I raise my head. 'And if I'm not going to be your wife?'

Joey blinks hard. 'Don't say that, Sophie.' He reaches to the back pocket of his jeans and pulls out a faded linen handkerchief. He unfolds it carefully, and then moves his hands close, so I can see. Nestled on the fabric, clearly antique but dazzling all the same, is a spectacular emerald ring.

My eyes sting. The ring is so beautiful, so perfect, this whole moment is the stuff dreams are made of.

'Joey?' I plead. I'm going to cry, any second now, but I don't care. 'What if I say no?'

He looks down at the ring, then back at me. 'Well,' he says slowly. 'Well, then you wouldn't be my wife. You'd be... my ex-girlfriend.' He swallows. 'And I suppose your mum is... one of my closest friends.'

There's no triumph in his face, no misplaced satisfaction. Just a determination and a knowledge that he's done it. He's kicked over the hangman's little stool.

Is clinging to him really the only way to prevent my plunge? A hundred thoughts cram my brain. They're buzzing and swarming, fighting for attention. Joey's telling me I have a choice. I can agree to marry him, put my inheritance money into his photography studio, make a reasonable future with a guy I've known for years. A guy who's funny, who gets on with my family, who apparently is more clever than he appears. A guy who knows stuff that I've been trying to conceal from almost everyone around me.

And if I don't marry him, that stuff will come tumbling out. The village will probably shun me. A pity, but I can move. My mother will never forgive me. Well, that's hardly the end of the world. But what will it mean for Kit? Will her university kick her out, if they find out she lied about her gap year? That's what gets me. That's what sets my jaw into a line: the thought of doing that to Kit, always knowing I had the choice, but put my own happiness before hers.

I can't do it. I won't let that happen, not when there's a way of keeping Joey on my side, keeping him contented and quiet.

I glance around the peaceful tea garden. There are a dozen shades of green here, in the grass, leaves and hedges. It's such a pretty colour. Slowly, I turn my eyes to Joey's hands. One more nuance of green: the emerald ring, boasting more brilliance and intensity than any of the other hues around me. The gem has an opaque depth, a beauty no modern ring could match. It holds some secrets of its own. Secrets far worse than mine, surely.

Joey follows my gaze, then reaches for my left hand and inches the ring towards my finger. 'Will you marry me, Sophie?'

I flick my eyes up to his, then look back at the emerald in his hand. 'Yes. Yes, I will.'

Chapter 32

I didn't reckon on the rapture that would engulf my mother on hearing the news. Joey's family, yes: his mother alone made enough noise to bring a restraining order down on their house, and his father kissed me on each cheek before opening a fresh bottle of limoncello.

But my mum is different. I've been so used to hearing how splendidly Kit is doing, and trying to shake off the knowledge that she wishes she never had me, that I've formed a careful layer of insulation around myself. So her reaction is all the more baffling.

'This is weird,' I say as we approach Wol's cottage. The pink hollyhocks seem to lean towards me, eager to hear the news. 'I don't feel right, barging in.'

'We're not barging in,' Joey says, giving three clangs on the door knocker. 'We're going to make her day.'

I look at the heavy wrought iron and can't ever remember using it before. I never needed to.

We went to the bank first, since it's Thursday and the chances were high that mum would be there. She wasn't, and nor were any customers, which might explain the sign on the door announcing reduced opening hours.

Marjorie, however, was thrilled to see us. She leaned so far over the counter I feared the alarm would go off, and Joey got a bonus look down her top.

'Your mum's up at Wol's,' Marjorie said. 'With the American chap. You know, what's his name, Charles. The one who inherited it.'

'Oh,' I said. 'Thanks.' I turned to Joey, hoping this would get me off the hook. 'We can tell her tomorrow.'

But he wasn't to be dissuaded. 'We'll walk over there. It'll only take five minutes.'

Under Marjorie's curious gaze, he propelled me out of the bank, along the High Street, and up the road towards

Wol's cottage.

The front door is opened by the man I remember from the bed and breakfast.

'Sorry to disturb you,' Joey says. 'We're looking for Erica.'

'Sure,' says Chuck. 'She's helping me with a few things.' He backs away inside Wol's cottage – I know it's not hers any more, but to me, it always will be.

Then mum appears, looking surprised. 'Oh! I thought you might be Amelia.'

Joey prods me in the back. 'Tell her, Sophie-kins.' He's grinning, certain of the praise that will cascade down on him.

'We're getting married,' I say simply, and I swear mum's toes leave the ground. Tellingly, she hugs Joey first. Then, of course, she hugs me, and when we step apart, I notice the creases which always seem to rumple her forehead when she looks at me have gone. Then the rest of her face creases instead, and she dabs her eyes with her forearm. It's as if we've announced that not only has she won the lottery, but Sean Connery wants to present the cheque.

'Oh!' she whoops, covering a whole octave in one syllable. 'Oh! You two! You two!'

The front path isn't big enough to hold all of us and she knocks Joey into Wol's lavender bushes. Watching her delight, I have to smile. Although I wonder, if she's like this today, how will she make it through the actual wedding? A bystander might guess she was marrying Joey herself.

'Excuse me,' comes a baritone twang. 'It seems there's something to celebrate.' Chuck looks amused at this rare display of British emotion unfolding on his doorstep. He introduces himself to Joey and I confess to having met him already, at Oak House.

By now, mum is sniffling into a handkerchief and I see Chuck squeeze her shoulder. Either Americans are considerably more generous with their hugs or this isn't the first 'sorting out' session they've had.

'That's awesome news.' Chuck nods approval at Joey.

I feel a flash of irritation: everyone is eerily smitten with my fiancé.

'Isn't it?' Mum puts her arm through Joey's. 'I didn't see this coming, Joe.'

We're agreed on that, at least.

'There's nothing here for a toast,' Chuck says. 'How about we walk on down to the pub?'

'Oh, no, that's okay,' I say, tripping over my words. 'It won't be open yet.'

Chuck looks at his watch. 'Jeez. What time do bars open here, then?'

'Don't be silly, Sophie.' Mum's forehead creases are back. That didn't take long. 'We'll tell Fergus it's a special occasion.'

'But – I haven't told Bella yet. I need to... go home, so I can... tell her.' Feeble, even to my ears.

'Tell her at the pub,' Joey suggests. 'Or call, on the way.'

'Is she going to be a bridesmaid?' Mum asks, but doesn't wait for an answer. 'With Kit? Oh, and your sisters, Joe, that would be perfect. And how about a little niece? We have to have a little one. She can wear ivory, to match the bride.'

Holy mother of hippopotamus. Every molecule of air leaves my lungs. It's been five minutes and already we're up to – what – six bridesmaids? I can't take it. I grind to an involuntary halt in the road outside Wol's cottage. I can't do this. I'm not going to the pub. I'm going to sit down, right here, and refuse to move.

But I do move. Joey's linked one arm through mine and the other through my mother's. She, in turn, has latched onto Chuck, so we're joined in a row, like something out of the Wizard of Oz. They can't make me sing and dance to the pub, but their momentum compels my feet to march. Even so, it's as if my shoes have been swapped. And every step feels like I'm pointing the wrong way.

~~~

Despite my prediction, Fergus is open for business when we arrive at The Plough. And he's clearly decided to stock up with champagne since our flying graduation: he produces an impressive magnum, which he then struggles to open. I see Chuck reach gallantly for his wallet to finance the first of the bubbly, which is generous but also embarrassing, as he isn't related to either Joey or me.

Avoiding the big television, which is now showing tennis instead of football, we troop out into the garden and claim the best picnic table. Mum makes a drama of swinging her legs in their tight work skirt over the bench, and I spot Chuck enjoying the view. I'm not so wrapped up in a bridal bubble that I'm oblivious to what's around me.

More customers are arriving at the pub, taking advantage of the incredibly warm weather. To me, it's oppressively muggy – this can't last without a storm. Fergus is apparently doing a good job of spreading the happy news: a steady trickle of villagers visits our table to express their good wishes. Some are probably only hoping to blag a free drink, but the resulting conversations are so chaotic, I've downed my champagne before I notice.

'I thought something was up!' The bank has been closed all of two minutes, but Marjorie has wasted no time in sniffing out today's gossip. 'Don't you make a lovely couple!' She beams at Joey and me. 'Erica, you're going to have such fun planning their wedding!'

Oh, joy. Maybe I can throw my mum in a room with Joey's and let them duel it out.

'And when's it going to be?' Marjorie asks, without pausing.

'Soon,' Joey answers, at the same time as I say, 'Not for a while.'

He pats my arm fondly and I look down, as stunned as if he'd hit me. Since when did he pat me like a pet?

'They only just got engaged,' Chuck says in his attractive drawl. 'There's quite a bit to discuss.'

I shoot him a grateful look, but his face is neutral as he surveys the pub garden.

Marjorie has her phone out. 'I'm calling Amelia.'

'Why?' I ask.

'Well, silly, you'll need somewhere to live, won't you?'

Mum looks thoughtful, then nods. 'Good point, they will.'

'That's okay,' I say quickly. 'No hurry for any of that. You really don't have to tell everyone, Marjorie.' By which I mean: stop blethering, this instant. I hadn't thought about not living with Bella any more. I look at Joey, hoping he'll back me up.

Surprisingly, he does. 'Yeah, no hurry for a house.'

I smile at him, then sag as he continues, 'Anyway, Amelia's sorting out the paperwork for my new studio. Sophie will have enough on her plate.'

But Marjorie's not interested in that. She'd rather speculate on the wedding, including whether we'll use the Sweeting church, who might do the catering and do we think we'll honeymoon in Italy.

My smile gets stiffer as we are visited by Saffron Sweeting's doctor, then the farmer responsible for the stray puppies. He reports that homes have been found for all of them and they'll be leaving their mother in a couple of weeks. Violet's taking the most mischievous one.

I can't help but wish I'd left my mother at eight weeks too. Suddenly, I'm public property, my low profile blown to bits, and she's loving every minute. Brian from the bakery pops up from nowhere, promising a special price on our wedding cake. I thank him, but the babble is becoming overwhelming. So, when I see Bella advancing across the garden with a cluster of clean glasses in one hand and a bottle in the other, I almost cry in relief. I texted her during the march from Wol's cottage, hinting about 'big news' at the pub.

'Are you okay?' she whispers, after the necessary beaming pleasantries.

I nod, squeezing closer to Joey to make room for Bella to wiggle and jiggle into the gap beside us. We're wedged in pretty tightly now.

'It's just a lot to absorb,' I say as Joey and the others begin to discuss his studio.

'You don't look like a typical bride-to-be, that's all.' Bella speaks close to my ear.

'I'm still in shock. Meanwhile, everyone's launched into wedding planning.'

'Your fiancé looks pleased.'

Fiancé. How did Joey morph from an old college boyfriend into my fiancé? Why didn't I realise the game I was playing, and how did I let the stakes get so high?

'Are you hungry?' Bella asks more loudly, refilling glasses from the fresh bottle of champagne. At least six hangers-on from the village are lurking by our table to have their glasses filled too. This is turning into quite a party. No doubt Fergus will be sending me a bill in the morning.

'Not really,' I shrug, but my answer is drowned by the simultaneous 'Starving!' from Joey.

Mum beams, as if she personally brought him up to be the strong, hungry lad he is today. This is especially annoying as she always looks disapproving when I mention hunger pangs. It's okay for Joey to make a pig of himself, but not her daughter. And she calls herself a feminist.

Bella starts to wriggle. 'I'll go and order something.'

'No,' I say. 'I'll go. I need to spend a penny.'

With much leaning and twisting, which almost deposits me on the grass on my backside, I vacate my spot and head inside the pub. It's a blissful escape. In here, it's cool, dark and quiet. I feel like I've entered the sanctuary of a church. Or, if that's too blasphemous, a wine cave at least.

My eyes are slow to adjust and it's a moment before I spot Lorraine at the end of the bar. She's talking to Fergus and I hear her say, 'I didn't see that coming.'

Then they both look my way at the same time; I'm pretty sure they were talking about me.

'Sophie!' she calls, and comes to greet me. 'Congratulations!'

'Thanks.' I accept her hug, which smells faintly of scones. She holds on a fraction longer than necessary, and I briefly contemplate begging for sanctuary at Oak House. Surely she has a nice gabled room with floral wallpaper, where I could hide for a few days until this hullabaloo dies down? The way this lot is carrying on, you'd think I just got engaged to Prince Harry. Any minute now a Newsnight helicopter will land on Saffron Sweeting's cricket ground.

But no helicopter is needed to broadcast my news. Instead, Lorraine spots someone over my shoulder and beckons.

'There you are!' she calls. 'Look who I bumped into. And Tom, you'll never guess!'

'Guess what?'

I turn, and there he is, giving me a smile so genuine, I feel I've been shaken like a rag doll. I don't know why I'm shocked; he's been in the village plenty of times before. And Tom meeting Lorraine for a drink on a pleasant summer's evening is hardly unexpected. But he's still looking at me, and the smile has reached his eyes. Instantly, I'm back in Scotland, huddled on the damp ground at the school, clinging to him like I never want to let go.

But I don't cling to him. I shove both hands deep in my jeans pockets and freeze as Lorraine says, 'Sophie's got some news.'

'Oh yes? What?' Tom parks himself on the nearest bar stool.

Lorraine doesn't answer immediately. She's suddenly uncertain as she looks from Tom to me.

'What's the news?' Tom asks, still smiling. 'What's Sophie up to now?'

It's Fergus who fills the gap, calling jovially from his vantage point at the end of the bar. 'Our Sophie's engaged, that's what.'

Lorraine bites her thumb. I look from her, to Fergus,

and at last to Tom. He's gone totally still, staring at me. When he arrived I thought he looked healthy and tanned, but I was wrong: he's waxy pale above his white shirt.

I swallow, glance back at Lorraine, then study my shoes. Outside, we hear the first distant rumble of thunder.

That's when Tom finally speaks. 'Engaged?'

I give my shoulders a shake, trying to appear nonchalant. 'Yes.'

'When?' he bites out.

'Yesterday.'

'Joey?'

'Yes.'

'Why?'

What kind of question is that? I stare at him and see his jaw is clenched.

'Why... would you do that?' Tom repeats, softly.

I clear my throat, taken aback by the intensity of his gaze. What's going on here?

Beside me, Lorraine murmurs something and retreats to the end of the bar. I see her put a restraining hand on Fergus's arm.

Tom gets off the stool and takes a step towards me. I take my hands from my pockets and fold my arms.

'Shit,' he says, and I see he's spotted the huge emerald ring.

I fold my arms the other way to hide it. I'm feeling more awkward by the second.

'Why would you do that, Sophie?' he asks again, his eyes raking my face now.

I shake my head. 'Why do people usually get engaged?' It's clearly a rhetorical question.

But Tom supplies an answer. 'Because you love someone,' he says. 'Because you care so deeply about them, being without them is unimaginable. Because they know every one of your hopes and dreams and fears, and they love you anyway.' He takes a breath and I see his chest fall as he continues. 'Because every moment you're apart, you think you'll die from the seconds ticking by until you see them again. Because when they smile at you, you feel like your feet lift off the ground. And when – when you actually get to hold them, it's not just your feet. Your whole body's flying.'

He finishes, but every muscle in his body is still tense.

I don't know what to say. *Hopes and dreams and fears.* There is nothing to say. Deep within me, something starts to unravel.

Someone comes into the pub and brushes past Tom to reach the bar. He blinks and gathers himself.

'So that's what you feel for Joey?' he asks, before his mouth sets in a firm line.

I lick my lips. Joey, my mother, my best friend, half the village, are out in the garden, toasting my engagement. *Feet lift off the ground.*

'Yes,' I say, dragging the word from my lungs.

Tom's eyes are fiery. 'In that case,' he says, 'I think I should be going.' He jerks his head towards the low, heavy door of the pub.

'Okay,' I say, silently signalling, *Don't.*

Tom ducks his glance for a moment, as if checking his body for a gunshot wound. Then he shakes his head, strides towards the door, and is gone.

Chapter 33

'I'm here to sign the papers,' I tell Amelia the next day, shaking raindrops off my hair. 'For Joey's studio.'

I don't believe in peeling a sticking plaster off slowly. Once a decision has been made, I'd rather get on with it, get the pain out of the way in a flash.

'Hello, Sophie.' She looks up from her computer. 'Goodness, darling, you don't look very excited about it.'

I flop down into one of her visitor chairs. The little coffee table is piled high with newspapers and property magazines. Likewise, Amelia's desk looks like there's been an explosion in a printing factory. She's listening to the Wimbledon commentary on the radio: the thunderstorm currently pounding Saffron Sweeting must have passed over London this morning.

'Well, Joey's excited enough for both of us,' I say, keeping my voice light.

Amelia stands, smooths her ketchup-red skirt, then perches on the front of her desk. A pile of paper wobbles as she does so.

'I heard you got engaged,' she says. 'Congratulations.'

'Thanks.'

If one more person asks me when the happy day is going to be, I might lose it entirely.

Amelia lifts one foot off the floor and twirls her shoe. 'It's a big change,' she says casually, as if simply talking about the weather. The rain's lashing against her office window now.

'Yes,' I agree, equally blithe. 'Lucky me.' I rummage in my bag for a pen. 'Lots to do.'

When I find a pen, it turns out to be from the Monboddo Arms. That trip already seems like months ago, not last week.

'You've heard what they say about stressful life events?'

Amelia examines a fingernail, then rubs it with her thumb.

'Huh?' I'm twisting the pen in my hands.

'Getting married, moving house, starting a business. Three of the most stressful things you can do,' she says. 'You've picked all of them.'

'You sound like Rainbow,' I say.

Amelia smirks. 'Well, it's true. Are you sure about the studio?'

No, I'm not sure. I don't want to own a photography studio. I don't want to sink Wol's money into property in Saffron Sweeting. And I don't want to be in business with Joey. 'Absolutely,' I nod. 'One hundred per cent.'

As I wait for lightning to strike me down, I notice the gaps between thunder are getting shorter.

Amelia's expression doesn't change, she just studies me. Meanwhile, the radio commentator is gabbling that someone has broken serve in the tennis.

'So, if you have the papers...' I prompt. For God's sake, can we just get this done?

Amelia inhales and walks back around her desk. A phone starts to ring, but she ignores it as she reaches for a file and starts to thumb through it.

'I was in The Plough that night, you know,' she says.

'Er, last night?'

Did she see Tom? Did she hear something? So much was going on, I can't be sure who was at the pub.

'No.' She pulls a document from the file, peers, and puts it back. 'The night you were telling everyone about your flying lessons. You were singing 'Up Where We Belong', as I recall.'

I clearly need to scale back my alcohol consumption. No wonder half the village has guessed my guilty little secret.

'I only mention it,' she says, 'because then, you really did seem excited. You couldn't stop talking about it.' She pulls the next document from the file, holding it between finger and thumb. 'The flying, I mean. And Tom.' With those last words, she pegs me with a wily look.

I squirm, but don't respond.

'I had a flying lesson once,' she says, looking off into the middle distance. 'A birthday present, from a rather wacky aunt.'

'Really?' That's so unexpected, I'm curious. 'You mean, behind the actual controls?'

'Oh yes,' Amelia says. 'She thought I might take after my namesake, you see.'

I'm not following.

'Earhart.' She gestures with her hand as if it's obvious, dazzling me with her cocktail ring. 'Amelia Earhart. My aunt thought it might be fun.'

'And was it?' I ask, already guessing. 'Fun, that is?'

'Darling, it was an absolute riot. A couple more lessons, I'd have been looping the loop.'

I grin. 'Don't tell Joey. He thinks women belong in the back of the plane, serving drinks.'

Amelia chuckles. 'That sounds like Joey.' She glances down at the paperwork and leafs through a couple of pages. Then she puts it to one side and rests her elbows on her desk so she can prop her chin on her knuckles. 'You remind me of me,' she says.

'Sorry?'

'I never really wanted to be Amelia Earhart. But I did want to be an actress.'

I frown. Where's she going with this?

'Then I met Michael.' She's looking in my direction, but her gaze is out of focus. 'He was ambitious, charming, everyone loved him.'

I begin rolling my Scottish pen up and down my thigh.

'Next thing I know, Sophie, I'm forty-something and divorced, staring at the bottom of a bottle for comfort.'

There's a pause, then I cough and stand. 'I'm sorry,' I say, 'I know you're busy.' Meaning, I want to get this done and get out of here, storm or no storm. 'If the papers are ready, can I sign them now?'

Amelia emerges from her reverie. 'Of course,' she says,

looking down at the contract again. Then she tuts. 'You know what... I don't think these are quite right.' She grins. 'I've been a bit distracted by that delectable Andy Murray. He's playing later, you know.'

Great, I think. The country's gone from football fever into a tennis tizzy.

'Can you pop back tomorrow, darling? We'll take care of it then.'

Fine, I think, as I open the door to step out into the deluge. As long as Amelia shoulders the blame, if Joey finds out I still haven't signed the wretched things.

Anyone would think he's nervous I'm going to change my mind.

~~~

I'm about six inches off the ground, munching listlessly on a complimentary strawberry, when I see him.

I haven't resorted to levitating, at least not yet. But my fear of flying is in danger of being replaced by a fear of wedding dress shopping.

Despite my protests, Joey's mamma has decided it's never too early to start searching for a dress. These things take time, she tells me: I must enjoy the experience and visit multiple shops, some of them twice. When Viviana got married, the dress took sixteen weeks to arrive from Italy and everyone was beside themselves in case it didn't get here in time. His mum, in other words, has a PhD in wedding planning and I am her newest project.

So, here I am, just one week later, in a posh but squashed shop on Green Street. Racks of impossibly long, frothy dresses, all in shades which remind me of white chocolate Toblerone, line the walls. The shop is so snooty we had to make an appointment, but since our little party has effectively filled the premises to capacity, I now understand why. Signora Williams is here, naturally, along with all three Anas. On hearing of this entourage, I dragged Bella into the throng to provide moral support. His family mean well, but this is hardly a day when I want to be steamrollered by a bunch of noisy Italians. And Bella didn't need much persuading. She's been sneakily reading wedding magazines at the hairdressers since she was fourteen.

The resulting rabble is a perfect camouflage for the lack of enthusiasm on the part of the bride. As I'm pushed, prodded and poked – and accidentally pinned a couple of times – my protests get steadily less convincing.

'I just want something simple,' I say as Fabiana and Viviana advance towards me with enough fabric to make a tent at Henley Regatta.

'Could I get a little privacy?' I plead as Luciana yanks back the dressing room curtain to give the entire party, plus two shop assistants, a view of me in nothing but knickers.

'Definitely not strapless,' I protest, seconds before being poured into a boob tube which leaves me literally breathless.

'Oh, So-fi-a! Così bella!' Mamma Joey's declared I'm beautiful about twenty times already today, which would normally be a nice ego boost, but is terribly confusing for poor Bella. Joey's sisters are doing better with their choice of adjectives, but even they've been dropping the B-word occasionally. And I'm deeply alarmed for Fabiana's chances of a successful fashion career: her admiration is directly proportional to the hideousness of each dress. The more vile the silk or satin hanging from my shoulders, the more she proclaims its delightfulness.

'What do you think?' Bella whispers as we consider a simple dress with beading on the bodice, in a soft champagne colour.

'It's not bad,' I admit, looking in the mirror. 'I don't look like death warmed up in this one. How much is it?' I try to reach the tag hanging from the back, but wobble dangerously on my little stool.

Because the dresses are so long, often with a train, the women in the shop insisted I clamber on this low stool each time I try a dress on, to get the full effect. Privately, I suspect their knees are killing them from all that bending and pinning, but so far I've complied. No doubt another reason to start dress hunting early is to give broken ankles time to heal, after brides tumble off the little stool. The shop boosts the chances of that by offering sparkling wine to brides and their henchwomen – sorry, bridesmaids. Thanks to the fizz, the exertion of climbing in and out of frocks which each weigh a ton, and the general lack of oxygen in this silk and satin cave, I'm sensing altitude sickness.

Bella leans close to tell me the price.

'You're kidding,' I hiss. 'Tell me that includes the zeros after the decimal point.'

'Nope,' she checks it. 'It's basically the price of a honeymoon.'

Now I really am feeling light-headed. Did Wol imagine that within a few months of her being gone, I'd be spending her money like this? Maybe if I play along for today, then I can say I want time to look at other options. Then I can sneak off on my own, or at least just Bella and me. Unlike Bella, I haven't spent a lot of time imagining my one-day wedding or the dress I'd wear. But on the rare occasion it did pop into my mind, I thought I might pick up a nice vintage dress, something from the fifties, maybe, with enough freedom for some serious dancing in the evening.

'So-fi-a, you look more perfect than I could imagine!' Mrs Williams' eyes are shining and she clutches Luciana's arm as if about to swoon. 'Do you think this is – the one?' She makes it sound like I've found a golden ticket stuffed in the bodice, making this the dress which will propel me into a lifetime of bliss with her son.

'Umm, it's very nice,' I say, still wondering how I got here and who this person is, in the mirror.

'It's gorgeous.' Bella smiles at Joey's mum. 'But before Sophie makes up her mind, she wants her own mum to see it.'

Bless you, Bell, I think. You are a total lifesaver. From now on, I will let you watch Doc Martin, eat your curries without wincing and always wash up when you cook.

Then I remember that I won't be living with Bella for much longer. Not once Joey and I tie the knot. I swallow and force a smile for my future mother-in-law.

'Sì, of course!' She still looks on the verge of tears. 'Your own dear mamma!' She sniffs, but manages to beam from ear to ear. 'And since you are English, you will have bridesmaids, sì? We are only at the beginning of finding dresses!'

I catch Bella's eye in alarm. She too is looking wary at the suggestion of dress shopping with the Williams family. She has reason to be fearful: tall, blonde, curvy Bella is pretty much the opposite of the dark, slender Anas. There's every risk that a style which looks ravishing on them will turn her into a circus elephant. Don't worry, I try to convey silently. You've watched my back, I'll watch yours.

At the same moment Fabiana discovers the cabinet of bridal garters, and starts pulling out torture instruments decorated with blue lace, I think I spot him. My little stool faces the ornate mirror, but from the corner of my eye I can see the street. I happen to look that way and for a fleeting instant, passing outside the window, I see broad shoulders, floppy hair, and a kind face. Tom.

I feel a tug in the bodice of the dress, as if someone has yanked at the lacing at the back. I have to talk to him. I don't know how he feels about me and I'm not sure if his words in the pub had deeper meaning. But I need to find out.

I topple down from the stool, landing awkwardly and twisting an ankle. The pain is irrelevant. I lollop towards the shop door and jerk it open. Behind me, a protest of Italian and English fills the air. But I don't hesitate. In my bare feet, I scamper into the street, hardly registering the chill of the pavement. Where did he go?

'Tom!' I call. That's him, about fifty yards away, walking briskly in the direction of Trinity Street. 'Tom!'

But the man doesn't turn. I bunch the dress into handfuls and set off at an awkward trot. Dammit, it's ridiculously unwieldy. No way am I buying this one. 'Tom!' I yell again.

The street is narrow and my skirt takes up the whole pavement. A couple of grey-haired women are emerging from Harriet's tearoom; they step aside, nudging each other. Across the road, a Japanese tourist spots me and reaches for his camera. I don't care. I'm closing in on Tom; he must have heard his name, he's pretending to ignore me. Well, fine. But I'm jolly well going to talk to him.

'Sophie!' That's Bella's voice, shouting from behind, but I don't look back. Even in this parachute of a dress, her running speed won't catch me.

A bike comes from nowhere, swerves, narrowly misses a bollard and subsides in a torrent of indignant bell-ringing. My right foot, the untwisted one, registers pain on the uneven cobbles. But I don't slow down.

'Tom! *Tom!*'

As he reaches the corner of Trinity Street, he pauses to look behind him before crossing the road. I'm mere feet away, and I grind to a halt as we make eye contact for a split second.

It isn't him.

Oblivious to the banshee in the wedding dress, the man switches his rucksack to the other shoulder, consults a guidebook, then saunters off towards King's College. I teeter on for a few more paces, then fizzle to a halt outside a shop that's ironically called Up & Running. There isn't even a doorstep I can rest on. In a rustling, defeated heap of dupion silk, the dress and I sink down to the pavement.

With one long sigh, I rest my head on my knees.

Chapter 34

It's not my first brush with the police. During my student days, a slight scuffle during demonstrations was a badge of honour. And you can't ride a bike around Cambridge for years without some over-zealous constable deciding that your lack of lights, or lack of respect for one-way streets, or, occasionally, your lack of sobriety, is worth a few words.

But I don't actually have a criminal record. Otherwise this would be much worse. They hold me for a few hours, while we wait for the woman who owns the shop to decide whether to press charges.

'It's just a misunderstanding,' I plead at first. 'I wasn't trying to steal it. Who'd be daft enough to run off in a wedding dress?'

The desk sergeant has tufty hair and two spots of pink on his cheeks. 'Yes, miss, but you did leave the shop wearing property that isn't yours.'

He seems awkward, probably more used to dealing with drunks from the bus station or wannabe football hooligans.

'I was coming back,' I protest. 'I wasn't wearing my shoes. Who'd make a sprint for it with no shoes on?'

The policeman coughs. 'Some might say that was part of your plan, miss. So you could run faster, like.'

Despite my agitation, I notice he's calling me miss. Can he be sweet-talked, after all?

'Sergeant,' I say, in my most persuasive tone, 'I didn't even have my bra on. What kind of thief leaves their bra behind?'

At this, the two spots of pink spread up to his hairline and down to his shirt collar. He glances at the bodice of the wedding dress, then rips his eyes away as if I might scream police harassment. Immediately, I feel bad for embarrassing him. 'Sorry,' I say.

The sergeant clears his throat.

'I was just trying to catch up with someone. You know, to have a quick word...' I peter out.

'But we haven't been able to verify that, miss, with the gentleman in question.' He looks down at his notepad. Not a tablet or an iPad, but an actual paper notepad. 'You haven't given us his name, either.'

'His name doesn't matter. It wasn't him. It was a tourist.'

The sergeant shakes his head. 'Well, it's out of my hands. Sit yourself down and I'll let you know when there's news.'

The dress and I do as we're told. I spread it around me as best I can, eyeing the hem which looks grubby from its unplanned excursion. There's no way I'm getting this one, now. Never mind. I didn't like it anyway.

~~~

'Oh – my – God,' Bella breathes as I emerge, dressed now in my regular clothes. She brought them from the wedding dress shop, scooping them up from the changing room floor. 'Are you all right?' She speaks as though we're escaping from the mob, not the fine upstanding boys in blue.

'Terrific,' I mutter. 'Thanks. Let's go.'

'Oh my God,' she says again, once we're out in the late afternoon sunshine. 'I'm not sure I've ever been in a police station before.'

'Right,' I say, not listening. I had been wondering who would come to bail me out, so to speak. I'm glad it was Bella, even if this was her first time inside the cop shop. For a while, I was worried it might be mum.

'Look who's here.' Bella points, perfectly on cue, and I stiffen.

Then I relax as I see the figure unfold herself from the low bench where she's waiting.

'Kit!' I call. 'What are you doing here?' She's supposed to be miles away, at a summer job in Melton Mowbray.

'I phoned her,' Bella says. 'I was worried about you.'

I hug Kit. 'You didn't need to come,' I say. 'I was only choosing a dress, not getting married.'

Kit and Bella exchange glances, then Kit speaks. 'Except, from what I hear, you weren't choosing a dress, were you?' Her voice is perfectly level and I'm not sure if she's having a go at me or not.

'Well, since you're here, shall we go to the pub?' I suggest. 'I could use a bloody drink.'

Are they doing it again? That glance thing?

'It's a lovely day. Let's sit on the grass, instead,' says Kit, swinging a paper bag. 'I brought snacks.'

I want to protest, thinking of the nearby Clarendon Arms or maybe The Free Press, but Bella chimes in. 'Super! Let's do that.'

With that, they propel me across the road and onto the grass of Parker's Piece. Kit settles elegantly with crossed legs, Bella lowers herself with a bit more effort, and I flop straight down beside them. I'd rather be knocking back a stiff drink, but it *is* nice to be in the fresh air after the dingy, bleach-scented police station.

Kit reaches into the bag. 'World-famous Melton Mowbray pork pies,' she announces. 'Plus crisps and gourmet lemonade.'

I get a whiff of pastry and decide I'm ravenous.

'Mmm,' I mumble after a few moments. 'S'good.' I flick crumbs off my top. 'So, how are things with you?'

Kit smiles stiffly. 'Fine. Everything's fine with me.' She looks at Bella.

They are definitely up to something.

'Soph,' Bella says, tugging the hem of my jeans to get my attention. 'What's going on?'

Casually, I pick up a bag of crisps and inspect the flavour. 'What do you mean? Nothing's going on.'

'You just got arrested for stealing a wedding dress.'

I snort. 'Pardon me, I did not. I wasn't stealing and I wasn't arrested.'

'Detained, then,' says Kit. 'Whatever.'

'It was a silly mistake,' I say. 'Bell was there, she knows.' I look for confirmation and am surprised by her grim look.

'Why did you run out of the shop?' she asks me solemnly.

I shrug. 'I thought I saw someone. I wanted to talk to him.'

'Who?' asks Kit.

'Does it matter?' I mash the crisp bag between my fingers.

There's a pause. 'Yes, actually,' says Bella.

'All right then,' I say crossly. They're like a pair of annoying wasps. 'I thought it was Tom.'

'Tom,' Bella repeats, with the satisfied look of a cross-examining barrister. She raises her eyebrows at Kit.

I yank at the crisp packet which flies open, showering us in cheese and onion flavoured shrapnel. 'So?' I say again, 'It's no big deal.'

But Bella's still on the case. 'Why did you need to talk to Tom so badly?'

'I don't know.' I stretch my feet in front of me and wriggle my legs. 'I just did.' My voice rises and I'm aware I sound defensive.

Kit scratches her neck. 'Soupie...' she waits for me to look up and acknowledge the nickname, '...why are you marrying Joey?'

'What kind of question is that?' I reach for my drink and take a long swig.

Kit pauses, then speaks softly. 'It's a valid question.'

'Jesus, Kit!' I turn on her. 'You sound like Tom!'

The words fly from my tongue before I can help it. This time, Bella and Kit don't try to hide their wide-eyed looks.

Nobody says anything for several seconds. Then Bella touches me gingerly, as if afraid I might bite. 'We're really worried about you.'

I don't reply. Maybe if I twitch my nose and screw up my face a bit, I can avoid crying.

'It's okay,' Kit says, shuffling across the grass to put a

hand on my shin. 'You don't have to marry him.'

'I do,' I gulp.

Bella speaks. 'No, you don't. Of course you don't.'

I take a long jerky breath. 'I do.' I drag my eyes from the grass and look at Kit. 'He knows.'

The hand on my shin retreats.

'I'm sorry,' I say. 'I blew it. He knows.'

Kit's pinching the skin between her eyebrows. That's her thinking pinch; I've seen her use it before big exams and her driving test.

'Shit,' she says.

Bella begins to fidget, but she doesn't say anything. Beside us, the food lies forgotten.

'What does he know?' Kit prompts.

'He knows I'm not an air hostess,' I say heavily.

Kit sniffs. 'Okay. What else?' She pauses. 'Sophie, what exactly does he know?'

When I don't answer, she carries on. 'Does he know about last summer? That I was – in the village?'

I frown. 'I don't think so. He hasn't mentioned it. But he knows I'm terrified of flying.'

Was terrified.

Bella clears her throat. 'Several of us know that,' she says tentatively. She's clever enough to realise there's a sub-text here, but too curious to keep out of it.

Kit's biting her thumbnail now. That runs in the family. 'Has he told mum yet?'

I close my eyes.

'Well?' Kit demands. 'Has he?'

Miserably, I shake my head. 'He says he won't, as long as...'

Bella's looking from my sister to me, clearly puzzled.

Kit, however, sets her jaw. 'As long as what?' she says slowly.

My nose is twitching for England. But it's no good. A fat tear rolls down my cheek. 'As long as I marry him.'

Bella gasps. 'I don't get it. What's going on? Why is Joey

blackmailing you?'

Kit ignores her. She scrambles to her knees and leans over me. 'Soph,' she says, urgently.

I don't look at her, and she squeezes my shoulder to get my attention. 'Listen,' she says again. 'You do not have to marry him.'

'Yes, I do.'

'No, you don't.' Her voice is steely.

By now, Bella looks like red ants have invaded her knickers. 'Will someone tell me what the fuck's going on?' she explodes.

I'm startled into looking at her. I don't think I've ever heard Bella use the F word before, not even when we were trapped in that cave and thought we might drown. Shocked, I find my tongue.

'Mum thinks Kit and I went round the world last year. If Joey tells her about my flying phobia, she'll know we didn't really go.'

Bella flaps both hands, clearly exasperated. 'And? So?'

'She can't know we didn't go anywhere,' I say, looking at Kit.

'Why not?' Bella's infuriated. 'What did you do instead?'

My eyes fill again. Bella tuts, then follows my gaze to my sister.

'Don't,' Kit says, changing tack. 'Don't marry him. I won't let you.'

I stare back miserably. A silent conversation passes between us as our pact unravels silently.

'She'll hit the roof,' I say eventually. 'More than the roof.' I swallow. 'She'll go into total bloody orbit. She'll probably never speak to us again.'

Kit shivers. 'We'll handle it,' she says. 'We'll manage.'

I give an inappropriate gurgle of a laugh. 'But you're her golden girl. You can do no wrong.'

'I don't care.' Kit's eyes are glistening now too. 'We'll manage,' she repeats.

Bella sniffs and looks like she might weep as well.

Soppy old thing: she doesn't even know what she's crying about. 'For pity's sake,' she says desperately, 'what did you do instead of going round the world?'

Kit sighs and looks away before nodding. 'Go on,' she says, her words firm. 'Tell her.'

Chapter 35

Kit and Bella think I'm asleep. They packed me off to bed hours ago, forcing me to imbibe a hot chocolate, with a sleeping pill they unearthed from the bathroom cabinet. It didn't work.

As the Saffron Sweeting church clock chimes eleven, I'm stroking the stiff taffeta of one of my vintage dresses. A deep turquoise, almost teal, I found it four years ago in a shop in Brighton. The bodice is boned and the skirt alone has yards of material in it. If I ever do get married, I think, I want to wear something like this.

I'm far too agitated to close my eyes or even to get back into bed. I need some air. In fidgety frustration, I sneak out of the house to pad my way through the deserted village streets.

The night is nearly still, with just a faint breeze stirring the trees by the river. The burbling water sounds louder than in the daytime, no longer competing with the noises of twenty-first-century life. I disturb a pair of sleeping ducks, and their indignant quacking makes me jump.

Overhead, the antique streetlights with their curvy necks give an orangey glow, but all the houses are in darkness. There's no blue flicker from late night television, no exhausted shift workers coming home. It's as if someone waved a wand and Saffron Sweeting fell into a deep, unruffled sleep.

The High Street is a black and white version of its daytime self. Every building is familiar, yet different in the shadows. Here, a fox trots across the road, busy with his nightly errands. I pass the malt house, huge and silent as always. The library dozes, any nocturnal adventures confined to the books on its shelves. Under the roof of a thatched cottage, a sole window is illuminated, but as I watch, that too snaps into darkness.

As I draw opposite the old vegetable shop, I pause. This is it, I think. This is what Joey truly wants. There's a skip outside: he must have started renovating already. He's planning to do most of it himself, to save money. I tilt my head and try to imagine his photography business. A black and white Saffron Studio sign. A tasteful grey awning to shade the premises from the sun. Beneath that, in the window, enlarged pictures of beautiful couples on their wedding day. Inside, Joey will patiently charm a baby, ready to capture first official photos to be sent to far-flung relatives. The baby will be fretful, uncooperative, but Joey will coo and cajole until the wee one turns blue eyes to the camera. The grateful mother will turn her own blue eyes to Joey and he'll tell her the beautiful infant takes after her.

A distinctive hoot floats along the street. The owl is probably hunting in the field by the abandoned malt house. I can't help but think of Wol. I miss her so much. Nothing seemed this difficult or this complicated while she was alive. Did she believe our secret was safe for ever, or did she know this day would come? What would she tell me to do?

There's a second hoot, much closer now. I look around sharply, half expecting to feel the swoop of wings. But the street is empty. Still, I have my answer. I square my shoulders, tug my cardigan more tightly around me, and turn for home as the Sweeting church clock strikes twelve.

~ ~ ~

My head is splitting. The sun pierces the bedroom window, gathering strength like a laser and then attacking my skull. Groaning, I lurch out of bed and stagger to the bathroom.

'What time is it?' I growl to Bella and Kit when I make it to the kitchen. If that heavenly, smoky smell can be trusted, they're sharing a breakfast of bacon butties.

'Bloody hell!' answers Stanley helpfully.

'About ten,' Bella replies, rolling her eyes at the parrot. Both her hands are occupied in steering a doorstep-thick sandwich to her mouth.

'You look rough.' Kit reaches for the HP sauce.

I grunt. I've no idea why she's still here, but I don't have any functioning brain cells to inquire. Although slow to act, that sleeping pill was as effective as a whack with an iron bar.

'Where are you going?' Bella calls as I open the front door.

'Out.' I close it softly behind me.

I've reached the High Street, the mild air refreshing my senses, when my stomach realises it missed out on breakfast. But I ignore its grumbles and carry on. I have something I need to do.

Compared with the night before, Saffron Sweeting is positively humming. The pleasant summer morning has brought villagers out to sweep front steps, walk dogs and chat with neighbours. A window cleaner is whistling from his ladder and, outside the pub, the fish van toots its horn to announce its arrival. The door of the post office is propped open, and I detect the aroma of fresh bread from the bakery around the corner. It's not Piccadilly Circus, but the place has a purposeful Saturday air.

And yes: he's here. Having seen the skip, and knowing that with the papers signed there's nothing in his way, I hoped I might find Joey at the vegetable shop. Sure enough, there are a couple of safety cones on the pavement and the door of the shop is flung wide. As I approach, I see Joey himself, dragging a length of old shelving out. Wary, I pause to watch as he hoists it over a saw-horse and proceeds to chop it to fit the skip. I'm out of his line of sight as the dust flies. At one time, I would have admired the view as he worked. But now, I just want him to finish the task, so I can approach.

'Joey!' I call as he heaves the pieces into the skip and turns to go back inside. 'Hey, Joe.'

He hoists his safety goggles up, looking surprised. 'Good morning! Come to help?'

His face is animated. There's already sweat under the

arms of his T-shirt, but he's alive with the excitement of the task. I know I'm looking at a man who can smell and taste his dream.

I swallow, pause, then force myself to move closer. He's grinning, still oblivious to the tension in me. I glance up and down the High Street. We're alone.

'Joey,' I say, my words rushed, 'I need to say something.'

He pulls the goggles off and blows dust from them. 'I heard about the dress shop,' he says with a chuckle. 'Mum can be a bit much sometimes. I'll talk to her.' He reaches out to give me a playful squeeze on the shoulder. Through his thick work gloves, his touch barely registers.

I take a breath that only reaches the top third of my lungs. 'That's not it,' I say, shaking my head. I'm frantic to get this over with. 'I – I can't marry you.'

'What?' He's leaning casually on the edge of the skip. I think I see him sway a little, before he pushes himself upright. Oh, boy.

'I'm sorry. I'm not marrying you.'

'Bugger,' he says, staring at me. Bewilderment settles on his face.

I look away. 'I'm sorry,' I say again. Then I remember I'm supposed to return the ring. 'Here,' I say, beginning to tug. It won't come over my knuckle without a struggle. 'Do you want this now?'

He takes the ring, apparently in shock. 'Why?' he finally manages.

'I don't love you,' I say quietly. 'And I don't think you love me, either. I shouldn't have let it get this far, I'm sorry.'

There, I've apologised three times. I've been gentle and honest, and not made a big scene. That should do it. I can leave quietly now, right?

Wrong. Joey is still staring at the pavement when another piece of shelving appears from the doorway behind us. Under it are legs in jeans. Male legs. He backs part way into the street, until the other end of the shelving can manoeuvre through the door. The person on this end has the advantage of being able to see where he's going.

'Hello, darling!'

Correction: see where *she's* going.

I almost choke. Adrenaline and bones are now the only things holding me up.

'Hi, mum,' I say weakly.

I should have known. Sorting out the mess inside the vegetable shop would be just her thing. Especially if Joey is the beneficiary. Although how she managed to rope Chuck in – yes, his are the legs I observed – I'm not sure.

'What's going on?' she says, frowning at Joey, who's leaning on the skip with both hands now and looks like he might throw up into it. I feel a slug of remorse, but plant my feet.

Then mum looks past me. 'Good lord, Kit, what are you doing here?'

I look back and yes, Kit is trotting up the middle of the High Street, ignoring a milk float which is trundling along behind her, waiting to get past. And behind that is Bella, half jogging, but stopping to walk and catch her breath every few paces.

'We came to see if everything's okay.' For once, Kit ignores mum entirely, pulling up several yards short and taking her sunglasses off to look directly at me. I see her glance flick to Joey before she turns back to me with a grimace of encouragement. Then she puts her shades back on.

Bella catches up and slithers to a halt beside Kit, hands on her thighs, almost panting.

'Everything's fine,' I say, and look directly at my mother. 'But I'm not marrying Joey.'

There's a second of screaming silence.

Then, 'What did you say?' mum splutters. 'Young lady, *what* did you say?' Her eyebrows have shot so high, they're in danger of disappearing into her hair.

'She said, she's not marrying me.' Joey's voice is a

hollow monotone which echoes around the skip. He still looks as sick as a parrot, and I see his throat working. Hopefully that's from the dust, not from my bombshell.

'Maybe we could use some sodas out here,' Chuck says quickly, backing away in the direction of the post office. Poor guy. He's barely been on English soil ten minutes and he's been dragged into a street scene that resembles West Side Story.

'Sophie, silly, you don't mean that.' Mum tuts, as if I'm just seeking attention.

'I think she does.' Bella, having got most of her breath back, chimes in.

Joey shoots her a hurt look. Then he turns to me, his eyes stony. He lets his gaze swing around to mum, then he looks back, meaningfully.

You bastard, I think. You utter bastard. The guilt I feel at dumping him ebbs away.

'I'm not marrying Joey,' I repeat, to give myself confidence, 'And I'm not an air hostess.'

'What on earth –' mum shakes her head. 'This is bizarre.'

Across the street, I see Violet poke her head out of the post office. Like a hound scenting the fox, she changes the sign on her door to read *Closed* and steps purposefully onto the pavement.

'Hey!' Chuck appears behind her, arms full of cans. 'I gotta pay for these, lady.'

'What do you mean, you're not an air hostess?' Mum sounds shrill now.

'I knew it!' Violet steps into the road so she can hear better. 'I knew she was lying.'

'Shut up,' Bella says mildly. 'Nobody asked you.'

I refuse to be deterred by the audience now gathered. The blood's pumping so fast through my veins, I need to say this now. And at least this way I'll only have to explain once.

'I tried to be an air hostess,' I say, willing my voice to hold steady, 'but I was rubbish. They sacked me when they discovered I had a flying phobia.'

Chuck whistles, then looks chastened as mum glares at him. 'Excuse me,' he says. 'Soda, anyone?'

We all ignore him. Further along the street, the fish man walks around to the back of his van and looks at us curiously. This little scene is more than he usually gets in Saffron Sweeting. He'll try to sell us a nice piece of hake, next.

'But you can't be scared of flying.' Mum looks genuinely puzzled.

I start to count down from ten, knowing that's roughly how long I've got.

But I haven't got past six when a dark green Mercedes purrs up behind Violet, who's effectively blocking the road. Thwarted, the car sits for a moment, then reverses smoothly into a space near the bank. Long, shapely legs emerge, followed by a deep cobalt shift dress and the rest of Amelia.

'Hello, darlings,' she calls. 'What's going on?'

I see her survey the scene, from the distant fishmonger, to Chuck with his arms full of contraband Coke, to Violet stationed in the middle of the street. Then there's mum, both hands on her hips, Joey leaning sulkily on the skip, and Bella with Kit, looking anxious but ready to pitch in if things turn nasty. 'Good God,' she says, 'has there been an accident?'

'No,' Bella says. 'But there's about to be.'

'Sophie's just jilted Joey,' Violet says cheerfully. 'And there's more.'

Amelia's eyes widen in poorly-concealed glee. Through long experience, she's aware that emotional crises often lead to property transactions. She leans on her car, swinging keys from one finger, waiting to see who her next client might be.

Mum is the first to oblige. 'You're talking absolute codswallop, Sophie Campbell,' she snaps. 'You can't be scared of flying.'

'I am,' I say again. 'At least, I was until recently. I've been getting some help.'

'Help?' Joey jeers. 'Yeah, is that what you call him?'

My mother isn't deflected. 'That's ridiculous. You're not scared of flying. Why, you and Kit went round the world together.'

I look at Kit now, my face full of question. She bites her lip but nods.

'Actually, we didn't,' I say.

Mum gives a high little laugh. 'Yes, you did,' she insists. 'You Skyped me from Shanghai.'

I don't want to hurt her. But there's no other way.

'We weren't in Shanghai. We didn't go anywhere.'

'But you were away for six months!' mum protests. 'All last spring and summer!'

Awkwardly, Chuck starts clunking the cans of drink down on the pavement. I'd love one, but it's hardly the right moment for a Diet Coke break. I run my tongue around the dryness of my mouth instead.

'No, we weren't,' I say. 'We were here all the time. With Wol.'

Violet gives a squeal. 'She was too. I remember, she was.'

'Shush,' Bella says, uncharacteristically rude.

But Violet won't be shushed. 'And not just you –' She points at me, then turns triumphantly to Kit. 'You've changed your hair, but *you* were here too!'

Amelia turns to consider Kit. 'I thought I'd seen you somewhere before, darling. And weren't you –'

'Shut *up*,' Bella looks like she might clout either or both of them. But everyone's too enthralled.

'Katherine!' Mum's incredulous. 'Is this true?'

Kit takes her sunglasses off. 'Yes, it's true.'

'Why weren't you travelling around the world, like you said? What were you both doing? Why were you in Saffron Sweeting all that time?'

I look desperately at Kit and shake my head. You don't have to do this, I'm trying to tell her. Let me handle it. I'll take the blame.

But Kit steps forward to stand beside me. 'Sophie and Wol were looking after me.' She speaks with calm authority, like a woman twice her age.

'Looking after you?' Mum repeats, just as Amelia says, 'Wol... of course.'

'What did Wol have to do with this?' my mother demands. 'Why did you need looking after?'

Kit's hand finds mine and she gives my fingers a squeeze. As I squeeze back, I sense her tremble. She's scared too, but she's not letting on. We went into this together and we'll come out of it together.

The little crowd of observers goes still. I swear every single one of us is holding our breath, and probably the fish man too. Finally, Kit speaks.

'I was having a baby,' she says.

Chapter 36

At Kit's simple statement, the blood drains from my mother's skin and keeps on draining until she loses the strength to stand and subsides onto the kerb. I turn to go. I've said my bit, a breach has been opened that may never heal, and I'd better start learning to live with myself.

'No,' Bella says, putting an arm around me. 'Stay a while. She'll have questions, when it sinks in.'

I glance at Kit. She's retreated to the opposite side of the narrow village street and has sat down neatly on the kerb too, as if waiting for Act Two to start. Mum hasn't yet said a word, and I'm curious to see Chuck sit next to her, not touching, but close enough so that she knows he's there.

Amelia and Violet are first to find their tongues.

'I remember now!' Violet gestures at Kit. 'You were in the family way when you turned up in the village.'

Kit pauses, then nods. 'I got pregnant,' she says. 'I decided to have it. Sophie helped me and Wol took us in.'

Amelia makes an exasperated noise. 'That's hardly a scandal these days, darling. Why the big to-do?'

Kit looks away. Maybe she isn't ready for this public testimony after all. I look across at our mother, knowing she can hear us even if her face is a mask.

'Mum had a high profile position at the bank,' I say cautiously. 'And in the business community too. She'd worked hard to champion education for girls... along with avoiding teenage pregnancy.'

Violet's eyes go from me to mum. She's a shrewd old thing and is no doubt calculating the slim age difference between us. No need to spell out my mother's own teenage mistake and how she's always blamed me for her missed opportunities.

Amelia puts her head on one side. 'She was on local television, wasn't she?'

'Oh!' Violet nods. 'Yes. Wasn't it after-school maths classes? In rural communities?'

'I'm not sure,' Amelia furrows her brow. 'I was busy getting divorced. Bit hazy on the details.'

As Violet's eyebrows arch, I wait for the snide remark about Amelia being busy with the bottle too. But she's still forming the perfect gibe when Joey speaks up.

'Maths mentors. For teenage girls,' he says. 'Lots of the bank staff volunteered. Erica won awards for it.' He's been leaning against the skip for the past few minutes, saying nothing. I'm surprised that he's still here. Now, he goes back into the vegetable shop, reappearing moments later with yet another fixture. Pulling his safety goggles down, he starts to break it into smaller pieces, bending each part savagely until it snaps.

'All the same,' Amelia says breezily, 'accidents happen, don't they?'

'Oh my God.' My mother gives a low moan and drops her head to her hands.

'Okay,' I say. 'We're not talking about this here.' We've made enough of a spectacle of ourselves for one day, washing our dirty linen in the middle of the High Street.

'Good call, Sophie,' Chuck replies, getting to his feet and trying to coax mum off the kerb. 'Come on, Erica. I'm taking you home.'

My mother, still sickly pale, shakes her head.

'You can't sit here, lovie,' Violet chips in. 'Come into the post office and sit down.'

'No,' says Amelia hurriedly, 'You can all come into Hargraves and Co. Much more comfortable.'

She squares up to Violet, both of them like cities vying to host the Olympics. They're both dying to have this domestic drama within earshot.

'No deal,' says Chuck, surprisingly firmly for an outsider. 'Give these Campbell women some privacy.'

We settle for moving a few paces along the street, to the bench outside the library. Mum sits down wordlessly and Kit perches on the back with her feet on the seat. I sit gingerly at the other end, muscles tensed.

'And the rest of you, clear off.' Bella glares at the hangers-on.

Violet tuts but, with a wary look at Amelia, turns away. Amelia pouts but also starts to retreat, albeit walking backwards so she doesn't miss anything.

'Wait a minute,' Joey says. 'Before I go.' He makes no effort to approach me, but jerks his head in my direction. 'This –' he unfurls a clenched fist and I glimpse the emerald, before he snaps his fingers shut and shoves the ring in his pocket. 'This doesn't change anything.'

What is he talking about? 'Er, Joey,' I say carefully, 'it changes everything.'

He surely doesn't think we're still a couple?

'You're still my main investor,' he says, his eyes flicking to those still listening. 'You signed the papers. You're legally committed.'

Oh, no. The stupid, stupid vegetable shop. His photography studio. He's right. I signed the bloody contract. Wol's money is locked in.

'Look –' I stutter.

He folds his arms, challenging me to continue. But his eyes are gleaming: he's cornered me and he knows it.

'Okay,' I say finally. 'Whatever.'

What a mess.

Amelia, now several backwards paces away, clicks her tongue. 'She's not, actually.'

'Not what?' Violet can't resist entering back into the conversation.

'Not legally committed,' says Amelia.

'I'm not?' I leap on her words.

Amelia shakes her head. 'Not as I recall.'

'How come?' Joey demands. 'What the f–' Glancing at mum, he amends this. '*What* are you talking about?'

'There's a cooling off clause, darling,' Amelia says smoothly.

'Don't you darling me,' Joey snarls. 'There is no cooling off clause in that contract.' He takes a step towards Amelia, who doesn't flinch. For the first time, I notice she's taller than him.

'Sorry, but there is,' she replies. 'I put one in. Investors have ten days to change their mind. That's Sophie, you see. She's your investor, she gets ten days.'

My mouth is open, joy threatening to bubble out as I look gratefully at Amelia. She wouldn't let me sign the papers, last week when I went into her office. She must have changed them.

'Nice one,' Kit says cheerfully.

'You bitch.' Joey spits on the pavement in Amelia's general direction.

'That's it,' Chuck says. 'Time out. Everyone, beat it.'

Amelia, seemingly satisfied, waggles her fingers at me and winks, then turns on her well-shod heel and heads for her estate agency.

Violet, who seems far more shocked by the latest exchange than news of an illegitimate baby in Saffron Sweeting, accepts Bella's suggestion that she walk the older woman back to the post office.

'And you,' Chuck fixes Joey with a glare, 'I'm watching you.'

Joey looks at me, opens his mouth to say something, then his shoulders sag. He shakes his head and turns away.

Chuck looks at my mother. 'You okay, Erica?'

She nods, finding her tongue. 'Thank you. Go.'

He hesitates, then, feeling dual stares from Kit and me, says, 'Call me.'

Mum nods again, and Chuck touches the back of his hand to her cheek. Well, I think, as he walks away, he's an improvement on the last one. And the one before that.

Then, there's a long, aching silence, the kind where breaking it is worse than enduring it.

~~~

Eventually, Kit finds some words. 'Mum, I only did what I thought was best.'

Our mother makes a strangled little noise. 'You didn't tell me,' she says in a half whimper. 'Why didn't you tell me?'

We didn't tell her because we didn't think she'd support Kit's decision to have the baby. I was convinced she'd try to talk Kit out of it.

Kit looks at me before answering. 'We... I just... couldn't. You'd have been gutted.'

'I'm gutted now!' comes the justifiable reaction, and I cringe. Guilty as charged.

'You'd made such a name for yourself,' I say hesitantly. 'You'd done so much work on girls getting their full education. Not... getting pregnant.' Like you did with me, I add silently.

'Mum, you were in the Daily Telegraph,' Kit adds. 'They called you a visionary.'

There's a pause. It's true: mum was a minor celebrity for a few short weeks, before the press moved on to a sports scandal. I consider mentioning Pompous Anthony, but decide against it. She can work out for herself that this would hardly have improved his chances of getting elected.

'But you could have told me!' she insists, tears in her eyes. 'What kind of mother am I, that you couldn't tell me?'

'We were just trying to protect you,' I murmur. 'Like you did with me about grandad, remember?'

Mum whirls around with such momentum, I think she's going to hit me. She doesn't, but the emotions of the last half hour are unleashed.

'That's ridiculous!' she cries. 'How on earth can you say it's the same thing, Sophie? It's completely different! Your sister had a baby, for God's sake! A baby. And you – you let me think you were backpacking and sightseeing and – and sipping espresso at street cafes!'

I want to run as fast as I can away from this bench, this

village, this woman. But I dig my fingernails into the soft wood and force myself to stay and to speak. 'No, mum, it's not that different. You didn't tell me how grandad died because you thought it would cause me great pain.' I break off, wheezing. 'And we didn't tell you about a baby being born, because we knew it would cause *you* great pain.'

As I hold my mother's gaze, I see a flash of understanding cross her face.

'Where – where is the child?' she asks, looking at Kit fearfully. 'Did it – did you –'

'Adopted,' Kit says, just above a whisper.

Mum flinches and closes her eyes. 'A boy or a girl?'

'Girl.' Kit has difficulty getting the word out. She's being brave, but I know the heartbreak of giving up her child is right below the surface.

'And... and the father? Does he know?'

Kit nods once.

'Who... who...' Mum's unable to finish.

Kit looks at me, but all I can offer is a small shrug of support.

'Ravi,' she says.

Mum blinks, then her lips make an 'O' shape. 'No,' she says. 'Not Ravi.'

As a kind but traditional Indian family, Kit's unwanted pregnancy would have been even more damaging to Ravi and his relatives than to our mother. It was pretty much the perfect storm.

'No...' Tears are running down mum's face now. 'No!' She's laughing now in the way people do when they're in agonising pain. 'Your maths – your maths improved so much. I told everyone you got into university because you were able to pass maths!'

The irony is indeed sour. The vast improvement in her numerical prowess was credited to the special rapport between Kit and her tutor. At least they found some time for algebra, I think ruefully.

'And you, Sophie...? You knew this was going on?'

There's an edge to mum's voice now.

Typical, I think. Blame me for my sister getting knocked up. 'No,' I say, attempting to keep the defensive rise out of my tone. 'Not till it was too late.'

'But you helped her hide it.' The accusation is plain.

'Kit wanted to have the baby. That was her decision.' I pause. 'I... offered to help. Wol helped both of us.'

'Oh, God.' Mum searches her pocket for a tissue.

She sobs for what seems like several minutes. Kit looks wretched too; her eyes are shiny and her lip is wobbling.

'Whatever I did,' mum says finally to Kit, gulping to be heard, 'to make you think you couldn't tell me, I'm sorry.'

Kit stares for a moment from her vantage point on top of the bench, then jumps down and hugs her. 'No, I'm sorry,' she says. 'I just didn't think you could take it.'

'What's her name?' mum asks.

Kit shakes her head. 'They told me not to – to name her.' Her misery spills over now into tears and she buries her head in mum's shoulder.

I'm feeling choked myself as I get to my feet. I should leave them to it. They have so much in common now: both mothers at eighteen, both with so much pain in their past.

'Hang on,' mum says, spotting me over Kit's shoulder. They untangle themselves, sniffing, apparently sharing one pathetic tissue.

My mother bites on her thumbnail. 'You told me you went round the world,' she says slowly.

I nod.

'But you stayed here, with Wol, so Kit could have the baby?'

'Yes,' Kit confirms.

'And then, Sophie, you went back to work as an air hostess?'

'No,' I say. 'I did some training, but when they found out I was terrified of flying, they let me go.' I sense it might not be the best time for further details.

Our mother nods slowly. 'And then?'

'Well, I couldn't tell you I was scared of flying. You'd know we hadn't been round the world. So I hung out here for a bit, with Wol. And Kit went off to uni, and things seemed okay.'

Mum frowns. 'Then?'

'Then?' I sit down again. 'Then Wol died. And you said you were coming back to the village, and Joey showed up and started asking questions... and I realised things were getting sticky. Too close for comfort.'

Now it's Kit's turn to nod supportively.

'But at least once I found out about grandad, I started to understand why I might have the phobia,' I say, beginning to make sense of recent months. 'And by then, I'd started to tackle the fear. I thought, if I got over it, I'd be able to get a stewardess job, and it might be okay after all.'

Mum shakes her head. 'What a tangled web, Sophie. I can't believe you'd lie like that.'

I flush, gripping the bench once again. I won't have any fingernails when today is over. 'I had good reasons, mum. I'm not sorry.'

And I'm not. Protecting my little sister and her secret was worth it. Kit's baby daughter is with good people. Ravi was saved from disgrace. And Kit still has a chance of a full life, an education and one day another family.

Mum takes a breath. 'But still. Whatever your reasons...' She looks genuinely perplexed. 'And even Bella was helping you! The shame of it!'

'Bella didn't lie to you,' I say quickly. 'Only by omission, maybe.' I stifle a smile.

But mum's not to be deflected. 'And other people too. That man I met at dinner – the pilot. You don't have a second passport, do you? He was covering up for you!'

I look at her. She's right. Tom allied himself with me when he had no idea what was going on, whether the game I was playing was good or evil, and who was on which side. When he had been so badly hurt by his wife's deceit, when he felt so strongly about telling the truth. When he had absolutely no reason to get involved.

I close my eyes. Tom. He's covered for me, coaxed me through my fear, comforted me and confided his own hopes and sorrows. He's cheered me up, cheered me on, and shown me I've got more courage than I ever knew. And he practically pleaded with me not to marry Joey.

I've been such an idiot.

In a flash, I'm on my feet. 'I'm sorry,' I say as my heart lurches, threatens to stop, then settles to a pounding urgency. 'I have somewhere I need to be.'

And then I'm off, running down the road, the wind whipping my face. There's so much raw power in my legs, that if I push myself just a fraction harder, I might find I can take off and fly.

Chapter 37

'Please. You have to tell me where he lives.'

Lorraine folds her arms. 'Sorry, Sophie. I'm not getting involved.'

'I know it's in Swaffham,' I say. 'At least, I think it is.' I'm kicking myself. The location of Tom's house hadn't seemed important before.

'Please,' I say again as Lorraine begins to close the heavy front door of Oak House. I'm ready to get down on my knees, if I have to. 'I've been to three of the garden centres. And I drove around Swaffham, looking for his car.'

Without wheels of my own, I helped myself to Kit's Morris Minor.

Lorraine's lips twitch. 'Which Swaffham?'

'I don't know!' Dammit: wretched villages with similar names. There's a Swaffham Bulbeck and a Swaffham Prior and maybe more I don't know about. 'The big one. Please, Lorraine.'

She sighs, wiping her already clean hands on her apron. 'I told you, it's none of my business. I'm not meddling.' Then, seeing my face crumple, she continues. 'Look, Tom's a terrific guy. He was my lifeline when Alistair died. I don't want to see him hurt.'

I look away, suddenly shy. Then I think, I've come too far to wimp out now. I meet Lorraine's eye. 'I'm not planning on hurting him,' I say softly. 'Far from it.'

But her expression shuts down again. 'That's not what it looked like, the other night at The Plough. I'd say you've hurt him already. Now, look, sorry, but I have scones in the oven.'

'I'm not marrying Joey,' I burst out.

Her eyebrows flicker up. 'You're not? Since when?'

'Since this morning. Please, I have to speak to Tom. I keep calling, but he's not answering.' I trail off, despondent now.

She gives me a long look. Then she reaches into the pocket of her apron and pulls out her phone.

'You're right,' she says, moments later. 'His mobile's off.'

'I told you!' I say, losing all patience. 'Which is why I need his address. Lorraine, *please!*'

She shakes her head. But her eyes are dancing. 'You don't need his address. You know where he is.'

'I don't!' What is she talking about?

'Come on, Sophie. You know where Tom's bolt hole is. You've been there with him, from what I hear.'

This is too much. 'No, I bloody haven't. What bolt hole?' I hope her sodding scones turn to cinders.

Now, she has the gall to laugh. 'You're a clever girl. You can figure out where he goes, when his phone is turned off.'

Lorraine's eyes are positively twinkling now. She looks at me meaningfully, then jerks her head towards the sky.

~~~

'No, I can't just call him up. Air traffic control would have my guts for garters.'

'Can you at least tell me where he's gone? Did he, er, file a flight plan?' I'm trying not to sound desperate, when all I want to do is stamp my foot.

'Dunno. If he did, it wouldn't be with me.'

I didn't think this through. The woman in the flying club office certainly isn't going out of her way to be helpful, but I believe her when she says she can't instantly locate Tom and make him come back. With the flying range of a Cessna, there are thousands of miles of sky where he could be. What can I do?

A man enters the small office, headphones dangling from his hand. He looks like he might be a flying instructor.

'All right, Agnes?' he asks conversationally.

Maybe if I buy a lesson, that will get me in a plane, and I can find out if Tom's on the same frequency. Will they lock me up if I try to talk to him on their precious aviation bandwidth?

'This, er, lady,' Agnes says, still eyeing me suspiciously, 'is rather anxious to locate Tom.'

'Tom? Tom Vine?' asks the man.

'Yes,' I nod eagerly. 'Do you know where he went today?'

The man walks over to the window and jerks his head. 'He's out there.'

'Where?' I scurry to look. 'I don't see anything.'

'When I got back a few minutes ago, Tom seemed to be going round the traffic pattern.'

'Going round the what?'

'The traffic pattern,' says Agnes, more helpful now. Maybe this man is her boss. 'It means he's taking off, doing the standard circuit, and lining up to land again.'

'Oh,' I say. 'Why would he do that?'

The man shrugs. 'Pilots like to practise it sometimes. Check their emergency drill, that sort of thing.'

'I don't understand.'

'You know,' he says. 'Engine out procedures, practise they can still land okay. Routine stuff.'

'Engine out?' Blimey, that doesn't sound routine to me. It sounds downright dangerous.

'Tom's been acting strange, these past few days,' says Agnes. 'Obsessing about every detail, going round the traffic pattern as if it's the only thing in the world that matters.'

Oh no, I think. He's got a death wish. He's up there trying to kill himself. And it's my fault.

'There he is now,' the man says, and I push my nose up against the window in time to see a white plane with red markings descending fast towards the runway. The wheels touch down, but it doesn't decelerate, it just keeps going, gathering speed. As the available runway gets shorter and shorter, it lifts off again and climbs back into the sky.

'We have to make him stop,' I say, looking at the others for assistance.

But they don't move. 'No can do,' the man says.

I blink back tears of frustration. 'All right,' I say defiantly. 'Fine. But you can at least tell me the tail number of that plane.'

~~~

The planes are landing from the south-west today. I pull out my phone and consult Google maps, desperately trying to get my bearings. I know I don't stand much chance of getting onto the airfield itself, not with those two already suspicious of me. And even if I could scale the fence and reach the runway, I'd probably be arrested before I got another glimpse of Tom's plane. I can't afford another brush with the law so soon after the wedding dress episode.

I swear quietly, waiting for the map to load. I just need to figure out... there. I see it. Coldhams Lane. I run back to the trusty Morris Minor: it starts first time. I throw the car into gear and within a few minutes have parked it badly at the side of the road, two wheels up on the kerb, hazard lights flashing. Coldhams Lane marks the edge of the airport and I've picked the precise spot where an approaching plane will fly over the road. There are even part-time traffic lights, to make vehicles stop if something big is coming in. This is close enough. It has to be.

I leap out of the car, run around to the front, and wait, straining my eyes towards the horizon. The sun is precisely where I'm trying to look, making it hard to see. I wish I had binoculars, or a telescope, or at least some sunglasses. Kit's wearing them, no doubt.

Then I see a shape. It's either a plane, about a mile away, or a bird, much closer. I can't tell. But it's coming right at me, and as I wait, it takes on the shape of an aircraft. I can even hear the low thrum of an engine. I tense, grab hold of the Minor's bonnet, and squint to see if it's Tom's plane.

It isn't. It's all wrong: larger, with jet engines under each wing. Damn. I hunch my shoulders against the noise as it flies startlingly close and disappears over the perimeter fence. Then I hear the engine noise change as the plane makes contact with the runway and brakes are applied.

There's no time to rethink this plan: another plane is approaching. This time, the shape is more like a Cessna. I'm at an awkward angle, but the colour looks right too. I bet it's Tom. I cross both arms above my head and make huge, sweeping waves, in the international gesture of someone on the ground trying to attract attention. The plane's coming in fast. I swing my arms as hard as I can, and at the last moment turn to see its tail. Yes: the letters match. It was Tom.

Did he see me? I crane my neck, trying to see the runway from my poor vantage point. The noise of the plane subsides, changes tone, then, almost instantly, it picks up again as the pilot pulls the throttle out. Standing on tiptoes, I see it take off from the far end of the runway. Damn. That was him, I know it. Didn't he see me? Or did he see me and choose to ignore me?

I grind my teeth. This is no good. I have to talk to him. I pace up and down the road, thinking. Can I scale that nasty fence? Maybe get myself next to the runway, where he can't miss me? Signal to him somehow? How long have I got? How long does it take to go round this thing they call a traffic pattern? Will it be two minutes or an hour?

Please forgive me, Wol, I think as, minutes later, I crouch gingerly on the roof of her beloved Morris Minor. The boot was too steep and slippery, but the bonnet was easy enough to clamber onto, and from there I slithered carefully over the front windscreen and up onto the roof. I'm clutching Kit's lipstick, which I found in the glove compartment after the boot yielded nothing but a pair of wellingtons and a first aid kit. But the lipstick is a good, deep plum colour. Perfect.

The vintage metal groans as I scrawl foot-high letters on Wol's beautiful car. I start with the end of his tail number: *JLW* for Juliet Lima Whisky. Below, I write *I LOVE*

YOU. Surely he'll see this?

I've barely finished and retreated to the relative safety of the car bonnet when I glimpse a speck in the distance. It shimmers, wobbles, then stabilises in the form of a plane. Can it be? I hold my breath, one hand shading my eyes. The shape grows bigger, doubling in size every second, until I'm in no doubt. It's him. *Please, Tom*, I think as I raise both arms again. Please see me here.

The hum becomes a roar, a huge shadow blots out the sun and I see wheels, so close I think they'll hit me. At the last moment I duck, slip, and sprawl on the car. Clinging on desperately, I gasp as I realise I'm still alive, then get gingerly to my feet. My legs are trembling, my courage fading fast, but I have to see if I succeeded. I straighten and look towards the plane, trundling down the runway. Now, I think. Now. Turn off. *Turn off.*

Juliet Lima Whisky slows and takes the first available taxiway. I whoop with delight. He saw me. He understands. He's parking the plane.

But the Cessna doesn't head for the usual parking area. There's a long pause while it sits, doing nothing, on the taxiway. My insides churn: this isn't normal, is it?

Then the plane begins to move again. It turns, goes back to the runway, and turns again, coming straight towards me now. My heart lifts; I wave my arms again for good luck. Then they fall to my sides as the plane makes one final turn so I'm looking at its tail.

'No,' I yell, unable to help myself. 'No, no, no!'

But the engine roars, drowning my howl as the Cessna accelerates to take-off speed. All I can do is watch as Tom climbs into the clouds.

Chapter 38

My fear of flying used to make me feel hollow inside. It made me shiver, and wobble. It turned my knees to jelly and zapped my strength as though I'd biked from Cambridge to London.

This is worse. I'm not shivering, I'm shaking. I don't wobble down from Wol's car, I slide in a helpless heap off the bonnet and onto the grass. My guts have been scraped out with an ice cream scoop, and I'm so exhausted I might as well have biked up Everest.

I know he saw me. I'm no expert flier, but I've been in that plane enough times now to know that, on final approach, I was unmissable. He saw me. He saw the message. And he kept going.

I don't know how long I sit there, leaning against the Morris Minor. I'd like to cry, to scream, to wail, but tears don't come. All I see is the shrinking silhouette of Tom's plane as it climbed skywards.

Eventually, the police turn up, alerted by air traffic control to a hazard on the road. I've been called many things, but I think this is the first time I've been a hazard. After they politely insist that I move along, I find several panicked text messages from Kit, who thinks her car has been stolen. Wol's not here this time to offer sanctuary. I have nowhere else to go; the only option is home.

But as I drive slowly into Saffron Sweeting, I know I can't face our house. I suspect mum's still there, and if Bella or Kit says one kind word, I'll crumple in a pile and never get up again. The pub is equally out of the question: after today's spectacle in the High Street, I won't have the nerve to be seen in the village for a while.

I change down a gear and steer the Morris Minor towards the river.

~~~

It's so peaceful here, by the ford. Having parked the car and found a relatively dry patch of grass to sit on, I feel my heart rate begin to slow.

There's hardly any traffic. Shortly after I arrived, a couple of cars splashed cautiously through the narrow river, but since then, there's been nothing. The water returns to its lazy burbling rhythm, and a short way upstream a heron waits stoically for his supper. I force myself to focus on a leaf as it floats past and continues its languid journey towards the sea. The sun has fallen behind the trees now, and the soft light is starting to fade. I realise this scene probably hasn't changed for a hundred years. Long after I'm gone, the stream will keep on flowing. As the water lulls me, I discover the numbness is a blessed relief. As long as I sit here, and as long as the river keeps rippling past, I can cope.

~~~

My watery trance is so soothing, I barely look at the car which arrives on the other bank. It stops a little way back from the ford, the engine still running. The driver has opened his door and stepped out before recognition swims to the surface of my brain. It's a grey Range Rover. And the man standing beside it is Tom.

I blink, tilting my head. Am I dreaming this? Have I hypnotised myself with the water? Is he real or merely an apparition?

The apparition takes a step towards the river, and calls out to me.

'Is there something I should know?'

The opposite bank is only about twenty feet away; he hardly needs to raise his voice to be heard. I scramble to my feet as I decide it really is him.

'Was that you at the airport?' Tom's expression is disguised behind his aviator sunglasses.

I nod wordlessly as the shock of seeing him starts to

crystallise into a tiny bead of hope.

'What the hell were you doing?' His voice sounds raw and angry.

My mouth is dry. 'I have to talk to you,' I call.

'You bloody idiot. You could have been hurt!'

'Please,' I try again, making an effort to speak more loudly than the river. I step closer to the water, wondering if I should just wade across to him. 'I've messed things up, but we really need to talk.'

He shakes his head and shouts back, 'There's nothing to say.'

'There is,' I holler, my voice stronger every moment. 'I've called off the wedding.'

Tom freezes. 'What?' He pulls off his sunglasses.

'I said, I'm not marrying Joey.'

His scowl vanishes. 'Why not?' He steps onto the pebbles by the water.

Finally, I have his attention. 'I made a huge mistake.'

He's so close now, I could almost reach out and touch him. If I had twenty-foot arms, that is.

I see him swallow. 'What kind of mistake?'

My breath is jagged. 'I'm in love with someone else,' I say.

'Who?' The word barely reaches me.

'You.'

Time stands still as I watch Tom close his eyes and dip his head. Then he turns on his heel, and with four long strides is back in his car.

I gape. Not again, surely? The gears crunch as he throws it into reverse and guns it back up the road, the way he came. I can't believe I got this so wrong.

But before I can react, there's a screech of tyres and the Range Rover hurtles forward towards the ford. It enters the water with an enormous splash, and a bow wave rears up from the front wheels. If the Morris Minor is now scarred with lipstick, Tom's car has probably sustained even more expensive engine damage. Still, it makes it through, skidding to a halt near Wol's.

As he jumps out, I see his chest rising and falling. He stops six feet away and watches me intently, hands clenched at his sides.

'I hope you're more careful than that in your plane,' I say, shocked into flippancy by the amphibious display.

He slams the car door shut, ignoring the shower of droplets. 'So it *was* you at the airport?'

'Of course it was,' I say. 'You saw me.'

'I wasn't sure. I've never seen that car before.'

We look at the powder blue Morris and I realise he never knew Wol or her car.

'And I thought that even if it was you, you were pulling some crazy stunt with Joey.'

'Joey?' I recoil. 'I told you, I broke it off with Joey.'

'So why did you write his initials on the roof?' There are deep lines around his eyes.

'They weren't his initials! That was your tail number!' I was so proud of that shorthand.

We stare at each other, the twilight deepening.

Then he opens his arms. 'Come here.'

There's a delicious thud as our bodies meet. I bury my head in Tom's shirt and feel the pressure of his arms around me.

'Sophie,' he mutters, and gives a long sigh.

I cling to him for a few moments, breathing clean cotton and soap. I rub my cheek against his shirt, sensing the muscles in his chest, just under the fabric.

'How did you know I was here?' I ask.

'I wasn't sure it was you,' he says, speaking into my hair. 'And I was pretty convinced they were Joey's initials. But as I talked to air traffic control, I realised I was repeating what I'd just seen on the car.'

I nestle closer.

'A small part of me began to hope. So I followed you back here.'

'Followed?' I frown up at him. 'No, you didn't.'

He gives a wry smile and raises his eyes meaningfully.

'Oh.' I get it now. From the air, a blue Morris Minor with lipstick on the roof would have been easy to track. I try to control my grin.

'Look at me,' Tom says, tugging lightly on the back of my top.

I tilt my face and the intensity I see makes my knees melt.

'Tell me again,' he says hoarsely, 'about the wedding.'

'It's off.' I lick my lips. 'It should never have been on. It was a terrible mistake.'

'You and Joey...?' He's still wary.

'Finished,' I say, my voice snagging. 'Over.'

He lets out a single groan and moves a hand to the small of my back, where he pulls my hips tight against his. My gasp at what I feel there is swallowed by his mouth on mine. His lips are warm and firm, and I know Tom can feel me shudder as he deepens the kiss. I reach up, grasping his shoulders, wanting to press against every inch of him.

When he finally releases my mouth, I'm breathing hard. With one arm still around me, he moves the other to my hair, stroking it as he kisses my forehead.

'You have no idea,' he says eventually, 'how long I've wanted to do that.'

Flushed, I look up at him. 'But... you kissed me in the plane.'

'Yeah.' A smile plays on his lips. 'And this time, you kissed me back.'

The words make my stomach flip again. His eyes look like they want to devour me.

'Take me somewhere private,' I touch his jaw, 'and I'll do more than kiss you back.'

Tom gives a low whistle, then looks at the Morris Minor. 'Can you leave that here for tonight?'

'Sure.'

Kit will forgive me.

He reaches for the door of his car. 'My place?'

'Perfect.'

~~~

But we've driven no further than Saffron Sweeting High Street when Tom swings the Range Rover off the road again. He bumps it up the kerb beside the abandoned malt house, and into the shadowy field there. The long, low building blocks the sliver of moon and we're now in almost total darkness.

'It's no good,' he says. 'I'm sorry.'

'What?' I'm alarmed.

'I've got to kiss you again.' He reaches to unbuckle my seatbelt.

Already leaning in, I have to laugh. 'Do you have a thing about confined spaces?'

'No,' he says, his voice husky. 'But I have a thing about you.'

This time the kiss is more awkward because of the gearstick and handbrake between us. But it's also more private: there's little chance of anyone seeing us here.

Tom leans over me and I feel another rush of excitement. As his tongue explores my mouth, my hands start to explore his back, his neck and under his shirt. I gasp in anticipation as his hands move under my top too. His fingers reach my ribs and I give a little moan, willing him to venture higher. He pulls his lips from mine so he can trail kisses down my throat, and lower.

By now my toes are curling. 'Yes,' I breathe in his ear, pulling his head to me. 'Tom, yes.'

Just as I'm thinking I want to climb in the back of the car right now, he stills his movements and holds me. My heart is pounding and I can hear his ragged breathing too.

'What is it?' I ask. 'What's wrong?'

'Nothing,' he says, 'but if I keep going, we're going to be doing it here in this field.'

So? I think. That sounds pretty good.

'Not quite what I had in mind for our first time,' he

continues, his chest still moving as he steadies himself. He pulls away from me, running a hand through his hair.

I make an effort to curb my panting lust. Perhaps he has a point.

'You had something in mind?' I echo his words, trying to lighten my voice.

'Sophie,' he says, reaching for my hand, 'I've had something in mind almost since the day I met you. You were the sexiest thing I've ever seen in that pet shop.'

'Oh, God.' My eyes widen as I remember. 'I thought you were the delivery boy. I practically ordered you to bring Stanley's food over.'

Tom sits back in his seat. 'Yeah,' he says. 'That was so hot.'

'Stop it,' I yelp. 'I'm sorry.'

'I'm not,' he says. 'Not one bit. And when you turned up at Lorraine's party, I felt like the luckiest bloke alive.'

In the darkness, I blush. 'Don't be daft.'

Despite the open sun roof, the car has steamed up and Tom lowers his window. I follow, and a mild breeze passes through the vehicle. A car goes past on the High Street but, back here in the field, we're perfectly secluded.

'But I didn't feel so lucky,' he says, 'when I couldn't work out what was going on with you. I knew you weren't playing it straight. I promised myself I'd walk away. Almost managed it too.'

I'm silent.

'I knew there was more to it than your fear of flying,' he says.

'Yes,' I admit. 'There was.'

'I kept hoping you'd open up and tell me. But you didn't.'

'I couldn't.' I gaze straight ahead.

'In Scotland, I thought you were close. When you learned about your grandad... You were so upset, I thought, she'll tell me now.' He swallows. 'But you kept pushing me away.'

'I'm so sorry.' I turn to him. 'It wasn't my secret to tell.'
Have I lost him?

'I can't...' He drums his knuckles on the steering wheel.
'I can't go forward with secrets, Sophie. After my wife... I'm
sorry, but I just can't.'

'I know.' With brimming eyes, I reach out tentatively to
touch his arm. 'I know. I can tell you now.'

Slowly, Tom's head turns. 'I hate myself for asking you,'
he says.

'Don't,' I say. 'It's okay.'

As quickly as I can, I explain how a fabricated round-
the-world trip was a cover story for something else entirely.

'I don't believe it,' he says, almost laughing with
incredulity. 'Your sister was that ashamed of having a baby?
In *this* day and age?'

'No,' I try to clarify. 'Not ashamed. It was just horrible
timing, and mum would have hit the roof.'

'Parents hit the roof all the time. She would have come
down.' His chuckle is ironic. 'All this, to keep a baby secret?
When a baby is the best type of news?'

I remember how much he wanted to start a family, and
send a guilty little thank you to his wife for not feeling the
same.

Tom shakes his head. 'And you... you were living a lie,
to cover this up?'

'I never intended it to get that bad. I thought I'd come
clean about not being an air hostess, sooner or later.' I
wince. 'But once the moment to tell mum passed, there was
never a good time to rock the boat. I just... let things drift, I
suppose.'

It sounds so lame. I look sideways at Tom, waiting for
him to judge me. This man places so much emphasis on
truth and openness.

'And then?' He speaks quietly.

'Then...' I sigh. 'Then Wol died. And the boat started to
rock all on its own.'

'I see.'

He doesn't see at all, I think. I turn my head away, looking at the darkness. I can make out the trees at the edge of the field, but no stars. I'm suddenly exhausted.

'You know,' Tom says, and the levity in his voice makes me look at him, 'I thought it must be something truly awful. I thought maybe you'd killed someone. I was just praying that whoever it was deserved it.'

I smack my lips together to stop a shocked laugh escaping. 'No!' I squeak. 'Definitely not.'

Tom exhales. 'And I'd just about decided that I didn't care, that I wanted to be with you no matter what you'd done, when you said you were marrying Joey.'

'I'm so sorry.' I close my eyes. 'He – he backed me into a corner. I should have been braver.'

I open my eyes again as I feel Tom take my hand.

'You were being brave,' he says. 'This whole time.' Then he pulls a face. 'But don't tell me any more about Joey, or he might wake up and find his teeth are missing.'

I laugh and look down. 'I'm sorry I wasn't honest with you. I do know... that it's important.'

He doesn't say anything, and I find one last ounce of bravery to search his face for clues. There, I see unwavering tenderness, with an edge of desire.

'I still can't believe you were hiding something so trivial,' he says.

'It wasn't trivial to me,' I retort. 'Or to Kit. Or our mother, for that matter.'

'No,' says Tom, making his voice serious. 'I get that. But it is to me. As I said, when you think the woman you love might have murdered someone, it's a lot to deal with.'

I gulp. 'Say that again?'

'What? That you bumped someone off?' His eyes are teasing.

'No.' I drop my gaze, then reach to tweak a button on his shirt. 'Not that bit. The other bit.'

'The bit about me loving you?'

'Yeah. That bit.'

Neither of us speaks for a long moment, then I raise my head to look at him.

'I love you, Sophie,' he says.

I swallow and nod. 'I love you too.'

The Saffron Sweeting clock chimes nine and, from a couple of fields away, there comes a faint but unmistakable hoot of an owl.

'What now?' Tom asks softly.

'Now?' I repeat as joy and longing rise up and threaten to overwhelm me. 'Well, unless you were serious about this field, I think you'd better take me home.'

Epilogue: Twelve months later

Finally, I see the lights: two red and two white, all in a row. Good. That means I'm neither too high nor – much worse – too low. This part's far harder than taking off. You'd think all you have to do is pop it down on the ground and then hit the bar to celebrate, but no, there are a dozen variables which can cause you to bounce along the runway like a kangaroo. And that's the last thing I want, with a special audience.

For the hundredth time today, I consult the clipboard strapped to my thigh. My speed's a bit fast: I ease back on the throttle. Lift the nose a bit... what else? Am I on the centre line? Yes. Okay. Here we go. The back wheels touch first, give the tiniest of bounces, then I ease the nose wheel down. Brakes now, steer with my feet, keep her straight...

The runway rushes past me, then slows. I choose the first taxiway and the Cessna turns obediently. I did it. I completed my first solo flight.

Now I see them. I was too busy, obviously, to look before, but there they are, gathered by the flying school.

There's Gwen, of course, my patient, fearless flying instructor. We found her after Tom refused point-blank to teach me.

'I love you to bits, Sophie,' he laughed, sweeping me up in his arms and spinning me around, when I told him that I wanted to use some of Wol's money to earn my pilot's licence. 'But I'm not having you arguing with me in the cockpit. Not until you're qualified, at any rate.'

It was probably a good call. Our relationship is still new and giddy; we're still finding our norms, including the best way to argue. It was best we didn't practise that at five thousand feet. Gwen stepped in with her own brand of tough love which reminded me of Wol. I flourished under her teaching style, which kept my brain so full of rules and procedures I almost forgot to be scared.

I bring the little plane to a temporary halt and contact the tower before going further.

'Taxi via Charlie,' comes the permission.

Next to Gwen, Fergus and Ingrid are attempting to keep an excited young spaniel under control. Named Biggles, he was probably only allowed onto the airfield because Ingrid refuses to be separated from him. His canine sister went to live at Six Mile Bottom, another brother to Saffron Walden, and the most zany of all has found a home with Violet at the post office. She's called him Mungo and he roams around the village at will. As a result, Stanley has learned a new word – 'Stay' – which he bellows at random intervals from his new perch inside the Saffron Sweeting Library. At least it's an improvement over *bloody hell*, and the children love reading to him.

I still need to get the hang of steering, but I do a reasonable job of returning the Cessna to the correct parking space. I can see them all now, waving a banner which says 'Sophie's First Solo'. There's a lot more learning to do before I get my licence, but today is certainly a milestone.

Bella's not here yet. She said she might miss it, as the course she's taking in food safety runs all afternoon. But she's coming over later, and, for once, Tom and I are going to cook dinner for her, instead of the other way around. Well, Tom is. I'll be pouring the wine.

Mum and Chuck sent a card from the Grand Canyon, which was more than I expected and brought a lump to my throat. Mum's lightened up a lot in recent months. She still talks wistfully about her lost granddaughter, but the acidity of her remarks is now tempered with hints about my own childbearing years. She'll have to wait a while for that. In the meantime, she and Chuck are on a three week tour of the western United States.

Before they left, she handed me something else: a grainy photo I'd never seen, of grandad and me in front of an old plane. It was taken just weeks before he died. Tom gave me a silver frame for my birthday, and it's now beside our bed.

I flip to the next page on my clipboard and begin my post flight routine. But I don't get far through it. As soon as I cut the engine, and the propeller stutters to a stop, the little crowd of supporters advances on the left wing. I extract myself from my headphones and seatbelt, flick the latch on the door, and tumble out.

'You did it!' Gwen and Ingrid call in unison. 'First solo!'

'My God, Sophie, I was almost sick watching,' Fergus laughs, and Ingrid swats him. Before Biggles left his mother, they went to Casablanca for a week. I know Fergus is plotting more trips, if he can persuade Ingrid to leave her dog.

'I'm taking a photo to send to Rainbow,' Ingrid says, brandishing her phone.

'Okay.' I pose for a moment, one hand on the plane. Rainbow's gone back to the States now, but her husband's company is going ahead with plans to open a satellite office at the Science Park. Amelia is beside herself with excitement, while the rest of the village cronies are braced for what they call the Yankee invasion.

'Jolly well done,' Gwen nods. 'Bit fast on final approach, but jolly good.' Gwen's not much of a hugger, but she thumps me on the back and I know that's her version of praise.

I turn to Tom, feeling shy. He's been so patient as I've recited CAA regulations each evening. He's looking at me with an odd sideways smile.

'How did I do?' I ask, fidgety for his approval. 'The plane's in one piece, so that's success, right?'

'Don't take this the wrong way,' he says, stepping towards me.

My face falls. That statement is always followed by blunt criticism.

He pauses. 'But my heart was in my mouth the whole time.'

'Why?' I scuff my foot, deeply disappointed. 'Gwen said

I did okay.'

Tom opens his arms. 'You did absolutely great. I'm so unbelievably proud of you.'

He pulls me into a hug and I take a full breath for the first time since taxiing for take-off. The moment I lift my head, his lips find mine and I wrap my arms tightly around this man who watched my back while I fumbled my secrets, unravelled my past and then took faltering steps to change my life.

'It's a good job I'm not teaching you,' Tom says as we come up for air. 'This would be most improper.'

'I don't care,' I say, pressing up against him once more. 'After all, us Campbell girls have a thing for our teachers.'

He grins his sexiest grin, then leans down to whisper 'Later' in my ear.

Gwen helps me check and secure the plane, then our little group turns towards our cars, Biggles straining at his lead to show the way.

'Incidentally,' Tom says, one arm draped across my shoulders as he strolls beside me, 'I have to go to Scotland next week.'

I glance up at him. 'Oh?'

'I was wondering if you'd do the honour of flying us there.'

I stop walking and turn to him. 'I'm not qualified.'

'You are if I'm beside you.'

'Really?' Tom and I haven't been in a plane together since I started lessons. 'You'd trust me to do that?'

He looks down at me. 'I'd fly to the end of the earth, with you at the controls.' His eyes are dark with tenderness.

My heart leaps at this vote of confidence and the love that underpins it. 'Maybe we should just start with Scotland,' I say.

'Okay. I know a really romantic hotel, if you're interested.' Tom pauses. 'In fact, the last time I was there, I fell in love.'

He squeezes my hand, and I recall the smooth whisky,

crackling fire and deep, squishy beds at the Monboddo Arms. 'File the flight plan,' I say with a smile.

I also remember the lone swan, skimming along the surface of that Scottish lake. And I understand now, if you stay true to what you trust, flying is no effort at all.

The End

From the Author

Independent authors like me rely on reviews from readers to help spread the word about our work. Please consider adding your review of *Secrets in the Sky* to Amazon, Goodreads and other online forums.

At the end of this book, you'll find the first chapter of *Saving Saffron Sweeting*. Set in the same village, this novel features new main characters and takes place one year after the end of *Secrets in the Sky*. You can purchase it at: http://mybook.to/sweeting

I love to connect with readers through my website and social media. Visit www.paulinewiles.com for news, bonus materials and special promotions. You can also sign up for my newsletter to be notified of new releases.

Saving Saffron Sweeting

Chapter 1

I was balanced on an eight-foot ladder with a mouth full of curtain hooks when I realised that my husband was cheating.

The individual pieces of the picture suddenly came together, making terrifying sense. I blinked hard, then stared at my knuckles, which were now white from gripping the ladder. But the image wouldn't subside. The picture I saw was James with another woman.

I was hanging curtains in my client Rebecca's bedroom, and the project was almost complete. This was great, as she'd been excited to give the room a whole new look after she'd recently come to the end of a long relationship.

'I'm ready to move on. Grace, I want a totally fresh look,' she'd told me when we met to discuss how I could help her. 'Something luxurious, maybe a little sensual. I don't plan on being single forever.'

I was still new in the design business and it was a huge deal for me not only to land a new client, but also one who had money to spend and some kind of clue what she wanted. My first few months had been a real struggle and I was starting to question my talents. Other business owners had stressed the importance of tapping my personal network to get things rolling, so James had spread the word around his office. Apparently, he had done a good job of promoting my abilities to Rebecca, his company's marketing manager. She had been great to work for and seemed appreciative of my suggestions. The only slight issue was that in the last few weeks she had been anxious to speed things up and get the bedroom completed.

Eager to please, I had been beavering away and attempting to charm my suppliers into hurrying. After getting the curtains up, I planned to hit the shops for accessories, and then the room would be ready for whatever action she had in mind.

My work had been interrupted by a knock on the front door of Rebecca's condo. I'd opened it to find a bubbly young woman, who presented me with a pair of pink stilettos.

'Oh!' she said. 'I was hoping Becca would be home. Can you let her know Kerry returned these?'

'I think she's at work,' I said, taking the shoes. 'I'm her bedroom designer.'

'Ooh, you mean the love nest? Can I see it?'

'Er, it's not finished yet,' I replied. 'I expect she'd rather show you herself.'

Kerry shrugged. 'Okay. I'll catch up with her.' She turned and was a few steps down the hall before she added, 'And tell her I want to hear all about Vegas and this James guy. He sounds delish!'

My mind was still on the curtains. I'd shut the door and put the cute shoes down, before returning to the bedroom.

Climbing back up the ladder, I thought, No wonder Rebecca wants to hurry this room. She's met some man in Las Vegas and needs her bedroom back. I was stretching to try to hook the edge of the curtain to the last ring on the pole when the dark feeling began to slither over me.

Did the ladder wobble? Had one of San Francisco's famous earthquakes nudged it? Or was the lurch, the sway, the feeling of my stomach dropping to the new wool rug, due to something else? I checked the new tear-drop chandelier hanging above the bed. As a British transplant to the Bay Area, I had spent the first couple of years diving under our dining table at the slightest tremor. But by now I had learned that if the light fixtures weren't swaying, the seismic jolt was all in my head. The glass drops of Rebecca's chandelier stared back at me steadily, not even winking, let alone dancing.

I had the presence of mind not to swallow my curtain hooks as I took a huge gulp and slid down the ladder. I slumped onto the new and naked mattress as I thought about my husband's recent conference trip to Las Vegas and how edgy he had been since. I remembered our paths crossing briefly in the kitchen, the first morning after his return.

'How was it?' I'd asked, digging through the drawer for my favourite cereal spoon.

'Okay, I guess.' He reached for the tea bags.

James seemed dispirited and I thought perhaps the industry analysts had given his company, a mobile security start-up, a tough time.

'Are you home this evening?' he wanted to know.

'Probably,' I called over my shoulder. I was already heading to my computer to check whether anyone had emailed for decor advice. Even at that hour, my mind was firmly on my fragile business.

But that day I'd been called by a potential customer to discuss her family room and, as was typical, she could only meet me in the evening. I was hard at work researching inspiration pictures when James came home, and within minutes I headed out to my appointment. After more than an hour of fruitless discussion on the merits of contemporary versus rustic style, I drove the forty minutes home across the Dumbarton Bridge to find my husband was already asleep.

With an uncomfortable feeling, I also recalled the previous evening, when he'd come home from work early and asked to talk to me, but I'd been flying out of the door to my women's networking group. This had been the pattern of life recently: we seemed to pass each other fleetingly, our schedules never lining up for longer than it took to brew a pot of tea.

And now I had learned that Rebecca had hooked up with someone called James in Las Vegas. My James had been acting oddly since he had returned from there. Keep calm, I told myself, it's probably fine.

But it wasn't fine. The third and ugly part of the truth was literally staring me in the face. Rebecca's favourite colour was purple and despite some reservations on my part, she had been adamant about using a strong shade of aubergine. We'd finally agreed on a sophisticated tan for three walls, painting the dramatic colour as an accent behind her bed. And although James usually showed precious little interest in any of my decorating ideas, we had been talking about Rebecca's project just before his trip, when we'd been in the kitchen long enough to empty the dishwasher together.

'How is your client list coming along?' he'd asked, shaking leftover water from a wine glass.

'Slowly,' I'd replied. 'Rebecca's bedroom is nearly finished but I don't have anyone lined up after her.'

He didn't say anything but had stretched over my head to put some plates away.

Happy to talk about my work, I'd let my brain run on. 'I hope it all comes together okay. That accent colour was such a bold choice.'

He'd pulled a slight face. 'Yeah, purple always reminds me of something my grandad would have had.'

I had dropped the topic, as I'd learned during our years together that James based most of his interior design dislikes on the vivid avocado and orange combinations in his grandfather's house. He thought any room featuring retro patterns or an accent wall was hideous.

Now, I leaped off the mattress as though it had bitten me on the behind. I was convinced I hadn't mentioned purple, aubergine or any other arty description for the colour behind the bed.

He knows what colour this room is. He's been here.

I was out of the house and into the car before I knew it. Days later, it occurred to me I should have stuffed Rebecca's hollow curtain poles with frozen shrimp. Of course, the clever moves always elude me at the time.

~~~

By the time I arrived at the Palo Alto office where James and his team were trying to create the next Silicon Valley success story, all dignity had abandoned me. I think my tears were already beginning as I lurched through the front desk area, empty because the company was too small to have a receptionist. In my haste, I then collided with the *foosball* table, which appears to be a required toy at every start-up with venture capital funding.

I spotted my husband – cropped, dark brown hair, shirt half untucked as usual – hunched over his keyboard, at the end of an untidy row of T-shirt clad computer coders. This gaggle looked barely old enough to have gained admission to Stanford University, let alone already graduated.

James looked up and noticed me. Surprise crossed his face, but was replaced with something I assumed was guilt. I could see how deep the lines in the middle of his forehead were getting these days, and how weary he looked.

'Purple,' was all I managed to utter at first. Terrific. Millions of wives over the centuries have faced this situation and all I could say was *purple*.

'Grace –' He stood and took my arm, trying to get me to sit.

I wrenched myself free. 'How did you know her bedroom is purple? How did you know?'

'Listen.' He shook his head. 'It's not what you think'.

Okay, so *purple* may not have been eloquent, but at least it was original. I saw red – as well as crimson, magenta and every shade in between.

'How could you?' I hissed. 'I know what's going on. And all the time, I've been decorating that sodding room!'

'Please,' he glanced sideways at the line of coders. 'Calm down!'

Fingers had frozen over keyboards. Curious youthful faces were turned towards us: James was a popular boss.

'You knew her bedroom is purple because you've been sleeping with her, haven't you? You've been sleeping with my client!'

'No, look, it wasn't like that.'

'No, you look. Look at this purple and tell me you've never seen it before.' I pulled the paint sample from my purse and unscrewed the lid. Dark and liquidly sinister, I waved it dangerously close to his computer.

'Okay, okay, I'm sorry. Please – calm down and let me tell you.' By now his dark brown eyes were wide with panic.

The whole office had fallen silent, but I saw that not everyone was watching us. Instead, some of them had turned to the far side of the room, as Rebecca stood and began heading our way. I realised most of them knew she had a part in this drama. And what about Rebecca? Was she half expecting this to happen? There I was, a total mess inside and out, and she appeared to be perfectly composed.

She came closer and I caught the eye contact between her and James. He had now turned paler than I'd ever seen, including the time he got food poisoning in Turkey and couldn't stand for three days. As she walked behind the desks of her co-workers, most of them didn't seem to know whether to freeze or flee.

'Look,' she said, 'let's not do this here.' Not a blonde hair was out of place.

'Where would you rather *do it*?' I snapped back, but my voice was quivering. 'Your bedroom? With my husband?'

James reached for me again, but seemed to change his mind and let his hand drop. 'I know you're furious right now, but it was just one stupid mistake in Vegas,' he said quietly.

'I don't believe you! You've been in her bedroom!' I was looking wildly from one to the other, sick with the thought of them wrapped around each other.

'Well, actually,' Rebecca had the nerve to put her hand on his arm, 'it's probably best that you know, Grace. It wasn't a mistake.' She glanced at me and I noticed for the first time an intense determination in her face. 'I'm so sorry, we didn't plan it this way. It happened after I hired you. But we can't help how we feel.' In her strappy beige sandals she was nearly as tall as James, and she barely needed to lift her pointy little chin upwards to gaze at my husband adoringly. 'The thing is, I care about you and I want to be with you.'

A collective gasp flew round the office, almost loud enough to drown my yelp of pain. I could sense the techie crowd reaching for their phones to post *Wild and crazy work love triangle* on their Facebook pages. I felt like I'd been whacked in the ribs with a cricket bat, but I registered through my tears that James was shaking his head in defeat. The little pot slipped from my fingers before I could think of throwing paint in their faces. Instead, it added a permanent souvenir of the demise of my marriage to the carpet and his Hush Puppies. Rebecca sidestepped smartly and her sexy sandals escaped the shower. Too bad.

Failing entirely to live up to my name, I turned and fled with as much poise as a double-decker London bus.

~~~

We spent the next two days in an ugly blur of sobbing, shouting, and silence. Not all the tears were mine: James followed me straight home and begged me to hear his side of the story. I heard but I didn't listen and I certainly didn't believe his lame attempts to blame his cheating on a drunken night of clubbing at the conference in Las Vegas. Did he really think I was that gullible?

He tiptoed around me for the first evening, then slept in our guest room and left early the next day. That was worse than the awkwardness of him being in the apartment: I knew he was going to see Rebecca and I was tormented by the thought. I wasn't even sure he'd come home again. But he did, to find me curled up on the sofa with a blanket, in pointed denial of the California sunshine outside.

'Will you please talk to me?' He approached hesitantly. 'I know this was really, really stupid but I need to tell you my side of things.'

'You mean you've got something original to say? Because up to this point, it's all looking like one big cliché to me. You cheated, you got caught, you're a lying bastard.'

He sat down at the other end of our Ikea sofa and I immediately tucked my legs under me, as if it would burn me to touch him. 'Grace, I didn't lie to you, I was trying to tell you!'

'Well, you didn't try very hard.' I could feel my eyes welling up yet again.

'Look, ever since I got back, I've been trying to get you to sit down.' He did at least have the decency to look distraught. 'But you've been so caught up in your business recently – there wasn't a good moment.'

He was staring at me intently and I could see the beginning of tears in his own eyes. He clearly hadn't shaved that morning and his shirt was even more of a crumpled disaster than usual.

'Well, excuse me for turning my back for five minutes to try and make some money.' I was firmly on the defensive, one hundred per cent the injured party. 'And in case you hadn't noticed, I was slaving away to finish a project for the woman you're sleeping with!'

'I'm not sleeping with her. It was just one time. One stupid bloody time. I'm so sorry.'

'I don't believe you. You knew about that goddamn purple wall.' I was looking around wildly, seeking my escape route. I didn't want to be in the same room with him.

'All right, so I happened to see her bedroom! That doesn't mean anything.'

'No, it means everything.' I was sobbing now. 'It means I'll never trust you again.'

I wish I'd had the panache to storm out of our

apartment in an expensive cloud of Chanel perfume. I wish I'd owned a Louis Vuitton bag to grab on my way to check into a luxury hotel, where I'd instigate a passionate revenge fling with a nineteen-year-old bellboy. Unfortunately, I clambered off the sofa with pins and needles in my legs and tripped over my blankie instead. Then I trailed soggy tissues across the floor and locked myself in the bathroom, where my only company was a dog-eared copy of *National Geographic*.

I had followed my British husband – and his job – from London to California, but my own attempt at the American dream had flopped. I'd been working crazily, had failed to see my marriage falling apart, and felt like a total fool.

I certainly couldn't afford to kick James out and stay in our apartment on my own. My so-called business was barely breathing. I had no idea how many months or years of scraping by might be ahead of me, if I attempted to build a list of design clients who weren't going to thank me by stealing my husband. Did I have the energy to move out, find a job, and rebuild my life in the fast-moving world of Silicon Valley? What the heck was I doing in this country, anyway? All I wanted was to crawl under the bed covers and hide, preferably with a packet of imported Cadbury's biscuits.

In the small, mocking hours of the next morning, I found myself unearthing a suitcase from the closet. With safety, seclusion and comfort food as my primary motives, I booked a flight home to England.

~~~

To continue reading *Saving Saffron Sweeting*, please visit:
http://mybook.to/sweeting